Field One

**SIMON
WINSTANLEY**

www.futurewords.uk

First Edition

ISBN-13: 9781518714627
ISBN: 1518714625
Library of Congress Control Number: 2015918364
CreateSpace Independent Publishing Platform
North Charleston, South Carolina

To Mum and Dad,
for their constant encouragement.

To Janet, Ben and Joseph,
for their constant support.

and

To those who look up at the stars
and constantly question.

PROLOGUE

For as long as Atka could remember, it had always been there: an ever-present Orb of light at the heart of the forest. Very few of the village Elders ventured this far in, preferring to live in the gloom away from the persistent glare of The Guardians.

From where he sat the Orb filled his field of vision, its cold ethereal glow warding off the darkness. Tonight, as every night, the coloured Sky-Spirits circled overhead, yet he was not afraid. If anything he felt reassured by their presence. A light breeze whispered through the illuminated trees; he shivered and moved his bare feet a little closer to his small camp fire.

Looking into the flames he recalled that night, many suns ago, when he had seen his first Guardian standing motionless within the Orb. In fear, he had fallen to his knees and bowed in reverence, averting his eyes. When he finally dared to raise his head, the silhouetted figure had turned and slowly receded towards the Orb's centre.

It gave him great comfort to know that The Guardians were real and were watching over him. Although he had returned to the same spot every night since, the Guardian had not reappeared. But Atka's spirit remained persistent and undeterred; he would again keep watch until sleep overtook him. He stoked the flickering orange fire; soon he would need to collect more wood if the fire was to last until morning.

He looked up to the Sky-Spirits and smiled, they always moved so beautifully, passing through each other exchanging hues and intensities. Some believed the Sky-Spirits were The Guardians themselves, able to shed their corporeal forms and fly among the stars.

Atka turned away from the glare of the Orb to look at the scintillating rings that surrounded his world, and the stars beyond. Many had speculated that The Guardians came from those stars and may one day depart from here, taking their followers with them.

Hearing distant thunder, Atka turned away from the stars to focus on the present. Puzzled, he saw there were no storm clouds. A second growl of thunder split the air, and he realised that the sound was not coming from the sky but from the Orb. Without warning, the ground under his feet began to shake and he fell. The Orb's once steady light was now pulsating and the Sky-Spirits had almost vanished.

The whole Orb began to shudder and then slowly vibrate towards him, the forest floor crumpling and breaking up in its wake. It started to push against the first of the surrounding trees, vaporising each in a brilliant flash of violet light. Then, just as suddenly, silence returned to the clearing and everything was still once again; although Atka was not there to see it, he was already sprinting back to the village to alert the Elders.

POWERS OF 10

15th March 2013

Neville Asquith had become irrevocably linked to the years of miserable financial austerity measures that had almost immediately followed the general election. The fact that his party had won by such a small majority had made it even worse; the British press had called it *'The best of two bad options'*. But for him to be Prime Minister now, of all possible times, was political suicide.

Over the past week, things had inevitably gone from bad to worse as the news had spread. With each briefing he gave, it had seemed that, rather than issuing directives befitting a true Head of State, he had been reduced to delivering statements to a press core that seemed to know everything anyway.

This morning had been different though. The news, that he could promise aid and relief to his own struggling country, was his to deliver. The press had listened attentively and, not having any foreknowledge, had no pre-prepared questions to bark at him as soon as he stopped speaking.

As he turned away from the briefing podium and strode across Downing Street towards Number 10, only then did the questions start to echo across the street. The sheer number of flashes, from the dozens of photographers lining the street, illuminated the classical Georgian architecture in front of him. Even now the video cameras must be capturing this, he thought; perhaps his place in history would be associated with today rather than the previous three years of political drudgery.

Neville turned back to the reporter-filled pavement and posed a hand in a Statesman-like wave, then returned to striding purposefully across the cobbles. As he approached the polished black doorway the attendant policeman stepped to one side and, as was custom, the door was opened from within.

Still smiling at the thought of his historic pose, he became dimly aware that the policeman was removing his hat. Neville slowed a little as he saw that the man's shaven head was adorned with a tattoo; a circle with a gap in the circumference, placed into which was a smaller, solid dot. The cameras continued to flash.

With a roar the man shouted, "Exordi Nova!", hugged Neville and pulled him back towards the open door.

The explosives within the man's vest detonated, instantly converting Neville Asquith's last embrace into a ball of white fire. The door, designed to withstand such a blast whilst closed, was powerless now that it was partially open. The initial explosion effortlessly blew the door inwards and tore through the hallway of Number 10. The extreme heat vaporised the closest civil servants within and spread fire deeper into the building. Outside, at the same time, the press were first impacted by fragments of flying bricks and ironwork, before being engulfed in the fire that had expanded across the street.

A second later it was all over. Where once stood an emblem of British democracy, there was now a shallow crater, above which stood the burning remains of a decimated Number 10.

ÖSKJUVATN LAKE

17th August 2009

The modified Bell 47G helicopter skimmed low over the glaciated landscape, its dragonfly shadow fluctuating wildly in size as it flew over the deep and shallow fissures in the barren terrain below, then cut northeast away from the Vatnajökull glacier. Ahead the landscape opened out onto the Askja caldera. Öskjuvatn Lake, now melt-water, sparkled in the late morning sun; ahead lay Lake Víti.

"This is it now, Sir," relayed the pilot over the headphones, his voice mixing with the high pitched whine of the rotors, "I'll set us down to the southeast. Alpha team are on site. Stay low when you exit."

In appearance Lake Víti was a circular crater with a geothermal lake in its basin. Such was the similarity to a lunar crater that NASA had used the area during training for the Apollo program to prepare the astronauts. However, the return visit today had a more terrestrial agenda.

On hearing the distant approach of the helicopter, the Alpha team returned from the crater and assembled in the makeshift operations tent. The Gravity Recovery and Climate Experiment, GRACE, launched seven years before, had yielded several candidate sites, but this one looked promising. Despite Iceland's volcanic nature, ground penetrating radar had confirmed there were no threatening magma chambers below it, and the high latitude excluded it from the possibly problematic effects identified at other potential sites clustered around the equator.

Whilst not strictly a military operation, the personnel immediately stood when the VIP entered the facility. A cold blast of air and an armed escort accompanied his arrival.

"GRACE up-link?" he asked the team.

The closest team member pointed to a laptop next to the radio station.

After a few keystrokes to admit entry, a screen displayed a world map. The familiar continent outlines were visible, but they were superimposed on what looked like a thermal image of the planet; hot spots were shown in yellow and orange whilst, at the opposite end of the spectrum, cold spots were shown in blue. However, unlike a thermograph, this display indicated gravitational anomalies. Öskjuvatn Lake, now displayed at maximum magnification, filled the screen with a solid, bright red.

The rest of the team stood by, hardly daring to breathe. Some started to shift uncomfortably as their guest repeatedly refreshed the screen. Eventually the most senior cleared his throat to speak, but was denied the opportunity; the guest suddenly stood, swept up the radio and headed outside, accompanied by his armed shadow.

Tuning the radio to the prearranged frequency he spoke: "Víti station."

"Go ahead Víti," came the reply immediately, *"channel secure."*

"Öskjuvatn anomaly confirmed, 56.9 milligals. Send the bridge."

1951

13th February 1952

Below a black sky, flecked with pinpricks of starlight, the Bradley Observatory dome was open. Being a clear night in Georgia, the thirty inch reflector telescope was again in use. Inside the dome, on a raised circular walkway, Howard Walker was writing up his notes on the evening's session. He was whistling a jaunty tune from the hit parade, the lyrics of which were questioning the altitude of the moon, when he heard the ground floor door open and footsteps climbing the cast-iron steps. He stopped whistling, and above its dying echo, Sam Bishop's voice came from below:

"Somewhere there's music."

"How near?" said Howard with a smile.

"How far, you mean!" said Sam reaching the upper walkway, "How far do I have to go to avoid that guitar-torturing record? Honestly, since my daughter bought that infernal record last week, she's been playing it non-stop. How can anyone think with all that racket?"

"Ha ha! You know he actually built his own guitar?"

"It's still a racket, and it'll never catch on," said Sam handing him an envelope, "Post for you."

"Oh, thanks. You know, I was thinking of running another - hey!" said Howard opening the letter, "Designation results!"

"Yes, I figured you'd probably want to see it."

Howard unfolded the letter, laid it flat on the worktop, and skip-read though it.

"Reference November 5th 1951... photometric astrometry plate result... blah - Ah!" he exclaimed, "Here it is...We have entered its provisional designation as..."

"Well?" smiled Sam.

"1951 VA," he beamed, "It got the 'A' !"

"Congratulations Kid!" he laughed, finding the enthusiasm infectious.

"I mean, we were bound to get the 'V', it was a November sighting," Howard grinned, collecting his notes together and stuffing them into his battered, leather satchel, "but to be the *first one* to find it... it got the 'A'! Told you didn't I?"

"Ha ha, you certainly did!" Sam stood to one side to allow him past, "Now clear out of here, you're whistling through my telescope time!"

"Betty's going to be thrilled!" said Howard, throwing the satchel over his shoulder and clattering down the iron steps, "Goodnight Dr. Bishop!"

The door clanged shut, leaving Sam in the peace and quiet of his own thoughts.

BACKUP PLAN

2nd March 2013

"Yes. I'll hold!" he said, through clenched teeth.

He was paying way too much for Datasave's online backup service and he wanted to make sure they knew how severely they were inconveniencing him by their continued ineptitude.

The phone line went quiet, and then there was more music.

'Perfect,' he thought.

It was as though it was purposefully designed to annoy customers even further. It was always some synth-rip-off version of the original track too. He felt the blood rhythmically pounding through his head, and a remote part of his brain noticed it was in sync with the music. Adopting the thousand-yard-stare normally associated with being put on hold, he took a swig from a can of flat cola and glanced around the room.

When he'd first moved in it had been pretty spacious, but the years of accrued newspaper clippings on the walls, piles of cannibalised tech, and stacks of old pizza boxes and magazines that rose in precarious columns now gave it an oppressive maze-like quality. Blackout roller blinds had been stapled permanently closed over the window frames to keep out sunlight and prying eyes. The only sources of light in this basement flat were a small fluorescent desk lamp and the computer monitors that cast long shadows on the paint-peeled ceiling. The fish tank, containing his only concession to living company, bubbled away quietly. He realised that whilst he'd been on hold the tank's automatic lighting had turned off; it must be evening already. Sometimes without that fish, a relic of a long-dead relationship, he wouldn't have a clue what time of day it was.

His anger veered momentarily towards remorse as he relived the memory of Kathcrine slowly closing the basement door on him for that final time. He hadn't wanted to stop his research, and she hadn't wanted to watch him slip into paranoia. He'd purged every byte of her data from his life that very day. From phone numbers to photos he'd erased her, but when it came to the pathetic fish he couldn't bring himself to get rid of it. He was snapped out of his reverie when the hold music suddenly stopped.

"I don't believe… you cut me off! Son of a…"

"Hello Mr. Davis? Thanks for holding," interrupted the technical support voice.

"Well yeah, about time…look," he recovered. He was sure it had been a woman before, but he'd been transferred so many times that it hardly seemed to matter. He was just drawing an irritated breath to explain everything again when the voice continued.

"We've checked into it and can verify that your files are still intact on our servers."

"Crap!" he spat, "I'm looking at the website right now and they're gone!" He hit the keyboard to refresh the screen, as if to show him the obvious absence of data. The screen dutifully refreshed showing him all his folders and files exactly where they should be.

"What…?" he muttered then twisted the chair around to get a closer look at the screen.

"We did have a minor power outage earlier today Mr. Davis. It's possible that the file records are taking a little while to come back online."

He couldn't believe it; on one hand it was a relief to have his data back, but on the other it wasn't the first time he'd had to make this call; his anger flared again.

"Look, this is the second time this week my stuff's gone missing; I pay a lot for the reliability you offer. And it's not reliable!"

"The power outage was quite beyond our control but please be assured that we take your data storage and retrieval very seriously; I can see from our records that you've been with us for quite a while, is it possible you're using the same router equipment from when you first joined us?"

"What? Er, yeah I guess, look what does that have to do with…"

"We've had reports of signal loss from those people using…I tell you what, why don't we send you a new router? It'll get round the signal loss problem and increase your connection speed?"

"And I suppose all this comes with a fee, right?" he clamped his hand over his eyes; you never got something for nothing.

"No, we'd rather you stay with us than go to our competitors, so on this occasion we'd pay for the upgrade"

He really hadn't been prepared for this response and felt suddenly guilty about his earlier outburst. It wasn't the fault of the poor guy on the other end of the phone line, and he knew it.

"Look I know this isn't your fault, you're just taking my call", he said resignedly, "but this stuff's important to me that's why I use you guys…"

"Of course, Sir", the voice reassured him, *"Now, the replacement router, does that option sound OK?"*

"Well that would be…great…I'd really appreciate it, thank you"

"Will you be at your place of residence tomorrow morning at 8.30? I have a delivery slot available and there'll need to be someone to sign for the equipment… the next available slot after that is…next Thursday at 4pm"

"Great, 8.30 tomorrow then!" he jumped in before the offer had chance to escape.

"If there's nothing else I can help with Sir I'll say goodnight," he concluded.

"Great, thanks."

He hung up and had the most amazing sense of relief. He'd been on the phone for over an hour but now this horrible situation was going to resolve itself.

•

The next morning he updated his video log, made a local backup of his most recent files on a memory stick and crossed the room to the illuminated fish tank.

"Morning, Penrose," he tapped on the glass. The goldfish resolutely ignored him, until the lid of the tank was raised.

"Feeding time, buddy," he smiled, then opened the fish-food container and sprinkled an extra large pinch of the flakes into the tank; he was feeling generous this morning. He watched for a moment whilst it languidly pecked at the surface of the water; there was something enviable about its simple lifestyle, no real worries, no burden of knowledge. The front door buzzer brought him back to reality. He stashed the memory stick back in the fish-food container, closed its lid, and put it back on the shelf.

Glancing at his watch he navigated through the cramped living space and walked down the narrow hall towards the door.

"Eight twenty-seven," he smirked to himself then opened the door.

A motorbike courier in black leathers stood there with the package in one hand and a mini clipboard in the other.

"Package for Davies?" he muffled through the crash helmet.

"Davis actually."

The courier turned the clipboard round to face himself and tilted his head sideways at it.

"Yeah. Davis. Sign and print here," he held out the clipboard and pen, then turned away apparently more interested in the quiet street than in his task.

The pen had run dry. Despite scribbling on a blank portion of the form, it wouldn't deposit another drop.

"You got another? This one's had it"

The courier just shrugged and turned his back again. Detecting he was not likely to get any further with this moron, he stomped back inside to get a pen of his own.

"Wait here," he shouted over his shoulder, "I'll get one that works".

He heard his front door slam behind him and turned to check.

The courier was standing at the end of the hallway and lowering to his side what appeared to be a gun. It was then that he became aware of a creeping cold sensation between his shoulder blades and he realised that he must already have been shot. The darkness folding in from the corners of his vision bled into the black leathers of the still advancing courier, and he fell.

He awoke on his own sofa with a faint smell of ammonia in his nose, feeling like he'd just been hit by a train. He tried to get up from the sofa but found he was restricted. On trying to glance down at whatever was holding him he realised that he couldn't move his head either.

"Please try to remain calm," came a voice from behind him somewhere. Rob recognised the voice but couldn't quite place it. He tried to speak but found he'd been gagged too. Footsteps approached from the direction of the voice and he felt hands holding the top of his head.

"I'm going to remove your gag so you can speak, please do not try to shout or scream or I will have to subdue you again. Does that option sound OK?"

It was that last phrase, *'Does that option sound OK?'*, that suddenly clicked the voice into place. He felt his head being lifted and the gag being removed.

"You're…Tech Support?" he managed groggily.

"No, Rob. No, I'm not Tech Support," he exhaled, "though that is indeed how we last spoke…" the man stepped from behind him now and he could finally see his assailant.

The motorbike helmet was gone and the leathers were unzipped to the waist, through which he could see a plain black tie and white shirt. With plastic-gloved hands, the man calmly poured a glass of water and dropped a drinking straw into it; then walked back over and crouched down at the side of him, uncomfortably close.

"My name is Benton and let me reassure you…" he said, angling the straw towards Rob's lips, "if I wanted you dead, we wouldn't be having this conversation."

"Then untie me and we'll talk, you bastard!" Rob's voice broke, despite his best efforts to sound menacing from his poor vantage point.

Benton sighed whilst forcing a smile. The British intrigued him, they were always so plucky. He'd seen much stronger displays of bravado and typically those situations ended untidily. Perhaps this would be one of the more straightforward ones.

"Rob, you are not tied in any way. I've given you a neuromuscular suppressant because you and I need to talk very calmly and I need your full attention - now have some water, a side effect is dehydration."

Rob watched as he delicately manoeuvred the straw into place and, after an initial hesitation, he sucked down the cold water. His mind, apparently the only part of him not completely paralysed, was racing to latch onto anything that might explain why this psychopath was torturing him. The man had obviously intercepted his phone call with Datasave, which meant it must be something to do with his data.

Involuntarily, Rob's eyes widened as he realised the full significance of Benton's interception; his data, The Data. He stopped drinking; a detail Benton immediately reacted to.

"Either you're no longer thirsty, or you've worked out why I'm here," said Benton, placing the half empty glass on the nearby table next to the package he had escorted, "and judging by the dilation of your pupils it's the latter."

Benton stood and walked around the room, "Nice idea, holding your evidence off site. Most people are too paranoid to let this sort of information out of their sight. Took two whole days to find a quiet way into Datasave. But no matter how many times we removed your files, you just *kept* putting them back. Last night we realised your persistence warranted a Level Two Intervention."

Rob's blood turned to ice as it began to dawn on him.

"No... *oh shit,* no!" he swallowed hard, then tears filled his eyes, "...you're a ...*Storykiller?!*"

Benton winced, partly because he felt it was such a crude reduction of his dedicated life, but mostly because Rob must have heard this term from someone else; and that must mean at least one other intervention had been conducted carelessly. Nevertheless his considerable experience allowed him to continue without displaying his frustration.

"No, not really Rob, I just manage information that's all."

Tears were now openly streaming down the side of Rob's head. From what few rumours he'd heard, 'Storykillers' were silencing awkward leaks in a cover-up that Rob and others had been researching. The scale of the conspiracy, along with a few actual plan details they'd unearthed, was beyond belief.

"Please…" he sniffed, "I'll stop…really…", his bottom lip vibrated frantically and the tears came freely, "…*please!*" he whispered.

Benton closed his eyes, put a finger to his lips and whispered.

"Shhh…it's OK. As long as the information is safe, I don't need to escalate my response. I'm not a monster," He picked up the glass of water and angled the straw again, "Look, have another drink and then we can talk things through, does that option sound OK?"

After a moment he withdrew the straw from Rob's mouth and set the almost empty glass on the table again. Bringing a disposable paper towel from his pocket he wiped away Rob's tears, then placed it into a thin plastic bag at his feet.

During normal conversations Benton would watch a subject for hundreds of involuntary body movements, in order to suck every last piece of information from their exchange. In the few seconds at Rob's front door an hour ago, he had determined that Rob would hold the clipboard in his left hand before turning to his right to go and find a pen. This had given him the necessary time to follow him undetected into the hallway and shoot the suppressor. Of course it had helped to plant the empty pen first.

The suppressant he administered to all his subjects was a true marvel; whatever reactions they had to his questioning, they couldn't physically turn away, which gave him an excellent read of their emotional leakage. It also kept them completely immobile during interrogation and was virtually undetectable in an autopsy; though if anything was discovered at that late stage it was quite within his reach to vanish that information too.

He studied Rob's face carefully now.

"I've taken the liberty of erasing the data from your computer, and it must remain that way."

Benton gestured towards the computer screen and, as he predicted, Rob's eyes followed, widening at what he saw. The firewall had obviously been disabled, as the screen was now awash with an array of dubious websites infested with viruses, spybots and malware.

Benton was now unwrapping his courier's package. Inside was not a replacement router but a selection of gun and explicit magazines, which Benton began to distribute randomly around the room.

"You're finding it difficult to breathe," he said, pulling some of the seedier centre-folds from their publications. He pinned them to the wall where Rob's newspaper clippings and maps had been just thirty minutes before, "hypoxia is another side-effect I'm afraid."

"Why…the..?" wheezed Rob, his eyes darting between the walls and his computer.

"In a few days you can either be discovered dead with your reputation destroyed in this…" he glanced almost theatrically round the room, "…den of iniquity…"

The theatrics, body language and blatant melodrama were all part of Benton's interrogation technique. He had never really fully understood why it was all necessary, but over the years it had arguably made him a more efficient communicator. He crouched at Rob's side again before concluding his performance:

"…or instead I can sit you up, and when the suppressant wears off," he lied, "you can clean up this mess and go on with your life."

Rob watched him tie a knot in the disposable plastic bag and stand up; there was something far too final about the action.

He knew at that moment that no matter which option he chose it didn't matter, Benton was not going to let him leave the room alive.

All his work would be buried; no one would ever know of the coming storm.

They'd all be like Penrose, swimming through what remained of their lives in ignorant bliss.

"What do you…want me to do?" he sobbed, blinking away the tears.

"Good. Other than the people you have contacted in your pursuit of Archive, I need to know if you have discussed the data with anyone else."

Benton's own research had been thorough, there should *be* no one else; but there was always the chance he had overlooked something. In his experience when people were offered the choice of exchanging information in return for extending their lives, they gave the information every time.

Rob's main discovery had happened months *after* he'd purged Katherine's data. She had rejected him but he'd loved her and wanted to protect her from all this. His protective instinct flared again now. As far as Benton was concerned his relationship with her had never existed. If he even mentioned her, Benton would still kill him to tidy up loose ends and then hunt her down too. He felt a moment's regret that he couldn't warn Marcus, but his options were limited and now his choice was clear.

He heard himself wheeze "There's no one…I don't know anyone," before fresh tears overflowed.

Benton was satisfied, "Thank you, Rob."

He pushed his hand under Rob's neck and raised him into a sitting position, thereby accelerating the paralysis. Rob's breathing became even shallower.

"You've been through a great ordeal, you should rest now," Benton smiled down at him.

Rob knew that he'd done all he could to protect her and with that knowledge came a certain amount of relief. His mind started to fog over and he felt comfortable, it was almost like falling asleep.

"Thank you…" Rob lied, "for sparing…my…"

Benton watched Rob close his eyes; the coma would take effect soon, and death four hours later.

He picked up one of the magazines, opened it to a suitably sordid page and placed it on Rob's lap. He picked up the disposable plastic bag full of Rob's life, re-zipped his leathers and walked towards the hallway.

Suddenly something didn't seem right to Benton; he turned to survey the room.

Something was out of place, but it wasn't anything he had done.

He closed his eyes and listened; the computer hard-drive was whirring, Rob's breathing was just about perceptible. And there it was, the faint hum of a fish tank's water filter. Benton crossed the room to the fish tank where the lid had been left open.

On examination he could see that there was still fish-food floating on the surface of the water. He picked up the fish-food container to add more food to the tank, then thought better of it; after all, the forensics of the room had to appear correct.

"Sorry, Fish," he tapped on the glass. He closed the tank lid and replaced the fish-food container on the shelf, then collecting his backpack he prepared to leave the room.

As usual he felt the slight tug on his conscience for what he had done. He did feel genuine pity for Rob and all the other individuals who had been through this process.

As if to silence his own internal demons, he justified his actions aloud:

"For the good of Mankind…"

Then he closed the front door.

THE FLC

2nd February 2010

Houston Mission Control was not, it seemed, without a sense of humour. The radio-shielding location qualities and technicalities of the mission had led to the Floyd Lunar Complex being established on the dark side of the moon.

It had taken 42 years, and almost twice as many missions, to haul each element from Earth to this remote location, undetected.

Mike Sanders had lost the poker game and so was on his way out to replace a CO_2 scrubber cartridge. The weekly cartridge service routine had been brought forward by a few days. It would be vital that all personnel were one hundred percent focussed on the first part of the FLC primary mission, and not distracted by a routine maintenance operation. The languid gravity allowed him to make elongated jumps, each one sending up curls of the ubiquitous grey moon dust into the vacuum.

"Never should have folded…" he grumbled into his suit's comm.

"… Don't be such bad loser…" came back Lana Yakovna *"…I win, you scrub!"*

He grinned and lowered the helmet's protective sun-visor; the term 'dark side of the moon' had nothing to do with sunlight. Signals from Earth couldn't directly reach this side of the moon so it was perfectly dark to communication and therefore ideal for Archive's mission. The only means of Earth contact was via a chain of repeaters terminating at the moon's eastern rim.

Behind him, most of the complex was buried under six feet of regolith, a measure designed to reduce the Sun's radiation and regulate the temperature within. Here and there were airlocks, portholes and antennas; artificial constructions with only a tenuous grip on the dusty surface. Even the presence of lunar rover tracks seemed hopelessly transient; the hostile environment seemed to actively resist human occupation.

He continued his jumps over to the rover, clipped himself to the frame, and pushed the dust-caked button to start the ageing electric vehicle. A bulb lit up on the control panel showing that adequate charge was available, so he set off for the scrubber site a few minutes away. He knew that sound couldn't travel in the vacuum of space, but he could never get used to the general lack of noise. The only audible clue he had that he was in motion was a mild low frequency vibration where the clips attached to his chest panel.

"I'll work out what your Tell is eventually," he baited.

"…Eventually…" she repeated calmly, *"…but, until then…"*

"Yeah, I know…" he laughed, and then in his best Russian melodramatic accent added, "Unteel then, I weel scrahb!"

Floyd Lunar Complex sat in a minor depression within the Coriolis crater, a tenth of a degree above the moon's equator. To his right, the north-eastern rim of the crater was eroded, forming a slope gentle enough that the automated Regodozers could enter and exit the site with comparative ease. He found it difficult to believe that work on this facility had begun with the Apollo program, but he knew from first hand experience that there was stuff up here date stamped '1968'.

He pitied the poor conspiracy theorists; NASA hadn't faked the moon landings, just the locations.

"FLC this is Sanders at Lima scrubbing station, switching to comms relay Lima," he reported, bringing the rover to a halt.

"Confirmed Mike," came Lana's almost conditioned response, *"go Lima in 3, 2, 1…"*

The communication channel switched to the mid-range network with hardly a click.

"Lima, check."

"Confirmed Mike, go get some fresh air."

"Copy that, keep the lights on."

He unclipped himself and looked out towards the west quadrant of the crater, to see the solar panel array gleaming like diamonds against the ink-black sky. Although the array was over a mile away, the lack of atmosphere on the moon meant there was no light diffusion over the distance; everything he could see was pin-sharp. He could tell immediately that there was a variation in the regular pattern of the solar array.

Under normal operation the panels were designed to actively orient themselves towards the sun, like sunflowers, so that the maximum amount of energy was always captured. At least one of the panels faced in a different direction to the others. A lunar day was approximately an Earth month; so the array had 15 useful days of sunlight in which to capture and store the energy, followed by 15 days of impenetrable night.

Up here every watt counted, so even a drop of half a percent could be significant.

"Lana, can you run a megawatt check on the array?"

"...We have problem?" Lana replied.

"Yeah, er, maybe. Looks like we've got tracking failure in section nineteen or twenty, probably only a few degrees off axis, but..."

"...I check now..."

"Copy that. Proceeding to the scrubber."

It had been decided in the early planning days that any form of oxygen storage or processing should not be located within the habitable units. If a fire were to start, then the abundance of oxygen may result in irretrievable damage. It didn't make the weekly maintenance routine an easy process though, unless of course you had a good poker face. He had just finished swapping cartridges when Lana reported back.

"All finish, Mike?"

"Just now. How's the array?"

"I have diagnostic running on nineteen-J, it was one day behind others."

"What, one Earth day? That's not poss…" began Mike, carelessly hop-walking back to the rover, "We're at T-minus 12 hours plus change, Lana. Give me a status check on Larry, Curly and Mho."

There was a small pause while Lana referred to her instruments.

"Mike, there is no change," she reported, *"We are at one-zero-two percent of nominal across all three firing chambers. Chamber three has variation of decimal zero five Tesla, but holding within parameters."*

"I don't like it. I'm going to take the rover and check it out myself. How can…"

"Negative!" interrupted Lana forcefully, *"I have already reset nineteen-J, we wait for diagnostic. Is protocol."*

"Protocol, my ass…"

"Ty blya! Is not just your ass!" she swore, *"Dlya blaga chelovechestva."*

This seemed to have the desired effect on Mike, who stopped and closed his eyes briefly.

"You're right… I'm sorry…" he re-attached his clips to the rover and looked out at the array, "…you're right Lana, 'For the good of Mankind'…switching to FLC local comms…"

FOUR

29th February 1976

Judy only just heard the doorbell over the music and chatter. She announced, to anyone that could hear her, that she would answer it. She crossed the living room, weaving her way through the guests of various ages, stopping briefly to pick up a carelessly dropped roller-skate and a paper plate with some half-eaten cake on it. She wiped her hands on a napkin and walked down the short hall where the small mirror helpfully showed her that a small piece of cake had also become caught in her hair. She hastily pulled the errant crumbs out, exhaled, and opened the door.

"Judy!"

"Hi, Dorothy! Come on in," said Judy, inviting her in and taking her coat, "the place is a madhouse! But the more the merrier!"

One or two of the guests gave Dorothy a wave and a smile, before becoming engrossed again, either in their own conversations or in looking through the family photo albums.

"Wonderful to see you Judy, you're looking well."

"You too. Is this another new coat?" she said, hanging it up.

"This ol' thing? No, I've…There he is! Birthday Boy!"

Miles ran up to her and stuck out his hand, "Hello Mrs. Pittman."

"Hello Miles!" Dorothy bowed slightly and shook his hand. She got the impression that he was suddenly trying to wipe a smirk off his face; an activity that hadn't entirely succeeded by the time he spoke.

"It's my first birthday!"

"Now I know that's not true, Miles!" laughed Dorothy. "I happen to know that you are four years old."

Miles nodded bashfully, "Four years and one day old! My true birthday happens every four years on the 29th of February because of the leap year. When I was born I was zero years old."

"You're a very clever young man!" she replied, turning to Judy, "I've said it before, and I'll say it again, mentally he's way ahead of his age group. Way ahead."

Judy drew a long breath. Dorothy mentioned it virtually every time they met, but her circumstances meant there was little she could do about it. She heard him chuckling and looked down to see him covering his mouth, his shoulders hunched in amusement.

"What is it, honey?" she smiled, "What's so funny?"

He managed to stop laughing long enough to tell her.

"I'm Miles, Ahead!" he giggled with glee and ran off to tell everyone at the party, one by one.

"Thanks for that Dorothy," she laughed, "he'll be introducing himself that way forever now!"

Dorothy laughed along with her, and the two of them stood watching him buzz between the groups of children and guests delivering his new favourite joke.

"He *is* bright you know, Judy," said Dorothy, laying a hand on her forearm, "Beyond his years. Why don't you let me have a word with my Bill, he could put a good word in at the school?"

"But the fees!" exhaled Judy. "You know I can't afford -".

She was interrupted by Miles suddenly rushing up, with a worried expression.

"Mommy! Mommy! Come quick! Laura's got a splinter in her finger, I couldn't help her and she's really crying!"

"OK, I'll come now," she lowered her voice slightly and spoke to Dorothy, "I may have to pull the splinter out. Can you keep Miles with you for a minute?"

"Of course."

"OK, Miles, you stay here with Mrs. Pittman," she said leaving them behind.

Dorothy crouched at his side.

"Do you think she will be OK, Mrs. Pittman?" he said, his bottom lip protruding.

"Oh, I'm sure she'll be just fine, honey," she said and began searching inside her handbag, "Tell me Miles, you like helping others don't you?"

Miles just nodded.

"It's a bit upsetting when you can't help, isn't it?"

Miles nodded and she put her arm around him to comfort him.

"Well, as a special thank-you for trying to help others. And because it's your *first* birthday…" she winked, "I have a little gift for you."

She pulled a small present out of her handbag and held it out for him. Miles took hold of the other end, but noticed that she hadn't let go. He looked up into her eyes to check that everything was OK.

"For helping others," she smiled, and let him take the small parcel.

Miles made light work of hastily ripping open the bright red wrapping paper, and then froze in amazement, his eyes drinking in the details.

"Wow! Thanks Mrs. Pittman!"

"It would make me really happy if you called me Aunty Dot."

"Thanks Aunty Dot!" said Miles without hesitation and hugged her tightly.

"You're very welcome, Miles."

Miles let her go and continued to study the gift.

"Do you know what it is, Miles?" asked Dorothy.

"Is it a coin made from silver?"

"That's absolutely right," she smiled, "only you must never spend it."

The thought of removing the silver dollar from its presentation case seemed abhorrent to Miles and he shook his head firmly.

"I will keep it forev - " he frowned as he discovered a new detail, "Why does this coin have two dates?"

"That's very observant Miles. Usually coins only have one date don't they? But this one is special, it celebrates two hundred years of liberty."

"Wow, that's a really long time!" he grinned and turned the coin over, "Is that a bell next to the moon?"

Dorothy nodded and simply watched him study the coin for a moment.

"What does *'e pluribus unum'* mean, Aunty Dot?"

"Have you heard of a language called Latin?"

Miles shook his head.

"Out of many, one," she explained.

RAIN

10th March 2013

It was raining, again, and the University of West London stood stoically amid the downpour; slate roofs and cast-iron guttering struggling to channel the current deluge. The Architecture faculty's fluorescent lights appeared as warped and rippled reflections on the black, wet concrete of the car park.

Kate Walker navigated her way across this shallow sea towards her car. In an attempt to keep her feet merely damp, she tried to travel between the patches showing least reflection. While she searched for her keys, the small umbrella in the crook of her arm did its best to direct the rain where it wasn't required. Rain began to dribble into her open handbag and over her students' assignments, so she hastily repositioned it to cover them instead of herself.

As she reached her car, the keys momentarily presented themselves before slipping from her wet fingers and dropping into the shallow puddle surrounding her foot.

"Dammit!" she exhaled, and stooped to retrieve them.

A fast blur in the darkness to her right became a violent push. Before she had time to react, her attacker had pinned her to the wet car.

"Scream and I cut you, yeah?" a low voice menaced in her ear.

Petrified, she managed a whimper, while feeling him rummage through her handbag.

"Nice phone," came the voice again.

Then, just as suddenly, she felt him release her and heard his fast footsteps splashing across the empty car park.

In a blind panic she fumbled for her keys within the puddle and somehow unlocked the car. She found herself gripping the steering wheel, shaking uncontrollably and her heart pounding. Then an animal noise began to erupt from her throat, quiet at first then graduating to a banshee scream as she repeatedly pounded the wheel. A little too late, campus security converged on her vehicle, but it was a further five minutes before they persuaded her to open the door.

Later at the campus security office, with a blanket wrapped around her, she became aware of the plastic cup of luke-warm, weak tea in her hands and a police officer trying to take a statement. Until then she had been trapped in her own memory, replaying the events again and again, trying to make sense of it. Why her? Had he somehow seen her smartphone?

Suddenly she noticed that someone was patting her hand and instinctively recoiled. The policewoman was crouched at her side and was in the middle of talking to her.

"...me to call anyone for you? A family member perhaps?"

"No... no, there's no one," she managed, still half in a daze.

"We'll also need to know what he's taken, sweetie," attempted the officer, handing her a complicated looking form, printed in a text size that made her eyes swim.

"What? Yes. Of course," she said taking the form.

"You look exhausted, let's get you home," said the officer, helping her to her feet, "If you're sure I can't help, I'll have an officer drive you home."

"Thank you... just sorry I couldn't remember more..." she began.

"It's alright, sweetie. Listen if you do think of anything, anything at all, just give me a call. Here's my card."

She found herself inserting her front door key into place and realised that most of the journey had passed in a haze. She glanced nervously around the quiet street, half expecting another encounter. In the distance was a police siren, its wail dropping in pitch as it raced away. She hastily opened the door, slipped inside, and dead-bolted it behind her.

She turned on all the light switches she could find. A distant part of her noted that it was only the primitive section of her brain that was making her crave the false protection of daylight. Another part of her also noted that she could do with something highly alcoholic from the fridge to calm her nerves.

She dumped her things on the kitchen table and was just returning from the fridge with a bottle of wine when her phone bleeped from within her handbag, signalling that an email had arrived. She froze mid step.

Her phone hadn't been stolen.

It was probably the most valuable thing in her handbag, but the mugger hadn't taken it.

"What the hell…?" she pulled the phone out of the bag and read the screen.

'I took nothing tonight. Rob killed. Check bag. Swap SIMM. Sorry Kate. Delete this message.'

She quickly checked the field marked 'From' and found it empty.

"What did I expect," she chastised herself, "the mugger's name?"

She re-read the message and realised that it had coincided with her arrival at home. Whoever had sent the message had quite possibly watched her return. Her logical side cut in and, after swiftly crossing the room, she turned out the living room light. She opened the curtain by an inch to peer out into the street, and waited for her eyes adjust to the sodium-yellow of the street lights.

If he had followed her home, she thought, he could have attacked her already. But he hadn't.

After a few minutes she had seen nothing unusual so closed the curtain.

'Check bag' she thought, recalling the message, and striding across the room she turned the light on again. Grabbing her bag she tipped everything out onto the kitchen table. *'Rob killed'?* She had only known one Rob, an ex-boyfriend.

'Rob killed'?

She emptied her purse and make-up bag. Nothing.

'Sorry Kate'?

How did he even know her name?

She sieved through the unmarked assignments, to see if anything was caught between them. Nothing.

It was unlikely to be one of her students, she thought, there was no connection to Rob there.

'Check bag' she thought again, and turning her attention to the bag itself she spotted a fresh rip in the lining. Without hesitation she tore at the rip in the fabric, widening it enough to push her whole hand in.

Her fingers closed around a smooth, slightly flexible, cylinder. Slowly pulling it from the bag lining she discovered a small container of fish-food.

Slumping into a kitchen chair she turned the container over in her hands.

"Penrose," she sighed, recalling the time she and Rob had won it at the funfair. He had thought it would be apt to call it Hawking, but she had countered with Penrose, and it had stuck. The likelihood of a fairground-prize goldfish living beyond a few weeks was low, but survive it did. In actual fact it had outlived their relationship. She thumbed through her phone's contacts until she reached his name, but hesitated before hitting the dial button.

Maybe he's OK, she thought, and then she would be the one who had made contact with him. What would he read into that? What if this was just some sort of mistake, or elaborate hoax? Immediately her logical side countered with the fact that someone had just gone to a lot of trouble to deliver her a single-lined message and a pot of fish-food.

She put the phone aside and looked at the little plastic container.

Could this really be the outcome of Rob's life?

Gripping the container firmly, she popped the top off and was greeted with a fishy odour. Immediately, old memories of Penrose and Rob's basement flat swam into her thoughts. As if to shake the memory she shook the container. Wedged into the flaky food was a tiny plastic bag and also what looked like a USB memory stick. She pulled both out, carelessly scattering flakes over the table top. On closer inspection of the diminutive memory stick, it appeared to have 128 gigabytes of storage.

"What are you hiding that needs so much space, Rob?" she said aloud, wiping off the remainder of the flakes.

She then unfolded the small plastic bag. Inside was a SIMM card.

Of course, she thought, *'Swap SIMM'*.

She picked up the phone again and re-read the message.

'I took nothing tonight. Rob killed. Check bag. Swap SIMM. Sorry Kate. Delete this message.'

She dragged the message over to the trash-can icon, but then hesitated.

"There's no way you're dead, Rob. But when I get my hands on you..." she threatened the icon, before letting it drop into digital oblivion.

It turned out that swapping the SIMM in her smartphone was not a straightforward operation. Eventually she resorted to mutilating a paperclip from a nearby student assignment, and poked the door open. Once she had inserted the shiny card, she had to restart the phone. Figuring it might take a minute or two, she crossed the kitchen to re-examine the contents of her bag in case she had missed some detail. She felt inside the lining again but found nothing more.

Once again her phone bleeped. A new message had arrived. Hardly daring to breathe, she picked up the phone and turned it over to read the display.

'Thank you for activating your new number. You have 500 minutes talk-time and unlimited - '

She exhaled with relief, it was just the SIMM activation message. The phone bleeped again and, still smiling, she looked down at the screen.

'Dont answr the dor'.

A second later her doorbell sounded.

2010

7th February 2010

In an attempt to prevent information leakage beyond the walls of the lecture theatre, the use of laptops as presentation devices was not permitted. The only format available was an ageing overhead projector; its halogen-white presentation surface threw a magnified version onto a screen mounted on the wall, and was the only light-source in the cramped room. The very simplicity of this type of projector had no doubt ensured its widespread adoption throughout the U.S. Air Force. The optics were too simple to fail so, with the exception of a blown bulb, there was nothing to break down. Stretched over the surface of the projector was a thin transparent film that could be written on, and scrolled from bottom to top. But, in order to leave no written record behind, delegates had also been asked to prepare slides rather than write directly onto the film.

General Napier stood to address the group.

"Your attention please."

The low murmurings quickly died down.

"I'd like to thank everyone for being here in person, ahead of Dr. Barnes' wider briefing shortly. So that everyone is on the same page, Dr. Patil please will you recap?"

"Thank you, General," replied Dr. Patil, approaching the projector.

He put the first of his slides onto the projection surface. It showed a simplified solar system diagram overlaid with the elliptical trajectory of a black, labelled dot.

"As predicted, Siva began its initial approach inside the orbit of Mars last year. Four days ago, February 3rd, the FLC attempted Siva deflection one. We have confirmed that, as expected, a second deflection attempt will be necessary in approximately 22 months. The FLC has already begun recharging."

He replaced the slide. It showed a grainy, potato-shaped image accompanied by a tiny, roughly triangular mass.

"This is our new immediate problem. When the FLC pulse hit the surface, a structural weakness within Siva caused a cascade fracture, detaching this shard," he said pointing to the smaller triangle, "designation 2010 CA, or Tenca."

At this point he removed the slide.

"As you know, we had planned for two further FLC deflection attempts in 2012 and 2014, each designed to course correct Siva away from Earth. The emergence of Tenca was not part of the original mission parameters."

He placed another slide onto the projector, it showed a diagram of Tenca accompanied by statistics relating to size, mass and density distribution.

"We have now had time to run the numbers across a wide error margin and based on our trajectory extrapolation we have confirmed that Tenca will be position coincident with Earth on February 15th 2013."

After an audible intake of breath, Bradley Pittman's Texan drawl came from the back of the darkened room.

"Where?"

"Best estimate is Novgorod, Russia," answered Dr. Patil.

"I'm no expert, but can't we just use that fancy moonbase up there to knock it down?"

Bradley Pittman was very much like his late father; blunt, confident and slightly larger than life. The Pittman family's wealth and business empire had been critical in establishing and maintaining Archive's various projects. In return Bradley's father, William, had been given assurances that his descendants would have a place within any conceived rescue package. As a major shareholder, it also gave Bradley a place at the discussion table today. However, many of the others present had bought their places through proven intellectual contributions to the project. Dr. Patil, being one of them, suppressed the urge to insult his lack of technical grasp.

"Mr. Pittman, the FLC has already confirmed that after the next Siva deflection due in 2012, they must begin recharging for the final 2014 deflection. Basically, if we use the FLC to deflect Tenca away from Novgorod in 2013 there won't be enough charge to fire our final shot in 2014."

"Shoot," accepted Bradley.

"Dr. Patil?" asked Bradley's daughter, Sarah, "From the scale indicated on your slide, Tenca's mass would be in the order of ten thousand tonnes?"

"Twelve," confirmed Dr. Patil.

"So destructive effects would not be planet-wide?"

"No, but it won't matter."

"No, I guess not. Thank you Doctor."

Like many of the Archive children, Sarah Pittman had been raised in full knowledge of the April 1st 2015 deadline. Knowing no other life, these children had accepted their privileged positions in Archive's plan without question. Their parents had ensured their day-to-day lives were sheltered and protected. So, with little of the outside world to distract them, they were extremely well educated and dedicated to fulfilling Archive's goals. In a sense these children were precision tools forged by their more blunt parents.

"Can somebody just cut through the crap and, like the General said, put me on the same page as you egg-heads?" blurted Bradley, "Where in the hell is Novgorod, Yakki?"

"It is about 260 miles east from Moscow," stated Alexey Yakovna.

Alexey, a successful mining magnate with as much financial might as the Pittmans, was already aware of the likely impact zone. Although the impact would occur in his home country he studied his map dispassionately. His contribution had ensured that in addition to his own assured survival, his daughter was at one of the safest locations off the planet - the FLC itself.

"I know we ain't got no critical Archive resources in Novgorod, so why all the ruckus? So what? A few Ruskies get knocked on their ass? No disrespect Yakki…"

Alexey was used to Bradley's obtuse nature and dismissed the mild slur with a raised eyebrow.

"Yes, my countrymen will dust off pants and carry on. Dr. Patil I have missed detail, yes?"

General Napier stood from his seat, prompting Dr. Patil to retake his.

"Each of Archive's projects depends on having a global population that is unaware of our preparation. The minute Tenca strikes Novgorod we lose containment. People will look up, share their damn phone-footage, panic. Even *we* can't cover up something that large."

"Shoot, General," cut in Bradley, "all 'cos we lack a little laser juice?"

Sarah winced. Although she was barely twenty she appreciated that the technology at the Floyd Lunar Complex was the product of decades of research, some of it her own, and not by any means a crude laser. In anticipation of her father's next question, she started digging through her printed notes.

"Sally, can't we just ship more 'dozers up there?"

"We'd need to increase the amount of strip-mined Helium-3 by… maybe… twenty percent," said Sarah, shuffling several charts around the table, "So, working backwards… allow a month before that for conversion… sixteen months mining time before that… Heavy payload Earth-Moon transit time, one month… Rego-dozer construction, six months…"

"Six months? Dang it Sal, we'll pay 'em overtime!"

"Dr. Patil?" said Sarah, ignoring her father's outburst, "Launch windows?"

"Seven months. September. Apollo 54."

A reserved cough came from the other side of the room, interrupting the conversation.

"We have a conflict of interests, Dr. Patil."

"My apologies, Dr. Chen," he replied with a very slight bow of the head.

"The FLC beta mission requires our, ah… cargo to use that specific launch."

The public facing Apollo program had ended in 1972 but Archive's missions had continued relentlessly, often in other countries. The significance of 54 in Chinese numerology, meaning 'not-death', had been the subject of heated debate several years ago. However, the timing and contents of Apollo 54 were now part of a long chain of mission dependencies, and impossible to move.

"Suggestions?" asked General Napier to the quiet room.

"Make the 'dozers work faster?" asked Bradley.

Sarah just shook her head, "They're at ninety percent tolerance already. Any faster and we'd risk burning out units and, as we've just discussed, we can't ship new ones up there."

"What, so that's it then?" Bradley glanced around the room, "Novgo bites the dust, and kick-starts two years of panic?"

"This briefing was to ensure that all options had been exhausted, before the main briefing begins in ten minutes," said General Napier checking his watch, "The simple fact is that our various projects are supported by a human workforce. No workforce, no Archive. We cannot afford to destabilise everything that Archive depends on. In order to keep Archive active we must unfortunately reveal at least some of it."

"This is not what we agreed!" began Dr. Chen.

"You're damn straight it ain't!" exploded Bradley, folding his arms.

The room erupted into a chaos of conversations. The General cleared his throat.

"Ladies and Gentlemen!" he shouted, silencing the room, "Your arguments should be levelled against that damn rock! It changed the plan. We adapt or we die. After February 15th 2013, like it or not, we will require the cooperation of everyone on the planet."

Perhaps unsurprisingly, Bradley Pittman was the only one to immediately voice the most obvious question.

"And just how in the hell d'you get seven billion people to do that?"

BOX

11th March 2013

S tanding in her kitchen, frozen to the spot, Kate felt a
rush of cold spread down her spine.

In that moment she didn't know which to fear most,
the doorbell sounding at the same time as the message had
arrived, or the message itself.

'Dont answr the dor'.

The doorbell rang again.

She swiftly switched the phone to 'silent', which seemed
to have the effect of switching the whole house to silence too.
Now individual sounds seemed heightened, isolated. Slowly,
she backed into the corner of the kitchen that was closest to
the back door.

From the relative safety of her kitchen she heard the
letterbox in the hallway squeak slowly open, but it didn't close
again. She realised that someone must be looking through it.

The phone vibrated loudly in her hand.

'Dont mak a sound'.

She realised she'd been holding her breath, and slowly released it. She also realised that the badly spelled messages were arriving in real time; whoever was sending them could see the outside of her house.

The phone vibrated again.

'Dont answr yr hous fone'.

As if on cue, the home phone in her hallway rang. After three rings her answering machine cut in. She heard her own outgoing greeting, followed by a beep. An unfamiliar voice began leaving a message:

"Er, Hi, Miss Walker this is campus security, we know you're staying with friends tonight, but please can you call us when you pick this up. Thanks."

She heard the letterbox squeak shut; evidently whoever was listening at her front door had heard the message and departed.

"This isn't right..." she whispered to herself. Campus security had driven her home, they knew where she was. She walked to the hallway to playback the message, but the smartphone vibrated several times in succession as multiple messages came in.

'He go to bak dor'

'B quiet'

'GET USB GET OUT'

She pocketed the phone and hastily dashed back to the kitchen to grab Rob's memory stick from the table. She could hear footsteps crunching along the gravel path that ran down the side of the house. Someone was about to break in through the back door.

She snatched her coat off the back of the chair and took long stealthy strides along her hallway to the front door. Taking a quick breath, she put her hand on the door latch.

"Dammit!" she muttered and doubled back along the hallway to the understairs cupboard door. As she pulled it open, she heard a soft knock on the back door.

She pulled a black canvas bag from a hook just inside the cupboard, put it over her shoulder, and closed the door again.

From the direction of the back door she heard the sound of keys being tried in the lock. The inevitable was only moments away. She reached out for the door latch and turned it.

The door didn't open. She tried again, tugging harder.

She looked up and saw that the door was still dead-bolted from earlier this evening. She was just reaching up to slide the bolt open when the sound of shattering glass came from the direction of the kitchen.

As swiftly and as silently as she could, she slid the bolt to the left; from the kitchen she could hear the back door being unlocked from the inside.

With the front door dead-bolt now free, she put her hand on the latch once more. She turned it and quietly pulled open the front door; at the same moment she heard the sound of the back door opening, and the sound of broken glass crunching under foot.

She slipped through the doorway and pulled the door behind her until it was almost shut.

She knew she had to get the timing of this just right.

Listening intently, she heard the characteristic groan of the back door's hinges as it was closing.

Just as the back door clicked shut, she gently pulled the front door closed.

She had no idea what time it was, but it must have been well after midnight. The street was dark and deserted, lit only by pools of yellow light that seemed way too far apart for her liking. Fuelled by adrenaline, she started to run down the street. Through a sheer act of will, she managed to slow her pace to a speed-walk. With her back to the house, she didn't know if she was being watched, so she had to try to act normally. Her pace slowed again. The immediate adrenaline rush had subsided slightly and she started to become aware of details around her again.

The phone was vibrating.

'MINICAB'

As she now discovered, in actual fact this last message had been delivered several times before, but her focus had been elsewhere.

She looked up and saw that she had walked past a minicab, the only one on the street. Retracing her steps she walked to the passenger side and bent to look through the window. The reflection of the streetlights, combined with the dim interior, had effectively turned the window into a mirror. Her pale face and mascara-stained cheeks stared back at her, prompting her to wipe at her eyes.

"I…er…" she began, crouching slightly to get a better look in.

Her reflection distorted as the electric window opened an inch. A low, throbbing, bhangra drum beat emanated from the darkness inside.

"Sorry, look, I think I've got the wrong -" she stammered, and started to stand up.

"Minicab for Walker?" came the driver's voice. He was holding his smartphone up to the window for her to see. The display was filled with his sent messages to her, the last of which read *'minicab', 'MINICAB'*.

She pulled on the rear door handle and, with a sideways glance towards her house, climbed into the dark interior of the car. As soon as the door was closed, the driver flicked the oppressive music off.

"Get down and shut up!" he said and, starting the engine, pulled off along the street back in the direction of her house.

From his beanie hat and glasses, to his skin colour, everything about him was dark. He wore a black coat turned up at the collar, part covering his stubble flecked cheeks.

She slumped down in her seat so her head was below the window line. From her position she could see the driver make a seemingly casual glance over at her house as they drove by.

"Did you leave your upstairs light on?" he called over his shoulder.

"What? I, no…" she managed, "Look, who - ?"

"Good," said the driver.

He turned a corner, then after about a hundred yards pulled to a sharp stop, "Time to ditch the wheels. Get out."

"Hey wait! What? We just - " she started, but he was already out of the car.

She ventured a quick check through the back windscreen, before opening her door.

She'd walked down this part of the street a hundred times before, but tonight even the distant traffic noises seemed more remote than she was comfortable with. She felt herself gravitating towards a nearby wall, almost as if she might gain some of its strength by standing near it. The driver had the front passenger door open now and stood with his back to her, busily pulling a rucksack up onto the seat.

"You got questions, yeah?" he said, not taking his eyes off the equipment he was packing, "Me too, believe it. But we gotta get off the street, 'cos in about five minutes, two things are gonna happen…"

She stepped away from the wall slightly and moved a little closer to the car.

"One," he said, briefly raising an index finger into the air, "the owner of this car is gonna realise it's gone."

"You stole the car?!" she whispered aggressively, backing up against the wall again.

"And two, your unwelcome guest will finish searching your bedroom. Hold this."

He thrust a black jacket at her.

"You mean that guy's searching my whole house?!" she hissed.

"He's looking for the stick, ain't he? Thanks to my 'Campus Security' message, he thinks you're staying with friends tonight, so right now he's searching your upstairs."

"That was you who called?" she said fiercely, "That guy is in my house. Because of you?"

He angrily slammed the car door and, throwing the rucksack over his shoulder, stepped so close that she could feel his breath on her face.

"He was gonna hit your house tonight, no matter what. All I did was change whether the police found your corpse or not."

The reality of it dawned on her and she fell silent, trying to take it all in.

"That guy. Is. Dangerous," he asserted, "Rob paid the price."

Despite the street lights it seemed darker. The cold of the pavement had apparently leeched into her feet and she shivered.

"Careless sod," he shook his head as if to clear a memory, then with resolve continued, "We gotta get off the street. Now get out of that stupid glow-in-the-dark beacon and put the jacket on."

Without argument she pulled her few belongings out of the pockets of her red coat, and tipped them into the canvas 'Go-bag' she'd rescued from under her stairs. Until this evening's events, she had completely forgotten about the bag. It had been Rob's suggestion at the time and she had tolerated it rather than get into a debate on the subject.

She pulled on the jacket and was surprised by its weight. There was something altogether more robust and protective about it, and it galvanized her spirits a little.

"Hat's in the left pocket," he said, adjusting his own.

He helped her tuck her long hair into the baseball cap, then they abandoned the car. He took her red coat, turned it inside-out, then unceremoniously stuffed it into a bush.

"What do I call you?" said Kate.

Without hesitation he replied, "Blackbox."

No doubt the stress of the night had got to her, she suddenly barked a laugh.

"Ha! No way in hell I'm calling you Blackbox!" she said, her eyes fixed on the road, "I need your name. You're asking me to trust you, so let's start with your name."

They walked on in silence for a moment, then she heard him clear his throat.

"Blake," he sighed, "My name's Marcus Blake."

DETAIL

11th March 2013

Level Four Interventions were perhaps Benton's favourite type; no time pressure, no conscience-pricking loss of life required, but still furthering the overall cause. Tonight's assignment was a Four; essentially, someone with surface information about Archive had crossed paths with a bystander. He had to investigate the exposure level of the bystander and add them to the watch list if he saw fit; or if the exposure was severe enough, elevate the intervention level for that individual.

He'd received his data package about twenty minutes ago: there had been a possible brush-pass outside the University of West London. Facial recognition software had returned a known alias, 'Blackbox', who had apparently mugged a certain Miss Walker in a car park. If it turned out to be an assault then local authorities would deal with it; but if information had been exchanged then he would need to act accordingly.

After assessing Miss Walker's house to be empty, gaining entry had been simple enough. He'd had to break a small glass panel to unlock the door from the inside, but his photo data returned to Archive Central would see a discreet Handyman deployed to the scene in fifteen minutes or less to fix the problem. He always found it incredible how often people would overlook a massive repair, simply because they weren't looking at it. This would be no different.

A sweep for data storage devices downstairs had only revealed a Wi-Fi router, which had meant there was probably a laptop upstairs. As he suspected, there was no password protection on the bedroom laptop. His plug-in analyser was already scanning the hard drives for relevant data and recording internet habits. From the looks of it so far, the search would come back clean. While he waited, he strolled around the room looking at the framed photos.

Pictures of university colleagues, small groups of friends and a framed Polaroid of a dowdy looking woman with a bundle of blankets, presumably containing a baby. Force of habit made him pry open the small frame to see if there were other photos stored in the back. People tend not to do that these days, he thought. In fact people tended not to print photos at all, preferring to catalogue their digital life and upload it to the 'security' of cloud storage for viewing later.

'Later,' he thought, sadly, '*What 'later'?*'

The move towards widespread, cheap, digital photography had of course been one of Archive's long term goals. It had made computer analysis so much faster. These days controlling information was all about speed.

Other than scribbled text on the back of the Polaroid, there was nothing of interest in the frame so he closed it back up and set it down on the bedside table. For a moment he experienced déjà vu, but then rationalised that there must be something familiar about this particular job. It was hardly surprising though, he'd lost count of the number of Level Four attendances he'd made. Turning off the light again he removed the analyser and headed downstairs; the Handyman had arrived and was sweeping up the broken glass.

"This it then?" the Handyman said, pointing to the broken panel.

"That's it," confirmed Benton.

"No door frame damage. Thanks."

Benton waved away the thanks with his hand and looked at the floor where he'd left partial footprints.

"Can you get rid of the…" he gestured.

"This isn't my first clean up, chief, don't panic," the Handyman replied dismissively over his shoulder.

Crouching down, Benton cast his eye over the dustpan containing the broken glass. There was something else in there too, light brown and flaky.

"You swept only the floor?"

"Of course," came the reply, over a mild pneumatic hiss.

Benton stood up and had a closer look at the table top; there were student folders dumped all over it. He was about to pick one up when he spotted more of the same brown flakes strewn across all the folders. He knew he recognised them from somewhere and quickly walked round to the other side of the table to get a different viewpoint.

Lying on its side was an almost empty plastic fish-food container. He was sure there were no pet fish in this house, but allowed himself the luxury of re-checking the ground floor. He was also sure he'd seen this brand of fish-food container recently. He suddenly realised that, in fact, he had seen this *exact* container before, at an intervention several days ago in a basement flat. The characteristic reddish-brown print was heavily worn away where the lid had been repeatedly prised open, a pattern of wear that could only have developed through *years* of use. Sure enough, when he examined the best-before date stamped on the base, it was eight years ago.

He'd been played.

In his long career it had happened only twice before.

Both times he'd managed to correct the oversight.

This was no different.

He stifled the burning anger that was unaccountably welling up inside him and turned to more immediate matters.

Could he risk the possibility of allowing the Handyman to report the failure?

He had to focus on limiting the damage.

Miss Walker was obviously never coming back, there really was little point in the Handyman repairing the door. He was fairly confident that he could compose a convincing data trail for Central that would explain why the Handyman's dead body was found at the scene of the break-in.

There was a wine bottle on the table, stabbing out from among the pile of folders.

"How much longer for the repair?" enquired Benton casually.

"My pick-up's in ten minutes," he said, removing a long shard of glass from the door, "Why?"

Benton quietly picked up the wine bottle by the neck.

To his surprise it was really cold, as though it had only recently been removed from the fridge.

This changed everything.

The cold bottle meant that his target was probably still nearby, hopefully he wasn't too late.

"Put some of these flakes on the floor when you're done," he said, pressing the fish-food container into the Handyman's glove and replacing the wine.

Although he didn't know which way Miss Walker was headed, he knew people. They would retrace old routes but try to stay away from the main roads. He pointed his car towards the darker end of the street and sped off. He turned left, away from a brightly lit housing estate and continued on.

A minicab was parked up ahead, already he could see that something was not ringing true; he pulled over and got out.

The minicab was parked with its wheels a good twelve inches away from the kerb and the road-side wing mirror was not folded in. On a narrow street like this he would have expected the true vehicle owner to park it more carefully. He could also now see that the doors had been left unlocked.

He walked to the front and placed his hand on the bonnet, it was still warm.

Taking a miniature torch from his pocket he shone it around, the bluish-white light picked out several tiny metallic objects littering the ground next to the passenger door. Crouching, he picked them up and immediately identified them as snapped phone SIMM cards. He collected them all anyway and made the appropriate notes to elevate Kate Walker's watch status. Casting the beam a little wider he saw a small pile of leaves lying on the pavement directly next to an evergreen bush; nature was rarely this tidy. A quick examination revealed a discarded and empty red coat matching the one he had seen in the campus security video. She was obviously getting assistance and the likelihood was that it was from 'Blackbox'.

He realised too why they'd dumped the car here, so close to her house; it was dark and there were no security cameras. For the time being he had actually lost them.

Turning off the torch, he angrily kicked several panel-buckling dents in the minicab's bodywork, before returning to his car.

CLOAK

11th March 2013

Marcus knew where they needed to go; it was a good twenty minute walk away, but it involved crossing through a town centre. In daylight they could blend in with the crowd, but in the dead of night under the glare of street lights and with empty streets, CCTV would pick them out in an instant.

"We gotta go through the centre," admitted Marcus, "no way round."

"OK, so..?" said Kate.

"So, I gotta assume he knows you had my help. Now they're scoping for two bods."

"And?"

"CCTV?" he said incredulously.

"Seriously?" she said, equally incredulously, "You're telling me they can work that fast?"

"You got no idea," he turned his back on her, shaking his head.

They had stopped in an alley that led out onto the brightly lit main High Street. A few feet away the thin veneer of electronic consumerism assaulted his eyes, whilst here in the alley the stench of over-filled bins, rotting food and urine filled his nose.

"What's in your fancy bag?" he asked, keeping his eyes on the street, looking for inspiration.

Kate unzipped the bag, she had tipped her own stuff into it earlier but the main pocket appeared to be divided into sections. Amongst other things there were a medical kit, more SIMM cards of various ages, a small padlocked pocket and an envelope of bank notes.

"What the hell were you thinking, Rob?" she mumbled, absentmindedly.

"What?"

"Nothing," she said, "We've got about a hundred in cash."

"Great. You got any credit cards?"

"Well, I've got my own… but can't they be traced?"

"Good point. Hand 'em over."

He still hadn't taken his eyes off the street, and merely put his open hand behind him to receive the credit cards from her. When she didn't immediately hand the cards over, his shoulders visibly sagged and he turned around to face her again.

"I'm not mugging you, Kate - "

"No, you did that already," she interrupted. It was the first time he had called her by name and just then she didn't know how to deal with the feelings. She closed her eyes and exhaled swiftly, "Sorry."

"Your cards are useless now," he continued as though nothing had happened, "Actually, no. Your cards are toxic now. Please give them to me, so I can save your life. Again."

She nodded and, conceding the valid point, pulled out the cards from her purse.

"Which one's got the lowest limit?" he asked.

"This one," she said pulling it to the front, realising what he was doing, "PIN code 2974."

"Good. Search the bins, I need a bottle and loads of newspaper. We need to disappear."

While he edged closer to the street, she moved back into the alley and started digging through the wheelie bins. She pulled out wet, soggy cardboard and thin, ripped, polythene bags filled with what smelled like soiled nappies. Finally she found a bag of glass bottles and lifted a few out. Dry newspapers were more of a rarity, and she was still searching when he returned.

"Your carriage, Madam," he mocked, presenting a bashed-up shopping trolley full of metal cans.

"What?" she said, not insulted, just puzzled.

"This is my new mate, Terry," said Marcus, stepping aside to reveal a dishevelled, hesitant, old-looking man, "He's agreed to lend us his trolley for half an hour, ain't that right Terry?"

They worked quickly to empty the trolley of cans, then helped Kate climb in. They piled about half the cans around her and, not having much newspaper, topped it off with a mound of wet cardboard. To the casual observer it would look like the same trolley that had entered the alley five minutes before. Marcus gave Terry fifty pounds and the credit card, with instructions on when and where to use it.

"Terry, you're a life saver," said Marcus, picking up one of the half-emptied bottles and scrubbing at the open end with his sleeve.

Terry simply hugged him, he would be able to eat for the first time in days.

"Good luck," came Kate's cardboard-muffled voice.

Taking a deep breath, Marcus stooped, and taking hold of the trolley handles quipped, "Invisibility cloak engaged…"

He pushed the trolley slowly out of the alley and staggered down the brightly lit street, being careful to swig from the empty bottle occasionally. The few people they passed on the streets looked straight through him, or perhaps studiously ignored him, completely ignoring his precious cargo.

COMPLIANCE

7th February 2010

Alfred Barnes poured himself a glass of water while waiting for Bradley Pittman and Alexey Yakovna to take their seats with the others. From the side of the room General Napier gave him a nod, and dimmed the lecture theatre lights. In response the noise level lowered. Alfred pushed his spectacles back into place. He estimated that there could only be perhaps forty people present, but this small number would shape everything to come.

He cleared his throat and, as the last few conversations stopped, he turned on the overhead projector to display his first slide:

How do we save our species?

"As a species we are reckless, short-sighted, and seemingly incapable of cooperating to save ourselves. And yet as individuals, self preservation is a persistent and dominating force. Why can't our species just be more like us? Right? This," he said throwing a thumb over his shoulder to the screen and shaking his head, "This is the wrong question."

He replaced the slide:

How do you persuade our species to save itself?

"Before I answer that, we'll need to go back a little way,"
He changed the slide again:

Chain

"As a species we've been surviving and adapting for a very *long* time. Through a mere quirk of branching probability, each and every one of you here today represents the most successful genetic outcome. Congratulations!"

Most of the delegates managed a short, but controlled, laugh.

"But there's a problem with being at the successful end of a million year old, biological, probability chain. The very method the chain uses to determine a *'successful outcome'* is now hard-wired into our genetics.

"And that's a problem.

"We carry a lot of *useless* evolutionary baggage. The adrenalin our ape bodies made to outrun a predator still floods our veins today when we get an annoying email. Our craving for foods high in fat and sugar, doesn't turn off in summer. Our fundamental, selfish, drive to have a bigger stick than the other apes? Well that's moved on a little, we want to own a better car than the other apes…"

There were a few polite laughs throughout the theatre.

"The point is that species level cooperation conflicts *directly* with each individual's *indomitable* drive to increase their own advantage."

He let this last statement hang for a moment in the hushed room.

"Put simply, I believe cooperation conflicts directly with self-preservation."

He took a sip of water before continuing.

"But what about those working to preserve the environment for future generations? Surely that's cooperation? Surely that's the voice of reason? Right?"

The auditorium remained silent as he changed the slide again:

Chains

"Wrong. It's just that old evolutionary chain using your voice. Don't forget, the chain *itself* has had to ensure its own survival too. It's had to survive encounters with other competing chains. It's happened before. The chain containing Homo sapiens won against the Neanderthals.

"It wasn't achieved through a war, them and us at each end of some big battlefield! It's just that our tools and forward planning were better.

"They died, we lived. Individuals perished, but our chain ensured its own survival.

"Sure, we can call our ecological actions altruistic, or self-sacrificing. But it's only our genetic chain, acting to preserve itself by cosily wrapping itself in human linguistics."

He took a swig of water and then added with a wry smile,

"And no prizes for guessing that it was *evolution* that gave us that language skill."

There was a smattering of appreciation here and there.

"So. Here we are," he continued, throwing wide his arms, "Slaves to our own genetic chain of success, stuck with who we are. We can't just choose to shrug off a million years of evolution just because we want to try on something new. No matter what we do, in a survival situation, each individual's instincts will motivate choices to improve their chances of survival."

He swapped slides:

Choice

"Now, if we assume that survival instinct will act to motivate an individual, only then will their mind step in to evaluate available options and make a choice. This might be a choice to run away. A choice to fight. No point us having an evolved threat detection system with no ability to act on it. What happens next could be called free will. Personal determinism. Choice.

"In simpler times, swinging through the high trees, our primitive ape brains were probably faced with a choice of two possible tree branches to jump to. If neither of the options were within our leap, we had to have the intelligence to reject both options, rather than leap to our possible death. Those that survived this basic intelligence test ensured that this life-saving skill was passed down the chain to us.

"But a few hundred thousand years later? It turns out it's not that helpful when you're trying to save a species. When people feel they have no viable choice, that primitive tree-clinging behaviour reasserts control to save us from making a potentially bad decision.

"The problem is that we don't *want* people to cling to the tree, we want them to leap. We want them to make a choice; because it's only in that moment of *choice* that we have the opportunity to interrupt the process and directly control an individual's rational mind.

"So how do you ensure that a choice gets made?"

He lowered another slide over the top of the original so that collectively they now read:

Illusion of Choice

This seemed to get assenting nods from some of the audience.

"Did you know that people will more readily choose from limited options if they feel they have a level of control over the outcome? Please note that I said *'feel'* that they have control."

He paused again here to allow time for the idea to translate.

"The reality of our dire situation is that when Tenca initiates panic in about three year's time, there will be very few real choices for people to actually make. What we're discussing today is engineering a social system that has the *semblance* of choice, but under Archive's control.

"To motivate people into making a choice from limited options, they will need to *believe* that their choice puts control back in their hands. On our part we will need to manufacture choices that are believable and cover a wide range of personality types.

"Finally, we move into darker territory. What if," he said turning the projector off, "What if the choice given is a questionable one? Uncomfortable. Perhaps immoral. What then?"

Whilst some of the delegates squirmed slightly in their seats, he changed slides and then turned on the projector again:

Authority

"Well, as I'm sure many of you know, in the Sixties social psychologist Stanley Milgram conducted an experiment concerning obedience to authority figures. It was an elegant experiment, worthwhile looking up if you get the chance. The exact results vary each time the experiment is reproduced, but the overall trend remains the same.

"He showed that when people were given the permission of an authority figure, they were more willing to make morally questionable choices. Issues of authority, choice and genetic predisposition to preservation, are all phenomena we'll need to utilise in this afternoon's Think Tank."

He changed slide again:

Fallen Veil

"On February 13th 2013, Archive's intricately woven veil of concealment will fall, and people's survival instinct will prompt action. Before they have time to think of their own alternatives, we will interrupt.

"We *must* provide them with a suitable range of choices that they believe are both within their control, and aligned with their personality type. We must then reinforce the validity of their choice by giving them the legal permission of a suitable authority figure. So even if individuals make a choice that could be considered morally questionable, we can mitigate the rejection effect.

"I'm sorry I have to put this into words, but in your sub-group discussions please put conventional morality to one side. We're not doing this to save any one individual. We are doing this..."

He put up his last slide:

For the good of Mankind

•

The afternoon Think Tank sessions were many and varied, with the delegates being split into six sub-groups to debate the mammoth social engineering techniques necessary to ensure the compliance of a global population. There was certainly no shortage of available Archive projects requiring a massive dedicated workforce. The problem was how to allocate people to each project in such a way that it ensured their voluntary, and lifelong, dedication.

Alfred Barnes was the only delegate with the authority, and indeed time, to move between sub-groups; a move designed to ensure compartmentalisation of ideas, keep a check on progress, and also allow him to steer people away from overly merciful thinking if necessary. It would be his responsibility to collate the delegates' recommendations and formulate the solution framework. After fourteen straight hours of debate he finally had all the sub-groups' contributions and needed to retire to quieter quarters.

Andersen Air Force Base had been the perfect choice as the summit location. With at least a thousand miles of Pacific Ocean surrounding it in every direction, it was remote enough to ensure the level of privacy that Archive required. The delegates' quarters were, by necessity, small and sparse; but despite the level of responsibility his position carried, he had insisted he was treated no differently. The bare, grey, breeze-block walls and hard bunk ensured there would be no visual distraction to his collation task overnight.

Just before midnight there was a sharp double knock on the door.

"Come in," he said, more as a formality than an invitation.

General Napier entered, which seemed to halve the small room's available space.

"Dr. Barnes."

"General. Please excuse the mess," he said, starting to bundle up piles of documents.

Napier waved a hand to dismiss the apology then plucked his hat off and hung it from a nearby peg.

"Hell of a day," he exhaled and sat down, fully occupying the room's sofa.

He brought out a flask of coffee and, after pouring himself a lid-full, passed it to Alfred.

"Hell of a day," replied Alfred, refilling his stained mug, "But not as bad as it'll be tomorrow."

The two of them quietly raised their drinks to each other, and then downed a mouthful.

"Do you believe a word of what you told everyone this morning?" said General Napier, flatly, "That we can control the thoughts and actions of seven billion people?"

Alfred took another sip before replying:

"In part, but the people I addressed this morning are as much a part of the population as anyone else on the planet. They themselves have to believe that they have both the permission, and the authority, to control others."

"Ha," General Napier actually smiled, something Alfred had rarely seen him do, "The illusion of control."

"How can I help you, General?"

Napier leaned back into the sofa and took a deep breath.

"I know you're due to deliver your report at the zero eight hundred hours briefing, but I was hoping to get some initial feedback."

Alfred sighed and picked up the pile of his most recent notes.

"The current projection from this afternoon's sub-groups is that ninety-six percent will comply with SRC - "

"The..?" interrupted Napier.

"Sorry, force of habit. 'Supplied Rationalised Choice'. The damned acronyms creep in. Fascinating really, initially acronyms are used to simplify verbal repetition, but later they become tribal language motifs that reinforce a bond betwee-"

"So four percent will not comply?" Napier interrupted with a cough, "They'll decide not to select from our allowed choices?"

Alfred drained the rest of his cup before continuing somewhat hesitantly, "My concern is that if the remaining four percent don't comply or, even worse, spread destructive conspiracy theories, then they could destabilise the social order we're trying to impose. Those who don't select one of our choices will be detrimental to our solution, and that makes them a problem. I'm afraid there's no delicate way of saying it - in order to save the ninety-six, four percent must be either coerced into compliance, or - "

"Culled from the population," completed Napier directly.

"Yes," Alfred shook his head in disbelief of the conversation, "The cold fact of the matter is that, as a consequence, we will need people who are willing to carry out the coercion or termination of those that won't comply."

Except for the low level hum of the air conditioning ducts overhead, the small room became quiet.

General Napier held his level gaze at Alfred.

Alfred grabbed a piece of scrap paper from the desk along with a pen.

"By definition we'll have no control over the non-compliant four percent. Right?" He began sketching a Venn diagram, of circles within overlapping circles.

"OK," said Napier angling his head to read it.

"So, the problem is that anyone who is actually willing to *murder* someone inside that four percent would need to be picked from within this nicely compliant ninety-six percent of the population," he pointed to the diagram.

"And this is a problem because..?" questioned Napier.

"They would have to be from within a subset of a very specific personality type," he said, scribbling more concentric circles, "They'd have to be willing to kill for an authority figure, whilst simultaneously persuading themselves that they are doing it for the good of humanity."

"It sounds like you're describing every soldier under my command..." said Napier, straightening his shirt cuffs in mild irritation.

"No! Sorry, you misunderstand me. Look," he interrupted, tapping a blank area of the diagram, "in addition to that they'd need to be independently driven but have absolutely no vested interest in their own long-term personal survival. That subset is *empty*! The personality-type doesn't exist."

General Napier shifted slightly in his seat, "Well that's not completely true. The 'subset', as you call it, is not totally empty. They are rare though..."

Alfred was momentarily distracted into silence.

"Until now," began Napier, "we've been dealing with a completely different problem - suppressing the knowledge of Archive's projects. In the process of doing this, certain *individuals* came to our attention that appear to demonstrate that very personality-type," he said gesturing to Alfred's circles.

"What? That...that's incredible!" stammered Alfred, searching for a blank pad of paper.

"Occasionally there have been members of the public who absolutely would not be dissuaded from spreading sensitive information. So on those occasions we sent in our *'ego-morphs'* to quietly contain or neutralise. Very dependable, very precise, zero residual presence."

"But that would make them..." he found some paper and started to scribble notes, "I mean their intelligence must be - "

"Astonishing," completed Napier, "One of their former handlers once told me that they're like an observation black hole - nothing escapes their attention."

"Incredible! I'd like to meet one. Their psych -"

"You really wouldn't," interrupted Napier, "Typically they attempt to coerce their targets from a distance, but by the time you meet one, your remaining life-span is apparently measured in minutes."

"So they're faster, stronger, or something?"

"No, not unusually so. But they don't need to be. They... anticipate."

This was too much information for Alfred to receive in one conversation, and he became suspicious.

He took off his reading glasses and folded them into his shirt pocket.

"You didn't come in here for my initial feedback, did you General?"

Napier simply sat, and waited for Alfred to reach the conclusion under his own steam.

"Your 'ego-morphs' - fascinating - but why tell me? What's the phrase you use? 'Need to know basis'. The only reason I would need to know about them is if they were relevant. At this moment. So, with all due respect, why are we having this conversation?"

"Fallen Veil, Doctor. Isn't that the way you put it? The day we effectively lose containment?" General Napier smiled, but it didn't quite extend to his eyes. "Very soon we'll be moving away from suppressing the knowledge of Archive's existence and begin herding people into their new, miserable, roles. At that point our ego-morphs will need a new function, that in almost every respect is still protecting the same goal. They will remove the influence of the four percent and protect Archive's interests at all costs."

He stood up and retrieved his hat.

"The reason you needed to know about them is because they are now relevant, specifically to you. They are a valuable resource and must be integral to your overall plan recommendations."

He presented Alfred with yet another buff-coloured folder. This differed from the crisp, brand-new ones he'd been accumulating all day; it was obviously very old, with layers of yellowed, aging sticking tape holding it together.

"Some additional reading material Doctor, your eyes only. Please, keep the coffee - I think you'll need it."

And closing the door, Napier left him.

The folder and contents were an inch thick. The page edges graduated from creamy-yellow and ragged at the top, through to bleached-white and pristine at the bottom. The front was completely covered in rubber-stamped text of various sizes and ages, indicating levels of privacy and authorisation necessary to read the contents.

"Cheapskates!" he remarked to the empty room, "Couldn't even replace the dog-eared fold…"

He stopped mid-sentence as he realised that, from the level of repairs this folder had gone through, there had been only a few owners in its long career. The information within it truly had been 'eyes only'.

He cleared a space on his cluttered table and placed the folder directly under the room's angle-poise lamp. The most faded, and presumably oldest, ink stamp on the cover read 'SIVA'.

The first pages, yellowed by the decades, were columns of numbers with what looked like a handwritten phone number scrawled in one corner. A few pages later, a now faded photo of the stars was annotated with an almost equally transparent name - 'HowardWalker'.

Alfred poured himself another cup of coffee, and started to read.

SUITS

10th October 1957

Howard and Elizabeth Walker lived in Atlanta, about five miles west of the Bradley Observatory. It was a fairly modest single storey home, with a small veranda skirting the front to provide shade during the warm summers. In their compact living room they were playing with their son who was busy trying to taste the shapes of various coloured wooden blocks and squealing delightedly to his parents' smiles. The pregnancy had been a difficult one but modern medicine had provided for them; and the delivery had had a surplus of expertise, including Howard himself who had offered helpful breathing advice before Elizabeth had been escorted into the delivery room.

"Blue," Howard said, holding the rectangular block for his son to see, "Blue. Cuboid."

He placed it down on the thick rug in front of him.

"Douglas?" said Elizabeth, miming 'where' with a puzzled expression, "Blue, sphere?"

Douglas immediately grabbed the blue ball that had been placed on the rug earlier in their game, and began biting it.

"Good boy, Dougie!" clapped his parents.

The front door bell chimed.

"Think he's going to be bright," Elizabeth gave her husband a peck on the cheek and headed towards the door.

"Going to be?" he half laughed, beaming at his son, "I'd say he's well on the way!"

"You're biased, remember your academic rigour..." she teased.

She opened the door to find two men standing a few feet away.

"Mrs. Walker? Sorry to disturb you, is your husband home?" said one of them.

"Sure, hold on one second. There's someone to see you, honey."

Howard scooped Douglas up from the rug and, half skidding on some home-made flashcards, walked over.

"Here, take Dougie will you? There you go little fella, thanks Betty."

The first thing that struck Howard was that the two men had identical dark grey suits.

"Yes, what can I do for you?"

One of them consulted a small clipboard of passport sized photos and then nodded to the other.

"Dr. Walker, we need to talk to you in private," he said, raising his official-looking identification card.

"Look guys it's getting a little late, I'd ask you inside to talk - "

"Not here," interrupted the slightly taller one, forcing a swift but tight lipped smile.

"What's this about?" asked Howard in a lowered tone, "Am I in some kind of trouble?"

"No," said the shorter one, "But we'd rather ask you nicely to accompany us, than make a scene here."

The taller one made a show of putting his pen back inside his jacket pocket, whilst obviously displaying the holstered gun at his waist. Registering the fact that Howard had now seen the minor display of force, he reassured him.

"Everything is fine Dr. Walker, and you'll be back, unscathed, by morning. Your wife and kid will be quite safe here, but your immediate assistance is required."

Struggling a little to keep up with the events, Howard glanced behind him to see Elizabeth on the sofa, busy bottle-feeding Douglas and apparently unaware of the conversation.

"I need..." he managed, "I need to let my wife know, and get a few things."

"Everything will be provided for you Dr. Walker," said the taller one and then, displaying a suddenly cheerful smile, called into the house, "Mrs. Walker? No, please don't get up, I can see you're busy with baby Dougie! It seems that someone broke in at the observatory so Howard's going to come with us and secure the premises. I'm sorry for the inconvenience, I truly am."

"Howard..?" she called.

"It's OK honey," he improvised, "I'll be back before Dougie's next bottle."

"OK, look, call me when you get there?"

He pulled on his coat and beamed a smile at her.

"You know me!" he said, pulling the door closed behind him before she had time to reply.

The shorter of the two men walked ahead of him to the waiting black car and opened the rear door.

"Please…" he gestured to the empty back seat.

Howard complied and climbed in. The door closed behind him and immediately the sounds of the world outside seemed to disappear. Inside the car the sound was deadened, muted, no doubt assisted by the expensive leather upholstery. The silence was broken for a moment as his escorts climbed in.

The shorter one tuned in the Bakelite two-way radio mounted in the dashboard, whilst the taller one picked up the handset. After the last of the whistles and pops were tuned out he clicked the transmit button on the side.

"Mother, Hotel Whiskey collected - Over."

By response, two beeps sounded over the dashboard speaker and, satisfied the message had been received, he hung up the handset and started the engine. As they started to drive, the taller one turned round in his seat to face Howard.

"You might want to get comfortable."

"But the observatory is just - oh, of course. We're not going to the observatory are we?" asked Howard, rhetorically.

"I'm sorry we couldn't tell your wife, but no we're going… somewhere safe."

"Look guys, what's this all about?" said Howard, almost apologetically, "I want to help but -"

"I've been authorised to give you this," he interrupted, handing over a thin, crisp, buff-coloured folder, "beyond that I don't know."

Howard took the folder; neat rubber-stamped letters across the top read 'SIVA'.

"Siva? I don't understand."

The taller one shrugged and turned again to face the front.

Howard opened the folder and found only a few pages inside, stapled at the corner. Most of the pages were filled with columns of data. He recognized them immediately as measurements of right ascension and declination relative to the Earth's ecliptic plane. Whatever the reason for his polite abduction, it would be linked with his expertise in astronomy.

One of the rows had been circled in red ink. A hand written note in the margin stated '2.5% traj. error!'

He flicked on through the pages, and came across a diagram of concentric ellipses labelled with the names of the inner planets of the solar system. Overlaid on this was an array of arcs that intersected with the orbit labelled 'Earth'. His heart skipped a beat as his eyes darted to find a date. He breathed a sigh of relief when he saw this was only a projection for some time in the next century. He flicked on again and this time found the only photograph within the folder.

Vague feelings of familiarity gave way to one of horrified recognition. He had the exact same photo mounted in a frame, at home. He was looking at a copy of his original 1951 plate photography, taken some six years ago at the observatory. His blood ran cold as he shuffled hastily back and forth through the pages, desperate to find answers. He came to the photo again, and just stared in disbelief.

"How long 'til we get there?" he said, impatiently drumming his fingers on the seat.

"In this traffic, forty minutes," came the shorter one's reply.

He looked again at the projected date. Early 2015. Doing the quick calculation he murmured "Fifty-eight years from now."

Overhearing him, the taller one let out a dry laugh, assuming he was still talking about the traffic.

He stared out of the window. His discovery of 1951 VA seemed like only yesterday, and yet here he was contemplating events in the next century. Looking again at the photograph and its accompanying text a thought crossed his mind; on a whim he used his finger to cover up the digits of his own century, and saw '51VA'

"Siva," he half laughed, "Of course."

•

When Howard had been marched into the draughty gym hall of Fort Gillings military base, he had immediately recognized

Sam Bishop, the astronomy mentor who had guided his early career. Given the ramifications of the potential threat, the briefing and location were disappointingly small; Howard was amazed that more people were not involved.

The further realisation occurred that he must therefore be one of the first ones to be aware of the discovery. There was no 'they' already working on the problem, he was present at the genesis of any solution that would follow.

Howard was escorted to the centre of the hall, where four chairs were arranged in a semi-circle around a large speaker with a black telephone moulded into the top. The armed escort then turned on his heels and marched out, the rubber soles of his boots squeaking slightly on the highly polished floor. When he was sure that they were alone, Sam spoke:

"How are you doing, young man?" he said, patting him on the shoulder.

"Not so young any more," he smiled, "Douglas is keeping us up all night. Good to see you again Sam."

"And how's Betty?"

"She's OK. We're struggling a bit with the house payments, she puts a brave face on it but I think she's finding it hard."

Sam just nodded.

"So why are we here Sam?" he said looking around the sparse surroundings, "Who wants to see us?"

Sam looked a little hesitant and gesturing to the basic chairs, invited him to sit down.

"It's me that requested you, Howard," he said almost apologetically.

"What?" Howard whispered, "You're military now?!"

"No, no!" Sam chuckled, "But I do have Eisenhower's ear…"

"Then…wait a minute…what?"

Sam waved away the interruption.

"The others will be here soon, so it's vital I fill you in on the details first. Understood?"

Howard nodded, feeling a little like he was a student again.

"You remember the 1951 VA print I gave you and Betty for your anniversary?"

"Of course…" replied Howard quizzically.

"Yes, well, in the process of getting it duplicated for you, I looked again at the exposure time and discovered a possible error in the trajectory - "

"The two point five percent - "

"Yes. I've since confirmed it using my own plates. 1951 VA, 'Siva', is a comet."

These details had been in the file that Howard had read on the way over, but to hear the words from someone he trusted seemed to make it all devastatingly real.

"It's all my fault," began Howard, slumping in the chair. "If only I'd - "

"Ha!" laughed Sam, cutting him off, "Sorry. Pardon my insensitivity, but no, it most definitely is *not* your fault."

Sam sat down in the chair next to him.

"It was a million-to-one shot that you were looking in that region of sky in the first place. It was your keen eye that picked it up. And had you not proposed to Betty that night, I'd have had no reason, sentimental or otherwise, to even look at the photo-plates again. So no, far from being your fault, we have you to thank."

Sam looked at the telephone and then after checking the clock on the wall, continued.

"I really will have to be brief, so putting sentimentality aside for a moment I need my best student to sit up and take note."

The authoritarian tone seemed to trigger an automatic response in Howard and suddenly he found himself alert and focussed.

"I brought you here Howard, so I could start to hand over my authority to you. You're the brightest I ever taught, your thesis on theoretical trans-lunar flight was beyond me, and you're personally involved with the comet's history. I know you'll work tirelessly to find a way to protect your grandchildren - "

Grandchildren; the thought had genuinely not occurred to Howard before. But thinking about it, by the time the comet was due to strike Earth, his son Douglas could himself have children as old as he was now.

"I don't understand Sam, if you say the President listens to you, surely you - "

"It's a young man's game," he cut in, "I need to make sure what I've contributed... counts in some way. Ike's a good man, he's exactly what we need. And because he listens to me, he'll listen to you when I'm gone."

"When you're gone?"

"Ah Howard, everyone has their time. This is mine. Doc says I've got about six months…"

"Wait, what? You're dying?"

"Everyone is dying. One day at a time," he smiled, "That's why you've got to make it count, kid!"

"Sam, I'd no idea," mumbled Howard, "Why didn't you say something?"

The hall doors opened and the same rubber-booted armed escort marched two more people in. Sam quickly turned to Howard and spoke in a lowered voice, "Time to step up."

"Gentleman," Sam stood to greet them, "your timing is excellent, we're about to receive the President's call."

The four of them took turns shaking hands and introducing themselves to each other, then on the stroke of six o'clock the telephone bell rang, echoing around the gym. As the others took their seats, Sam Bishop lifted the heavy handset and listened.

"And to you too, Mr. President," came his one-sided reply, then after another pause he added, "Understood. I'll open the conversation to multi-person now."

Sam turned a large knob on the speaker box, so that the indicator pointed to 'Multi', and a small red bulb above it lit up.

"Mr. President you are now speaking in conference."

"Good evening, Gentlemen," came Eisenhower's voice over the crackling speaker.

"Good evening, Mr. President," they replied, almost completely in unison.

"By now you will have read the files provided by Dr. Bishop on the potentially devastating event that will befall our world should we fail to avert it. But avert it we must, we can have no loftier goal. Following the Russians' launch of their Sputnik satellite last week, we believe they are already aware of the issue and may be developing a program for space occupation. Therefore, in your search for solutions, I vow to put the resources of this office at your disposal.

"Despite the personal reactions you will be no doubt be experiencing, I must order you not to spread information beyond these walls without my authorisation. The news will only instil panic in those we will be trying to save. I would please ask you to focus only on today. We must move forward now with quiet determination and have the courage to make the intellectual strides necessary to create a living archive for the human race. Or our generation alone will be counted among the lucky ones."

During the remainder of the telephone conference, the word 'Archive' was chosen to represent the colossal undertaking; mostly because of Eisenhower's own reference to a 'living archive', but also because the word in isolation would mean very little to anyone who overheard it. However the need for a covert communication framework was still discussed in order to further reduce the probability of the project being discovered accidentally.

In order to protect the global population from panic, Archive's projects would need to slowly unfold over more than half a century. Despite this, it would also require advances in scientific knowledge and technology to progress at a rate faster than at any time in all of recorded history.

Vast sums could be channelled from the world's governments into Archive, under budgets loosely termed 'Defence'. But appropriating the knowledge, expertise and resources to allow technological development to expand at a geometric rate would require the involvement and the instant private funds of billionaires.

In the two hours following the telephone call, a shortlist of those likely to fit the strict 'delegate' profile, was prepared. At the top of the delegate list was William Pittman, and with good reason. The exact worth and scope of the Pittman family empire could only really be estimated, as their various enterprises spanned the globe. This was of course the main reason Archive had elevated his status to delegate number one.

Sam Bishop took Howard to one side of the hall and handed him an address on a piece of paper.

"William Pittman's requested that you meet him. He's read the official brief."

"Already?" he whispered, somewhat in awe at the speed with which his rough notes had been turned into a Presidential brief, and delivered to the first delegate, "Look, Sam, I don't think I'm really qualified to - ".

"Look around you, Howard," said Sam in hushed tones, "How could anyone be *qualified* for something like this? You know the details better than anyone. This is where it all begins. You have to get on board with this now. This starts with you."

Sam knocked once on the hall door, and within a few seconds the armed escort entered the hall again.

"Sir," he said, snapping to attention this time.

Sam looked pointedly at Howard, and then at the piece of paper he was holding in his hand. Howard caught on, and clearing his throat, he stood up straight.

"Thank you," said Howard, and with as much authority as he could muster, presented the paper, "Please drive me here."

•

In stark contrast to the Fort Gillings gym hall, The Pitstop seemed a welcome and lively place. In fact when Howard's escort dropped him at the entrance he felt sure that there must be some mistake, and spent a good few minutes waiting outside, feeling completely out of place. It seemed ridiculous to him that such a prominent industrialist would want to meet here.

"This is stupid," he muttered to himself and, checking again that he was at the right address, made his way down the ironwork steps to the basement establishment.

A bar ran along one side of the long room and along the other side were several open-sided booths, with seats inside facing each other. Down the centre were more open tables and chairs. The place was loud with the buzz of conversation and jukebox music, but not rowdy. Not sure who or what he was looking for, he just stood and glanced around the lively scene. After a minute he decided it had been a mistake and turned to leave, to find himself almost walking into a man nearly as wide as the door.

"Howard Walker? Bill Pittman," he introduced himself, thrusting out a forceful hand.

"Hi, good to meet you. I wasn't sure I had the right place. How did you know it was me?"

"Don't know anybody who goes drinkin' with a beat up satchel of paper," he smirked, pointing at Howard's now aging leather bag, "Now, what say we get ourselves a drink?"

Howard laughed, it was probably the most normal thing anyone had said all day, certainly the most grounded. They walked over to the bar, where a bartender slid to their assistance.

"Good evening Mr. Pittman, Sir. The usual?"

"Nope Patrick, I think we're gonna need the strong stuff tonight. Me an' Howie need a quiet conversation."

"Of course, right away. Will you need the room?"

"A booth'll do just fine."

The bartender nodded and then strode across the room to evict a couple from a secluded booth in the corner of the bar. He compensated them with a bottle of champagne and cleared the table with such efficiency that Howard got the impression that this was not the first time he'd done it.

"All ready for you, Mr. Pittman," intoned the bartender and with smooth proficiency he guided them over to their new seats. Howard watched with amazement and felt a little guilty at forcing someone to give up their place for him. Although Bill was not academically well read, he could read people, and made a mental note of Howard's expression.

"I guess you come here a lot?" asked Howard, sliding into the seat on one side of the booth.

"Nope, but I own a load of these places," he smiled, taking up the place opposite him, "It carries a little weight."

As if on cue, the bartender reappeared and deposited two small glasses and a bottle of whiskey, and then he was gone again without a word. Bill opened the bottle and poured out a finger measure for each of them, then pushed a glass over to Howard.

"Oh, I don't really... alcohol and me, I..." Howard tried to excuse himself.

"Listen Howie, I very much wanna hear what you got to say to me, but I sure as hell ain't gonna do this cold sober. Now you raise your glass an' take the edge off."

From the look in Bill's eyes, refusal was not really an option. The look was not one of menace, if anything it was of sincerity.

Howard squared his shoulders and raised his glass to match Bill's, then both downed the whiskey together. Bill placed his empty glass on the table with a firm hand, while

Howard collapsed into a coughing fit, hoarsely commenting how strong it was.

"Good man!" said Bill with a wide grin, and poured a second measure each, "D'you have kids Howie?"

"Just the one," he managed through a second, smaller, coughing fit. He pulled out his wallet and flipped it open to show the photo of his wife holding their baby, "That's my Douglas. How about you?"

"Yep," smiled Bill, similarly presenting his photo, "Bradley's my pride and joy."

Bill pulled out his cigarettes and a matchbox, and started digging out a match from the sliding tray.

"Sorry Howie," he apologised, offering him the packet, "d'you smoke?"

"No, not really...I - "

"One vice was enough for tonight huh?" he joked, flaring a match off the side of the box.

"No, I can't... that is, er," Howard looked away awkwardly, "we can't afford... money's kind of..."

Bill glanced at Howard's hands, still absentmindedly thumbing over the photo. On impulse he blew out his match and put away his cigarettes.

"Please don't stop on my account - " Howard started.

"Whole world's about to change Howie," he interrupted, leaning across the table, "We gotta keep an eye on what's important," he said tapping Howard's photo with his own heavy wallet.

Holding each other's stare, the two of them exchanged a sincere nod, before sipping the whiskey.

"Now, why don't you lay it all down for me?" Bill said glancing at Howard's satchel.

"OK," began Howard, pulling out reams of paper and notes, and spreading them over the table, "When I first detected Siva, I identified it as an asteroid, but with a mere two and a half percent trajectory error, we'd actually be looking at a comet instead, with a decaying elliptical solar orbit, and strong probability factor of Earth position coincidence sometime in…" Howard stopped, Bill was shaking his head.

"Howie," he sighed, "this ain't a test. I know you can tell one end of a slide-rule from the other. Whatever fix you come up with I'm guessin' we're gonna need a whole heap o' cash. So that's what I do, I'm the guy with the deep pocket that'll kick start it. But I'm a simple man, so simplify."

The alcohol had already started loosening Howard's tongue and he was finding it easier to speak his mind, even if his mind had been simultaneously slightly dulled.

"We don't have good enough instruments yet but some time early in 2015, the comet Siva, will collide with Earth. Catastrophically. How's that for simple?"

Saying it out loud made it seem preposterous to Howard.

"See? That weren't so hard," Bill concluded bluntly.

"We've got fifty-eight years to either destroy Siva before it gets here, or find a way to get off the planet."

"Or both," said Bill knocking back the remains of his whiskey.

"Both?"

"My Grandma, God rest her, always used to go on about not carrying all your eggs in one basket. If we're talking about the human race, shouldn't we oughta have more than one basket?"

Howard looked blank, evidently he wasn't used to the drink.

"Howie, we gotta shoot that comet down, but plan on getting off this ball o' rock too."

"That deep pocket of yours had better be pretty deep."

"I might need to dip into some of my other pants," he grinned, then pulled a pen from his coat and wrote a telephone number across the top of one of Howard's pages.

"This is my direct number," said Bill buttoning his coat, "Call me tomorrow afternoon, so we can make a plan. You're a decent man Howard, I think Bradley and Douglas are going to grow up to be good friends."

"I hope so," said Howard, gathering up his papers again.

"Did you drive over here Howie?"

"No, the escort dropped me here."

"I'll have Patrick arrange a car for you," smiled Bill, "Been a pleasure."

They shook hands and while Howard gathered up the last of his papers he saw Bill have a conversation with the attentive bartender.

During the long drive back to Atlanta, the surly driver hardly seemed to say anything. This suited Howard just fine, the burden of the knowledge he had acquired over the last day had been immense to say the least, and he tried to use the time to work out what he would say to Elizabeth. No matter how he tried to construct the sentences in his head, he could never imagine looking into his wife's eyes and saying them. The car turned down his street and his attention was once again drawn into the present.

"It's number twelve," he called to the driver.

The driver pulled into the empty driveway of the Walkers' house, turned off the engine and got out. Howard opened his own door and climbed out too.

"Thanks for the - " he began.

"Sign at the bottom," interrupted the driver, handing him a clipboard.

After Howard had signed the form, the driver handed him a copy and started to walk back down the driveway.

"Your keys are in the ignition," he called over his shoulder.

"My keys?"

The driver didn't reply but turned up his collar and, muttering under his breath, started to walk to the nearest bus stop. Howard quickly found the keys, on which a brown paper luggage label was tied. A hand-written note on one side read:

'Thanks Howard, talk soon. B. Pittman'.

CAPITOL HILL

25th May 1961

Under Eisenhower's instruction, the National Aeronautics and Space Administration had been formed in 1958, and since then had operated under Archive's direction. Of course NASA was not the only such acquisition. In the four years since the briefing in the cold gymnasium of Fort Gillings, Archive's reach and influence had expanded to encompass vast areas of scientific or geographical advantage in pursuit of the long term goal.

Six months after Archive's creation, a quiet memorial service was held for Sam Bishop. But prior to that he was true to his word and took every opportunity to elevate Howard Walker to a position of trust with regard to the Oval Office.

For his part, Bill Pittman sank his personal and industrial fortune into every aspect of Archive. But there came a day when he confided in Howard that their space endeavours were rapidly approaching the limits of concealability, both in terms of his creative accountancy and the sheer number of physical assets that were being created.

"We need to wave the Stars 'n' Stripes, Howie!" he had commented, "Bring it out into the light. Give the good folks o' the U. S. of A. something they can get behind. And maybe cough up a little cash too!"

In the winter of 1960, the members of Archive were faced with a difficult decision. They realised that with Eisenhower's term of office coming to an end, and with a potential change in political party, they could possibly lose their previously unquestioned support.

The future of humanity could not be placed at the mercy of transitory political allegiances. For Archive to have long term viability it would have to operate outside of Presidential authority. Despite recognising the validity of the logic, it was not something that sat well with Howard's conscience, and the immensity of the authority it obviously carried troubled him deeply.

Today at Capitol Hill, a little over four months after being sworn in as the 35th President, John F. Kennedy was giving his address to the Joint session of the United States Congress, announcing full Presidential support for one of Archive's key projects.

Howard, Elizabeth and their son Douglas sat overlooking the House of Representatives chamber. Douglas, now four years old, sat between his parents. As usual he had his notepad and pencils with him; he'd spent most of the address drawing a stick-like tree with branches and then smaller twigs. Elizabeth leaned over to see what he was drawing.

"That's lovely," she whispered, "What is it, honey?"

Douglas considered his sketch and added some small circles before replying, "Maybe tree."

"That's very good Dougie," she smiled, gently ruffling his hair, "but normally we put the fruit at the end of the twigs…"

Douglas just returned a puzzled expression, as though she was the one who had got it wrong.

"Shhh!" pleaded Howard quietly, "This is the part Betty. Silverstein reckons this is the one that will swing it."

"…the dramatic achievements in space which occurred in recent weeks," Kennedy was saying, "should have made clear to us all, as did the Sputnik in 1957, the impact of this adventure on the minds of men everywhere, who are attempting to make a determination of which road they should take. Since early in my term, our efforts in space have been under review. With the advice of the Vice President, who is Chairman of the National Space Council, we have examined where we are strong and where we are not, where we may succeed and where we may not."

Howard held his breath and leaned forward in his seat, as Kennedy continued:

"Now it is time to take longer strides; time for a great new American enterprise; time for this nation to take a clearly leading role in space achievement, which in many ways may hold the key to our future on earth."

The chamber responded with applause, as did Howard and Elizabeth. However, Douglas was fully occupied, having switched to colouring pencils. He busied himself colouring each of the circles; green for those closest to the trunk of his tree, yellow where the branches forked and then finally, out by the twigs, red. A little over a minute later his colour coding exercise was completed to his satisfaction and he proudly held it up for his dad to see. His dad quickly glanced at it and smiled before turning away again to concentrate on the man who was still talking.

"First," Kennedy continued, "I believe that this nation should commit itself to achieving the goal, before this decade is out, of landing a man on the moon and returning him safely to the Earth. No single space project in this period will be more impressive to mankind, or more important for the long-range exploration of space; and none will be so difficult or expensive to accomplish. We propose to accelerate the development of the appropriate lunar space craft. We propose to develop alternate liquid and solid fuel boosters, much larger than any now being developed, until certain which is superior. We propose additional funds for other engine development and for unmanned explorations; explorations which are particularly important for one purpose which this nation will never overlook: the survival of the man who first makes this daring flight. But in a very real sense, it will not be one man going to the moon; if we make this judgment affirmatively, it will be an entire nation - "

Douglas caught the end of this sentence and tugged at his dad's sleeve excitedly, "Are we all going to the Moon?"

Elizabeth could see her husband's irritation and answered for him, "Let's wait and see, honey."

WEEKEND

19th August 1966

The Walkers had moved to Orlando, Florida in the summer of 1965 in preparation for NASA's AS-201 unmanned test flight in February of the following year. Howard's deeper involvement with key projects within Archive had meant he was spending an increasing amount of time out at Cape Kennedy. Eventually Elizabeth had been the one to suggest moving the family out there so that there could be some semblance of family time.

Even though she had felt incredible guilt, she had sold the idea to Douglas on the basis that the construction of a new Disney World theme park had just been announced. Douglas had always loved the mouse cartoons and following a private visit to the studio had become fascinated with the very idea of animation; the concept that it might take an animator an entire day to draw something that would last only a 24th of a second in real time, appealed to him. Indeed he had filled a notebook with detailed sketches on the subject; and in the bottom right corner of each page of the book were a series of stick-man figures that, when flicked through, created the illusion of a jumping man.

All expenses of the relocation had of course been covered but leaving behind family and friends had been a wrench, particularly for the then eight-year-old Douglas who found it difficult to make friends.

However, a year later the move had not solved matters. The reality of the situation was that being closer to the Cape meant that Howard just worked longer and longer hours.

One night, Howard had arrived home at around eleven. Elizabeth, almost on autopilot, began her routine for making cocoa.

Howard hung up his coat, took off his shoes and crossed the hallway to their large living room.

Elizabeth added the cocoa to the warm milk, poured it into the two cups and then carried them through.

Howard reclined on the long padded leather sofa and closed his eyes.

Elizabeth put her cocoa down on the table and sat in the single armchair opposite.

She had tucked Douglas into bed several hours ago and the house was now completely quiet.

She took a sip of her cocoa, and placed it down carefully again on the table.

The clock on the mantelpiece marked the long seconds.

"You need a vacation," she implored, "We all do. Or at least some time away from the Cape. It's too much."

Howard sat upright and leaned forwards earnestly.

"The AS-202 launches in five days! If we can get this right we've got a real shot of getting to the moon, Betty! It's not a good time to take a break. Look, we'll just get past this launch and then we'll go away, just the three of us. I just need to get past this - ".

"There is no 'past this'!" she snapped, "There will always be another stage, a next test!"

She dashed from her armchair to sit next to him. She looked at him intently and took hold of his hand.

"Howard, you're spending so much time preparing for that godforsaken future, that you're forgetting what's here, what's now! What use will a saved future be if we don't even have the present? Sometimes I don't know what we're protecting anymore!"

"I'm trying to protect that boy!" he hissed, pointing upstairs, "I'm trying to protect our son!"

"Your son hasn't seen you in weeks, Howard!" she cried, "While you're out saving the world, you're missing the reason you're trying to save it!"

"Do you think I don't know this? Do you think that I don't wake up every single morning feeling the weight of it all? The responsibility? The guilt? The thought of how impossible a task *all* of this is?" he slumped back in the sofa, "I feel it, Betty. Every minute, of every single day."

He glanced over at the clock and the framed comet photo, both of which appeared to be forever watching him.

"If I had seen it earlier, we could be years ahead now. Do you have any idea what it's like to know that you made a mistake that could mean the human race…" he trailed off, then suddenly threw his hands in the air. "And yet here we are. Part of the elite. The saved ones. Living our lives in comfort, the best money can buy. It makes me feel an utter fraud, Betty. I have to work. It's the only way I can justify being in the program. I have to make this right."

The truth of it was that Elizabeth fully understood and felt it every day. In fact she felt it more acutely because she could tell no one. Ever since the day Howard had turned up with a free brand-new car, hers had been the more difficult life. To know the ghastly inevitability of the future events but be unable to act upon it. To raise their son, shielding him from the truth, and maintain the pretence of a normal life. All the while knowing that despite her best efforts, her son would face an uncertain future; one that she could never adequately prepare him for.

Of course, as ever, she said none of this; she had to be the constant, the stabiliser for the family.

Regretting her loss of temper she simply put her arm around her husband and held him close.

"I don't deserve you Betty," he whispered, and kissed her on the forehead, "I'm sorry. I just…"

In response she just squeezed him tighter, "It's OK. I know."

They let their cocoa go cold, settling instead for the warmth of each other's company in their bedroom. In the darkness they both found themselves focussed in the present. After a few minutes of lying in the comfortable quiet, Howard whispered:

"One day we'll have to tell Dougie the truth."

"One day," she conceded, "but for now, let him dream."

The next morning they were awoken by a telephone call, requiring Howard to drive out to the Cape again. Elizabeth packed a lunch for him, while Douglas ate breakfast.

"They said it should just be the morning," Howard said and planted a kiss on her cheek, "I'll be back after lunch."

She just raised a cynical eyebrow, handing him the small paper bag.

Finishing up a spoonful of his cereal, Douglas quickly rifled through his latest notebook to find the right page. The page had one of his many tree-like diagrams, with coloured circles throughout it placed at the junctions of branches.

"Dad?" he asked, placing his finger at the base of the tree.

"Yes Dougie?"

"What day is it today?"

"It's Saturday."

Douglas traced his finger up the trunk and out along one of the branches.

"Will you play catch with me in the yard?"

Howard shot Elizabeth an apologetic glance.

"I'm afraid I've got to go to work again."

Douglas blinked several times, his eyes shifting back and forth along his diagram.

"But it's Saturday…" he said quizzically.

"I'm sorry Dougie," he crouched down to meet his son's eyes, but also to avoid Elizabeth's, "The rest of the world won't wait for me, so I don't have time to play right now."

Douglas studied his diagram, then traced his finger back along the branches to ground level.

"I understand, Dad," he said, quite genuinely, "I have to work now too."

With a furrowed brow he turned away from his father and climbed the stairs, turning to a new blank page in his notebook as he went. Despite the emotional conflict Douglas was feeling, he reached quite a logical conclusion.

If his father didn't have time to play with him, he would have to make time.

It was a simple thought that would rise to dominate the rest of his life.

JOTTER

22nd August 1966

After dropping Douglas off at school, Elizabeth was tidying up around the home when she found a NASA jotter. Although identical in appearance to her husband's notebooks, she recognized it as belonging to Douglas because it had a serial number on the outside; Douglas was meticulous about such things.

Once a week her husband would bring home a new, blank, paper jotter for him. Such a simple perk of Howard's job, yet something which brought great joy. They could only have cost a few cents to make, but they brought such a smile to her son's face that you would be forgiven for thinking they were made from a precious metal.

Elizabeth placed the jotter on top of her laundry basket and went upstairs to return it to her son's room.

When they had first moved there, Howard and Douglas had built a bookcase specifically for the purpose of holding the jotters. They had spent an entire weekend assembling it from planks of pine, wood-glue, and screws. At the end of the project there were three redundant screws, and Douglas had been about to throw them away. On the way over to the bin, his dad had coughed loudly to get his attention.

"But we've finished…" he began, puzzled.

"There are no left over pieces Dougie," he said and then presented him with a small matchbox, "There are only pieces that we might need later."

Douglas took the box gingerly.

"Go ahead, slide it open!" he smiled.

Douglas pushed the matchbox drawer open to find a small metal plate with 'Douglas' inscribed on it. The letter 'O' had been replaced with a zero, to make it look more like a part number. Douglas beamed and hugged his dad, seemingly unable to speak. For the eight-year-old it was one of the happiest days in his life.

Howard had simply asked the manufacturing facility to letter-punch his son's name onto a piece of scrap aluminium and drill a hole at each end; but he had no idea that the end result would have such an astounding effect on his impressionable young boy.

"I love it, Dad!" he said, eyes still glistening.

Together they picked a place on the side of the bookcase where Douglas would be able to see it every time he walked into his bedroom, then they used a screwdriver to fix it in place. Douglas was left with one single screw. He held it up so that his dad could see it.

"I'm going to save this for… later," he smiled and put it into the matchbox.

That had been over a year ago; the jotter now in Elizabeth's hands was numbered 54.

She crossed the room to the bookcase, its top shelf was almost full but another four shelves below stood empty and ready. Other kids might have filled the remaining shelves with other toys and books, but Douglas had always maintained the space, knowing that one day he would fill it. In fact Douglas had very few toys or trinkets to distract him; there were a few playthings from before their move, but his time spent in Orlando was under-represented in terms of toys.

Checking the burgeoning library on the top shelf, she saw that the jotter she held was the most current one. She casually flicked through it. Throughout the many pages were his familiar tree sketches, notes crowding the remaining space.

The layout was different though, the tree drawn on each page was more or less in the same position, aligned with those that came before it and those that followed. Douglas had never spoken about the meaning of the coloured circles standing at the junctions of the branches, and Elizabeth had never really paid much attention to them. She had always assumed it was just his endearing way of drawing the tree's fruit. Whilst the trees were familiar enough, the new structured layout allowed her to see their true meaning.

As she flicked through the book, different coloured pathways through the tree lit up; each coloured circular decision node connecting onwards to a new sub-branch of further possibilities. She flicked through it several times and realised that the book as a whole represented all the available outcomes that would follow from an initial state.

These were not 'maybe' trees. They were possibility trees.

Or more precisely, one single possibility tree. There was no key to explain what the various colours represented, but presumably they meant something to Douglas.

In her brief search for some sort of clue into what the tree was evaluating, she looked at the back of each page too and found a series of simplistic figures. It appeared to be another of his stick-man animations. Turning the book over she flicked through the pages, and saw the basic animation come to life.

Inside a circle were a stick-family with simple smiley faces, which no doubt represented Elizabeth, Howard and Douglas. A ball appeared to pass between the stick-man and the stick-boy.

Elizabeth smiled at the simple execution of the idea, then she noticed a second detail. Outside the circle was a cartoon-like tree, a cloud, and an 'm' shaped simple depiction of a bird in flight.

This in itself was not odd. Douglas had created far more complicated flick-books before, complete with moving rockets and cars. What was odd about this animation was that, while life continued inside the happy bubble for the family, on the outside the bird remained rock steady and motionless against an immobile cloud.

APOLLO 8

21st December 1968

The Apollo Program, first initiated following Kennedy's speech back in 1961, had reached yet another mission milestone: nothing less than a manned flight to the moon. Not to set foot on it, but to orbit it and test systems ahead of the landing that was scheduled for the summer of 1969. Today, four days before Christmas 1968, Apollo 8 sat fuelled and ready on Launch Pad 39A at Cape Kennedy. The Tower standing alongside it acted as fuelling mechanism and as access lift for the crew. In the moments before Lift-off, the crew access gantry and support services would be fully retracted, leaving the craft standing truly alone; but until then it maintained its delicate umbilical link.

The Apollo 8 spacecraft was divided into modules, each fulfilling different segments of the mission. At the top was the cone-shaped Command module. Commander Frank Borman, Command module pilot Jim Lovell, and Lunar module pilot Bill Anders would be calling this claustrophobic space home for the next six days. Beneath them was the Service module, housing reaction control assemblies, environmental control systems, and the high-gain, deep space antenna.

Under this was the space reserved for the Lunar module, which would ultimately carry astronauts down to the surface of the moon. However as the lunar lander would not be used on this mission, an equivalent mass had been placed aboard to ensure that the equations of flight worked identically.

The remaining four-fifths of the spacecraft was all propulsion, split into three stacked stages. Each stage was equipped with engines designed to sequentially activate during specific modes of flight; beginning with the lowest and largest, the one that would lift itself and everything above it off the launch pad.

The voice of Jack King, at Launch Control, reverberated out across the Cape, "20 seconds, all aspects we are still GO at this time, T-minus 15, 14…"

The gathered crowds, some of whom were aware of Archive's involvement, looked on with renewed concentration, as if their sheer act of will would guarantee a successful launch. Their efforts were rewarded with a fireball emerging from under the launch pad, slowly at first then in a rush of orange and white.

"… we have ignition sequence start, the engines are on. 4, 3, 2, 1, 0. We have commit, we have… we have Lift-off, Lift-off at 7.51 am Eastern Standard Time."

Under the combined thrust of five F1 engines the immense spacecraft began to re-balance the forces at work. The downward thrust increased and, a few seconds into the burn, completely cancelled out the effect of Earth's gravity on the craft. The continuous downward force then overcame the effects of inertia and the immense mass began to move with an almost impossibly slow speed.

"Lift-off. The clock is running," reported Borman from within the Command module.

"Roger. Clock," confirmed Capsule Communicator, Mike Collins at Houston Mission Control.

The spacecraft had now begun to demonstrate its phenomenal acceleration as, barely ten seconds after Lift-off, it had cleared the Tower.

"Roll and pitch program," Borman reported.

"Roger."

"How do you hear me Houston?" checked Borman, over the deafening thunder beneath him.

"Loud and clear," smiled Collins, eyes glued to the mission clock.

The initial shouts of celebration following the launch were short lived because, while everyone present was overjoyed to see the result of years of planning and dedication spring from the launchpad, the mission came first. Once more, a studied focus had settled across Mission Control. Collins cleared his throat:

"Mark Mode 1 Bravo, Apollo 8."

"Mode 1 B," copied Borman.

"Apollo 8, you're looking good."

"Roger."

At just over a minute into the flight, and despite having to battle gravity for every vertical inch, the spacecraft broke the sound barrier. Such was the spacecraft's speed that the air above it had no time to disperse; and after the initial sonic boom, a rapid and continuous succession of thunderclaps followed, filling the air around Cape Kennedy with a crackling raw energy. The spacecraft tore on through the clear blue sky, the long-range cameras relaying its historic ascent back to Mission Control.

"Mark Mode 1 Charlie, Apollo 8."

"Mode 1 C," Borman verified.

"Apollo 8, Houston. You are GO for staging," Collins stated, "Over."

"Roger," said Borman.

After a mere two minutes forty-one seconds, the lower, first stage, engines explosively detached themselves. Viewed from the ground a small flare of light from the engine was momentarily visible, before a much larger but equally brief explosion appeared to engulf the spacecraft. The crew, sitting atop this controlled detonation, continued their mission. With incredible understatement, Borman simply reported "Staging."

Having given the upper stages a speed of over six thousand miles per hour, the first-stage engine's forty-two mile vertical leap was complete. The Earth's relentless gravity reasserted its grip, forcing the spent first stage of the rocket into a long arc bound for the Atlantic. The upper stages powered on with the ascent.

Below, quietly observing the event from a private booth, were the Pittmans and Walkers. The eleven-year-olds, Douglas Walker and Bradley Pittman sat smiling and comparing notes, whilst their parents sat watching the achievement that neither of them could ever publicly declare.

Bill Pittman poured some whiskey from his hip flask into the lid cup and handed it to Elizabeth Walker.

"I'm real sorry Howard didn't get to see it, Betty."

A completely random car accident had claimed Howard's life six months ago. He had been waiting at a stop light when the truck had slammed into his car from behind. The sheer momentum had thrown the car forward into two lanes of fast moving traffic. It served as little comfort to later learn that by all accounts he hadn't suffered. The funeral had been a discreet affair, no burial with honours, no parades, no recognition of a life given in service to the long-term goal of saving the human race. Elizabeth knew that it could not have gone any differently; for Archive to remain effective, her husband's death could be given no more attention than any other member of the public.

Already a delicate boy, the effects on Douglas had been even worse. He retreated even deeper into his own thoughts; others at school began to treat him as a strange outsider, mistaking his intense academic concentration and silence, for weird eccentricity.

Once again, Bill Pittman had stepped in and insisted that he make arrangements for Douglas to attend the same private academy as his son Bradley. Over their lives the boys would have to spend a lot of time in each other's company, and ultimately take over their parents' Archive responsibilities. As it turned out, the arrangement worked well for both boys, and they had fallen into an easy friendship. Today Elizabeth was relieved to see her son smile again for the first time in what seemed like months.

Bill nudged her and then raised his flask.

"Bottoms up!"

Elizabeth smiled and gazed out to the steadily growing vapour trail.

"In both senses of the word!" she said, pointing up.

The two sat in a comfortable silence.

"It's sad in some ways," she sighed.

"Oh?"

"What we'll do eventually is to make space travel so ordinary to the public that they'll look at it with no more wonder or curiosity than watching someone take the bus."

She took another sip and watched the receding spacecraft.

"Eventually," she said, "no one will even appreciate what we've accomplished."

"Ah, Betty," consoled Bill, "The best magic is always done while nobody's looking!"

He raised his binoculars to sight the now miniscule dot containing the first of humanity's hopes, and then continued:

"And what we need right now, more than anything, is nobody watching what we're doing."

PERSPECTIVE

11th March 2013

Having to remain motionless for what seemed like hours had allowed the cold to saturate her bones, and Kate felt sure that her shivering must be shaking the cans that were concealing her. From her perspective, she could hear everything but see virtually nothing. Every so often Marcus would stop whilst a new can or bottle from a nearby bin was added to the shopping trolley. She had to hand it to him, in terms of maintaining the cover, he was thorough.

However the longer they were on the street, the more danger they would be exposed to; simple danger like the light rain that had started. Normally it would have been little more than an inconvenience, but under these circumstances it could prove deadly. Soon the sodden cardboard above her would offer no protection, and start to channel the water onto her. Her toes were already either numb or wet, she couldn't tell which.

During her silent transit she occupied her time trying to assemble the night's events.

Rob had data that was obviously so dangerous that people had killed him for it, but then failed to find it. Marcus had wound up with the data and then carried out a bizarre reverse mugging in order to give it to her, rather than use it himself. Now a killer with intelligence-agency style access to CCTV and credit card data, was hunting them; while she was being pushed through a town centre in a crippled shopping trolley.

In her exhausted state the pieces just simply wouldn't fit.

Whilst she could not see out, she could tell that the ambient light had suddenly dimmed to almost black. The rattling of the trolley was echoing off walls now. They must have cleared the town centre. Almost in anticipation of her starting to move, Marcus placed his hand on the cardboard.

"Not yet," he murmured.

She could hear him lifting bin lids and perhaps kicking over bottles on purpose. Then her metal cage lurched off again, she felt it turn a corner and then pick up pace. The light drizzle had become a downpour and she could feel the sopping wet cardboard begin to mould around her face.

"Just a bit longer!" he said over the clatter of the cans.

She tried to hang on to the cold metal of the trolley beneath her and realised she couldn't feel her fingers any more. The trolley lurched to a crawl again. She closed her eyes against the rain and, in the welcoming darkness, felt sleep beckoning her. Her senses were getting quite blurry and she couldn't really tell what order things were happening in. She heard what sounded like a metallic door squeal open or closed, and felt the trolley spinning. She could also hear an echoing voice calling for someone called Kate. Suddenly it became a lot lighter and she had the sensation of being shaken. The loud voice was back again too, telling her to do something.

"Kate! Wake up!" shouted Marcus into her face.

She awoke with a start, sending cans toppling to the floor - her eyes were now wide open, desperately seeking familiarity but finding absolutely none.

"It's OK! It's OK," Marcus was saying to her, "We made it."

"Made..?" she said blankly.

Trying to make sense of it, she looked around her. They were in a small lock-up with a metal swing door at one end. The cans in the trolley shifted slightly beneath her.

Almost as if events were loading into her mind in reverse order, the evening reconstructed itself in her head, and she sat bolt upright breathing rapidly.

"Hey!" Marcus reassured, now holding her shoulders to steady her, "Safe. We're OK."

Her breathing slowed a little, and she experimented with blinking again.

"Let's get you out of there," beckoned Marcus, "We gotta get you into something dry."

He pulled her up and helped her to clamber out. Once on her own two feet, she looked around her. Dangling from a bent wire in the centre of the ceiling, a single light bulb cast a dim yellow glow into the room. The light didn't quite reach the corners, which seemed blacker than black. Around her were a combination of disused filing cabinets and electrical equipment.

"This way," said Marcus, guiding her away from the light.

Without the glare of the bulb, her eyes adjusted to the gloom and she could just make out a doorway shape ahead.

"Where are we?" she coughed through the musty odour.

"Don't freak, OK?" said Marcus, flatly, "Nobody's gonna look here..."

He twisted the door handle and pushed hard. The door appeared to be slightly too big for the surrounding frame, but after a second push it grudgingly jarred open.

It took a second or two to mentally consolidate the new, slightly odd, perspective, but then she realised she knew this place very well.

They were in Rob's basement flat.

•

She felt like a ghost revisiting a past life, an illusion amplified by her walk through a doorway that, in her day, used to be a solid wall. As she walked further into the flat, it felt like stepping into an old memory; the essence of the environment she had known was still here, but the intervening time had somehow smoothed away the sharper detail. There were things here from a time after her departure that blurred her recollection of the place.

"Here, get dried off," said Marcus, putting a large towel around her shoulders, "You OK?"

She nodded and started to towel her hair dry.

"I need the memory stick," he said holding out his hand, then added, "Please."

She opened her canvas bag, and pulled it from a side pocket.

"Here," she said, handing it to him, then walked into the main living space.

Rob's long computer bench was still there but the screens, that were once so much a part of the ambient lighting, were now dead. Although the fish tank lights were now off, Kate could see Penrose bobbing around at the bottom, occasionally flapping a fin. Despite everything, the goldfish had survived, completely ignorant of the world beyond its transparent walls. Its vacant stare seemed to bore an accusing hole in her.

"I didn't believe him - ", she began, "I had no…"

"Don't," he cut in, "He was keeping you safe."

Marcus walked back to the door and with an effort persuaded it to close. There was no visible handle or door frame, so it sat almost seamlessly within the wall. The only clue to its presence was a string-thin line of torn wallpaper outlining where the doorway was. Without the paper tear, it would have been undetectable. At about eye level a bland looking picture had been hung to complete the illusion. Marcus saw her looking.

"Rob kept a lot hidden - " he shrugged.

"I didn't even know there was a door there…" she said.

"It was his panic exit," Marcus pointed back at the door, "If he saw trouble, he could get out quick."

Kate walked round the flat trying to find some old curio, a photo, anything that she might connect with, but found it to be an emotional vacuum. There was simply no trace of her involvement in his life. At all. There were piles of newspapers, more than in her day, stacked in high columns; but there didn't appear to be anything personal. She took the jacket off, draped it over the sofa, and scrubbed at her hair with the towel. She had accused Rob of paranoia and over time had convinced herself that his conspiracy theories were merely delusional. On the basis of her own logic she had left him.

She let her gaze wander over the room; as it settled again on the fish tank she realised that she hadn't asked the most obvious question:

"When did it happen?"

"Dunno exactly, only found out about a week ago," said Marcus, searching his rucksack, "We were gonna meet up in the... the usual place, but when he didn't show, I clocked something was up."

He pulled a chair out from under the kitchen table, dragged it to the corner and climbed up on it. In the ceiling directly above his head was a foot-wide hole exposing a variety of different sized cables. He now busied himself attaching his own cables to those in the hole, using what looked like fat, plastic bulldog clips with LED lights embedded in them. He spotted her puzzled expression.

"I've been nicking power from the flat upstairs - can't run the risk of this place making a signature," he said dismissively, climbing down again.

"Did Rob leave any clues or anything? Maybe he's just on the run - " said Kate quickly walking over to Marcus, hopeful that all of this was somehow a hideous mistake, "He might've got spooked by something? Maybe he isn't dead!"

Marcus lowered his eyes and took a deep breath. He had already lived through a week of hell, but for her this had just happened. He explained to her that, according to the local newspaper, Rob's body had been discovered by the upstairs neighbour, and that the police had taken his body away. In reality he knew this was completely false; Marcus himself had found Rob. In order to keep the death hidden from the authorities, he'd had the harrowing and traumatic experience of stowing Rob's body under piles of cardboard in one of the darker corners of the lock-up. He was having a difficult enough time dealing with the events and reasoned that Kate was in a more fragile state than him. This was a conversation best left until they were a long way from here.

"Kate, you need to listen real careful, OK? A Storykiller took Rob's life trying to find this data," he said, holding up the memory stick in front of her, "Whatever is on here was so important he was willing to bloody die for it! We need to know what's on here. Fast. Or we - will - join him."

"You already had the bloody stick!" she exploded, standing upright and sending the chair scraping across the floor, "Why give it to me?! Why drag me into all this?! Just plug the damn thing in and read it! Why can't -"

"It needs *your* fingerprint!" he said, then stepped closer so that he could whisper, "That's why you're here!"

Her immediate confusion drained her angry momentum and she was unable to speak. It seemed that with the arrival of each new piece of information the situation was becoming less, not more, resolved.

"Sit down. We're up against it," he said, checking his watch, "but I'll tell you what I know, OK?"

While he booted up his laptop he recounted how he'd broken in through the panic exit and told her of the staged conditions he'd found within the flat. The intention had obviously been to discredit Rob but he'd spared Kate some of the more sordid details.

Then, carefully avoiding mentioning the body, he told her how he'd found the memory stick. On one of the few occasions that he'd visited Rob, Marcus had happened to spot him hiding a memory stick in the fish-food container and Rob had explained himself with a one-worded shrug: 'Breadcrumbs'.

"I gave it a quick check on my laptop but I couldn't get round the fingerprint scanner," continued Marcus, "I didn't want to hang around here but, before I could get home, I clocked a whole bunch of cops outside my house."

"So?"

"So these cops had riot shields and a hefty door ram. I saw them bust my door down, but I didn't hang around. Except for this rucksack I lost everything in my life right there," Marcus seemed temporarily lost in a moment of regret, before taking a big breath and putting on a forced smile, "Ah screw 'em! They ain't getting through my encryption anyway."

"So you've been staying here since?" asked Kate.

"Didn't really have a choice," said Marcus, "I couldn't use any of Rob's kit, so it slowed me down while I looked at the memory stick line by line. Took me 'til yesterday, but I found an ASCII marker."

"What's an asky?"

"Doesn't matter, it's just a bit of text, but it was your name and the letters UWL."

"UWL, so that lead you to the university?"

"Yep," he said, though again this was only a partial truth.

When he wasn't trying to pursue Archive, Marcus scraped a living through selling data; the digital skills involved were easily transferable. A month ago an anonymous client, 'Chalkmole', had requested the web browsing habits of thirty people, Kate Walker being among them. In the course of his duties, he'd easily found her clumsy online footprint along with her place of work.

Only when he'd found Kate's name embedded on Rob's memory stick, had Marcus put the two pieces of information together; then realising the jeopardy she was in, he'd felt compelled to act.

"The stuff on that stick is obviously important," Marcus continued, "I didn't know how much time I had, but as nobody was watching the university, I - "

"- you forcibly *donated* it to me - in the car park," she completed on his behalf.

"Sorry."

"It doesn't matter now, I - "

"No. I'm saying sorry 'cos to get to you quickly I made mistakes. The only reason your home got busted tonight is 'cos I got picked up by CCTV. I'm sorry."

Marcus plugged the USB stick into a spare slot on the side of his laptop and a security screen presented itself.

"OK," said Marcus, angling the laptop to allow her to scan her finger, "Hang on, which finger?"

"I think I know..." she raised the middle finger on her left hand at him. The finger tip had a completely smooth, rectangular, patch of skin running through it, "Tell you about it some other time..."

She placed her finger on the USB's small scanning plate, and an animated hour glass displayed on the laptop screen along with the words:

'Processing - please wait...'

After five seconds had passed she started to believe she'd made a mistake.

Suddenly the security screen went black.

Then clear white text appeared:

'Hey fish-face - long time, no sea...'

DROP

24th December 1968

After a flight time of over seventy hours, Apollo 8 began lunar orbit insertion, starting the process of trading its momentum for a new, stable orbit. As viewed from Earth, it passed behind the western limb of the moon and for the next fifty-four minutes no communication would be possible.

For those watching from Earth there was something slightly irreverent about wilfully voyaging out across space and attempting to tame mankind's closest celestial neighbour. Despite knowing the physics of the trajectory in play, it did not prevent every member of Apollo Mission Control from feeling a distinct sense of unease as the remote spacecraft was apparently silenced by the moon.

Within ten seconds of the predicted emergence of Apollo 8, communication was re-established, and everyone breathed a little easier. However, this was only the first of the manoeuvres, each designed to allow the moon to assert more of its gravitational grip on the tiny craft. During the mission they would periodically lose and acquire direct communication, as Apollo 8 orbited its goal.

After four and a half hours, just before communication would again be interrupted by Apollo 8's transit behind the moon, Capcom at Houston called Apollo 8.

"Apollo 8, Houston, over."

The radio signal, travelling at the speed of light, took approximately one and a half seconds to reach the distant spacecraft, and the response took just as long to return.

"Roger. Go ahead," said Borman.

"Roger. Frank, we'd like to know about the water chlorination. Have you - when was the last time you chlorinated the water? Over."

They knew that communication between ground and craft could easily be intercepted, so this pre-arranged code phrase had been used to signal to the crew that the next phase of the mission was a go. Borman had to reply with the suitably innocuous phrase to communicate that he understood.

"Jim .... a little and it smelled like a bucket of Chlorox about an hour ago."

Already, Apollo 8 was beginning to head away from Earth and begin another journey behind the moon. Part of the message was garbled, so Houston verified.

"Apollo 8, Houston, say again."

"I said Jim spilled some of that chlorine and it smelled like a bucket of Chlorox in here a little while."

"Roger, understand," satisfied that the message was delivered, Houston continued. "We have two and a half minutes to LOS and all systems are looking good. Everything is looking just fine down here, Frank."

As predicted, the loss of signal occurred on time and the three crew members aboard the Apollo 8 fell temporarily silent. The only sound within the cramped Command module was the background noise of the Service module below them, regulating the delicate atmosphere and temperature.

"Houston, Apollo 8, over?" checked Borman.

No reply.

"Good, we're dark. Bill, you good to go?"

"Good to go Frank," reported Bill Anders manoeuvring himself over to the console, "Clock running, T minus 40 minutes."

"Jim?"

"Good to go."

The Lunar module was not required for this mission, but in terms of experimental rigor, equivalent mass had been placed aboard to ensure that conditions would be identical to those of the lunar landing scheduled for the following year.

At least that was the official line delivered in public. If 9027 kilograms of redundant dummy mass had to be raised from the Earth to the Moon, the reasoning within Archive was to give it an active mission profile. Far from being a mere flyby practice for the planned lunar landing, Apollo 8's primary mission was to deliver its precious payload to the dark side of the moon.

SPACE PROGRAM

21st December 2012

At the centre of the Floyd Lunar Complex was a drum-like rounded cylinder. In part, this central drum had been constructed from materials dropped by Apollo 8, 44 years before, but with each successive mission the Complex had slowly spread out. Growth, of course, had meant personnel.

Archive had made it a matter of minor misdirection to ensure that the world focussed on the three Apollo astronauts that made each round trip, rather than the extra man stowed away in the Lunar module who would remain behind. By the time Apollo 17 had concluded its mission in 1972, five men had been covertly transported to the lunar surface. Theirs was the unenviable task of picking through Apollo 8's lunar drop package for rations and laying the foundations for Archive's expansion.

Within the first year of establishing a basic hub on the moon, Archive realised from the experimental data that the initial intention to create a functioning lunar colony for thousands would fail. However, one area of success was the confirmation of Helium-3 within the upper layers of lunar regolith, carried there from the Sun over billions of years by the solar wind. Consisting of two protons but only one neutron, Helium-3 was theorised as pivotal in the development of nuclear fusion, and its abundance on the surface of the moon would make its acquisition a minor concern.

At the time, the barriers to nuclear fusion had not yet been overcome. Similarly, the theory of converting and focussing laser light to produce a deflective force, was still in its infancy. But Archive could plan for the day when it would become a reality. The FLC was redesigned to become an open framework capable of accepting solution 'modules' as they became ready. On July 4th 1976, the optimistically named Lunar Colony 1 was renamed The Floyd Lunar Complex in preparation for its new role.

The size of the proposed solution modules meant a redesign of spacecraft, and by 1981 the first Space Shuttle had flown, paving the way for larger payloads to be lifted to Earth orbit. The Shuttle consisted of an aircraft-like Orbiter vehicle and two solid rocket boosters, all mounted on a bullet-shaped, cylindrical tank. Standing at over 45 metres high and 8 metres in diameter, this tank was very much the backbone of the assembly.

During flight, the massive external tank supplied liquid oxygen and hydrogen to the Orbiter's main engines. Combining this with the thrust generated by the solid rocket boosters, allowed the whole assembly to reach the upper atmosphere. When the solid rocket boosters exhausted their fuel they detached and fell to Earth on parachutes. But the external tank would still keep delivering liquid fuel until the Orbiter could reach orbit; then once empty it would be ejected and burn up during re-entry to Earth's atmosphere. However there was nothing in the Orbiter's schematics that categorically *required* the tank to be ejected. In keeping with Archive's 'multiple efficiency' principles it was a design feature that would be capitalised upon.

On August 30th 1983, under the cover of darkness, the first of the Shuttle's night missions began. The launches themselves could never be concealed, but the fact that the external tank was not ejected could be obscured from view. At the appointed time, the Orbiter crew reported the separation of the tank back to Mission Control, but instead carried it into orbit.

Drawing on the accumulated knowledge and engineering skills of the Apollo program it became a straightforward, if somewhat expensive, operation to outfit the hollow tanks with their own remote guidance and propulsion systems. Between then and December 2nd 1990, six night missions were undertaken. By 1991, all six cylindrical tanks had been painstakingly manoeuvred into place on the lunar surface, radiating out from the original central drum. Before the Helium-3 harvesting Regodozers had pushed tonnes of radiation-shielding regolith over the top, Floyd Lunar Complex had resembled a six-legged starfish.

•

The interior of the Drum at the centre of the FLC served as a combined living and sleeping quarters for the crew, and ensured that any of the mission-critical surrounding limbs were quickly accessible in the event of an emergency. The Drum was little more than 3 metres wide, but was 5 metres tall, and divided into an upper and lower deck. The upper deck had six bunks, arranged around the circumference, which were accessed from below by slim ladders built into the surface of the wall; but at one-sixth of Earth's Gravity most of the crew could make the 2 metre vertical leap up without effort or without resorting to ladders. The only downside to the arrangement was the risk of failing to strap in before sleeping; falling out of bed from this height could still give you a nasty shock and bruises to match.

The lower deck, in addition to holding an auxiliary FLC control console, was given over to a basic dining area and food preparation galley; though in practise the microwaveable ration packs needed little actual preparation. The dining table and seating also functioned as the crew's briefing room, secondary medical bay, and game area.

They still kept time with Houston, so by their clock it was around 7pm on Friday 21st of December 2012.

Today was the second of three firings on Siva.

The first had taken place in the February of 2010, and the last would take place in two year's time. This was to be the crew's last relaxation period before the deflection window.

The Christmas decorations put up around the lower deck were modest and a concessionary nod to the Earth-based festival. Up here, the sparse nature of their arrangement meant there could be no Christmas Day surprises, nothing that hadn't already been seen by someone before. The same went for personal space. The intimate living arrangements forced upon them by limited resources had all but removed the concept of privacy. The crew knew each other well, both mentally and physically.

"Snake Eyes!" beamed Eva Gray, sitting back grinning.

The others just rolled their eyes and tutted. She said the same thing every time she got to play that particular domino.

"Not funny, Gray," frowned Cathy Gant while sorting through her pile, "We don't need bad luck hanging around."

"Actually, I think it's good luck," chipped in Leonard Cooper.

"Oh?"

"Snakes were important to the Mayans…" he stated, arranging his stack carefully.

"OK Cooper, this snake'll bite," Cathy eyed him suspiciously, "Where are you going with this?"

"Well, Kukulkan was a Mayan snake deity linked with the equinoxes - and today is, well, a special equinox."

"Oh yeah! I read about this in the last download, did you see it?" cut in Mike Sanders, "The Mayan calendar ends today!"

"Well, the Long Count *resets* today," Leonard corrected, "but yeah, you could read it as end."

"Apparently there's been a load of Mayan Prophesy nuts predicting the end of the world," continued Mike.

"Well…" Cathy glanced at her watch, "If we mess up the firing, there's still time for us to end the world today!"

Around the table, the smiles faded quickly, and there was an awkward silence.

"As I was saying," ventured Leonard trying to put the conversation back on track, "it's time for a new Long Count, a new beginning. And, Mayans or not, we're here to kick-start it."

"Well put, Lenny," said Mike, and raised his small beaker of water, "To us Pioneers!"

They all followed his lead in raising their beakers, then took a slurp from the embedded plastic straws. After a few turns of each player adding a domino to the chain, Eva felt the need to break the silence, again.

"D'you ever think of those first guys?" she said, "The real Pioneers?"

"Anders, Lovell and Bowman?" offered Leonard.

"Borman," interrupted Mike, "You're thinking of that movie!"

"Oh yeah, 'Monkeys and Monoliths' wasn't it?" teased Leonard. He knew the actual title well, but enjoyed winding up Mike too much.

Mike threw a domino at him. Here on the moon there was less gravity to drag projectiles into a downward arc, so despite travelling horizontally at speed it was vertically off target, and sailed harmlessly over Leonard's head.

"You're such a noob, Sanders," stated Cathy with a smirk.

"I mean," started Eva again, "they came here with nothing! No homing beacon, no guide corridors, nothing. They flew here in a can with nothing but the vac-suits on their backs."

"I'd trade places like that," said Cathy, clicking her fingers, not looking up from her stack of dominoes.

"What?" said Eva, "Not enough adventure for you up here, Gant?"

"It's not that," she replied, "They got to go home - "

"Here we go," mumbled Leonard, shooting a sideways glance at Sanders, "another Gant Rant."

"The Apollo guys got a heroes welcome. They got to live out the rest of their lives, before any of this crap happened, so yeah, I'd trade."

It was certainly true that in the early Apollo missions the astronauts were welcomed back as heroes. But during the four decades that followed, each astronaut to arrive on the moon had done so in the knowledge that they would never return to Earth. They had given their lives in service to build a better future for the human race; one they would never see for themselves.

The current crew were the latest in this long chain of lunar occupants. However, if they were successful in their mission, they would be the first group to actually leave the surface. This in itself had a cruel irony. Despite daily exercise regimes in Chamber 4's gym, the long-term effects of low-gravity muscle wastage had effectively made each of them exiles from their home planet. The likelihood that they would ever walk on the Earth's surface again diminished with every passing day.

"Sorry guys," said Cathy, gesturing to the feeble Christmas tree cut-out fixed to the bulkhead, "time of year I guess."

She placed a double-two domino at the end of the chain and exhaled flatly, "No change. Apt."

"D'you think they knew what they were starting?" said Eva, as undeterred as ever.

"Course not, they thought they were going to build a New Eden!" said Cathy, gesturing around their grey living quarters. "A place where we could begin again. A glass-domed tropical paradise! Did you ever see the early artist sketches?"

A low dual tone sounded from a wall speaker, which was something of a relief for the crew who were eager to focus on something more tangible. Leonard retrieved the domino that Mike had thrown at him and tossed it back with a grin. Mike caught it mid-air and returned it to the box.

"Hey, Lenny, try not to shave any more chunks off Siva this time."

"I'll have a polite word with Floyd!" he grinned, and headed towards his airlock, "I'll tell him to wear his glasses…"

'Floyd' was the crew's nickname for the FLC's Shen500 series computer. Floyd ran many of the day-to-day processes but also the main Siva deflection system. Its accuracy had been improved significantly for the firing today, thanks to a recent shipment of faster processor chips. But two years ago, inadequate sensor resolution had been blamed for the creation and trajectory of the Tenca shard.

Tenca's creation had begun a three-year countdown to an impact somewhere in Russia.

The crew had all received counselling from Earth-side therapists, absolving them of responsibility. However, something of a gallows-humour had since developed between the crew; a form of psychological defence against the brutal truth that Siva had already begun its remote onslaught against the Earth.

The dual tone sounded again.

"Crew to engineering stations," came Lana Yakovna's command, followed a second later by, "Please."

Cathy and Mike looked at each other, with raised eyebrows.

"Pliz," imitated Cathy, pursing her lips, "Manners, that's new. The Ice Queen thaw-eth?"

With a wry smile she left the Drum. His curiosity piqued, Mike walked to the wall panel and pushed the reply button.

"Where are you, Lana?"

"I am on chamber Mho."

Mike glanced upwards and out towards her location, visualising the primary firing chamber beyond the grey wall of the Drum.

"What are you doing up there?"

"I find oshibka."

Lana only tended to make linguistic slips under stress, but he'd worked with her long enough to translate.

"What kind of error?"

"Mho was show power drop, but is only sensor glyuk."

"Glitch?"

"Da, Glitch."

"Is everything OK, Lana, do you need me to check it out?"

"All is OK now, Mike. I see you at control, thank you."

The wall panel clicked off and he was left alone in the metallic Drum.

Lana had earned her nickname of Ice Queen owing to her extreme self-control, and some had even speculated that Lana was a borderline ego-morph, but glitch or not, something about the experience had obviously unsettled her. Despite the constant, regulated temperature, Mike felt a shiver.

"The sooner we're out of here the better," he announced to the air, before heading off to his monitoring station.

Radiating out from the Drum, the cylinders had additional internal airlocks in the positions previously occupied by the Shuttle's intertanks. These functioned to compartmentalise the chambers in the event of a breach. Before leaving Earth, the exact shape of the technologies that would eventually occupy each of these 'solution modules' was unknown, but the fact that humans would need to navigate their interiors could be planned for. In fact several of the cylinders arrived with pre-constructed walkways welded along the inside. The thin, lightweight, metal flooring was designed for lunar gravity use, but during the initial flight-phase the metalwork also functioned to reduce liquid turbulence within the fuel tank.

Mike climbed to the upper level using the thin aluminium ladder, made his way along the metal gantry to the control panel labelled 'Curly' and pushed his ID key into place. The intercom on the panel activated and almost immediately the dual tone sounded.

"Lana Yakovna. FLC control. At this time I ask you for a go, no-go. Stations check in."

"Mike Sanders. Clockwise containment beam. Go."

"Cathy Gant. Counter-clockwise containment beam. Go."

"Eva Gray. Central sublimator beam. Go."

"Leonard Cooper. Observatory. Standing by."

"Houston, FLC," reported Lana, "all stations report ready. Over."

Lana's signal made its way through the chain of equatorial repeater stations that joined the FLC to the Earth radio-relay at the moon's eastern rim. After three seconds delay, Houston's reply arrived back at the FLC.

"FLC, Houston, Good to hear your voice."

"And yours also, Papa."

Everyone knew Alexey Yakovna was Lana's father, and that it was his position within Archive that had given her the privileged FLC posting. But Mike knew from first hand experience that her cool intellect and faultless logic were reasons enough to have her in command. In truth everyone here had ridden in on a ticket paid for by their parents' contribution to Archive. However, it bothered him that she had referred to him as 'Papa' over open comms. It didn't seem detached enough for her.

"Earth-side telemetry looks good," Alexey continued, "Siva has maintained cyclic spin and trajectory remains within decimal zero zero two percent of delta vee."

"Roger Houston. And Tenca?"

Even allowing for the communications delay, the reply time seemed slightly longer than usual to Mike.

"No change."

Lana's reply time was more noticeable, it was at least two seconds before she spoke:

"Roger, understand Houston. All stations report ready, we are good to go with second stage firing on Siva. Do we have commit from Houston?"

"You have commit FLC."

"Confirmed Houston," reported Lana, "Final station check."

Each station checked in as before, with no changes.

"Roger FLC, you are go for Floyd lock-out."

Mike found himself crossing his fingers and staring intently at the speaker in the control panel, just as he had during the first firing two years ago. The vast amount of observational data taken over previous decades now allowed Siva's location within the solar system to be predicted to within a metre; an astonishing feat given the distances involved - the equivalent of being able to predict the position of a football in flight within an area the size of France. When it came to the precise moment, Floyd would automatically control the actual firing on Siva. Floyd could determine the coordinates and firing instant down to the nano-second, something the human crew could not do in real time. To ensure that Floyd was dealing with a closed system, human intervention had to be locked out at the last moment.

"Personnel lock-out in 3, 2, 1," Lana relayed, "Floyd autonomous control established."

"FLC, Houston, we confirm lock-out."

The heart of the Helium-3 fusion process required that matter was turned into energy; its containment therefore could not be constructed from matter, as it would be consumed in the process. The containment was achieved by the manipulation of a high density electromagnetic field. As the fusion reactor came online Mike felt the slightest of tugs on his whole body, as the magnetic field exerted a force on the miniscule amount of iron in his blood.

"Containment field is active," reported Lana, "Fusion injection is underway."

"FLC, Houston, we read fusion event."

Although nothing visibly changed in the chamber Mike had an increased sense of anxiety. The idea of a human hand being absent from the control gave him a distinct feeling of unease. Control panel lights winked on and off, but despite the incredible power under his feet there were no other external signs that the device was even running. After the first firing, the others had expressed similar opinions, except Lana of course.

Then, without fuss, a low vibration transferred through the decking plates beneath him, coming from the general direction of the Drum, and Mike realised that the process had begun.

•

Long before their installation at the FLC, the principle of using tractor beams like the ones perpetuated by science fiction movies, had been evaluated in an Archive lab. Using a laser beam with a doughnut-shaped cross-section, and controlling the inner and outer ring temperatures, it was possible to push small amounts of mass using the beam. The drawback was that it relied on the laser heating the air in the vicinity of the beam; it worked well on Earth but in the vacuum of space it would be made redundant.

The concept of using individual photons within a laser to transfer their momentum to an object was also well known. The vacuum of space was ideally suited to this process; with no free-floating dust or atmospheric particles to interfere with the transfer of photon momentum, all of the energy transferred by the beam would impact its target. With the appropriate rate of photon emission one could move mountains, albeit over the course of many centuries; the time-scale of Siva's arrival made this solution impractical.

The solution arrived with a twist - literally. By altering the *spin angular momentum* of the light within a laser beam, electrons within it could be given a corkscrew twist. By using a second laser with an opposing spin and higher temperature a self-contained light-tunnel could be created. The tunnel operated in a similar way to the doughnut tractor beam, but crucially would allow a third, high powered, beam to travel through its centre.

This third beam, confined by the tunnel around it, would transfer all of its energy to the surface of Siva, creating a local area of superheated particles and debris - in effect a miniature atmosphere. The corkscrew-like radial momentum of the light-tunnel would also be transferred to the superheated particles, effectively swelling the radius of that atmosphere at the surface.

The more the atmosphere grew, the greater the amount of superheated particles could be pushed against by the light tunnel. The longer the three beams could be maintained, the larger the atmosphere would become, and the greater the push against Siva would be.

Despite being the culmination of decades of research and development into repulsion technology, the crew themselves had light-heartedly nicknamed the clockwise laser corkscrew 'Curly', the anticlockwise 'Larry', and the central sublimator beam 'Mho'; the spelling of the latter being at Houston's insistence that there should at least be some reference to actual physics at the station.

The only truly moving part at the FLC was the Prism assembly directly above the Drum. The Prism's function was to combine the three different lasers into one directional targeted beam. When not in use, and to protect it from dust and radiation, the Prism was covered by a protective cowl.

Now, in the lead up to firing, the motors whirred and began the process of sliding the cowl aside to permit the Prism's exposure to space. The cowl locked into place leaving the Prism peering out into the night.

From the Observatory cylinder, Leonard Cooper monitored the beam output and Siva itself, using a combination of remote cameras and the optical tracking telescope.

"Houston, Observatory," reported Leonard, "Estimated beam activation in T-minus fifteen seconds."

"Roger FLC."

Leonard refreshed the telescope view of Siva, and zoomed in on the predicted impact zone.

"Activation in 3, 2, 1."

A peculiar effect of using lasers in a vacuum was that the beam itself was not visible to the naked eye. On Earth, with atmosphere and dust, even a low powered laser beam would have appeared as an impressive coloured lance. But here, with nothing to interfere with the beam, the only visible feedback would be from Siva's surface itself. A high tone emitted from his console, paired with a solid green light.

"Houston, Observatory. Instruments report activation. Stand by."

Glancing over at the Prism monitoring screen, he could see minor dust particles caught for a moment in the beam before being vaporised in brief sparkles of intense light.

"Houston, we have particulate sublimation confirmed at the Prism. Now verifying target acquisition."

Turning to the spectral analyser he overlaid the results on the telescope view and zoomed in. After a few seconds the screen updated to reveal a bright white disc on the visible eastern limb of Siva, accompanied by a sharp radiation spike in the superimposed thermograph.

"Houston, initial Siva beam contact confirmed. Stand by."

Leonard's screen updated again, showing a much larger disc of light. The surface of Siva must be burning fiercely right now, he thought. Checking Siva's trajectory and spin readouts he found that already both had been altered; the coupled spiral beams were even now exerting a force on Siva, pushing it ever further from Earth.

"Houston," Leonard couldn't help but smile, "Surface sublimation cascade event confirmed on Siva."

Everyone at the FLC could hear the Earth-side jubilant cheers, relayed through their individual station speakers. Leonard's smile cracked into a wide grin, even in this desolate lunar location it was hard not to be affected by the sounds of laughter.

"FLC, on behalf of everyone on Earth we thank you for your early Christmas present."

"Mayan Calendar reset," he quipped, "Happy New Year, Houston."

TRAJECTORY

15th February 2013

Seven weeks after the second firing on Siva, Tenca neared the end of its long elliptical collision course with Earth. Archive had known for three years that this day would arrive, and that there was nothing that could prevent it. Using the FLC laser to deflect Tenca would have imposed an untimely drain on FLC's fusion reactor, preventing it from operating at peak output for the final Siva deflection next year.

At the time the decision was made to allow Tenca to strike, the predicted impact zone was centred around Novgorod, Russia. In the light of more precise readings from the FLC, Archive now knew that final impact point would be some 830 miles east, in Chelyabinsk. As agreed, no prior warning was given to the population.

In the morning following Valentine's Day, star-crossed lovers across Russia woke to find a star crossing their skies. Appearing at first as though a tiny slit had been opened in the fabric of the sky, it grew in length. As the slit grew, a slice of brilliant white light began to bleed from it, and at the leading edge, a ball of fire as bright as the sun began to grow.

So bright and fast was the burning meteorite that shadows of buildings swept the ground with such speed that it appeared an entire day was passing in a matter of seconds. The sound of distant thunder echoed in its wake while a white vapour trail hung in stark contrast to the otherwise empty blue sky.

Although damage was reported across three thousand buildings and schools, against all reasonable odds barely a thousand casualties occurred; most of these due to the effects of the airburst from the meteorite entering the atmosphere, causing windows to shatter and walls to collapse.

The final impact at the unpopulated Chebarkul Lake left merely a twenty foot hole in the ice, but the larger impact was to the social media networks which exploded with mobile phone footage and eyewitness accounts, from all over the Ural region. Over the following weeks, as predicted some three years earlier, Archive began to lose containment as people turned their eyes to the skies.

RESOLVE

11th March 2013

In Rob's old flat, less than a mile away from Benton, Marcus and Kate sat staring at the laptop screen.

"Hey fish-face - long time, no sea?" read Marcus, "What the hell does that mean?"

Before Kate could reply, a video log began to auto play, filling the full screen. Looking at the picture she tried to work out where it had been recorded from. It showed a slightly blurred empty seat with the edge of a brightly lit fish-tank just visible on the left-hand side of the screen. She turned around to look at the darkened flat; the empty fish-tank and the dead monitor beyond. Rob's hopelessly empty seat faced the now inert webcam. He must have recorded it right here, she thought.

On the video log a hand moved into shot, momentarily covering the lens. When the hand moved away, the image was in focus and then Rob sat down into shot. Kate sighed and bit her lip; the years following their split had not been kind to him. Gone was the man who had a reason to consider his appearance.

In his place was a man with dark circles under his eyes, untamed hair and stubble to match. He was mostly lit by the bluish light from the monitor, giving him a pale, gaunt appearance. He shuffled slightly in his seat, then looked directly at the camera into Kate's eyes.

"Memory stick header video file, March, er, Second, 2013. 8.15 am. Still researching 'Archive'," he said making air quotes, "and why it's trying to suppress the Chelyabinsk meteorite findings. I mean, seriously, this thing is *out there* guys, what's the point?"

Kate glanced over at Marcus who was nodding. Without taking his eyes from the screen he murmured "Meteorite - came down in Russia 'bout a month ago."

Kate remembered seeing shots on the news but recalled little more than that. On the screen Rob cleared his throat and continued.

"So, a new thread came in last night from Shades141 and verified by Blankspace, apparently there's another Archive hotspot being built in Iceland, referred to as 'The Node'." At this point Rob raised a sarcastic eyebrow. "Imaginative. Anyway, the location's in the zipped file. OK, so, Breadcrumbs. Replacement high speed router delivery this morning in, er, 15 minutes. Rearrange meeting location with Blackbox, the Gasworks is possibly compromised. Stay low."

Rob leaned forwards, again his hand covering the webcam and, after a little microphone rustle, the feed went dead. On the screen a box then opened up containing several other folders. Marcus leaned in further to get a better look at the contents.

"Do you mind if I…?" he said, pointing at the screen.

Kate shook her head and stood up, away from the table. With no particular sense of direction she wandered out towards Rob's darkened workbench. She placed her hands on the shoulders of his chair, allowing it to take some of her weight. How many times had she stood on this very spot, facing his computer screens, peering at his latest subject of fascination? Today those screens stood dark, reflecting only herself and his empty chair. She knew the moment must come, and succumbing to both emotion and exhaustion, her eyes began to water.

"Hey. Shh…" Marcus said from beside her.

She started for a moment at his sudden proximity.

"I'm, OK," she sniffed, wiping her eyes hastily. "I'm OK. You, do your… on the…" she gestured to his laptop.

He put an arm around her and led her away from the bench. He guided her past the kitchen to Rob's bedroom and found a blanket to drape over her.

"Rest in there, I'll wake you in a - "

"The hell you will!" she snapped suddenly, "That data's not leaving my sight!"

She straightened her back and stared Marcus squarely in the face.

"I want to see it," she sniffed, scraping tears from her face, "I want to see it all."

Some of the folders had familiar looking names, but navigating past ones labelled Chelyabinsk and NASA, she clicked on 'The Node'.

•

Benton had been driving the dark streets for several hours but still hadn't located Kate Walker or her accomplice, Blackbox. Earlier, Kate's credit card had been used to withdraw cash from an ATM, but this turned out to be a false alarm. The homeless man Benton had apprehended said he'd found the card, but had no adequate explanation of how he knew the PIN number. Correctly assessing that Blackbox had created the situation as a diversion, Benton had continued his search pattern. He had to admit it; he found Blackbox's behaviour fascinating and was looking forward to a long conversation with him.

This fascination was becoming a distraction for Benton; the concept of anticipating the enjoyment of an interrogation was a new one. He did not usually experience these feelings.

Normally he kept his emotions in check with minimal effort. For him there was no valid logic in allowing primitive urges to influence his decisions and single-minded pursuit of the goal. However the events of today had actually riled him, and he found himself acutely aware of expending his valuable mental resources on subduing two distinct emotions, anger and panic. It was a sensation with which he was completely unfamiliar, and it disturbed him.

Perhaps he was running low he thought, so he pulled the car over to the side of the empty street, and retrieved a case from his jacket's inner pocket. He popped it open, exposing three, small, short vials of a whiskey-coloured liquid, and a place to rest his finger. The small mechanism in the case pricked his finger and the digital display responded with a percent value almost instantly. He'd certainly had lower values than this, but decided to top up. He removed a single vial and loaded it onto the case's injector mount, then pressed the flat side of the case against his thigh.

"For the good of Mankind," he heard himself say, and pressed the injector button. The thin needle plunged straight between the fibres of his suit and into his flesh. It would be a few minutes before any effect would be detectable, he just had to clear his thoughts and let it do the work.

As he put away the case, his phone screen lit up. Automatically he checked his surroundings through the tinted windows before keying in his access code. The usual icons presented themselves but then disappeared, to be replaced by a black screen. A second code pad then presented itself, accompanied by the word 'Ego'.

This could only be a direct communication from Archive Central. It was rare, and an indication that a large scale event was about to happen, or had already begun. He keyed in his sixteen character pass-phrase and waited for the authentication. After a moment the code pad itself disappeared leaving a single line of text for Benton to read:

'Fallen Veil'

Benton understood immediately. Archive was informing all personnel that containment of the knowledge surrounding Siva was failing. His mission now was no longer to keep Archive secret, but to remove the influence of those who would not comply with Archive's new social order.

He actually felt conflict.

He had failed to complete his primary mission to shut down a potential Archive-damaging source, but his instructions were clear; he must now stop his pursuit of those seeking Archive, and switch to protecting Archive's system that would allow for the survival of the human race.

Yet he found himself unable to disconnect from this evening's events. He had been fooled and had allowed the pair to escape with an unknown amount of data.

For the second time in as many weeks he had the suspicion that he'd missed something. Unbidden, the Polaroid he had handled earlier in Kate Walker's house flashed into his mind. The injection was apparently starting to take effect.

He got out of the car and stood in the darkness, then closed his eyes.

He then pictured Kate's room around himself, and began to mentally move around the same space again. The university colleague photos. The laughing groups of friends, with a monument in the background, Eiffel Tower. No, too small. Las Vegas then. The coiled bead necklace on the dresser. The framed Polaroid next to it. Reinforcing his earlier actions he mimed opening the back of the frame whilst picturing the memory. No other photos stored behind the one on display. The scribbled text on the back of the photo.

A few hours ago he had only glanced at it, now he had to try to resolve it, but in his mind's eye it was still blurred. Allowing his current senses to drift slightly he became aware of the sounds in the street around him. In the immediate vicinity he could hear an argument going on in a house nearby, a little further out a dog barking, the distant traffic starting again for the dawn commute. The household dispute had apparently become a little out of control and he heard a glass smash.

Remembering the sound of the Handyman sweeping up the broken glass provided an additional memory anchor. Still within his memory, he glanced down again at the back of the photo, this time recalling the sound of the broken glass swept by the Handyman. He mimed lifting it closer to his face, and this time the text resolved itself.

'Betty & Baby W, Sept. 10th '82.'

He replayed his examination of the woman in the photo, and the source of his earlier déjà vu revealed itself. Her features were a little older than he remembered, but her eyes hadn't changed. The 'Betty' in the picture was without a doubt Elizabeth Walker.

His eidetic memory began shifting and delicately re-structuring the new information, visualising how it fit into his already detailed historical knowledge of Archive's personnel.

He knew that Elizabeth had married Howard Walker in 1955.

Howard Walker had been instrumental in the formation of Archive, following his discovery of Siva. But shortly before the Apollo launches, a traffic accident had silenced his brilliant, but apparently troubled, mind.

The event had caused Elizabeth to act out of instinct to protect her only son. By all accounts Douglas had been devastatingly bright and she had enrolled him in the Pittman Academy's accelerated education program. As a graduate of this program Douglas had been quickly absorbed into one of Archive's exotic science projects, thereby guaranteeing him a place in any final rescue solution.

Even by Benton's high-functioning standards he considered Douglas Walker to be worthy of note. If Douglas had only lacked the weakness of compassion then, in all likelihood, he would have been labelled an ego-morph too.

Benton mentally moved down one generation.

In 1981, Douglas had married Monica Dean, another Archive specialist. Compartmentalisation within Archive meant that Benton did not have detailed knowledge of other project areas. Monica Dean's history was only visible to him where it intersected the Walker family tree.

However, from the small amount of location data he had on Douglas and Monica during the 1980's he was willing to extrapolate that the 'Baby W' in the photo was their daughter.

He opened his eyes again and breathed the cool air of the dawn.

In the comparative calm he formed a new personal directive.

Given that his new mission would be to protect Archive's new social order mechanism, he reasoned that Blackbox still represented a threat. But if Kate Walker truly *was* the baby in the photo then, even with her criminal association to Blackbox, she would be of value to her parents.

That also made her valuable to Archive.

The conflicting logic evaporated.

He must retrieve Kate, and Blackbox must die.

Through a twist in his logic he could extend the deadline of a failed mission by converting it into an Archive-defending new one.

He downloaded a supplementary data package to his phone, to cover the shortfall in his knowledge of the Walker family tree, and then removed the tracking chip from the phone. He had always known it was there, but until now it didn't serve him to remove it. It would prove a hindrance now.

He then wrapped it in a piece of paper from the glove compartment, crossed the road, and dropped it into a postbox. When the letters were collected later today, the chip would be kept in motion for hours at the sorting office - more than enough time to achieve his objectives. Assuming he was successful he could then report back to Archive Central for his change of duty.

With a renewed sense of optimism and determination, Benton drove off towards Dover, and the home of Kate's mother, Monica Walker.

CHAOS THEORY

14th February 1980

Douglas Walker had chosen the restaurant himself, from a list of about twenty that Archive had vetted as being safe locations. However his assigned bodyguard, the ever-present armed shadow, was never more than ten feet from him, which made most locations arguably safe. Whilst he wasn't actually worried, he was a little agitated. He was of the opinion that worry was just the human mind coping with the fact it couldn't evaluate all the possibilities of a situation; but he had always rationalised that if you knew what all the possible outcomes were then you didn't need to worry. Douglas was confident he'd evaluated all possible outcomes of tonight's meeting. When the moment came to act, he had all the relevant paperwork and hardware at his disposal.

The restaurant table he'd chosen was quite secluded, and the gentle bubble of conversations at other tables seemed to provide an air of conviviality and warmth. When the time came, it would also become a useful conversation-masking noise. He'd arrived earlier than planned, so to pass the time he sat solving and jumbling a Rubik's Cube. Though it was a relatively new toy, he found it a worthy distraction; not a puzzle with trivial solutions, but sufficient combinations and permutations to preoccupy his busy mind.

A cough from his bodyguard alerted him that his guest had arrived. He nodded to acknowledge the signal and replaced the re-scrambled cube into his pocket. The guest and her bodyguard were escorted through the well-ordered room to his table. Her bodyguard then took her coat and discreetly positioned himself a little out of earshot. Douglas, always a little clumsy when it came to etiquette, stood and waited for her to take her place. Once satisfied she was in position he sat down, noting that his heart rate was a little elevated.

"This is a lovely place," she smiled taking in the surroundings, "how did you find it?"

He opened his mouth to answer but she followed up.

"No, let me guess!" she grinned, then leaning forward she whispered, "Archive gave you some to choose from?"

He looked a little sheepish, "Well, I…"

"Seriously?" she giggled, but then spotted his reaction, "I'm sorry, it's lovely. No really it's lovely."

The return of the waiter had the effect of defusing the situation, and after they had ordered he politely backed away, leaving them alone again.

"I had a terrible time getting here. My driver George," she nodded over to her bodyguard, "managed to make a wrong turn off Oxford Street. He went round Soho Square a few times, either to get his bearings or to check out the shortness of the girls' skirts. Seriously they must be freezing. But I guess they don't stand around on the streets long though, do they? Busy times. Money makes the world go round! Then we had to find a place to park up and… Sorry, I'm talking too much aren't I? It's just that, well I'm a bit nervous…"

"Why are you…?" he began.

"Well it's just that, er… it doesn't matter."

"Monica, you're perfectly safe. Between your George and my Henry back there, they've got us covered."

"It's not what - " she began, but then seemed to change her mind. A knowing smile crept from the corners of her mouth and her shoulders relaxed a little, "It's perfect."

It was a little earlier than he had expected, but he knew the moment had arrived and he reached into his pocket for the hardware and paperwork for his presentation.

"Monica Dean," he began, dropping to one knee and presenting an opened engagement ring box, "After thoughtful consideration I have these for you."

With one hand still holding out the ring box, he presented her with two small white envelopes marked 'Yes' and 'No'.

A smattering of polite claps came from other restaurant guests. Claps that were quickly hushed by the simple action of both bodyguards standing up and looking in their direction.

Monica retrieved something from her purse, then leaned down to look into his eyes. As she kissed him gently on the lips, her perfume swamped his senses and Douglas thought he might explode with joy. But when she withdrew she was holding out her own small red envelope, it was marked:

'External Variable'.

He was genuinely confused. This was not part of his multi-branched decision tree diagram.

"It's OK," she beamed, and ran her fingers down the side of his face, "open it!"

Hesitantly, he opened the envelope and took out the card that was inside. It simply read:

'No Douglas - Marry Me!'

From his lowered perspective, the soft candlelight caught the dimples in her cheeks and she beamed down at him with an effortless charm, completely disarming any anxiety.

"A woman's prerogative!" she shrugged. "Leap year."

His eyes darted back and forth, his blinking was erratic, and she knew he was trying to re-calculate routes along one of his complex decision trees. Within a second or two he appeared to have found a solution.

"My answer and my oath within," he smiled and, returning the 'No' envelope to his pocket, re-presented both the ring box and the small envelope marked 'Yes'.

She took it and held out her left hand. Carefully he pulled the ring free from the soft grip of the box and holding her hand steady, slid it onto her extended finger.

This time, the other restaurant diners seemed not to care about the bodyguards and proceeded to applaud. One man, joining in the clapping rather too enthusiastically, succeeded in knocking over a champagne bucket, sending ice cubes flying over neighbouring tables and onto the floor. The bodyguards reacted instinctively and stepped forward past Monica and Douglas to act as a protecting wall.

Seizing the opportunity, Monica grabbed Douglas by the hand and pulled him to his feet. She planted a quick kiss on his surprised face and dragged him in the direction of the kitchens, before the bodyguards had time to notice.

"What are you doing…?!" he gasped.

"Embracing the chaos!" she whispered loudly into his ear, then pushed him through the swing doors, past the startled staff in the steamy kitchen, and out to the cold night air.

It was a busy night on Oxford Street, but the London black cabs were out in force, eager to transport Valentine's Day couples to their covert venues. An exhilarated Monica flagged down a cab and bundled Douglas inside.

"Where to?" asked the driver over his shoulder.

Still breathless from the improvised sprint, Monica looked up at the somewhat bemused Douglas. For her, this was a much needed adventure away from the ever watchful eye of Archive; for him it was the very first time a spontaneous event had been put in motion without his careful evaluation and consideration. He had no emotional reference on how to deal with it, at all.

After a moment just looking at each other in silence, they burst out laughing.

"Hilarious, I'm sure," muttered the mirthless cab driver who after all was spending Valentine's night alone, "Where are you folks heading?"

"Shall I give you a list of approved Archive hotels?" she whispered into his ear, "Or can I choose?"

It occurred to him in that moment that every one of his life decisions had been fed to him. Temporarily glimpsing the bars of his invisible cage, he realised that his path through the many branches of his life was not truly his alone.

His normally present frown of consideration lifted and he turned to face Monica.

"You choose! Time for a new tree."

Long familiar with seeing his detailed multi-branched non-linear diagrams, she knew exactly what he meant.

The newly directed cab fled on with purpose now up Regent Street into the cold night, while a police car siren wailed in the opposite direction, unaware of them. The initial euphoria of their escape from their bodyguards had subsided a little now, and Douglas found himself with a shoulder propped against the cab door, and holding Monica close. He was stroking her head when a thought occurred to him.

"How did you know I was going to propose?"

"Oh Douglas," she laughed again, and held his hands, "my darling Douglas, you're a brilliant man, but when it comes to affairs of the heart you're absolutely hopeless!"

He couldn't help laughing now, she was right, but it didn't concern him. The myriad alternate possibility diagrams he'd calculated for the evening collapsed leaving behind only the certainty that she loved him.

"I had it all worked out too..." he said, running his thumb over the tiny diamond inset within her ring.

"I'm sure you did... but sometimes you have to add a *little* chaos into the equation," she said furtively.

THE NODE

9th February 2010

General Napier had taken the retrofitted Hercules transport plane from Andersen Air Force Base yesterday, following the Siva briefing. The first of three firings on Siva had been a success, but the presence of a detached shard had proved so significant a risk it had been given its own designation. It had been determined that the shard, Tenca, would impact Earth somewhere in the Russian Urals, roughly three years from now. At that point, despite all the military might at his disposal, information would move faster than it could be damped and Archive would lose containment of Siva's existence. If even a fraction of the human race were to be saved, it would become necessary to defend Archive's interests at all costs. The briefing given by Alfred Barnes on saving the species followed by his report on the Think Tank had proved enlightening, but there was still a long way to go.

One of the reasons for Napier's visit to the Node was to check that adequate preparations were underway to secure the facility against physical incursion.

The ruthless Icelandic terrain streamed by outside the cockpit. The ten mile exclusion zone surrounding Öskjuvatn Lake had been put in place following the confirmation of its gravitational hotspot. At the time, scare stories had been released to convince the public that it was a volcanically active area, which for the most part had worked. The terrain was so inhospitable that most people never even ventured into the exclusion zone. Those that did, often perished in the cold long before arriving at the Node's gates. Those unfortunate enough to make it, were made to disappear.

But six months on, Napier had considered it prudent to add camouflaged gun emplacements. The unmanned ground-to-air missile defences dotted around the exclusion zone, were tasked with terminating all inbound unauthorised transport, be it ground or air based. Indeed Napier's Hercules itself had been targeted before the appropriate access codes were transmitted to pacify the system.

"We're cleared for landing, Sir," relayed the Captain over the headphones.

Napier had spent the entire journey wading his way through a thick folder of recommendations from Dr. Barnes, and looked up for the first time.

In the distance lay the hastily built, but not makeshift, runway. Their approach was such that their landing would initially take them beyond the Node, before taxiing back. The heavy drone of the four engines changed pitch and he felt a slight tug in the pit of his stomach as they began their rapid descent. To his left, the southern portion of Öskjuvatn Lake swept into view. In the midst of the lake, on a wide plateau of volcanic rock, stood the Node. By no means complete, its domed nature was already quite distinct. A framework resembling lines of latitude on a globe was already in place, interspersed with smaller vertical walls appearing to radiate out from a central point. All over the structure, minute sprays of hot sparks flew, each one the signature of a busy soldier at work. Temporary support buildings were arranged around the circumference of the island and accompanying them were the busy personnel, resembling ants dashing between sugar cubes; both dwarfed by the Node's 'half grapefruit' proportions.

Taking care to stay above the hundred knots stalling speed, but still land on the short runway, the Captain expertly brought the next load of construction material and the General down to ground level.

"I believe congratulations are in order, Captain," said Napier, unbuckling his harness, "30th mission?"

"Sir," he nodded, now focussing on taxiing back to the main compound, "21st flying this route."

"Good man," Napier said shaking his hand, before stepping out of the cockpit and preparing to disembark.

The Hercules arrived at the hangar and a swarm of personnel began unloading the cargo. Napier stepped out onto the composite tarmac and, finding his bearings, headed off in the direction of the main gate.

The main gate acted as a precautionary barrier to slow down the approach of any hostile force, it was the only entrance point through an otherwise unbroken perimeter fence that surrounded the circular Öskjuvatn Lake. Inside the fence were six observation towers, whose sole purpose was to protect a thin, wood and iron bridge. This bridge ran for about a hundred yards from the shore to the Node's island, and was the only means of entry to the facility.

Until its completion, access to the Node was beyond even his clearance. Not that it mattered, the main thrust of the experimental work and preparation for the voyage was being conducted in the surrounding support buildings. Napier dutifully submitted to searches and signed the reams of paperwork necessary to gain him entry to the bridge. Overall he was satisfied with defensive progress, leaving him free to concentrate on the main focus of today's visit.

With a discreet hiss, the airlock re-pressurised behind him, leaving him in a quiet but chaotic looking lab. Everything in the lab was arranged to sit outside of a yellow and black hazard-tape circle stuck to the floor. Inside this circle sat a large metallic grey box, perhaps ten feet to a side. The box had another airlock attached to one side, and a small observation window in another. A window shade was currently drawn over it, but Napier could see the room within was dark. On the floor, within the circle surrounding the box, were various collections of plants, glass test-tubes filled with different heights of liquid, and portable data recorders; all arranged within a grid of electrical cables laid out like bicycle spokes.

"General Napier?" came a voice from somewhere behind the box, on the opposite side of the lab.

"Yes," he confirmed, "Dr. Bergstrom?"

Taking care to walk around the outside of the circle, she crossed the lab and extended a hand to General Napier.

A small part of him always expected people to salute him, but over the years he'd grown used to shaking hands with civilians. The fact of the matter was that Archive was not a military operation, but had used the substantial pre-existing military infrastructure to support its population-saving goals.

"So this is the Mark 2?" said Napier, scrutinizing where a large portion of funding had ended up.

"It certainly is," she said proudly, the barest hint of her Swedish ancestry in her accent.

"Smaller than I thought."

She smiled, "You were expecting to see the actual hemisphere?"

He glanced down again at the yellow and black hazard-tape marking out a circle around the chamber.

"For the purposes of the Mark 2, we don't need to build all the way out to the edge," she explained, and on seeing Napier's eyes still assessing the construction, she added: "But we did spend four dollars on the floor tape..."

"I'm not here in the capacity of budget oversight, I - " he broke off when he saw her quiet amusement, "Oh. Yes. Very good, Doctor. Long flight."

He hadn't expected levity from Anna Bergstrom. Their few written communications so far had always been fairly perfunctory and had in no way indicated that she even had a sense of humour.

"Is he up?" Napier said, gesturing to the lowered window shade.

"Not yet," she answered, picking up a small writing board and marker pen, "but the shade is only down for six minutes in every twenty-four, so we should not have long to wait."

She wrote 'Gen. Napier' in block capitals on the writing board, then crossed the lab to where an easel faced the chamber's observation window. She placed the board on the easel then returned to join Napier.

"Can't believe we're still using this thing to communicate," he grumbled.

"Ah!" she snorted, "That is physics for you General. We can bend, but not break!"

A flicker of movement came from the window.

"Ah, here we are," she smiled and pointed to the chamber.

The shade now up, a similar sized writing board had appeared within the observation window. It read:

'No. Sorry. Close to breakthrough. Need 2 more cycles. Power stable.'

Napier exhaled and checked his watch.

"Do you mind if I…?" he gestured to a nearby desk.

"Go ahead," she said over her shoulder, re-crossing the lab to the easel. She picked up a red marker and, without removing the writing board from the easel, drew a diagonal line through her previous message.

"How long has he been in there?" he asked, laying out his briefing notes over the table.

She hesitated slightly before replying, "A whole day."

Her answer caught him a little off-guard. He knew the maths of the situation so it shouldn't have surprised him.

"Rations?" he asked, looking over to the chamber, "Oxygen?"

"Both red-lining. He must be close to the solution now. I've not seen him this driven."

Napier stood, a trait that made him feel able to take control of a situation. But she waved for him to re-take his seat.

"He knows what he's doing. In two cycles - "

"I should remind you, Doctor, that Douglas Walker is, absolutely, not expendable. If oxygen levels - " he began forcefully.

"And I should remind you, General," she cut in pointedly, "that the power supply is *internal* to that chamber, and we must wait for *him* to exit."

Napier knew this was true and forced himself to stand at ease.

"My apologies, Dr. Bergstrom."

"Not necessary, really. It's like this every week here," she soothed, "But, in matters of available time, I trust him implicitly. Now, why don't I send out for some refreshments? I think when Dr. Walker emerges we'll all need to re-fuel."

Without waiting for a reply, she lifted the handset of the nearest desk phone.

•

Part way through their civilised cups of coffee, a low, repetitive, bleeping noise issued from the console in front of Anna.

"Excuse me," she turned to face the screen, "Mmm, Gaussian field strength has dropped three percent…"

She snatched up a handheld device and walked directly towards the tape markers on the floor. Holding the device out towards the chamber, the needle of the dial flicked fully to the right.

"Fan! Fel skala!" she swore, then flicked a switch on the side. "Ya. Now thirty percent drop. The field is collapsing, he's coming out now."

She turned around and grabbed a handheld oxygen cylinder from the medical rack, mounted just outside the circle on the floor. Still holding the device out towards the chamber she called out the readings:

"Ten percent… five… Field strength, zero. Move in!"

General Napier, glad to be on his feet, was already at her side when the chamber's airlock began to cycle. A green light flashed on above the door and as Napier pulled hard at the handle, Anna dashed forwards with the oxygen. However, as the heavy airlock door squeaked open, Douglas was standing calmly looking at the pair of them with an expression of mild confusion, seemingly unable to understand what all the fuss was about.

"Douglas?" Anna asked with a frown.

"I'm fine," he reassured them with a frown that matched hers, "There's over a cycle's worth of supplies left. Really. I'm fine. What's going on, have I missed something?"

"You had us concerned Dr. Walker," replied Napier, moving to stand at ease.

"Yes, General Napier was quite concerned for you," she delivered, the only hint of sarcasm being a slight twinkle in her eyes, "So, are we any closer?"

"No field inversion. We're going to need *much* faster processing," he shook his head, "But I did get us a ratio of 360 to 1."

HARD LINE

11th March 2013

"We need to get this information to somebody," said Kate, determinedly.

Marcus sighed and returned from peering out through the crack in the stapled-down blinds of Rob's flat.

"Yes. Absolutely," he frowned, and then added sarcastically, "maybe we should take it to the police? Or the government? Or maybe, yeah, let's give it to the C.I.A., they'd know what to - ".

"Don't!" she cut in angrily, standing up away from the laptop.

"Well, what do you suggest?" he argued back, in a suppressed whisper, aware that the neighbour in the upstairs flat may be alerted to their presence, "The Authorities ain't there to bloody protect us! There's too many of us. They're here to manage us, like cattle."

"You sound just like my mother."

This seemed to have the effect of silencing him.

"You, my mother, even Rob," she continued, "All convinced that - "

"All convinced that what?" Marcus jumped in, "That someone might kill you for the sake of data?"

He let the question hang in the air.

In the silence, they heard footsteps stop on the pavement outside the flat. Marcus glided swiftly across the room to the crack in the blinds and peered out again. From the low perspective of this basement flat he could see a pair of legs, which then moved off again down the street. As the legs got further away he could see they belonged to someone who had stopped to light a cigarette.

"It's OK," he said, "Just some guy."

"Isn't there anyone you could reach out to? You know, someone in your network?"

"Network?" he said incredulously, converging on her, "This ain't the movies! Ain't no network! It's just you, me and that stick!"

"Can we make a phone call from here?"

"D'you not hear me?" he grabbed her by the shoulders.

His action seemed to ignite a fire in her, and she pushed him away, hard, into the wall behind him. Once she had him pinned loosely against the wall, she shoved at him again to make sure he got the message.

"Do you not hear *me?*" she asked, and pointed to the hole in the ceiling. "You said you've been borrowing bandwidth and electricity from the upstairs flat. Do they have a phone line?"

"What?"

Marcus had always preferred to keep his communications methods mobile. During his time here he hadn't used

Rob's conventional landline in case it had raised the alarm somewhere. The thought of using the *neighbour's* phone line had genuinely never occurred to him.

"Can we tap into their phone line to make a call?" she asked.

"Maybe…" he shrugged himself free of Kate's hold and moved over to the kitchen, to mull over the idea.

"When Rob had his phone line put in," said Kate, following him, "I remember him saying that the number had different starting digits to the others on the street…"

"Yeah, local exchange numbers went non-geographical when they ran out of digits," said Marcus, climbing onto the kitchen chair again to access the hole in the ceiling, "So?"

"So, if Rob's phone number was being monitored, the neighbour won't be in the same bank of numbers on the exchange, right?"

Marcus grinned, and for a moment Kate saw a glimmer of hope in their situation.

"Sweet," he pushed his arm further into the hole and began to feel about for more cables, "I told you though, I can't call no-one."

"There's someone I know," she said, steadying the chair, "We don't really get on that well, but I know I'd be taken seriously."

"Alright," said Marcus, "who you gonna call?"

Resisting the urge to reference a 1980's movie that Rob had once insisted they watch together, she replied, "My mother."

"Bad call," he said immediately, "If that murdering son of a bitch knows who you are, he'll definitely try to get to you through your family first."

"How do you know that?"

"It's what I'd do," he said shrugged, coldly.

She thought about it for a moment and could see his logic.

"Then we should definitely do it," she reasoned, but seeing his puzzled expression, she explained herself:

"We have to assume that he knows you're with me, right?"

"Right."

"So, he knows that you would advise me *not* to contact my mother."

"OK…" he ventured, hesitantly.

"So, as far as he's concerned, there's no reason I would choose to contact her first."

"Now, hang on…" he began, not liking the direction the conversation was going.

"I've not spoken to her, in what, maybe a year? He would *have* to assume I'd reach out to friends and work colleagues first, before I'd call my mother."

Marcus seemed caught in a dilemma, and lapsed into contemplation. It was Kate that broke the stalemate and provided them with some much needed direction.

"The way I look at it, the worst thing we can do, is to do nothing. The longer we stay put, the greater the likelihood of discovery. The longer that we *alone* know this information," she said pulling the memory stick from the laptop's socket, "the greater the personal risk. There are no good options to choose from here. Only least bad ones."

"OK," admitted Marcus, "I'm out of options."

"Glad you agree," she said pocketing the memory stick, "because you'll be needing my fingerprint to access the drive again."

In response Marcus just smirked. If nothing else, he'd convinced her of the very real predicament they were in; the fact that they were about to call her mother was not ideal, but he'd have to live with it. A few moments later he'd found the relevant cable.

"Pass me that clip," he pointed to his bag.

"This one?"

"To the left. Blue."

She pulled the clip out of his bag and a long thin cable trailed after it, with a phone jack roughly soldered to the other end. He took the clip from her and fumbled about in the ceiling again.

"Is your Mum far from here?"

"Dover," she replied, unknotting the thin cable, "middle of nowhere."

"Hmm. Ah, got it," he said, finding the neighbour's phone line.

He climbed down while Kate went off to find Rob's landline phone.

"I don't suppose you have a spare phone in that bag of yours?" she called.

"Nope," he shook his head, following her.

"Rob had this annoying habit of cable-tying everything together..." she said crawling under his workbench. Sure enough, the cables were neatly ordered, and bound together in bundles. No doubt the groupings had made some sort of sense to Rob at the time, but it slowed her progress having to pick through dozens of grey wires, and years of accumulated dust to find a phone cable. Eventually she found the one she needed and traced it back to an extension cable; she freed the phone plug and handed it to Marcus.

Marcus took it and then made sure he had her attention.

"Once I cut off the neighbour's line, the clock's tickin'."

"What clock? I thought they couldn't trace it?"

"Once I clip these cables then, real soon, the neighbour's gonna figure out their phone's bust. They call for repair and..." Marcus gestured around himself and the massive hole in the ceiling, "they find all this."

"OK," Kate frowned, "So we get our stuff ready to go first."

Marcus nodded and started gathering the few things he'd unpacked. Kate walked past the sofa and stopped to pick up the Go-bag that Rob, in his wisdom, had packed for her. The thought occurred to her that maybe he had packed one for himself but never had time to use it. She put the bag over her head and managed to snag her hair in the strap.

"Dammit!"

"Alright?" said Marcus, pushing the laptop into his bag.

"Yes, fine. Listen, when you broke in here, did you ever find, I mean did Rob have a Go-bag?"

"Good point. I'll check around."

"OK," she said picking up a pair of scissors and heading towards Rob's bedroom, "you check. I've got to do something first."

Marcus pushed aside the small hanging picture on the back wall to expose a ragged hole with a door handle inside. He gave it a tug and the concealed door reluctantly opened for a second time that night. "OK, I'll make a start, he probably stashed it in here."

She crossed the bedroom to get to the small en-suite bathroom, and turned on the light above the mirror. Steadying herself on the sink rim she studied her reflection. Her long limp hair fell like damp black curtains either side of her ashen face. Assuming that she would need to travel and not be easily recognised, she knew that she would have to change her appearance.

"You've looked better, Katie," she said, looking her reflection in the eyes.

Over the course of the night, her mascara had smudged itself out into large, dark, circles surrounding each eye.

"Perfect," she said, semi-sarcastically. Then on further study, changed her mind, "Perfect."

Turning her head from side to side, she ran her hands through her bedraggled locks and took a deep breath.

"Desperate times," she whispered to herself, then started to chop away at her hair with the scissors.

Long strands started to fill the sink, until the longest hair on her head was no longer than her thumb. She wiped the remnants of old lipstick off her mouth on a towel, and then re-applied it with precision. The stark contrast between her eyes and mouth now looked deliberate and, for anyone not looking too closely, would be mistaken as a fashion statement. To complete the effect, she stripped out of her blouse, and pulling open Rob's wardrobe, looked for a suitably aggressive looking T-shirt, or jacket. The wardrobe did not disappoint. By the time Marcus returned, carrying another black bag, her appearance had shifted significantly.

"Rob's bag was - Shit!" he cried out and half stumbled away from her.

She grinned; his reaction told her all she needed to know.

"Pick something from the wardrobe, then let's make that call," she said and stepped out of the bedroom past an open-mouthed Marcus.

•

Marcus clipped the phone plug into the socket, "Clock running."

Kate picked up the receiver and was greeted with a dial tone, "OK it's working."

She pushed the digits on the handset and waited.

"It's ringing," she said, covering the mouthpiece.

"Good," said Marcus and pushed a button on the phone's base to turn on the speakerphone.

After three rings Marcus frowned, "You got the right number?"

"Of course I got the right - "

"Urgh! There better be a damned good reason why you're calling me at three twenty," came the voice of Kate's mother, *"Who is this anyway? Your number's not display -* "

"It's me, Mum. Kate."

There was a pause.

"Kate?"

"Yes, Mum."

"OK, hang on," Over the speaker they could both hear Monica Walker sigh, followed by the sound of her manoeuvring herself into a more comfortable position. *"Right. All this time, and you pick, three twenty in the morning, to call me."*

"Yes I know. Listen - ".

"Can I give you a call back? It's just that - ".

"Mother, they're trying to kill me!" she yelled.

Marcus winced and glanced up at the ceiling, ears straining to hear any noise from the upstairs flat, and simultaneously any response from the other end of the phone call.

"What d'you mean 'they're trying to kill you?'!".

"Rob's dead, Mum. They killed him. They killed him trying to get hold of a memory stick!"

Again, the pause.

"Where are you?" came her mother's voice.

Marcus shook his head.

"I'm safe. Sort of."

"Yes, but where are you?" her mother cut in.

Marcus glared.

"I'm… I'm on my way to you."

There was another long silence. Kate hit the speakerphone button, and covered the mouthpiece.

"Does this hack have a delay?" she whispered to him, pointing at the cable.

Marcus shook his head again, then re-activated the speaker.

"Kate, don't go to the police. I'll meet you at the Monument. You know the one I mean?"

It took her a moment to realise that her mother was being deliberately vague on purpose.

"The one where… we used to meet Dad?" she replied, equally cryptically.

"Yes. Now, how quickly can you get here?"

Marcus flashed two fingers, frowned and then put up three. Then mimed a steering wheel.

"Two, maybe three hours. It depends what car we take."

"OK. I'll get things ready for you. I hope your silent escort, who's listening in, keeps you safe."

"How do you know - " Kate began.

"This isn't my first dance darling. Stay safe and hurry."

The phone line went dead, and Kate replaced the handset.

"I meant depending on traffic," said Marcus, re-miming the steering, "it's about two or three hours to Dover."

"So we don't need to steal a car then?" she asked directly.

"No!" Marcus objected, "Don't profile me, I don't make a habit of boosting cars alright? Last night was -"

Kate held up a hand to stop him speaking, "So how do we get a car?"

"What d'you mean?" he turned to point towards the emergency exit, "We'll take Rob's."

In all her time with Rob, they had never had a car, or so she had thought. He had always argued that it was pointless in London, and preferred to use public transport.

"Did he have the car when he knew me?" she asked, following Marcus out through the exit and past piles of cardboard boxes and filing cabinets, "How could I not know?"

As they neared the metal swing door at the end of the lockup, the car came into view, along with a shopping trolley half filled with cans and wet cardboard.

"Guess you didn't clock the car on the way in," said Marcus, pushing the trolley to one side, "you were well gone. Had me worried."

The car was a modest silver-grey hatchback; small dents and chips in the paintwork and several patches of rust on the door frames told Kate it was, at least, second-hand. Marcus pulled open the driver-side door and turned the ignition key. The starter motor stammered and, miraculously, the engine grudgingly coughed into life.

"Will this even make it out of London?" she asked.

"Unless Her Ladyship would prefer to travel by trolley again," he replied with a mocking bow.

INVERSION

11th March 2013

The cuboid monument itself was not that impressive in terms of stature or precious materials. Barely two feet high, the solid block of stone stood inside a rough patch of earth, set a little way from the edge of Samphire Hoe cliff. As Monica walked up the incline towards it, she could see the Dover Strait open out beyond, and felt the stiff, cold, wind begin to pick up. These days she felt the cold more, but today it bothered her less.

Although the monument had only been there a few years, time had been hard at work rounding its corners and text. She brushed away some of the dirt within the words *'Douglas Walker'*, and then looked out towards the sea. Somehow it seemed rougher and more cruel than yesterday; its chaos of grey reflecting the dawn sky above.

She used to adore chaos, the sense of freedom it gave her to act unpredictably or tangentially. But as she had grown older, she had come to realise that chaos was only fun when there was a strict system to deviate from. Life *itself* was chaos now, its pattern almost indiscernible from noise. Like the ships on the rough sea below, her life had become harder to navigate. There seemed fewer absolute values to navigate by, merely a shifting seascape of grey morality.

Seagulls glided overhead. A few, with wings outstretched on a thermal air current, seemed to defy gravity and hung motionless in the air. Temporarily they appeared frozen in time, separated from the chaos of the churning sea below. It reminded her of a time when Douglas had explained a concept to her using a childhood flick-book he'd made.

She became aware that a voice was calling from behind her, muffled by the wind.

She turned and saw two people walking towards her. The closest one had spikey black hair and make-up like a bizarre cartoon panda.

"Mum?" called Kate.

"Katie?" Monica called above the wind. "Katie, what on earth have you -"

Her daughter suddenly embraced her. It wasn't the sort of reunion Monica had been expecting at all, but she felt the simultaneous rush of relief and redemption overwhelm her.

"I'm so glad you're here!" she whispered into Kate's ear, "I've missed you so much! I'm sorry..."

"No, I'm sorry..." said Kate, looking down at the tiny monument engraved with her father's name.

Over Kate's shoulder, Monica spotted the man who had accompanied her daughter, and she stiffened a little.

"Who's your friend?" she said quietly, continuing their hug.

Marcus spotted that he was being watched and stepped forwards, palms raised.

"Not that this ain't emotional," he gestured to the pair of them, "but can we go somewhere else? You know, like somewhere less exposed and ball-freezing?"

The Walkers broke their hug and turned to face him. When Marcus had changed clothes back in London, Rob's wardrobe had yielded a less coherent outfit than Kate's. He wore baggy light cotton trousers and a long-sleeved grey T-shirt proclaiming 'Anti-social Networking'. He stepped forward extending a hand to shake.

"I'm Marcus Blake."

Monica eyed him for a moment before accepting his hand, "Monica Walker. Where's the car?"

"In the lay-by, back down the hill."

"Plates?"

"Took them off," Marcus confirmed, slightly offended that she would even ask.

"You leave anything in it?" said Monica, looking at them both in turn. When they both shook their heads she turned on her heels and headed away from them, "Good, we'll walk back to my place. In case you're wondering, Mr. Networking, five minutes."

Kate stole one last look at the monument overlooking the white cliffs.

"Bye Dad," she whispered under her breath, then followed her mother along the coastal path.

•

Yesterday, Douglas Walker had celebrated his 56th birthday. Anna and a few others had insisted that they mark the occasion. They had managed to get a few balloons together along with a basic cake. Not having 56 candles to put on top, Anna had placed three candles followed by three holes, and told him to think in ones and zeroes. It made him smile again now. He picked up one of the balloons and stared through the window of Hab 1 at the Node.

After nearly four years of continuous construction the structure was nearing completion. Gone were the showers of sparks peppering the once exposed framework; instead a super-sized crane, in itself a major construction project, was lifting complex-curved panels into place, fifty metres above the small island that the hemisphere now dominated.

Whilst the solid part of the construction was almost complete, he knew his contribution to the project still had a long way to go. If the Floyd Lunar Complex succeeded in its final firing on Siva next year then, in theory, everything here at Öskjuvatn Lake would be irrelevant. But Archive always planned for the worst.

He didn't know if it was a perspective peculiar to him, and he was aware of how others saw him as peculiar, but he found birthdays curiously poignant events; he found himself often in deep introspection about paths he'd taken in life, and the alternatives he'd discarded as 'non-optimal'.

Not that he looked back on his choices with any measure of regret. In any given situation he was able to look beyond the immediate decision to the branch of possibilities that it unlocked or, more crucially, denied; so by his own argument, regret was not a possibility. And yet he found the idea of rejected choices wasteful; his decisions, albeit necessary, killed off entire trees worth of alternative outcomes.

Before making a decision, in his mind's eye he could see hundreds of possible futures branching out from that moment, existing simultaneously along side each other. The inherent perfection of being able to hold all possible decisions open, forever, seemed to have an unassailable beauty. So to knowingly collapse billions of possible branching future outcomes in the process of making one decision, weighed heavily on him.

He had started to notice too, over the years he'd spent here, that the number of decision branches had been reducing, as though eventually a nexus would be reached. No new information was entering this isolated closed system; and in the absence of a little chaos to add complexity then a singularity, a final decision, was an inevitability.

He found himself, not for the first time, revisiting the night he had proposed to Monica. The infectious nature of her smile, and the mischievous sense of chaos she had brought into his closed-off world. A second image flashed into his head, of his daughter giggling uncontrollably as Monica tickled her. As if his mind were providing an unwelcome antidote to the happiness, he remembered that he would never again hold them close -

The balloon burst in his hands.

He looked down at the remnants of the balloon, noticing the tiny droplets of moisture sticking to what was once the inside surface. He became peripherally aware of Anna Bergstrom entering the room and starting to speak.

"Ah! There you are Douglas. Napier has called an assembly," she said and peered down at the popped balloon, "It seems that someone does not know their own strength - "

She spotted the look on his face that she had seen several times before, and waited patiently. After a few seconds Douglas seemed to become aware of his surroundings again.

"Oh, Anna. Sorry - "

"Quite OK. What do you need me to do?"

"How's your Whitney-Graustein theorem?"

She gave him a skewed look, "Fine. Thank you for asking."

He held up the remains of the balloon, and then deliberately turned it inside out.

The smile creases around her eyes and mouth slowly straightened, and she grasped his arm.

"Herregud!"

Douglas nodded and started to walk quickly towards the door, "I need to speak with Napier."

"What? Wait!" She called after him, hastily grabbing another balloon from the table before running to catch up with him.

•

Kate placed her head against the ceramic tiled wall and let the fast, hot water pummel the back of her head. Less than a day ago her long hair would have directed the water down past her waist, but with her shorter crop it streamed down through her eyebrows and over her cheeks and chin. Running her hands through what remained of her hair, she stared down; the sheets of water pouring off her legs and arms ran black, and swirled past her feet into the drain. Only now had she begun to get back the feeling in the tips of her toes. After scrubbing at her cheeks to remove the last of her fashion-statement mascara, she just stood in the warmth allowing the steam to surround her, whilst her aching muscles drank in the water's heat.

She couldn't tell how long she'd been there, questions flooding her mind, but the water now ran clear. She could hear a gentle knocking.

"All OK, Katie?" came her mother's slightly muffled voice, from the other side of the bathroom door.

"Yes, Mum," she called back, through the noise of the running water. It was almost like she had never left home.

Feeling slightly more human she dried herself off, hung up her towel and slipped into the bathrobe her mother had lent her. The trauma of the last day now seemed surreal, distant, and as temporary as the dirt she had washed away. She stepped out of the shower enclosure and padded barefoot across the warm floor. Looking at the bathroom door, it now seemed ludicrous that she herself had wedged the back of the bathroom chair under the door handle to prevent anyone entering.

She pulled the chair back to resume its decorative occupation, slid the privacy lock and opened the door. She hadn't really appreciated the amount of steam she'd generated until it went billowing out into the slightly colder upstairs landing.

Marcus was just reaching the top of the stairs and instinctively she gathered the bathrobe lapels closed.

"Don't flatter yourself," he smiled, before squeezing past her into the bathroom, "I'll be down in five."

He closed the door and she heard the lock slide over, followed a few seconds later by the sound of a chair being dragged. Evidently she was not the only one feeling insecure.

She crossed the landing to the spare room and sat on the bed, towel-drying her hair, more a force of habit than a necessity now. This had been her room once, and without really thinking about it she had managed to position herself at the exact spot on the bed where she could see the dressing table mirror. She found it incredible to think that somewhere in her brain were these old, seemingly insignificant, behaviour patterns being re-activated without her awareness. She wondered what other patterns she had already fallen into, in her first half hour here.

On her bed was a small pile of jeans and tops, with their price tags still attached. Having left no clothes behind when she moved out, she made a mental note to ask her mother where they had come from. Holding up combinations of clothing against her body she studied the approximate effect in the mirror, then chastised herself. Old patterns again. This was not the time for assessing fashion. She pulled on the two things that were in her hands last, then headed downstairs to the kitchen.

A freshly brewing teapot sat on the table accompanied by a set of bulky looking mugs. The washing machine churned in the corner of the room, and her mother was fetching some milk from the fridge.

"Mum, have you got some scissors so I can cut off these tags?" she asked, tugging at the light cardboard labels.

"Sure," Monica replied whilst lugging over a chunky, thick laptop, "top drawer - "

"Next to the sink," she remembered, "of course."

At that point Marcus walked in, dressed in clothes that still didn't quite suit his demeanour but at least were warmer.

"Ah, you found the clothes I left out? Best I could do I'm afraid - "

"It's cool, thanks - " he started.

"I'm washing the clothes you both arrived in. You never know if -"

Kate's hand reacted instinctively, darting to her hip to find the pocket where she had stored the memory stick. Just as quickly and with sickening panic she realised that pocket containing the memory stick was busy drowning in the washing machine.

"The data!" she shouted, dashing across the kitchen and scanning for a way to stop the washing machine, "Marcus, help me!"

He started to run across the kitchen, but Monica realised their incorrect assumption.

"Hey!" she shouted, rolling her eyes, "I've got it right here! It's safe."

Kate and Marcus froze, and turned to look at her.

Monica, a little confused, returned their stares, "When you were a kid I always used to check your pockets before putting your clothes in the washer. Force of habit I guess."

They both exhaled gratefully. But their sense of relief was short lived.

"It's very odd though," Monica continued, "When I plugged it into the computer -"

"You did what?!" shouted Marcus, now scrambling around the kitchen table, "It's protected by an -"

"Yes, I know, an A.E.S. 256 bit key encryption cipher," Monica continued, "driven by a 16 point bifurcation modal fingerprint scan, and multi-overwrite erase fail-safe…"

Both Marcus and Kate seemed dumbfounded at her apparently sudden expertise, and with open mouths opted to sit down in silence on either side of her. She angled the laptop for both of them to see the screen. It was then that Kate saw that her mother's thick laptop was in fact a radiation-hardened military-grade field computer.

"…and from the looks of this ASCII-string right here, it's waiting for your fingerprint, Kate."

"Mum?" she began, loosely pointing at the hardware.

"Yeah, what's with the mil-spec?" joined in Marcus.

"OK. So you'll need to stay calm. Both of you. But I need to explain a few things," Monica replied, pouring the tea. She handed her daughter the first mug, then poured the second.

"Mr. Blake, you're very clumsy," she said, pushing the mug across the table to him.

"What? I don't…" he replied, clearly confused and glancing back and forth between the two women.

"You left your fingerprints all over the memory stick…"

"What are you talking about? Only Kate's scanned her finger, I ain't dumb enough to scan my own - "

"No. Not those fingerprints," she said pointedly, tilting her head and waiting for Marcus to catch on, "The drive also had a machine ID code recorder. Your laptop ID code showed up in that sector."

"So what?" he retorted defensively, "What use is that ID code to anyone?"

"It was useful to me," she said, pouring the tea into her own mug and stirring in a spoonful of sugar. She noticed his defensive posture and reassured him, "Stay calm, you're quite safe. I couldn't be sure when we first met, up on the cliff top, but your ID code is an exact match."

"For what?" Kate cut in, unsure of what was unfolding in front of her.

"An exact match for someone I - " she momentarily searched for the appropriate word, "hired."

She took a sip of her tea, then looked over the rim of the mug at Marcus.

"Hello, *Blackbox.*"

Marcus stood up from the table and backed away. Kate wheeled around in her seat.

"You *know* him?!" she spat.

"Know him?" she said calmly over her tea. "Of course I know him. He doesn't know me, personally that is, but I know him."

Kate was now on her feet and also backing away from the table.

"Bull*shit!*" shouted Marcus, nervously edging closer to the door.

"Sit down Marcus!" Monica raised her voice, putting the mug down on the table loudly, "I said you'd have to stay calm. You only know me by my alias."

"You're not making sense Mum, please - " said Kate quietly, not knowing who to turn to.

"You know what?" said Marcus turning towards the door, "Screw this."

"*Chalk Mole,*" she called out.

Marcus stopped dead in his tracks.

"You know me as Chalkmole, Mr. Blake," said Monica calmly, "Please. Both of you. Sit down."

The washing machine clicked and fell quiet, leaving only the wind outside the window to highlight the uncomfortable silence. Marcus slowly returned to the table, eyeing them both suspiciously.

"You're Chalkmole?"

Monica nodded, and took another sip of her tea.

"Thought you were a guy," he muttered.

"Good," said Monica simply.

"Chalkmole, Mum?" said Kate, edging closer to her, "What the *hell*? I thought you worked for Eurotunnel - "

"I'll come to that," she sighed, "Marcus, you couldn't have known, but it complicates matters considerably by you bringing Katie and the data here. My plan was to keep her safe."

"I didn't bloody know that you *were* Chalkmole, did I?"

"It doesn't matter now Marcus. At least she's here now."

"Yeah. You're welcome," said Marcus, sarcastically, "Well done Marcus for savin' my daughter from Mister Psycho and getting her out of London, undetected, with the memory-stick-of-death. My pleasure, don't mention it."

"I'm trying not to mention it, Marcus," said Monica calmly, "That little stunt you pulled at the University campus - "

"They raided my fucking house! I lost everything! The campus was my only choice!"

"You dragged her into this!" said Monica, her composure starting to fracture.

"She was already bloody *into this*!" shouted Marcus, pointing at the fingerprint scanner, "Mister Killer broke into her house - "

"Enough!" yelled Kate, banging her fist on the kitchen table, "Mother. Start talking. What are you keeping me safe from?"

Monica exhaled and looked at the kitchen clock.

"We really don't have time to do this here."

"Make time," said Kate, stubbornly folding her arms and sitting back in her chair.

The statement interrupted Monica's line of thought, "Your father used to say that - "

"Yes, yes, I know, before he died - "

"Damn it Katherine!" Monica cut across her, suddenly unable to hold her composure, "Your father's not dead!"

Even the wind outside the windows appeared to fall quiet. The only sound now being the distant seagulls hovering above the cliff edge. Kate held Monica's gaze, and began to see the look of sadness in her mother's eyes. She could also see something else, it was relief.

"But, the accident?" Kate stared at her mother, looking for something to cling on to, "The memorial service… his, his monument, out there?"

"I had to, it was the only way I could be sure they wouldn't come after you."

"You keep saying this! Make sure *who* wouldn't come after me?"

"Archive."

Marcus shot Kate a look across the table, a look that she returned with equal realisation.

"Rob mentioned Archive," said Kate pointing at the memory stick, "I think it was a folder too."

Monica took hold of Kate's hand again, "I will tell you everything, I promise, but we need to know what Rob found out. They may be on the way already."

"Who?!"

"Darling, please! I will explain, but, please..." Monica gave up her seat opposite the computer screen, and encouraged Kate to take her place. As before, Kate placed her finger on the scanning plate and waited. Again the screen went blank, before Rob's message appeared.

'Hey fish-face - long time, no sea...'

As before, his last video log began to play.

"Memory stick header video file, March, er, Second, 2013. 8.15 am. Still researching Archive, and why it's trying to suppress the Chelyabinsk meteorite findings. I mean, seriously, this thing is out there guys, what's the point? So, a new thread came in last night from Shades141 and verified by Blankspace, apparently there's another Archive hotspot being built in Iceland, referred to as 'The Node'. Imaginative. Anyway, the location's in the zipped file. OK, so, Breadcrumbs. Replacement high speed router delivery this morning in, er, 15 minutes. Rearrange meeting location with Blackbox, the Gasworks is possibly compromised. Stay low."

The list of folders popped up again.

"Here they are," said Kate, and stood to give access to her mother, "that's all we found."

"First things first," Monica began typing strings of characters into a text box at the bottom of the computer screen. Marcus tried to follow her approach, but quickly became lost. Within a few seconds a dialogue box opened on the screen with a progress bar, illustrating the percentage of files that had been processed.

"The files," said Marcus frowning at the screen, "They were copy protected, how did you -".

"Ah, but I'm not copying... I'm defragmenting the drive," she raised her eyebrow, "But the re-assembled fragments end up on my drive not the original."

While Marcus marvelled at the digital sleight of hand, Monica beckoned Kate to follow her into the living room next door.

"It will be a few minutes," she said over her shoulder, "make sure it doesn't skip any sectors."

The living room didn't appear to have changed since the last time she was here. The low ceiling seemed less pronounced in here than in the kitchen, and the large plump sofa and cushions almost filled the entire space, but it somehow made the room seem cosy rather than cramped. The only ornaments present were on the mantelpiece above a quietly crackling fire, and around the room, oversized frames held small photographs and pictures. No new photos seemed to have been added since she had left.

"I've been dreading this moment you know, but to be honest it'll be a relief," said Monica sitting on the sofa, and then mumbled to herself, "How far back do I start?"

"Why don't you start by telling me why you've had Mr. 'Blackbox' following me?" she said pointedly.

"Marcus was the last of several people I've had following you."

Not for the first time today, Kate felt that explanations were not making things simpler. She just stared at her mother, beginning to wonder who she actually was.

"For your own protection I couldn't tell you back then, what I have to tell you now," Monica continued, "After your Dad's memorial service, I kept tabs on you. It was easier while you were still in the school system, but it got harder when you left it. I had to resort to more, indirect, methods. Mr. Blake was one in a long line of, well paid I must say, observers."

A thought had occurred to her daughter because Monica could see her whole posture change. Her folded arms, tilted head and pursed lips, told her what she was thinking.

"No," Monica shook her head, "Robin, 'Rob', was not one of them. But that in itself was a challenge, keeping you out of Archive's radar -".

"Stop! Just, stop!" Kate suddenly found her voice again. "Who the hell is this Archive, and why do I need so much protection from them?"

"Monica?" Marcus called from the kitchen.

"Hold Alt Shift, then press F5," she called back, knowing what he was about to ask, "Then come in here, I only want to explain this once and it's best that you hear it too."

She stared around the room hoping for inspiration. Her eyes settled on a simple photo of a flower.

"Do you remember that picture?"

"What? Er, I guess. Didn't Dad give it to you?"

"That's right," Monica smiled.

"All very romantic, Mum, but like you said, we don't have time."

"It's relevant; and like both you and your Dad said, we'll make time."

Field One

5th April 1989

"OK, you and me both know that I flunked biology," exhaled Bradley Pittman, "so, what am I looking at Dougie?"

Douglas walked to the projector screen, extending his telescopic pointer, then turned to face the gathered group. With one hand he shielded his eyes from the glare of the slide projectors he'd set up for the presentation, and with the other he pointed at the images.

"OK," he cleared his throat, "Can we go back one slide please Anna?"

"Both projectors Doctor?" asked a slightly nervous Anna Bergstrom. She was still in her first week of induction to the program but, despite her obvious intellectual suitability, she was still finding her feet socially.

"Yes please," said Douglas, virtually squinting to make out her silhouette among all the others.

The slide projectors mechanically clicked, unloading the slides from the apertures. Then, rotating the carousels of slides into place, reloaded the previous slides. Both slides showed a bright pink flower with a yellow centre.

"Cosmos bipinnatus," began Douglas again, "a flowering herbaceous plant. We selected this type because of its already short germination time, typically nine days, and flowering at around two to three months."

Douglas nodded to Anna, who then re-advanced the slides.

"Both of these specimens have similar test conditions, 75 degrees Fahrenheit, soil at a pH of 6, and sunlamps to provide steady and continuous warmth and light. Brad," he addressed him personally, "they're two pink flowers that start to grow quite quickly if you look after them."

"Now that weren't hard, was it?" smirked Bradley.

"Initiation criteria - " began Douglas, then adjusting to fit his audience continued, "Starting conditions are the same for both flowers. Both were watered before the clock was set to zero."

Douglas looked out towards Anna and waved a hand for her to advance the slides. As prearranged, she began advancing the slides in pairs, so that the development of both flowers could be seen simultaneously.

"Here we are at twelve hours. No apparent change in either specimen. One day. Two days. No change. Three days. No change - ".

"Brilliant," muttered Bradley, "A lesson in how things stay the same."

One or two stifled chuckles came from around the room, but Douglas was used to Bradley's scientific irreverence and continued.

"We switch now to every two days, and you'll notice we've zoomed in a little to capture detail. Now at twelve days. Fourteen - ".

"I can hardly stand the anticip-" began Bradley, but his usual ebullience evaporated as the slides continued to change.

The image on the left showed virtually no change from the initial conditions, but the image on the right now began to show a marked difference. A small green shoot had pushed its way through the surface of the soil. In the next image the stem had thickened. In the next, spindly, gutter-shaped leaves had sprung out.

"Now at twenty-two days," continued Douglas. "Wait for it."

Suddenly a flower bud was replaced by a bright pink flower. The image on the left was only now showing signs of life, with a green shoot starting to emerge from the soil. But the image on the right showed a vibrant, yellow-centred flower in full bloom. The flower head became larger and began to sag under its own weight, then just as suddenly as it had emerged, it collapsed and turned brown. Douglas raised his hand to signal Anna to stop.

"Day thirty," smiled Douglas, "One month."

"So?" said Bradley with a furrowed brow, "You invented a flower that grows three times quicker?"

"No," he said plainly, and nodded to Anna.

The left image disappeared, leaving only the decaying flower on the right. The next slide zoomed out slightly, followed by another zoom out, so that the laboratory equipment surrounding the flower came into view. Douglas himself was visible in the next slide; standing next to the apparatus, he was tipping a small beaker of water onto the rotten flower below. But the timing of the shot showed that instead of the water hitting the flower, it was deflecting around it.

It appeared that the flower and its container were surrounded by a small transparent bubble, and the water was running over its surface.

"What you're looking at, is a Chronomagnetic Field."

The silence only lasted a few seconds before Bradley Pittman managed to assemble a few words approaching an actual question.

"Surely this is some kind of -"

"I can assure you, this is not any kind of photographic fakery, Brad," he said, pointing at the image. Douglas then turned to face him, making sure he had his full attention:

"The flower inside the Field was proceeding through time at three times the rate of the one on the left."

"Oh, come on Doug!" he blurted out. "Seriously?"

"Seriously," said Douglas, his expression not changing one bit.

"Come on!" he laughed, glancing back around the room, "Back me up here? You all in on this little joke?"

"Brad," Douglas said earnestly, "You've known me since we were kids. I'm serious."

He *had* known him a long time. Bradley still had vivid memories of sitting next to Douglas watching the Apollo 8 launch, on a cold December morning of 1968. He knew that when it came to counting cards, Douglas was a natural; but one thing was for certain, he had no poker face. Bradley stared at him, trying to read any hint of deception in his eyes. He got nothing.

"Shoot," he said resignedly, and leaned forward to take a closer look at the image. He studied the image carefully, glancing back and forth at Douglas "So. What? This doohickey field makes things age faster?"

"No. Well, yes." Douglas scratched his temples, "I mean, no. It's all relative."

"For crying out loud Doug!" protested Bradley, "Straighten it out for me, or I'm relative-ly walking out the door!"

"OK, look," he nodded to Anna.

The slide carousel clicked again and the image of Douglas disappeared. Then two new slides arrived, again taking up positions on the left and right of the projection screen. Both slides showed simple graphs, illustrating how the flowers had grown as time passed.

On one graph, a line steadily rose from the bottom left to the top right.

"This is our 'normal' flower," said Douglas, pointing at the graph, "If we had let it grow, it would have reached the full height in three months."

"OK, with you so far," frowned Bradley, rubbing his chin.

"Good, now look at this slide," said Douglas, directing his pointer to the other graph.

This one had a similar straight line but it was much steeper, so the graph only took up one third of the slide's width.

"That's the flower inside the field thingy?" asked Bradley.

"Yes. As you can see, the line is much steeper because from our perspective it only took one month, not three, to reach the full height."

"So. Like I said, it grew faster?" said Bradley still frowning.

Douglas paused and, not for the first time, wondered if it was only the Pittman family's fortune that was guaranteeing Bradley his place in Archive's matters.

"Look, imagine for a minute that you *were* the flower," said Douglas, trying a new approach. "You go into the Chronomagnetic Field for three months. During your somewhat isolated vacation you don't do anything faster than usual, from your perspective everything is normal. But, when you come out of the Field, you find that outside your little bubble, only one month has passed for everyone else."

The frown lifted from Bradley's forehead.

"So, if I was inside that bubble. You guys outside would be moving real slow?"

"Well technically, we would *appear* to be moving really slow, relative to you. But yeah," conceded Douglas.

"And to you guys outside the bubble I'd *appear* to be moving real fast?" ventured Bradley.

"Exactly," smiled Douglas.

"OK, I think I got it. I dunno how in blazes you're doin' it Dougie, but I think I got it," Bradley smiled, almost triumphantly, but it subsided quickly as a new thought pushed its way forward, "Except…"

"Except what?"

"Surely time is time?"

Before Douglas could respond, a frustrated but suppressed hiss in Swedish came from the back of the room.

"Anna?"

"Please Doctor Walker, I excuse myself!" she started, "But…"

With a little effort, and trailing the electric cable behind her, she picked up the whole slide projector showing the steeper graph, and lugged it around the right hand side of the room. She positioned herself to be within a few inches of the projector screen, but then pointed the projector obliquely along the screen at the first graph. It took her a few seconds to find the correct angle to stand at, but eventually she was satisfied. Despite the graphs showing two different time periods she had found a position where the first and second graphs overlaid each other perfectly.

"Same time, different perspective," exhaled Anna.

Bradley looked from her, to the projector screen, then to Douglas.

"Now why didn't you explain it like that, Dougie?" said Bradley, "*That* makes perfect sense. I need a coffee."

Douglas simply closed his mouth.

While Bradley went to fetch himself a cup of coffee, a general murmur of discussion spread between the delegates in the room. Most of them were aware of the research Douglas was conducting, but many of them had virtually dismissed the project as exotic theory. Few could have guessed the level of its progression in the physical world, but the few images they had seen so far was now fuelling a heated network of discussion around the table.

"That was extraordinary, Anna," Douglas whispered to her, while lacing film through the film projector they would need next.

"I know it is not how the Chronomagnetic Field functions," she replied, returning the slide projector to its stand, "But Mr. Pittman did not need to understand the physics."

"No?"

"No," she whispered, "he needed a solution-shaped answer. He just needed to *think* that he understood."

Douglas just smiled, he'd never seen Bradley placated so easily before.

"It was trivial really, I only had to think in three dimensions to simplify things for him," she shrugged, then leant closer to Douglas so she could lower her voice further, "Also, he was slowing things down!"

When they reconvened a few minutes later, the mood in the room seemed to have changed. The general level of restlessness had reduced, and there was an air of inquisitiveness. It seemed to Douglas that people were more willing to engage with each other, instead of simply passively absorbing what was considered to be just another presentation, in a long line of presentations.

"Dr. Walker?" came the voice of Dr. Chen. "What are the limitations to the size of this Chronomagnetic Field?"

"None, as far as we can tell, except for practicality," Douglas shrugged.

"Please explain?"

"OK, the amount of power required to maintain the spherical Field is proportional to the cube of the radius - "

"Forgive me, surely it is proportional to the square of the radius?" Dr. Chen cut in.

Anna raised an eyebrow at Douglas, who stood back to allow her to answer.

"The *surface area* of a sphere is proportional to the square of the radius. But the *volume* inside a sphere, the physical space within the bubble, the amount of matter within the bubble, varies with the cube of the radius."

"Of course, my apologies," he conceded with a slight bow of his head.

"So if you double the radius," added Douglas, "then the power requirements go up eight-fold."

Even Bradley whistled at that point.

"Mmm," said Dr. Chen, "Then, does the Field have to be spherical?"

Again Anna stepped forward.

"We only see the Field as a sphere, but this is because higher dimensional orders resolve to be symmetrical in all directions," she said factually, but noting no reaction in Dr. Chen she added, "Yes, it has to be spherical."

"Why can't we see the bubble itself, Doug?" asked Bradley.

"At the scale of this experimental sphere, the thickness of the Field wall is much thinner than a soap bubble, but it contains virtually no matter, so light can't - "

"No," interrupted Bradley, "I mean why can't we go see it, y'know, right now?"

Douglas shot Anna an uncomfortable glance.

"We can't see the apparatus at the minute," said Douglas hesitantly, "it's engaged with a second experiment. But we have some footage, taken from that experiment, to show you."

Douglas turned off the room lights again, and crossed swiftly to the film projector. He was dimly aware of Bradley quipping to someone about popcorn, but his main focus was on the content of the footage. Douglas was usually acutely aware of branching possibilities and planning for their outcome; but he hadn't even conceived of the outcome of this experiment, and it had left him a little uncertain.

"It will be OK," Anna reassured him, "it is necessary for next stage."

Douglas started the projector and the film flickered into life on the screen. Anna nodded with an encouraging smile, and he started to describe the footage.

"This is the second apparatus, you'll note it is about twice the size of our first experiment."

He heard a Texan drawl mumbling words to the effect of 'eight times as much power' to his nearest neighbour, and for a moment was glad that Bradley had actually learned something today.

"Is that a...?" someone had whispered.

"Yes," he replied to the room in general, "it's a mouse cage. But built to fill the spherical space of an activated Field."

A lab coat covered arm lowered a mouse into the cage through a trapdoor on top, and placed it on a small circular platform at the exact centre of the cage.

"The test subject was sedated beforehand to," he hesitated, "to minimise any distress, and provide a stationary point of reference."

The mouse lay asleep and behind it, also on the platform, was a small LCD digital clock. The arm withdrew from the cage and closed the trapdoor.

"The clock is there to show us the amount of time passing inside the Field, relative to the control clock in the top left of the screen. The flash you'll see in a moment is where the film becomes temporarily overexposed. We suspect this is something to do with the activation of the Field."

The film flared brighter for a moment and then the clock inside the cage started to move faster than its counterpart outside. The mouse twitched and then its whiskers became a blur.

"As you can see the subject successfully regained consciousness, and mobility."

It began to scurry back and forth around the small platform, pausing once or twice to try gnawing at the clock; but in the accelerated time-frame of the sphere, the mouse appeared to exist only as a series of trembling poses linked by blurred lines of movement. After scurrying to several places around the circumference of the platform it then peered over the edge.

"We think it was looking for a way down, at this point," said Douglas, and having seen the film several times, closed his eyes.

The mouse moved forwards slightly, seeing the cage floor below. Before it could jump down, it juddered and fell from the platform. However, instead of hitting the cage floor it was flung to the right at tremendous speed and was shredded to pulp. There were a few intakes of breath from around the room.

Douglas shut down the projector, and walked from the room.

"I'd say my vacation in that bubble just got postponed," said Bradley with a dry smile, "Excuse me a minute folks. Anna, why don't you run the movie again for everyone? Get some pondering going?"

He made his way past the others at the table and went out to find Douglas. He didn't have to look very far, Douglas was sitting on the corridor floor, with his back against the grey wall.

"Mind if I join you, buddy?"

Douglas gestured to the carpet tile next to him.

"Thanking you kindly," said Bradley, awkwardly lowering himself to the floor, "I mean it looked like it was going well, it woke up in there, and did its thing. You normally plan things so - I mean - any idea what the hell happened?"

"Some," said Douglas, "You have to understand, there's no way I could have planned for an outcome that - ".

"Hey, it's OK Doug," he consoled, "Your outcome-blindspots are rare as hen's teeth! In all the years I known you, I only seen it happen, like, twice but I know how it gets to you. So we lost a mouse - big deal!"

"It's not the mouse-paint cage decor I'm concerned about Brad!" he spat out, "We'll need to work out why it exploded, obviously, but that's not the problem!"

"OK then, why don't you tell me what's gettin' up in your hair?"

"You remember me saying the footage was taken from the experiment?" he asked rhetorically, "Well that's the problem, the experiment is still running, I can't shut it down."

Bradley sat in thought for a minute, "OK. Level with me. Is it dangerous?"

Douglas looked up from his study of the floor, "What? No. It's just that for the Field to work, the power source has to be *inside* the Field."

He waited for Bradley to connect the dots, but he seemed unable to.

"Brad, your new prototype generator is *inside* the Field. When the experiment started, the Field was activated by remote control, but now the signal to deactivate it can't get through. I can't turn it off from the outside and - ".

Bradley was actually shaking with laughter.

"Oh, buddy! You are one in a million, I tell ya! Screw the generator, I'll build another!"

"But, the cost was -"

"Nah, screw it! When's the generator gonna run out of juice?"

Douglas hesitated, "Sometime in June."

Bradley just collapsed in a fit of laughter, slapping Douglas hard on the shoulder, before stamping his feet on the floor. "Dougie, that there is *the* most funniest thing I ever heard!"

His laughter was infectious and soon the pair of them were unable to stop. After a few seconds, Anna emerged from the room with a puzzled look on her face, only to see them both red-faced and giggling.

"Is everything alright?"

Bradley nodded before blurting out, "Ol' Dougie's left the keys in the ignition - and locked himself out of the car!"

VALENTINE'S DAY

14th February 2013

Lana, Mike and Cathy were gathered round the auxiliary FLC control console in the Drum, waiting for Houston's live up-link, when the airlock gave its characteristic breathy hiss. Eva came through the door first, her cheeks flushed red, followed a moment later by Leonard, pulling up his jumpsuit zip.

"Well I hope you cleaned up after yourselves," Mike smirked.

It appeared to be hard-wired into the human DNA; there was something about the remote location, isolation, and low number of people that triggered the desire to procreate. Something the five crew of the FLC knew intimately well. They were all aware of the fact that raising children here would be an impossibility and potentially lethal; but the primitive drive was a persistent force and they took appropriate steps to ensure that such tensions were relieved, without judging each other.

"Leave the poor Valentines alone," consoled Cathy, in a mocking tone.

Leonard and Eva joined the others without comment. It wasn't their first time, but of all the various permutations they seemed most comfortable with each other.

"How long till the live-link?" asked Leonard.

"Not long enough to use the airlock again," uttered Cathy.

"What is your problem, Gant?" Eva rounded on her.

Cathy just shrugged. Lana, spotting the exchange of looks, cut across the interference.

"Focus! One minute."

The live-link had been scheduled months in advance, and was using an array of various satellites in synchronous orbit around the Earth to view the approach of Tenca, Siva's breakaway splinter meteoroid. As usual the FLC was following Houston time, but while for them it was 10.15 on Thursday evening, it was already 9.15 on Friday morning for the people of Chelyabinsk - now the confirmed impact region.

Upgrades to Floyd's tracking abilities had confirmed that Novgorod would escape Tenca's impact. After taking into account atmospheric friction and drag, it had predicted the new impact region in the Russian Urals with an error margin of less than one tenth of a percent. Lana Yakovna's mood had lightened considerably following the news, Mike guessed that she must have had family in Novgorod, but they had never spoken about it. Tonight however she was again as tense as everyone else. Siva was about to demonstrate a small sample of what was to come.

"FLC, this is Houston," came Alexey Yakovna's voice over the console panel.

"Houston, FLC receiving," Lana replied.

"FLC be advised we are transmitting audio only, visual feed will follow agreed chain of satellite coverage."

"Houston, understood. We are standing by."

The monitor screen suddenly flicked on, but the picture was very dark. Lana reached over and turned out the working light for the Drum, leaving only the console lights and the dim emergency LED lighting surrounding the airlocks to illuminate the space. The crew stood silently in the dark and waited for their eyes to adjust.

"Houston we are receiving pictures," Lana reported, "please confirm they are from J-Sat 21."

The crew had largely become used to the delay of signals making their way, first around the moon, then across the empty space to Earth; but tonight standing in the dark and quiet, each of them felt the passing of every second. Leonard felt Eva's hand slip into his, and he squeezed it gently.

"FLC, J-Sat 21 confirmed," came the reply.

The absence of ambient light in the Drum now allowed them to see the detail in the picture. Pinpricks of light were scattered randomly over an otherwise black screen. It was Leonard who spotted it first. He let go of Eva's hand and pointed to the top right of the screen.

"There!" he said and began to diagonally trace his finger across the screen.

Tenca itself was not yet visible, but it appeared to temporarily turn off the stars as it passed in front of them. By mentally joining the winking dots, Tenca's trajectory revealed itself. The stars stopped winking to black, as Tenca moved out of range of the satellite's camera.

The screen now changed to a new view.

"FLC, AE35."

"Houston, confirmed," Lana said quickly, before pointing to the screen and questioning Leonard, "Here?"

"Yes. I think that's the long axis we're seeing," he said pointing to a thin white line of sunlight reflecting off its surface. The sliver of light became shorter, then disappeared. Sensing the others shift a little, he explained, "It's spinning. Just as we thought."

It was one thing to read data and piece together the appearance of Tenca from spectral analysis, but it was quite another to see it using human eyes. The crew jointly drew a breath.

Several more screens followed, each showing similar glimpses of silhouettes and highlights from edges as Tenca proceeded relentlessly to its goal, until suddenly the viewpoint changed radically.

"FLC, ISS Node 3 Cupola. Long range," reported Houston, indicating that the view was now coming from the International Space Station. There was a faint blue glow to the bottom of the screen, indicating that the Earth itself was somewhere just out of view.

"Here we go," exhaled Mike, folding his arms tightly, as though it would afford him some protection.

Lana tugged nervously at her earlobe, and repositioned her headset, "ISS Long, confirmed Houston."

Suddenly they could see it, lit by brilliant sunlight and tumbling end over end. Only now could they begin to appreciate any sense of scale. Leonard estimated that Tenca was rotating once every eight seconds, in the hard sunlight he could see the crisp dark shadows chasing over the rifts and valleys in its surface, before being plunged into the darkness of a four second long night. It was difficult not be in awe of the sight. Perhaps for the first time Leonard found himself picturing the possibility of Siva, hundreds of times larger, appearing in this very spot two years from now, if they failed in their mission.

Hundreds of sparks suddenly erupted over its surface.

"Entry? Already?" Mike called to Leonard.

"No," he shook his head, "Satellite annihilation."

The sparks continued for a moment longer as Tenca ploughed on through a cloud of satellites, utterly decimating most and sending others on to create new collisions with their neighbours. Surrounding the area where Tenca had punched through the satellites, the crew saw several smaller explosions detonate simultaneously. A few seconds later Houston reported:

"ISS confirms DCP activation."

Three years ago, when news of Tenca's separation from Siva reached Archive, construction began on a set of orbiting explosive devices. Not there to destroy Tenca, even then they realised it would still be impossible to stop, but to assist in damping the spread of debris. Debris Cascade Protection was a network of shaped charges, designed to obliterate any satellite casualties caused by Tenca. The DCP units directed explosive charges back towards the intrusion point. The idea was to create a fire-break in space, stopping the spread of debris from causing a chain reaction of collisions in orbit.

The feed cut to another of the cameras onboard the ISS, this one showed the curvature of the Earth's atmosphere in the lower part of the screen and Tenca entering from the right at speed. Almost instantly the dark shape began to glow white hot, as it started to enter the atmosphere.

"FLC, be advised Tenca is now in ablation phase, expect interfer- " the remainder of the audio was garbled.

Then the crew saw it.

Initially it looked like they were watching the re-entry of an Orbiter Space Shuttle, an atmospheric shockwave building at the leading edge, graduating into an incandescent glow. But then Tenca flared, seeming hundreds of times brighter than before. The camera aboard the ISS followed it, tracking its motion as it began to pass directly underneath it. Clouds, possibly a mile wide, were being aggressively smeared in its wake as it continued its slice through the upper atmosphere.

Over Chelyabinsk that morning there was virtually no cloud cover. The ISS had a perfect view as Tenca began to boil the water in the atmosphere into steam, leaving a motionless, hanging trail of vapour and meteorite debris behind; a final death-cry etching itself into an arc through the sky.

The atmosphere fought back, creating friction and heat; within a few seconds it was enough to split Tenca apart. Rapidly the other fragments, previously shielded by being on the inside, became exposed to the violent tearing of the air, and began to flare white hot themselves. A long line of fast moving smaller meteorites, slowed by their entry, became purely ballistic now and continued their bullet-like trace towards their target.

At that point they went out of the range of the cameras aboard the ISS and the screen switched to black, leaving the crew in the darkness of the Drum. Perhaps it was the stress of the situation but everyone could hear Cathy trying hard not to laugh.

MICE AND MEN

23rd July 2000

Lionel Waightes woke slowly.

Immediately he could feel a pounding in his head. In his ears was a high-pitched ringing, a persistent background noise just on the periphery of what he could hear, but seeming to drown out any other sound. He opened his eyes and was met with darkness. He reached up to rub his eyes but found that his wrist was restrained. So was his other wrist and, as he now discovered, his head and legs. Events started to come back to him, the most recent first.

He remembered the anaesthetic being administered, that must be the source of his headache, and then he recalled a priest rambling on about his soul. Working back, the memory of being strapped into the chair swam into view, and the looks on the faces of those gathered to witness his execution. Only then did the thought hit him that he was not, in fact, dead.

"Hey!" he called out into the darkness.

He could tell from the small echo that the walls had to be close. He'd learned that particular awareness in his years of waiting on Death Row. Had there been a last minute reprieve? Was he back in a holding cell? No, the darkness was too perfect, even in solitary confinement there had always been stray light leaking in from somewhere, even at lights-out.

"Hey!" he shouted again, thrashing out with his arms and legs. His legs could move a little more than his arms, but his arms appeared to be clamped tight to whatever chair they had him strapped in to. He was also pretty sure that he could feel things attached to his skin.

Without warning the lights came on, and he closed his eyes tightly against the brightness. Gradually he managed to flicker his eyelids open, and found that the light wasn't as bright as he thought. He could now confirm that he was lying in a reclined position, and above him was a plain white ceiling. On that ceiling he could see a sign which read:

'Stay Calm. Compliance = Life.'

He heard a pneumatic hiss and found that his head had been unclamped. He raised his head to look around the room.

He was no longer in the chair that had held him during his execution; this one was more basic, more metallic, less padded. He saw that his limbs were indeed restrained by impressively reinforced tubular metallic cuffs. The cuff around his right wrist was fairly plain, but the one around his left wrist apparently had a syringe embedded in it, pointing down into his arm. As he flexed his left hand he was convinced that he could feel the syringe's metal needle between the fibres of his muscles. A sharp but momentary pain confirmed this as the syringe's plunger popped up and the cuff unlocked itself, springing open to release his arm.

He swore loudly, bending his arm at the elbow, and flexing his fingers repeatedly into a fist. With the release of his arm he could now lean forward a little more, and instinctively reached out to free his other hand. On the cuff around his right wrist, was an unlabelled small button, he hesitated for a moment before pushing it, half expecting there to be some awful consequence.

The cuff sprang open and for the first time he could fully sit up. Ahead of him he saw his own reflection, staring back at him in a large mirror. Being no stranger to interrogation rooms with mirrors along one side, he correctly assumed he was under observation. He flexed his left hand again, then extended his arm out towards the mirror. Clenching his fist he extended his middle finger in the direction of those he assumed must be beyond the mirror.

The first and most obvious thing that he could see was they had shaved off his hair and beard; but they had also put him in a plain grey jumpsuit. By the looks of the numerals on his chest, he was inmate number 23. For the first time since waking, he considered his position; he'd been brought back from the dead, or at least been snatched back to life before actually dying, but by who or what he didn't know. He looked down at his ankles, still bound to the chair by the metal cuffs. Sitting between the cuffs was a sign, drawn in black ink on white cardboard:

'Tablets for your headache.'

He looked around the room, and over in the other corner was a small shelf with a beaker of water on it. He lifted up the cardboard sign, the only thing not fixed down, and saw a button to release his ankles. After freeing his feet he swung around to sit on the edge of the reclined metal chair. He still felt a little disoriented and he had a funny taste in his mouth, no doubt another side effect of the anaesthetic. He swirled some iron-tasting saliva round his mouth, then turned to face his unseen observers. Taking aim carefully for the centre of the mirror, he spat out the yellowish contents of his mouth, then watched with satisfaction as it began a slow dribble downwards.

Perhaps this was some form of torture. Stage an execution only to be brought back to life, before presumably doing it again and again. He'd never break, he told himself. It was now a badge of honour that he had never revealed where he'd buried their bodies. He would never allow those grieving relatives the closure. It gave him too much pleasure. More so now, he'd come back from the dead, which was more than he could say for them. He smiled squarely at mirror, and bowed slightly.

The headache seemed to be getting slightly worse so he walked the six feet over to the wall-mounted shelf. There was a plastic beaker containing water and some tablets next to it. He tossed the tablets into his mouth and took a swig of water. As he swallowed he noticed a small folded piece of paper, which presumably the water had been standing on. He turned it over in his hands and found more writing on the reverse side.

'Do not remove the tag from around your neck.'

Looking down he saw nothing around his neck, but after pulling down the chest zip on the jumpsuit, saw that they had concealed it inside. He pulled it out and studied it. On the thin metallic chain was a small electronic device looking like a pocket calculator, but instead of a keypad there appeared to be a small, bluish, crystal protruding from the surface. The calculator-like display showed the digit '6'.

"You talkin' about this?" he shouted, swaggering back over to the mirror, "Huh?"

He grinned and yanked the tag from around his neck, breaking the chain.

"You talkin' bout this?" he taunted, tapping the tag against the mirror, "You wan' it? Huh?"

He sneered, then flung the tag as hard as he could across the room, so that it smashed against the opposite wall. He turned, triumphantly, and walked away from the mirror.

Alfred Barnes paused the playback of the observation tape. With no possibility of remote control through the Field walls, it had been Alfred's responsibility to devise a set of automated machine actions, to accompany a set of sequentially revealed suggestions, based on the subject's personality.

"My report details the remainder of this experiment. We're still waiting on the lip-reading translation because, as you know, the Field prevents sound transfer; but his aggressive body language seems to conform to my behaviour prediction. That said, up until this point, Subject 23 has been the most successful outcome so far. Gross and fine motor skills, language, cognitive function, personality, all unimpaired."

The others nodded and there were general noises of agreement from around the table. They had all of course received detailed reports before the briefing but for most of them it was the first time they had seen the actual physical proof.

"The pre-injected isotope, along with the Biomagnetic pendant, successfully anchored Subject 23. He was able to walk around inside the Chronomagnetic Field with no ill effects. Whatsoever."

"Hmm," said Bradley Pittman, "Right up 'til the dang fool ripped his tag off."

"Well, yes," confirmed Alfred, "ideally we wanted the test to run a little longer, but he strayed outside the influence of the Biomag, or more accurately he *threw* it away from him. At that point the granularity of the Chronomagnetic Field became significant -".

"You ain't kiddin'!" said Bradley, his hand darting forward to un-pause the video.

Lionel Waightes progressed no further than two feet away from the mirror. Suddenly he appeared to vibrate uncontrollably and was ripped into a cloud of red chunks that flung themselves against the right hand wall. There were several gasps from around the room and Alfred was sure he heard someone retching.

"There was a reason I stopped the video!" Alfred snapped at Bradley, re-pausing the footage, "The written details in my report should have been quite sufficient to -".

"Yeah, well the numbers only go so far Freddy!" he interrupted, slapping his palm on the papers before him. "Ethically I got no problem, what-so-ever, using that convicted, murdering, sonuvabitch to advance our research! But if we're gonna have to wear these damn tags for the whole journey I think everyone should see the consequences."

The room remained quiet, everyone considering the combined horror, fascination and scientific advance they had just witnessed.

"Excuse me, Dr. Barnes," said Dr. Chen, who had been studying the report. "The report does not detail why this, ah, 'granularity' exists inside the Field."

"OK, I'm not the Field expert here," replied Alfred, "but according to Dr. Bergstrom, as far back as Subject 12 she suspected that the Field was not uniform throughout. It's possible that there are pockets where the Field is less dense. Without direct measurement inside the Field, it's impossible to tell if these pockets are randomly spaced, or have a geometric pattern. But what we *do* know is that the Biomag and isotope combination appears to allow the subject to move between the pockets, without becoming unanchored."

"I see," said Dr. Chen, "This recording is, I assume, played back slower than normal?"

"Yes," said General Napier, "This was also a trial of our new high speed digital video recording equipment. Without it you'd be watching a fast moving blur."

"So, from the display, I note too that the chronometric gradient has been increased?"

"Yup, we're at a ratio of six to one. Six hours in there," said Bradley, pointing at the video clip, "means only one hour passes out here."

"In theory," chipped in Alfred, "if Walker can fine-tune the Field, then we could have ratios of hundreds to one!"

"Truly astonishing. It is a pity we could not congratulate Dr. Walker in person."

"Unfortunately Dr. Walker ain't available at the moment, but I'll pass on your gratitude," said Bradley, knowing only too well that Douglas knew nothing of the human trials, and would see the ethics of the situation entirely differently.

"Forgive me again," hesitated Dr. Chen, "clearly this result is of extraordinary significance, and I do not want to spoil the celebration…"

"But?"

"I am still unclear on the practical application," ventured Dr. Chen.

"Excuse me?" said Bradley leaning forward.

"If time itself could be made to move hundreds of times faster inside the Field," he began, "then anyone inside it will grow older faster. But for us out here, how does it help us?"

Bradley raised a questioning glance to the other end of the table, and General Napier gave him a nod.

"OK," said Bradley, turning again to face Dr. Chen, "Now that we know this thing works, we can put a man inside it. That means we can do research *way* faster."

"Research into what?" replied Dr. Chen, closing his copy of the report.

"Everything," said Bradley, for once quite straight-faced, "We got less than fifteen years before Siva comes a knockin'. The most valuable resource on the planet is time. My Texan bucks can buy a whole heap o' hardware, but they can't buy more time, cos there ain't any."

"Think about it," Alfred joined in, "With the correct attenuation of the Field, we could make time move fifty or perhaps *a hundred* times faster in there! Think within your own area of expertise in computational analysis, Dr. Chen. Imagine the performance boost to just *one* of your Shen5 multi-cores, running *a hundred times faster*."

Dr. Chen raised an eyebrow.

"So in a decade," Dr. Chen quickly worked things through, "We could have up to a thousand years of preparation time within the Chronomagnetic Field?"

"I can see where you're going with this," said Alfred, shaking his head, "As I understand it from Dr. Walker, because of power generation requirements, the largest size we could build one of these Fields is a hundred yards wide. Now even if we did build one, and filled it with people, then we still couldn't store a thousand years worth of food and resources inside it."

"Hmm," said Dr. Chen scribbling a quick calculation, "plus at the end of its journey, it would have sustained at least forty generations of humans. Not feasible."

"Never thought 'bout it like that, but yeah," nodded Bradley.

"Then I must ask my question again. With more borrowed time, what things require research?"

"OK, for starters, Nuclear Fusion," began Bradley, "My daughter Sally, she's only ten, but even she knows we started Floyd Lunar Complex on the moon cos of all the Helium-3. Fact is we can't use a shovel-full of that moon-dust till we know how Fusion's gonna work. Then there's Gravity, Cryo - ".

"Gravity?" cut in Dr. Chen.

"Yes," said Alfred, "Every Field test so far, has resulted in the subject being thrown to the right when they, er -"

"Un-anchor?" said Dr. Chen, diplomatically.

"Yes. Dr. Walker thinks it might be a factor of location, or more specifically *our* location on the planet, and our compass orientation, which hasn't changed since the first tests on flowers."

"We may have to move the entire test chamber," shrugged Bradley.

"To where?" asked Dr. Chen.

"We don't know yet," admitted Alfred, "we need to survey the globe for gravitational hotspots -"

"My NASA boys are lookin' into it," Bradley said, then added with a smile, "But it could speed up their calculations if you could send over a crate-load of your Shen-Five Deep Thinkers. We'll set 'em up in the Field and see how fast they fly!"

"I have no wish to see my Shens fly across the room like your test men!"

"Sorry Dr. Chen, it's just an expression," smiled Alfred, "Bradley just meant that we'll see how fast they perform. Machines and inorganic matter are perfectly safe. It's only biological matter that seems to be affected."

Dr. Chen looked at the paused video again. In stark contrast to the blood-caked walls, the free-standing chair and glass of water were completely unscathed.

CONVERGENCE

11th March 2013

"**A**t ease. Please sit," General Napier walked to the front of the Node's small assembly hall. In theory it was just large enough to brief all the personnel present at the Node, but this morning only a select few had been invited. Those present broke from their discussions and moved to sit in fold-up chairs, facing a makeshift podium. He was about to begin his briefing but saw two empty seats. As if on cue the doors at the back of the hall opened and Douglas Walker bustled in, carrying his ever-present stack of paper folders under one arm, followed a few seconds later by Anna Bergstrom carrying a blue balloon.

"General I need to -" began Douglas making strides towards him.

"It will have to wait," he held up his palm.

"No you don't understand -"

"I'm sorry, Doctor. This takes priority," he said holding up a small briefing card. Not that he needed notes, he'd known this day would arrive and knew the consequences and actions that would follow, but he found it helpful today to have a prop to hold.

He cleared his throat while Douglas and Anna shuffled into their seats.

"Thank you," he began, "We have been issued with formal notification that as of zero four hundred hours today, Fallen Veil conditions are now in effect."

As he predicted, questions erupted from around the hall. He waited for a few seconds before raising his hand again to stop them.

"Please. I can answer all questions, one to one, but first I must brief you all."

The amount of background noise diminished, with the exception of an impatient jiggling foot belonging to Douglas. After Napier looked in their direction, Anna placed a hand on his knee and, following the surprise of the physical intervention, Douglas stopped.

"Over the past few weeks," Napier began, "we have managed to conceal the connection between the Chelyabinsk meteorite and the Tenca splinter. In particular we were able to suppress the reverse-calculation of Tenca's origin at Siva. However, at twenty-one hundred hours yesterday, Siva was independently sighted by the Ankara University Observatory in Turkey. It didn't take long for students worldwide to correlate Siva's trajectory with that of the Chelyabinsk meteorite. The images and trajectory data went viral, and Archive lost containment globally by twenty-three hundred hours. In accordance with Fallen Veil protocol, the Heads of States will be briefing their nations independently and simultaneously later today at eleven hundred hours GMT."

Colonel Beck had arrived quietly at the back of the hall, so Napier took the opportunity to deflect what he assumed would be one of the next questions.

"If you wish to view the briefing for your specific country," he said, pointing loosely towards the rear of the hall, "please let Colonel Beck know and he will open up an incoming channel for you."

Several heads turned to acknowledge his arrival. Beck was a solid six feet tall, but did not have the same larger-than-life aspect as Napier. He had been introduced to the Node a year ago to coordinate the construction schedule and oversee site security, managing to alienate most of the key personnel along the way. His brusque, direct manner made Napier look positively cheerful by comparison.

"I should point out," continued Napier, "all that has happened is that Archive is no longer a concealed organisation. Its preparations will now continue in public, in most cases assisted by the public. However, this facility is isolated enough to be considered invisible. There will be no public input here, so you will continue to work towards Departure Day as though nothing has changed.

"It has always been the assumption that if all goes well with Floyd Lunar Complex then our task will have been, thankfully, redundant. But until we receive such information our deadline is only two years away, and we must do everything possible to be mission-ready beforehand."

This last statement was delivered whilst looking at Douglas, who responded by nodding and tapping his stack of papers. He opened his mouth to speak, but Napier got there first.

"Unless there are any other joint issues, that concludes the briefing."

Most of the questions that immediately flew at Napier were related to the safety and protection of the facility. He deftly calmed the fears of many by asking Colonel Beck to recap the virtues of the heavily armed perimeter defences and the ruthless Icelandic terrain surrounding it.

After patiently waiting for a lull in the questions, Douglas raised his hand.

"General?"

"Yes, Doctor," he replied, a little impatiently, "Will this not wait until this afternoon?"

"No."

"OK," he sighed, "you have our attention Doctor."

Douglas hastily swapped placed with Napier and then made his way to stand in front of the podium. He tried to gather both his papers and his thoughts together - it would probably be tricky to focus people on scientific matters, so soon after news of Fallen Veil. But he would have to try.

"OK," he began, "as you all know we've been tackling the two issues of chronometric gradient and incident field projection within gravitational maxima -"

He stopped, realising that many of the conversational shortcuts he and his colleagues used on a daily basis would be useless to his current audience. He glanced over at Anna, who simply waved her balloon. He waved her forward realising that this was one of those occasions requiring one of her *solution-shaped* briefings.

"The very first 3-to-1 ratio Field allowed plants and mice to travel 3 times faster through time," she began, "The much more powerful Mark 2 version allowed us to travel 60 times faster than normal."

In the interests of simplifying the message, she skipped over mentioning her isotope that had actually made human travel possible.

"When we're not using the Mark 2 ourselves, the Field is put on an internal timer and the Shen500's sit within the 60-to-1 Field trying to find higher ratios. The highest theoretical ratio we have found so far is 360-to-1."

"So why aren't we using it?" asked Colonel Beck.

"The Mark 2 Field generator cannot be upgraded any further," explained Anna, "Even with all 64 of our Shen500's, the 60-to-1 is not fast enough to run through all the permutations required to reach a solution before Siva gets here."

"We need to build the Mark 3," stated Douglas, plainly.

"Impossible," came Beck's frustrated voice, "We'd have to deploy valuable resources away from the Node's construction."

"I want to hear them out," said Napier, "So, am I hearing you correctly? The Mark 3 would be able to travel *360 times faster* than out here?"

There were a few appreciative whistles from the middle of the hall.

"Yes," continued Anna, "360-to-1."

"And that would give you all the time you need to find the solution?" Napier frowned.

"Solutions," Douglas corrected, "There are two last obstacles to overcome."

"Given the ultimate geometry of the Node and its power core," Anna explained, "We hypothesize there may be one more relative speed ratio above 360-to-1 that will be accessible to us. Somewhere around 1000-to-1."

This time the hall remained silent.

"Dr. Walker, you said there were *two* last obstacles," said Napier, "what's the second?"

"OK, theoretically you could spend *decades* inside the Field, but then when you emerge you would find that only a *week* has passed out here. This is not a solution that will allow us to skip over the impending devastation. We still need to solve Field *inversion*."

"Field inversion is like being able to take our existing Field," Anna held up the balloon again, "and turn it inside-out, but without destroying the Field's complex surface."

She could tell from the mass of frowns that everyone was mentally trying to turn the balloon inside-out without popping it.

"Or to put it another way," she tried, "once you're inside the Field, make time pass more slowly than on the *outside*."

This explanation seemed to lift the frowns.

"OK then, with a 'Mark 3' how long would it take to solve your two problems, Dr. Walker?"

"Two years," he stated plainly.

It didn't seem possible, but the room fell even quieter. Everyone here was acutely aware that if the Floyd Lunar Complex failed in its primary mission then Siva would impact Earth, also in two years.

It was Anna who saw everyone's misinterpretation of the statement.

"Two years *inside the Field*," she corrected, "If we build the Mark 3, we'll have 360-to-1 compression. From your perspective the mission would take only *two days*."

General Napier had been loosely keeping track of the theoretical developments at the Node, but with the imminent disclosure of the various Archive enterprises his attention had been spread quite thin. Ever the pragmatist he pushed on relentlessly.

"How long to build the Mark 3?"

Douglas rifled through several pages within his folder then, as expected by everyone who had known him long enough, became suddenly caught in introspective analysis before resuming the conversation.

"Five months, six days."

Napier was slightly unprepared for the answer, "What? No range, just an exact number?"

"My level of precision is not always appreciated," said Douglas sheepishly, before adding, "Plus or minus three days. Leaving one year and seven months until Siva's arrival."

General Napier nodded at Douglas and Anna, and then turned to Colonel Beck.

"Build it."

•

Monica was surprised that, of the two of them, Marcus had accepted the truth more readily than her own daughter. For Marcus, the idea that there actually *was* a reason that the world worked the way it did, and that there *was* a veil covering privileged information seemed to fit very comfortably within his own world view.

For Kate it was much harder, more personal, and of course she was having to deal with issues of her father's death, or lack of it.

From Monica's fragmented recollection and basic descriptions, Kate couldn't yet fully grasp the long-term purpose of her father's work. The real world application of having crops grow at an accelerated rate seemed somehow mundane to Kate. It all seemed to contribute to an overall air of confusion that had suddenly arrived in her life.

What she found utterly preposterous was the notion that *her parents* had been, and possibly still were, working for an organisation with the directive of nothing less than saving human life by any conceivable means.

"I couldn't tell you," Monica continued.

"Why the hell not?" Kate snapped.

"The moment anyone knows about anything to do with Archive, they are in danger."

"*You're* still here," she bit back.

"That's, different," she hesitated, even now desperately trying not give her daughter more information than she absolutely needed.

"And at what point were you going to tell me that a comet is about to wipe out the planet?"

"If all goes to plan, it won't do."

"So you *weren't* going to tell me?" she fixed her mother with an accusing stare.

The wind outside had picked up again, rattling through the wooden shutters that were folded back against the side of the cottage. Marcus had joined them in the living room a while ago and had been sifting through Rob's files on Monica's laptop; but despite the sudden quiet he didn't dare to look up.

"Do you know what a burden this knowledge has been?" said Monica softly, "To know, exactly, the moment when life on Earth may end? Have you any idea what that does to you as a person? Never being able to tell anyone? I couldn't do that to you. If Siva missed us, then I'd have pointlessly filled your life with misery and worry."

Kate had nothing to counter with, but she could begin to glimpse the terrible logic that had undoubtedly been torturing her mother for so long. From the corner of her eye she noticed Marcus sit upright and turned away from her mother.

"Er... Rob's Chelyabinsk folder," said Marcus, "There's a whole load of Solar System diagrams in here."

"Let me see," said Monica, reclaiming her laptop from him, "These charts are from all over the place... New Delhi, Adelaide, Beijing... they're all showing the same thing."

She looked through all the diagrams; each one was attempting to trace the Chelyabinsk meteorite back to its point of origin. They all referred to it being position coincident with another astronomical body; although they all had different names for that body, they all agreed on a date.

"February 3rd 2010," said Monica, handing the laptop back to Marcus, then stood to warm herself in front of the living room fire.

"Let me guess, the Chelyabinsk meteorite originated at Siva?" said Kate.

"I'm sure of it," Monica stared into the fire, "Rob was completely out of his depth, he got too close. This has to be the reason why Archive silenced him. Him and anyone who sent data to him."

The wind outside was now accompanied by the distant sound of low thunder, and the light coming in through the lace curtains seemed to be more grey than before. The low, orange light from fire couldn't quite chase away the shadows of the small room, but as Marcus looked into it he had a thought.

"The destruction at Chelyabinsk was tiny, 'cos the meteorite was small. But Siva's huge, right?" asked Marcus, "If they were both in the same place three years ago, wouldn't that mean the smaller one came *from* Siva?"

"But if that's the case," continued Kate, "then isn't that moon base you mentioned supposed to be stopping meteors?"

"My information is at least a decade out of date," admitted Monica, "but I'm guessing they would have to wait for the Moon and Siva to be in the right place, before they could take action."

"Or they took action," joked Marcus, "and that's what chopped a bit off…"

Monica nodded, tentatively mulling over the idea.

"You're actually taking me seriously?" said Marcus in disbelief.

Monica just stared at him, "It would explain why Archive are still trying to silence the story. The meteorite over Russia blew their cover. It's possible that Chelyabinsk is a catalyst event; one that Archive know they can't conceal from discovery, but need to delay as long as possible."

"Just wait a minute," said Kate, "Even if a bit of Siva somehow became detached, how do you explain it reaching Earth *two whole years* before the rest of it?"

Monica had known about Siva for so long that the idea of curved trajectories and orbital paths seemed commonplace; but for Kate this information was merely a few hours old.

"Siva has been getting closer to Earth for the past sixty-two years," Monica explained, "but it hasn't been in a straight line. In 1951, possibly even before, Siva got captured in our Solar System's gravity. Since then it's been looping around the Sun."

"Like an orbiting planet?"

"No, it's not that stable. It cuts across the orbits of the inner planets in a sort-of ellipse. But with each loop, the Sun's gravity pulls it closer in, and the ellipse gets smaller."

"So, eventually," Kate concluded, "Earth's orbit and Siva's ellipse will coincide."

"April 1st 2015," confirmed Monica, "Unless the *men on the moon* can push Siva out of our way. Now, if the Chelyabinsk rock somehow separated from Siva, back in 2010, then it *could* follow a tighter path towards Earth."

"So the Russian rock got here before Siva will," stated Marcus.

Between the three of them they deduced that, at the very least, Archive must have known of the *existence* of the Chelyabinsk meteorite at some time before the impact, but had chosen not to warn anyone. Marcus had also pointed out that Archive couldn't have known the precise impact point in Russia, and must therefore have been quite willing to accept the possibility of entire cities being destroyed.

"Archive serves to ensure the survival of the human species, not the human population," Monica stated plainly, waiting for Kate and Marcus to absorb the statement.

"They have too much power now. Even in the early days, Archive knew," she continued, "if Siva reached Earth, then they would have to choose."

"Choose?" said Marcus.

"Choose who would live."

By inference, both Marcus and Kate realised that in making that choice, Archive would also determine those who would die.

"I know this because in 1989 we had a close call," Monica went on, "Earth's orbit is 365 days and Siva missed us by just six *hours*. Of course back then they called it '4581 Asclepius'..."

"I don't remember that!"

"No, but you probably *do* remember going to a birthday party with hundreds of other kids."

Now that she thought about it, Kate *did* remember the party and the slightly odd fact that she had taken a pink suitcase full of her best clothes and toys. It had been a rush to get there and they had used an elevator to get down to a brightly decorated, but windowless, room.

Monica could see the realisation dawn on her daughter's face.

"It was the Whitehall deep bunker," said Monica, suppressing a shudder, "one of the scariest days of my life. We managed to reach the bunker before they'd sealed the doors, but many didn't make it. I can still remember the yelling as the door forced itself closed. I think the event provoked Archive to prepare in other ways too; within a few weeks they took reproductive samples from all personnel, me and your Dad included."

Despite the warm temperature of the living room Kate felt a rising chill, as her mother continued:

"I realised that by the time Siva reached Earth, you'd be thirty-three and I'd be a stately fifty-eight. We would both be, how can I put this delicately, 'beyond our prime'. We wouldn't make the cut. They already had genetic samples; we would be disposable."

It made a certain cold, logical sense to Kate; with limited resources only a few percent of the population could ever be saved in person.

"That's why you and Dad wanted to get us out."

Monica nodded gently, "I realised we would have to make our own preparations."

"But let me guess," said Marcus, "Nobody just leaves Archive?"

"No, leaving is easy," replied Monica "Leaving *alive* is harder. It took careful planning and preparation, but by 2001 we were ready."

For Kate, 2001 was burned in her memory as the year she lost her father. She was suddenly confronted again with conflicting feelings of both profound loss and also shinning hope that he was still alive.

"We reached a compromise, you and I could go, but your Dad had to stay until he completed his work."

"All this time I thought you both worked on the Channel Tunnel. I mean isn't that why we're here in Dover?" said Kate pointing to the ground beneath her feet.

"It was one of the reasons we moved here," she started to explain, but then decided against it, "Your father and I put our plan into action and Archive allowed you and me to leave."

"How come they let you walk out?" asked Marcus.

"Part of our preparation was to amass information," she replied, "I made a very public demonstration of my knowledge to Archive. I arranged for information to be leaked about an Archive project, a project that I should not have had any knowledge about."

"If they're as powerful as you say, then why not just kill us?" countered Kate.

"Because I told them that if we died of anything other than old age, then everything I knew about all their other projects would automatically be made public."

"Why, what else you got?" chipped in Marcus.

"Nothing," said Monica simply, "but they don't know that."

"Ballsy," he complemented.

"Wait a minute," started Kate, "If Archive is not able to contain the news about Siva, and it has to reveal what it's been doing all these years, then…"

"Archive will have no secrets," completed Monica, glad that Kate could see the problem, "My threat to reveal them is powerless. We lose our protection."

The crackling of the fire and another grumble of thunder was punctuated by four knocks on the front door.

•

On the drive to Dover, Benton assessed his options. Monica Dean was essentially ex-Archive, a position that very few people were allowed to occupy whilst still alive.

From the data he'd absorbed, she had allegedly ensured her continued survival by taking steps to automatically reveal Archive's interests in the event of her death. Whilst no digital proof was ever found, she had once demonstrated her power by revealing a small amount of knowledge to the press. Archive had successfully quashed the chaos, but her demonstration had been enough.

However, in a few hours the whole world would know of Archive's existence, so Benton reasoned that the majority of her bargaining tools were about to evaporate. But he also knew that there were NASA offshoots and also an Icelandic project that would remain covert. He did not know how far Monica's knowledge spanned, but knew for certain that he should not be the cause of any project failure.

All too suddenly the road ran out, and he realised that her house must lie off a footpath. He looked up at the sky through the windscreen, and was greeted with a slate grey wash. Sometimes he hated this country.

He decided he would probably run with the 'lost American' introduction, to gain confidence. Reaching into the glove compartment he pulled out a beat-up looking map and his suppressor side-arm. Satisfied that he was now prepared, he loaded his suppressor into the holster-pocket inside his jacket, and cracked the door open.

Immediately he was surprised by the amount of noise that assailed his ears. The fresh, cold, wind bit into him, almost forcing the car door closed again, but he pushed harder and stepped out. The seagulls raucously bickered, rising and swooping on the thermals of the cliff edge. He walked carefully up to the edge and peered over. The tide's destructive force was busy smashing itself against the chalk face. The broken, rocky, fruits of its labour laying drowned in its swell.

The coastal path went in two directions, and a little way to his left a woman was ambling along towards him. She dragged a reluctant, tiny dog on a lead behind her. Perhaps she could help him.

He stopped to conspicuously look at his map, then glanced up and down the coastal path, before turning his map around. He sighed deeply then awkwardly folded it under one arm. He detested the performance but knew it was necessary for his exchanges to be believable.

"You lost?" the woman asked with a smile.

"Ha ha," Benton replied, pushing his accent a little harder for the avoidance of doubt, "what gave it away?"

"You're American?" she said, tugging her dog to heel.

He mirrored her smile in reply, "Ha ha, yeah!"

"I wouldn't stay out here too long, deary. There's a storm coming."

He looked out to the thickening clouds over the sea; the pathetic parallel between the weather and Archive's imminent announcement was not lost on him. He gave a short laugh for the woman's benefit.

"Is that right? Guess I better find my cousin's house quickly then," he lied, "I'm looking for Samphire Cottage, I don't suppose you know -"

"Monica Jones!" exclaimed the woman, "I had no idea she had family in the U S of A!"

It was the wrong surname, Benton realised, but that in itself was not surprising if she wanted to retain local anonymity. Now he just needed to know which direction.

"You know my Monica?" he acted dumbfounded, adding for good measure, "Well bless my soul!"

"Ha ha, yes I know Monica, we sometimes bump into each other when I'm out walking Henry, here, past her house," she gestured to her right along the path.

Now he knew the direction.

"How old is Henry?" he smiled, starting to crouch and holding out his hand to the dog.

"Oh, he's an old trooper like me," she began.

Benton sprang up from his crouch and pushed her hard off the cliff. The lead snapped taught and the dog followed her. There was no sound other than the relentless pounding of the tide on the broken rocks. In the moments before the brief conversation, he had quickly scanned the area for witnesses. There were still none now. He liked remote locations. Isolated. Controllable. All things considered, he persuaded himself that he had probably done the old woman a favour. He turned and continued along the path.

After five minutes walking he saw the cottage directly ahead, perched on the cliff, looking out over the Dover Strait. He considered for a moment the hubris of any human who would build a house so close to this magnificent force, knowing that the continual erosion would one day drag it downwards to join the jagged rocks below. Just as quickly the thought was gone, people did this all the time. Benton concluded, not for the first time, that either they considered themselves masters of nature, or they simply did not plan far enough ahead.

Even at this distance he could see that inside the front porch of the cottage was a pair of black Wellington boots. It was likely she was at home. He would have to play this very carefully. The one thing in his favour was the fact that they had never met.

As he continued his approach he kept an eye on the lace curtains drawn over the window. He did not detect even a twitch and so continued to walk towards the house. Maintaining his performance, in case anyone was watching him, he started to glance back along his route, and then back at the map, turning it around in his hands as if to verify his location.

Shaking his head one last time he made his way hesitantly to the front door and, raising the ring-shaped brass handle, he knocked four times.

•

Monica was the fastest to react to the rapping at the front door; given her age Kate thought she was still remarkably sprightly.

"Marcus!" she hissed, beckoning him over to a small monitor, semi-concealed behind some books, "Recognise him?"

The black and white monitor displayed a man standing outside the front door, holding a map, but Marcus found it difficult to get a good look at his features. Inconveniently, he appeared to be standing with his back to the door. Monica gave a light snort and flicked a dial on the monitor to change channel. Now the reverse angle from the front of the porch flickered into view and Marcus could see the man's face, the front door behind him.

"That's him," he whispered.

"OK. As we discussed, Marcus," she said, keeping her voice low, "Kate, go with him. Now."

Without really thinking, she deferred to family hierarchy and obediently followed her mother's instructions. Evidently during her time in the shower, Marcus had received a briefing that she knew nothing of. Another of her mother's protection mechanisms, she guessed.

Kate watched her mother stride purposefully across the living room, picking up a walking stick and a pair of oversized reading glasses. Marcus raised a finger to his lips and escorted Kate into the kitchen. Out of her sight, she could now only hear her mother in the hallway.

"I'm coming, just a minute."

Kate thought she sounded older now, and immediately pictured her hobbling towards the door with the walking stick, wearing the large glasses. Marcus was quietly retrieving a small case from one of the kitchen shelves, so she tried to focus on her mother's voice.

"Hold your horses," she was saying.

Outside, Benton was growing impatient. He found this, in itself, a little alarming. He only experienced impatience when his mind was deprived of input, if he didn't receive it then he couldn't plan ahead. He concluded that something must be out of place. He heard the front door latch rattle, and resumed his persona. The door was opened by an old woman, far older than he had been expecting.

"Yes my dear?" said Monica.

He could tell that the walking stick was obviously well used from the shininess around the grip area, and the mud stains around the base were consistent with those on the Wellington boots he had seen just inside the porch.

"I'm awful sorry to bother you, Ma'am," Benton said, simultaneously chastising himself mentally for adding the 'Ma'am', the accent was strong enough already without the need to add a subservient flourish, "I seem to have gotten myself lost."

"You from America then?" said Monica, adjusting her glasses.

The glasses were preventing him from getting an accurate read on her eyes.

He smiled bashfully and glanced down at her feet, while pretending to check the map. She was wearing a pair of those ridiculous slippers that the Brits loved so much.

"Ha ha! Yeah, I'm from the States, what gave it away?"

He realised too late that the dirty, man-sized boots in the porch were far too big for this old woman's feet.

"Ha ha," said Monica, still inhabiting her character, "The give away? It was the gun in your pocket."

The pretence was dropped in an instant and he reached for the suppressor inside his jacket.

The woman had taken a step back, perhaps preparing to run away.

That could work to his advantage, he thought, shots to the back were easier to deliver anyway.

But now he saw that she had taken a step back in order to point her walking stick at him.

No, he realised, she wasn't pointing, she was aiming.

Monica squeezed the handle and twin coils of wire leapt from the hollow end of the walking stick, delivering a ten-thousand volt charge straight into the man's chest. The man folded to the floor instantly, unable to stop his muscles convulsing as the charge continued to drain into him.

"Marcus!" Monica shouted.

Marcus ran through the living room to meet her at the front door.

"Now!" she shouted.

He grabbed hold of the twitching legs with his rubber gloved hands, looped a sturdy plastic cable tie around the man's ankles, and pulled it tight. Monica released the handle and the man lay groaning.

"Hands," she instructed Marcus, her finger still hovering over the trigger.

Marcus cable-tied the man's hands together, dragged him into the house and hauled him onto the sofa.

While Marcus secured the cable-ties to the sofa, Monica made light work of stripping the man of his possessions and laying them out neatly on the wooden table. After they were satisfied that he was fully restrained they joined Kate in the kitchen.

"I've given him a sedative," Monica said, ignoring the look of incredulity on her daughter's face, "If he turned up here looking for you, then he's after the data on that stick, and we can fix that."

"I can hear a 'but' coming," Kate replied.

"But, if he's here looking for me, then it's only a matter of time before things get a *lot* worse."

"How can things get any worse?" Marcus stared at her.

"I'm not just talking about worse for us. I mean worse for everybody."

Monica drew them further away, before continuing in half-whispered tones.

"If he's been sent to kill me, it means that Archive aren't afraid of my threat to expose them. If that's true then it means they're going to unveil, well, everything about their operation. We're not protected anymore, and when the announcement is made…"

"Social anarchy?" Kate completed.

Marcus was shaking his head. "Hang on. You said that moon-base thing up there still had time to take another crack at Siva? I mean haven't we got, like, another *two years* before it gets here?"

"Panic," sighed Monica, "If Archive had managed to maintain the silence around Siva, they could've avoided planet-wide panic. Now they'll go to their Plan B."

"OK then," said Kate, "let's find out who that man is here for. Marcus, can you hack his phone?"

Marcus was a little surprised to be given such direct instructions, but after Monica reinforced Kate's request with a nod, he plugged the phone into his own laptop and began work.

In preparation for the man's interrogation, the Walker women absorbed what they could from the recent information they had acquired.

"I understand," said Kate after a while.

"Good, because if he's here for me - "

"No, Mum," she interrupted, and said it again looking directly at her, "I *understand*. I understand why you and Dad, did what you did. I couldn't have known."

Monica's eyes began to fill up and she simply patted her daughter's hand, "I have had to hope for the best, but plan for the very, very, worst. You have no idea -"

"Mum, I -"

"Oh, it's OK!" Monica half laughed, "I'm glad you had no idea! We did everything we could to make sure nobody knew. You included. I'll take it as a compliment!"

Kate continued making notes on possible connections between Rob's data and the information she knew now.

"I don't know how you and Dad managed it," she began, "spending your lives looking over your shoulder."

"I've had help from my underground network of course."

"Is there anything they can do to help us now?"

"I've used every willing contact from my time inside Archive, to help further my preparations for the days ahead. But if possible I'd like to keep them isolated from me."

Just at that moment there was something about her mother's use of the word 'isolated' that resonated with her. Through the chaotic cloud of information Kate had been exposed to, she began to see a thin filament connecting several pieces of information. She double-checked her notes and recalled her mother's conversation from earlier on.

"You said Dad suspected that gravity had a connection with his crop experiment?"

"I doubt that after all this time it's still being used to grow crops, but yes, he thought gravity was tied up in there, why?"

"OK," said Kate, organising her thoughts, "well, look at this…"

She opened up a folder on the laptop and showed Monica what looked like a thermal image of the planet, with hotspots indicated in red and orange.

"Which one is this?"

"It's the output from the GRACE mapping project from 2009," she began, "The hotspots here, and here, show areas of stronger gravitational pull."

"Yes, I remember this now," said Monica.

"OK, one of those gravity hotspots is in a place called New Britain, just east of Papua New Guinea."

"So?" said Marcus.

"So, it's just off the Equator."

"Still ain't getting it," Marcus shrugged.

"You wouldn't build a new facility anywhere it could get hit by a meteorite."

"Who's talking about building facilities?" frowned Marcus, starting to become irritated again.

"I'm coming to that. The other hotspot is *way up here* just outside the Arctic Circle. Well away from the Equator."

She looked at her mother and Marcus, but wasn't sure they had made the connection.

"In Rob's video, his contact *Blankspace* verified that something called 'The Node' was being built in Iceland," she said, jabbing her finger at Iceland's location on the map. The whole area was a red hotspot.

"If you're going to keep something secret…" Kate began.

"…put it somewhere isolated and inaccessible," Monica completed, looking out of the window to her own wind-swept landscape beyond.

"That gives us something to bargain with, right?" asked Kate.

"Possibly," said Monica, apparently still deep in thought, "It depends if Archive intend to reveal what they're doing in Iceland. Marcus, what did you get from his phone?"

"Not much," he admitted, "These guys are ghosts."

"What did you get?" Kate pressed.

"The phone designator script reads 'Benton', presumably his name - "

"Mmm, not necessarily," Monica deliberated, "but carry on."

"He got a coded message last night."

"Saying?"

"That's why I said coded, I don't know," said Marcus, irritably, "I know it's got two words, six letters in the first word, and four in the second. But that's it."

"Any ideas, Mum, six four?"

Monica shook her head, and picked through the rest of his belongings; an item that looked like a gun, a case containing two vials of a brown liquid, and a well worn coin. There wasn't much to go on. But 'not much' may be just enough she thought. It would mean giving away the last of the information she had withheld from her daughter. But, in a few hours it probably wouldn't matter anyway.

"OK," Monica spoke with resolve, "Time to move him."

Having no clue what thought processes she had just been through, both Marcus and Kate were a little confused.

"Er, move him to where?" asked Kate hesitantly.

"To meet my friends in the underground," she turned to Kate, "I've been preparing for a long time, I thought we'd have a lot longer, but we've got to go now."

"So we're just gonna take Mr. Killer for a nice sleepy drag down the cliff to the car?" frowned Marcus, "'Cos last time I checked, you didn't have any wheels."

It took Monica a moment to realise the source of their confusion, after all she knew the structure of the house very well. She stood up from the table, and began pushing it aside. Then she walked over to her old fashioned phone on the kitchen worktop.

"Or are your buddies gonna come here?" continued Marcus.

Monica lifted the receiver and stuck her index finger in the rotary dial. She placed her other index finger in front of her lips.

"Quiet now children," she said in a deliberately lighter tone, "Mummy's on the telephone."

She dialled a zero, her finger tracing a long circular arc around the dial, but instead of letting go she held it there. After a few seconds she reacted to a voice on the other end of the line.

"This is Chalkmole. Open the guest bedroom."

Kate watched her replace the receiver and a moment later she felt a thump under the floor. A tile in the kitchen floor popped up exposing a handle and Monica stooped to pull it. The tiles remained stuck to the surface of the door which opened up in the middle of the kitchen floor.

"We'll need to move quickly," said Monica, who had started collecting things from around the kitchen and placing them into a bag, "that sedative will start to wear off and -"

She broke off when she realised that both Kate and Marcus appeared to be frozen in place.

"Oh for heaven's sake! You have no trouble with the idea of men on the moon, but I show you a concealed tunnel and you fall to bits."

CHAMBER 4

11th March 2013

Cathy Gant stood before the Z-bank. The cryogenically frozen zygotes, samples of Earth's genetic materials, had been transported here and retro-dropped along with Floyd's next generation processor chips. It hardly seemed six months since the last Floyd upgrade. Surely, she thought, there must come a point when the chips couldn't be made to operate any faster. She was at a loss to explain how the leaps were being made with so little development time between each release.

She ran her hand over the cool surface of the metal. Should Siva be successful in reaching Earth then this project, yet another Archive failsafe, would be a possible means of returning humans to Earth.

"What are you doing, Cathy?" came a voice from behind her. Despite the airlock cycling she hadn't heard anyone enter, and was temporarily startled.

"Damn it Mike! Don't creep up on me like that!"

"Sorry, Cathy, I… Look is everything OK?"

Cathy appraised his expression.

"Did *she* send you?"

"Who? Lana?" he said, genuinely puzzled.

"Yeah, Ice Queen."

"What? No. Look, Cathy, d'you want to talk?" he shrugged, "I had my session with the Earth-side shrink and - "

"Fucking hell Mike!" she screamed, pulling her own hair, "What can *anyone* down there *possibly* tell me, that'll make me *feel* any better, after what we saw?"

He was taken aback by her outburst and was contemplating how to respond, but she wasn't finished.

"We saw that rock stab Russia right in the gut, and Houston reports that everything is *fine*? Give me a break!"

"Cathy, we know there were casualties," he managed, "but there were so few, that - "

"No, Mike!" she stared levelly at him, "We were *told* that there were only a few."

"What difference would it make, Cathy?" he countered, "Hmm? We're a quarter million miles from Earth, on the dark side. All we know is what comes to us by the relay. We have no choice but to operate on what we know. I have to believe that if we fail, then they're doing their best to save as many people as possible down there."

She drew close to him and whispered, "That's what bothers me Mike."

"Cathy," he put his hands on her shoulders, "you're not making any... I don't know what you mean..."

She placed her hands on his forearms, bringing him closer, and she looked into his eyes.

263

"Have you even stopped to think what *'For the good of Mankind'* actually means?" she whispered, "Mike, does anyone even know anymore what the 'best thing' for mankind is?"

"It's not our decision to make," he said, as gently as he could.

"Then whose is it?" she whispered, but hearing someone approaching she improvised by leaning forward and kissing him.

Eva stepped through the open airlock.

"Well this is cosy!" she smiled knowingly at Mike, "I'm really happy for you. Both of you actually."

Cathy returned an embarrassed looking smile.

"Eva, I..." Mike started, a little flustered.

She held up a hand to wave away his protestations.

"I've been buzzing your comm panel for the last minute, eventually I had to come and get you. Lana's called a meeting in the Drum. Fallen Veil."

PARTING

16th July 1968

William Pittman was poring over the evening's newspaper while eating his evening meal. In five month's time NASA would launch Apollo 8, Archive's most public but covert venture yet; it pleased him to find that an article on the space program appeared on page five of the newspaper, well out of the limelight. What was pleasing him less was the front page news.

"Remember Judy?" his wife was saying from the other end of the polished oak table.

"What, uh yeah, I guess," muttered William, "what 'bout her?"

"Well she's getting married to that nice young man, John Benton and I want to get them something nice."

"Sure, whatever you wanna do's fine by me," he said dismissively, and returned to studying the day's stocks and shares. The protests over the French Nuclear tests in Moruroa had been playing havoc with the day's trading. And as a major shareholder in Archive's financial foundations, he was more than a little preoccupied this evening. He forced a chunk of steak into his mouth and chewed hard.

"She says he's really clever, he's been to university."

"Well, hot dog," said William, trying to sound like he was joining in with the conversation.

"I know she's desperate to start her own family -"

"For crying out loud, Dotty!" he shouted, slamming his fork down, "I don't wanna hear 'bout that sort o' thing!"

Dorothy wiped the corners of her mouth with a napkin and left the table quietly.

"Dot?" he sighed in exasperation, but she had already left the room.

He chewed his way angrily through the remainder of the steak. The nuclear weapon tests at Moruroa had of course been Archive's cover story to disguise a nuclear *fusion* test. So far the results had proved disappointing. Which of course would mean that more of his family's billions would be sucked up. He genuinely didn't mind spending the money, he reasoned that there would be no point having dollar bills left in his pocket if, or when, Siva hit the Earth, but he hated wasting money.

The telephone in the hall began to ring, echoing off the marble flooring, and when Dorothy didn't answer he realised he would have to make the trip himself. He pulled the napkin from around his neck, threw it into the gravy on the plate, and crossed the hard floor with purposeful indignation.

"Yeah, what is it?" he answered, "Aw, hell no. When?"

Howard Walker had apparently threatened to go to the Houston Daily News about Siva. William could probably use his influence with the editor to keep it out of print, but it would be costly.

"When did he leave?" he sighed, "OK, I'll deal with this."

He hung up, shaking his head and mumbling to himself, "Ah Howie, what're you doin'?"

Pulling out his wallet he dug out a piece of paper with a number written on it. He was supposed to have committed the number to memory but hadn't yet made time. He dialled the number and waited.

He'd often spoken with Howard about the burden of knowledge, and the fact that there were occasions when concealing the truth was better than panicking the planet. They had spoken about the possibility of failure, too; and the sad fact that anyone not buried deep underground when Siva hit, would in all probability die.

When the conversation had turned to the idea of building underground survival spaces, he'd asked Howard to look into the feasibility of converting several of the Pittman mining operation sites around the world, into generational bunkers. It looked like the pressure had finally got to his friend. The problem was that this close working trust they'd built over the last decade was now a liability to Archive.

The call was picked up at the other end.

"Hi, look this is Bill Pittman," he began, "I need a, dang it, what's the phrase you guys use? A level one intervention."

William gave the man the details of Howard Walker's car, the instructions to carry it out immediately, but not the exact instructions on how the fatal accident should be engineered.

He hung up and stood in the quiet hall. With only the relentless ticking of the grandfather clock for company, he murmured the words that were supposed to provide solace and absolution, "For the good of Mankind."

The words did little to appease the guilt, tugging at his insides. Howard Walker was not the first to be silenced, and he would not be the last. In a voice that only he himself could hear he added, "I'm sorry Howie."

"Hey Dad," came a voice from behind him, "everything alright?"

William quickly turned to see his son halfway down the stairs, and couldn't be sure how much he may have overheard.

"What?" he replied, plastering a grin on his face again, "Yeah, absolutely son! Now I see you got your catching mitt there. You wanna go outside so we can chat a while?"

"Only if you got time, Pops"

"For you Bradley, I got all the time in the world."

POKER FACE

25th December 2013

Mike manned the auxiliary FLC control console, as was protocol during any moonwalk activity, and glanced around the grey walls. The pathetic excuses for Christmas decorations were once again hung around the lower deck of the Drum, though it had done nothing to improve the ambience.

In a year's time the FLC would already have made its third and final firing on Siva, hopefully correcting its trajectory away from a direct impact with Earth. Until that time however, the crew were continuing to work hard at fulfilling the requirements of keeping the base operational; from maintaining the CO_2 scrubbers and solar array, to shepherding the Regodozers as they toiled to extract the Helium-3 from the grey landscape; there was always enough to distract the crew from their isolation.

"FLC this is Yakovna at Lima scrubbing station, switching to comms relay Lima," reported Lana.

"Confirmed Lana," said Mike, "go Lima in 3, 2, 1..."

There was a slight crackle, then Lana's voice continued, *"Lima, check."*

"Confirmed Lana."

"Just tell me one thing," came Lana's voice, *"How did you know I had nothing?"*

She was referring to the crew's Christmas Eve poker game, in which she had attempted to bluff her way out of scrubber duty. It had taken nearly three years for Mike to spot her Tell, and he was determined to relish every minute of it.

"What? And give away my only bargaining chip?" he smiled, "No way!"

It seemed that Lana didn't feel like responding just then, she was giving him the radio silent treatment.

"Don't be such a poor loser," he added, grinning to himself.

A moment later, Eva came into the Drum, he could see immediately that there was a problem.

"What is it?"

"It's Gant," said Eva breathlessly, "she's locked herself inside the external airlock, and she's disabled the comm panel!"

Thinking back, Mike remembered a fevered outburst from Cathy; he'd found her alone in Chamber 4 shortly after Tenca had broken up in Earth's atmosphere. The comm panel had been disabled then too.

"OK," said Mike, "take the headset, Lana's at the scrubber, stay on comms with her. Get Leonard to meet me there?"

Eva nodded and sat at the control panel, Mike grabbed a message board and pen and dashed out of the Drum, closing the airlock door behind him. If there was a de-pressurisation event, the Drum would need protection.

ISS

28th August 2009

"*Confirmed STS-128 you are go for docking procedure.*"
"Roger ISS," said Commander Charles Lincoln, "transferring guidance control."

The Discovery Space Shuttle edged nearer to the joint docking port of the International Space Station, an empty fuel tank still attached to its underside. Under daylight operation conditions the tanks were discarded, burning up in the Earth's atmosphere, but today's night launch had provided the necessary cover of darkness to haul the last of three tanks into orbit.

"Guidance control is external," reported Pilot Valery Hill.

The ISS was a testament to function over form; various spur-like chambers and solar panels had been added over the years, extending outwards from a long central axis composed of smaller sub-modules. With its cargo bay doors open, Discovery began the process of aligning with the end module, arranging itself to form an ungainly right-angle to the axis of the main structure.

The docking clamps engaged and a small vibration transferred through the hull.

"Docking ring engaged," reported Charles, "Begin environment check."

From her position in the cockpit of Discovery, Valery looked up.

To her it looked like she was at the base of a tall ISS-shaped tower; floating directly above it she could see the now familiar triangular metal framework. From her viewpoint the ends of the previous two cylindrical Shuttle tanks looked like discs, arranged at two corners of an equilateral triangle. The third corner lay open, ready to receive the last tank. Over the next six days the final empty tank, identical to those making up the majority of the FLC, would be manoeuvred into position within the framework.

When complete, the three tanks would run parallel to each other along three sides of a prism-like structure, joined by a series of walkways and airlocks. In open space the exact sizes of things could be deceptive but she estimated that despite its width the ISS would easily have fitted within the enclosed space of the triangular framework it had helped to create.

"ISS, we show pressurisation complete," Charles reported, "please confirm."

"We confirm, pressurisation complete. Cycle airlock."

"Cycling airlock," he stated by return and, silencing the comms, followed Valery's gaze, "You think we'll be done in time?"

"Every time I come up here, it always seems that progress is so slow," she shook her head, "but I think once this third chamber's in place things'll speed up."

"I hope so," said Charles knocking on the control panel superstitiously, "I wouldn't want to be orbiting when the big day comes."

"By then," she said, looking around the cramped cockpit, "we'll be long gone from here."

MARK 3

17th August 2013

The new Mark 3 Field capsule was appreciably larger than its predecessor and a closer fit to the spherical nature of the Field that held it. Douglas had argued that Anna should remain outside the Field, she had argued that he was an old curmudgeon and needed somebody to give him alternative opinions. She was also the only one capable enough of understanding, and in some areas now surpassing, his knowledge of the Field geometry in play. To intentionally maroon her in the relative slow motion of normal time would be, in her words, 'a waste of an excellent mind'.

General Napier had insisted that the departure should be done with a sense of occasion, although Douglas had not really seen the point. From the perspective of everyone in the newly constructed hangar, designed to shelter the Mark 3 capsule, their journey would only appear to take a couple of days. Inside the Field however, two whole years would pass. Napier had said from that perspective it was comparable to a tour of duty on the International Space Station, which had similar issues of limited resources and cramped conditions. Not that the Mark 3 was unpleasant, every effort had been made to make their voluntary incarceration as comfortable as possible.

Whilst inside, Douglas and Anna would be attempting to solve the issue of Field inversion. The current technicalities of forcing time to move faster on the inside of the Chronomagnetic Field were, by any standards, an incredible feat. But the Field would only be of true use if its operation could be inverted.

In all likelihood, if Siva actually impacted with the Earth then it would usher in a new ice age. Only by allowing time to move much *slower* on the inside of the Field, would a single generation of occupants of the Node be able to skip over thousands of years of planetary time.

Douglas and Anna knew the calculations could be done, it had always been a simple matter of time. Whenever the previous Mark 2 had not been scheduled for their research, the chamber had been used extensively to advance the development of computer chip speed. Within the Field, months of design could be prototyped in mere days; which in turn created faster processors, which in turn were used to design even faster ones. Although the temporal ratios had fallen some way short of the 'hundreds to one' promised to Dr. Chen three years ago, the sixth generation of his processors were now capable of calculations at least five-thousand times faster than the original Shen5 chip-set. Douglas and Anna had sixty-four of them working in parallel, but the sheer scale of the Field inversion mathematics would still require up to two years to solve.

As had always been the case, the power source for the Field had to be placed within the Field itself. They had activated it only a minute ago and Anna was staring in amazement out through the observation window to the hangar beyond.

"I can never get used to it," said Douglas watching her, "Of course it's a lot slower out there this time, but even with the Mark 2 it was always a little, er, unsettling."

"It's one thing to know the maths," she shook her head in wonder, "but to *see* it…"

Anna looked again at the people in the hangar. As it had turned on, the expansion of the spherical Chronomagnetic Field had displaced the air suddenly. Flocks of paper hung almost motionless in mid-air. Several polystyrene cups of coffee had been blown off the monitoring desks, releasing dark-brown glossy liquid to grow like roots through the air. Everyone had their eyes either fully closed or were in the process of beginning to blink.

"To them," Douglas gestured, "we've been gone for one-sixtieth of a second. Our presence at this window a moment ago hasn't even registered in their retinas yet."

"We're invisible," Anna smiled.

While Anna studied the frozen faces of the people outside, Douglas flicked through his NASA jotter. During almost half a century the pages had yellowed, and become more fragile; some had fallen out and were now held in place with sticky tape, which itself was now brittle and discoloured. His decision trees filled every page; possibilities within possibilities, played out in minute detail, but all with one goal. He turned over the jotter to look at the series of drawings he had penned as a child, and flicked through the pages to bring them to life once more. Inside a circle were a stick-family with simple smiley faces, representing Douglas and his parents. A ball appeared to pass between the stick-man and the stick-boy, whilst outside the bubble, the world waited for them, forever frozen.

"I made time," he said quietly to himself, thinking of his father and the childish wish he had never fulfilled.

Anna had been so fascinated with the view that she missed what he had said. She turned to him and saw the contemplative look on his face.

"I'm sorry that Monica and Katie aren't here," she said.

"I was actually thinking about my Dad," he shook his head, "Too many have died."

When Monica and Kate had left Archive, he had stayed on to complete his work. But shortly after the Node was relocated to this quiet, remote area of Iceland, correspondence had abruptly ceased.

Suspecting foul play, he had confronted General Napier demanding that they reinstate the channels of communication. It had been Bradley Pittman in person who had delivered the devastating news of their crash.

The horrific photographic evidence he provided was enough to persuade Douglas it was truly over.

The following months had been the blackest he had known and in the depths of his depression his research had fallen to a dangerously slow rate. Eventually they had flown Anna Bergstrom in to assist him, and together they had slowly put the program back on schedule. Eventually she had become as indispensable as anyone else.

Douglas straightened his shoulders and took a deep breath.

"We've got about an hour before they start the light cycle," he said with resolve, "Let's get started."

•

The blast of air, produced by the sudden expansion of spherical Field, blew a few papers into the air and tipped over a few half-empty coffee cups. The Mark 3 was undoubtedly bigger, so the air blast was to be expected; General Napier wondered for a second what the blast effect would be when the full sized Node began its journey.

After emerging from the original Mark 2, Douglas had given feedback on his time inside. He had found it difficult to maintain a regular sleep cycle if the normal 'circadian' rhythms of day and night were missing. Taking this and other feedback into consideration, the hangar surrounding the Mark 3 had a built-in system to mimic the light levels of a standard 24 hour day. Owing to the enormous time frame difference though, the lighting would cycle in the hangar every 4 minutes. Just over two and a half minutes of daylight were simulated in each cycle, before the hangar lights dipped to black.

General Napier could see from the readings that the Field was stable. He signalled Colonel Beck to give the order.

"Two minutes to blackout," called Colonel Beck, "evacuate all non-essential personnel."

The desk phone rang.

Napier checked the extension number shown on the phone's display; moving his hand to hover over a large button labelled 'abort'.

The 'abort' button couldn't deactivate the Field from the outside, but it would trigger the whole lighting simulator to emit an extremely rapid strobe pattern. Even at the accelerated time frame within the Field, anyone would see day and night passing in seconds and could close down the Field if necessary.

With his hand still hovering over the button, he picked up the handset.

"Gate House, this is a priority line."

"My apologies, Sir," came a nervous voice from the other end.

"Well?"

"Perimeter Defence Station four has intercepted two travellers."

The personnel manning those stations were well briefed in the procedures of turning away unwelcome visitors, but from the tone of the call, Napier knew there must be something more.

"Connect me to them."

There was a light click and a new, but equally hesitant voice answered.

"DS4, Sir."

"Report."

"We're holding two visitors, claiming to have... very detailed knowledge, but their pass-phrase is out of date. Protocol says that -"

"Who are they?" he cut in.

"I don't know, Sir."

"Well have you asked them?" he said starting to feel his blood pressure rising.

"Yes, Sir. He says he will only speak to General Napier, sorry Sir."

Anyone willing to walk up to a remote defence station, with knowledge of the inside of the facility, and mention Napier by name would obviously need his direct attention.

"Let me speak to them."

"Sir, protocol dictates that - "

"I wrote the damn protocol. Put them on the horn. Now," he insisted.

There was a pause while the visitor was escorted to the phone.

"Here he is now, Sir," came the voice, followed by a muffled noise as the handset changed hands.

"Who am I speaking to?" said Napier in a direct tone.

"My name is Miles Benton," came the self-assured voice, *"I've brought Dr.Walker's daughter to visit The Node."*

Napier moved his hand away from the 'abort' button and spoke quietly.

"I'll send transport for you," he said, then carefully replaced the handset.

The lights inside the hangar suddenly started to fade, and in another moment he was left in the dark.

AIRLOCK

25th December 2013

When Mike reached the airlock he could see Cathy inside, frantically trying to climb into her spacesuit. He tried pushing the comm button to speak with her, but it did appear that the comm panel had been deactivated, just as Eva had said. Sound communication through the glass of the airlock panel was impossible, so he prepared to use his message board and pen, as was procedure in the event of audio failure.

Cathy saw him and she made swift strides over to the glass. Mike could see that she was obviously yelling, but from his side of the airlock door no sound reached him. Her eyes were bloodshot, and she had a deep scratch down her cheek. She backed away from the glass and started pointing repeatedly at the panel on the front of her spacesuit.

Mike started to write the words *'Stay Calm'* on the board, but then noticed that she was making a hand gesture mimicking 'telephone', whilst still pointing to her chest panel. She could only mean the short range radio built into each suit. He reached inside the neck hole of the nearest spacesuit to retrieve the headset and activated the channel. Immediately the air was filled with Cathy's screaming voice.

"…behind the whole thing! She's going to kill us all!"

"I hear you Cathy!" he shouted over her, to make himself heard, "Calm down, why don't we just talk about it, I'm -"

"The bitch locked me in here!"

Mike knew that each airlock had a safety override and could be opened from the inside. Evidently in her agitated state this was eluding her.

"OK, so open it up again from your side," he said as calmly as he could.

"That's what I'm telling you Mike!" she screamed, "Eva's disabled the fucking comm and locked me in here! The override's disabled!"

Mike was already at the internal control panel, it only took him a second to realise that he couldn't open it either. The airlock had been locked into a diagnostic cycle, it showed thirteen seconds and was counting down. At ten seconds a small high-vis light began to flash every two seconds, indicating that the external door was about to open. Mike pulled the headset on again.

"Cathy I can't stop it!"

"I know!" she yelled pulling the helmet over her head and locking it into place, "You have to stop her Mike! She going to -"

Cathy's voice turned to static, and although he could see her mouth move he couldn't make out the words.

"Quickly Cathy, repeat. Over."

The static continued to hiss from the headset, but he could see that she wasn't speaking to him anymore. She had turned to face the airlock door that was swinging open. The short range radios did not suffer from interference during airlock operation, which left only one alternative. The communication was being deliberately blocked. He thought back to his brief conversation with Lana at the scrubbing station only moments before, when she had apparently given him the silent treatment. It was possible that *all* communications were down.

He retraced his steps towards the Drum. The inner protective door was still closed, and after trying to turn the handle he concluded that it had been locked. He tried pushing the button on the comm panel, and found that it emitted a tone. So the communications were being selectively disabled, he thought.

"Eva?" he called.

"Yes Mike?" came her calm reply.

She had evidently anticipated his return and locked him out.

"Eva look," he improvised, "obviously the two of you have had a... falling out, but Cathy's trapped outside. I've lost comms with her, and she could be in real danger out there."

"That's such a shame," she continued, emotionless, "she was so... useful."

"Eva, please, let me in," he said, "We can discuss it. I know that Cathy can -"

"No. You'd only try to talk me out of it," she delivered, "Goodbye Mike."

The comm panel clicked off.

Instinctively he jabbed at the button again, but despite the tone, Eva did not reply.

"Talk you out of what?" he shouted at the closed door.

Thoughts clamoured for his attention. She had said Cathy had been 'useful'. Presumably then, Eva had been planning this for a long while, and Cathy had somehow unwittingly assisted her plan. Assessing the situation, he knew he was stuck in Chamber 4 with no means of direct entry to the Drum or the rest of the facility beyond. Although Floyd's main control centre was in Chamber 6, Eva had chosen the auxiliary station inside the Drum presumably in order to control access throughout the station. And it appeared to be working, he thought. He knew Lana was possibly on her way back from replacing the CO2 scrubber cartridge, and at least Cathy had made it out of the airlock in one piece. Hopefully she would rendezvous with Lana. That left only Leonard unaccounted for.

The awful thought occurred to him that perhaps Eva and Leonard were working together. If that was true then Leonard could be anywhere, either within the FLC or out there. That last thought tipped Mike's decision and he hurriedly started to don his spacesuit. In here he was trapped, but outside there was at least a small possibility of him regaining some form of control.

Hearing a click behind him, he whirled around.

Nobody was there but he saw that, in his brief absence, the airlock had concluded its forced diagnostic cycle and the internal lock had clicked over to the unlocked position. He tried manually cycling the airlock but it appeared that Eva had already considered that option and disabled it. He looked around, racking his brains for inspiration.

COFFEE

17th August 2013

Napier knew it would take at least ten minutes for Benton and his guest to be flown from Defence Station Four to the main gate, but even with this time he felt unprepared. From his own working knowledge of the ego-morph program he knew what to expect. Their analytical skills were so well tuned that they never missed a detail, which included reading the mannerisms of those they were with. Their interactions with those around them could only be described as flawless, either for the purposes of interrogation, or blending in during long-term operations. He had met others before, of course, but not this particular one. However, the prospect of meeting one in person always unsettled him.

And then there was the potentially problematic issue of his guest.

The reason Archive had maintained such a powerful hold over Douglas Walker and his research was because they had convinced him that his family was dead. Shortly after the facility had been relocated to this gravitational hotspot in Iceland, Bradley Pittman had made the arrangements for Monica Walker and her daughter to meet with a Level One Intervention. But there had been complications which had meant their survival had to be ensured, in return for the continued concealment of several key Archive ventures.

If Douglas Walker saw his daughter alive then they could lose all control over him. For the time being, Napier thought, he didn't have to worry about that, Douglas was safely contained within the Mark 3 Field for the next two days. All he would have to do was ensure that Kate never entered the hangar.

However, if Walker and Bergstrom succeeded in solving the issue of Field inversion during their time-compressed two day trip then there would be no problem. As soon as the data was safe they would no longer need to maintain control of Douglas. And if things became difficult then, although regrettable, they would no longer need any of the Walkers. Monica's threat to reveal Archive's interests had largely evaporated after they had voluntarily gone public about most of their endeavours.

Most. Napier thought. Most of their endeavours. However, there was still the Node, and the ISS. With well over a year to go, he still had to protect them from prying public eyes. When Monica had left, these facilities had not even begun, but she had once demonstrated that despite being on the outside, she knew things. Things that she shouldn't have. Napier would be the first to admit that an unknown unknown was dangerous. For the time being he would have to continue to treat her as a viable threat.

He returned his attention to Benton, reviewing his notes on the office computer. A few days after Archive had gone public, Benton's tracker had been found at a London postal sorting office, but he had not been seen since. Benton's file, along with a few others at the time, had been closed as missing in action.

It was not without precedent. Even before Fallen Veil, sometimes ego-morphs would embed themselves too deeply within an operation and simply run out of Metathene. Without regular doses of the whiskey-coloured liquid, they tended to become unfocussed and suicidal. After their initial psychological priming, it was the only control mechanism that Archive had over their otherwise autonomous existence.

Dorothy Pittman, Bradley's mother, had first pioneered both the drug and the technique back in the seventies as a way to shape and direct the minds of young, impressionable children. She made her selections only from the brightest, which went some way to explaining the focussed intellect of the end result. Looking at the age on file, Napier could see that Benton may even have been among the first.

He could hear the lightweight helicopter's rotors winding down and gathered both his thoughts and paperwork. He surveyed the office to check if he'd left any unintentional information on show, but nothing immediately sprang to his attention.

All too soon, there was a soft knock at the door. Napier straightened his uniform and picked up a random folder from his desk.

"Enter," he said firmly.

Benton was led in and behind him was, unmistakably, Kate Walker. Both were handcuffed.

Napier dropped the folder back on the desk, and gestured casually to their restraints, "I think we can dispense with those, don't you, sergeant?"

Benton turned his head and took in the decor, while their handcuffs were removed. Kate's eyes darted anxiously between Napier and Benton, while massaging her wrists.

"Please," said Napier pointing to the two empty chairs on the other side of his desk, "have a seat. That's got to have been a long journey. Sergeant, please can you bring some coffee?"

"You have coffee here?" said Kate, unable to stop herself. Since the collapse, coffee was rare.

"Yes," smiled Napier, then addressed the sergeant again, "and the milk and sugar."

Kate was obviously impressed, but Benton's expression hadn't altered since he'd entered the room. Kate sat heavily into her seat, while Benton purposefully lowered himself into his. Now turning his attention towards the General, he spoke for the first time:

"General, I believe Archive may have lost a Walker. I'm returning this one."

Napier could almost feel the assessing gaze cut through him, "Thank you Benton, we were -".

"Where's my Dad?" exploded Kate, succeeding in making Napier jump. But his composure returned almost instantly.

"Miss Walker," he smiled with sympathy, "we both know that your father died tragically and -"

"Don't!" she shouted, this time slamming the desk with her fist and standing up, "I know you're holding him here!"

Technically, Douglas Walker was holding *himself* inside the Mark 3, thought Napier with a sense of irony.

The door flew open as two armed guards reacted to the noise. Framed in the doorway, their sidearms were raised.

"Stand down," Napier instructed, then turning to Kate said, "Sit down."

They stepped aside and a tray with coffee, milk and sugar was brought past Benton to Napier's desk. Napier stared at the guard, who was nervously trying to re-holster his sidearm, and motioned for them both to leave the room.

"You can't blame me for trying, Miss Walker," he said lifting the pot and pouring the hot black liquid into a mug, "We went to a lot of effort to ensure your father remained safe from those who wanted to -"

"Use him?" she completed with an accusing stare.

"Protect him, from those who wanted to prevent the completion of his work, I was about to say," Napier attempted.

"Is that why you have him working on The Node?" she fired.

Napier poured out a second mug. He'd given instructions that they should be blindfolded during their transit to the main gate, so he was sure that they hadn't seen the Node itself. But knowledge of the name, if not its purpose, was apparently out there already. He handed Kate the filled mug and she began to drink it greedily.

"The fact is that your father is on a research expedition for a couple of days. You're welcome to wait for him, I'm sure he'd be delighted to see you," Napier suggested, raising the mug to his mouth.

"I wouldn't do that, General," said Benton, leaning forward and pointing to the mug.

Before Napier could reply, Kate slid sideways out of her chair and fell limply to the floor. During her fall, Benton leaned forward, caught her mug, and replaced it quietly on Napier's desk.

Napier froze, his mug still poised.

"Apologies, General," Benton smiled, "Unfortunately, a moment ago, I only had time to drug the pot. We both know she was asking too many questions and I could see you were getting a little uncomfortable. She will be fine, I assume she is worth more to you alive?"

Napier just nodded, amazed at the ego-morph's apparent speed and resourcefulness.

"Good," said Benton, "I don't mind admitting it gives me a certain amount of... yes, *satisfaction* to tie up this loose end. I'm formally reporting for Archive reassignment."

Napier allowed himself to set the mug down on the desk, grateful that the ego-morph was still under Archive direction. It still took him a few more seconds to regain his authority.

"Good, thank you Benton. Where did she get 'The Node' from?"

"From a now terminated underground network," said Benton, "For the good of Mankind."

Napier recognized the phrase and nodded.

"Though there is the possibility that Miss Walker's mother is aware of the Node's location," Benton reported.

"That damned bitch always finds a way to keep her neck from the noose," Napier grumbled.

For the time being he had to assume Monica Walker would have taken precautions to ensure automatic disclosure of the Node; her termination was no longer an option.

"I have to assume you have some form of holding cell on site, General?" said Benton, dragging Kate from the floor and hauling her over his shoulder, "Where would you like me to put her?"

ARIADNE'S THREAD

8th February 2010.

Alfred Barnes put the folder down on his desk among all the other notes, and reached for the flask of coffee that General Napier had left with him a few hours before. He poured the remainder into his heavily stained mug and drank it all in a few mouthfuls.

He had just spent the better part of two hours reading through the thick 'SIVA' folder. In a few hours more he would be expected to present his solution for assuming the social order of the global population. The bare, grey, breeze-block walls of the Andersen Air Force Base stared back at him offering no help.

He pushed his glasses up above his eyebrows and rubbed his eyes. He needed some fresh, or at least different air. He also needed to walk; it would help him think, and perhaps he could also find some more caffeine along the way.

Napier had been right, the ego-morphs were too useful a resource to waste, and would definitely be part of his recommendations concerning social control. He found their origin fascinating.

In 1951, long before Archive had even been given a name, Sam Bishop had come across the evidence of Siva in a photographic plate taken by a student of his. Bishop had realised the significance of the discovery, but also the importance of discretion. Given the scant 64 year time-scale involved, he also knew that if the human race was to rise to the challenge of escaping Siva then it would need to become smarter. And do so faster than evolution would allow.

From his reading of the file, Alfred surmised that despite the illegality, what had actually followed was five years of unapproved drug development and trials on expectant mothers. The cortical booster was designed to significantly increase brain activity within the foetus, allowing neural connections to be formed more easily and permanently.

After the birth, every baby in the trial had been 'vaccinated' with a substance called Metathene; this counterpart drug was designed to work with the gene-level cortical booster already present within the child, and activate increased cognitive abilities.

Apparently it had not worked as predicted.

In all the test subjects, mental abilities were significantly increased, but the effect was temporary. For the child's superior cognitive functions to persist required regular doses. Not only that, it was addictive. The drug could not be manufactured fast enough for the hundreds of test subjects, so only the most promising were picked to continue receiving it. Their progress was carefully monitored by creating an academy where such high level scrutiny would appear commonplace.

As the years progressed, a disturbing correlation was found. What the children had gained in terms of logic and cool intellect, they had lost in empathy and creativity. They could absorb vast amounts of information and complete their given tasks to perfection, but they lacked the inspiration to think in new directions; directions that may have helped to escape Siva.

However, Archive, already deep into the development of the space program, spotted an opportunity. The subject's lack of empathy extended to their own ego. If the subject deemed the logic within a goal to be consistent, then they would irrevocably follow it until they reached the end of the task. Even if that meant self-termination. With the right doses of metathene and appropriate mental re-conditioning, the ego-morphs had proved essential in the initiation of the Apollo program, and the wider task of maintaining Archive's anonymity.

Alfred Barnes reached the end of yet another grey, breeze-block corridor. Right now he could do with some mental stimulation of his own, he was pretty sure he'd been going in circles.

"Why is it so hard to get coffee in this maze?" he sighed into the air, leaning against the wall.

In his exhausted state he began to picture the base as a mythological Greek labyrinth, with dead ends and wrong turns. He noted to himself that, on some level, it must obviously be reflecting his current mental state. He couldn't tell at what point his journey into fantasy had begun, but now he pictured the beautiful Ariadne handing him a ball of grey thread. So this was to be a Greek Mythology daydream then, he thought. Now he could wander the maze, trailing the thread behind him. Wrong choices he'd made would now be easily visible, and eventually he would find his way to the exit. *'Eventually'* would take too long though, he realised. His position in the maze, now criss-crossed with thread in all directions, lacked fear and urgency. As if on cue, the Minotaur appeared; it completed the myth and began to pursue him, relentlessly, through the maze until it irrevocably reached the end of its task. As he turned to run, the multiple wrong choices of thread caught round his ankles, knotting and slowing his escape. Just before the monster of the maze reached him, the threads tangled suddenly and he fell.

He awoke suddenly, facing the same grey walls, realising that he had never actually left the room.

But now he had his answer, probably not the one that Archive was expecting, and it certainly left conventional morality firmly outside the door.

CHRISTMAS EVA

25th December 2013

"Happy Christmas," Eva whispered into Leonard's ear, "hope you liked your present."

Leonard laughed quietly, "I'll give you yours later!"

"I like it when the Ice Queen goes out," she said zipping up her jumpsuit, "it gives us longer to play."

"Damn," he said through a smile, zipping up his own jumpsuit and patting his pockets.

"What is it?" she drew close to him again.

"Must've left my ID key in the Drum."

Eva quickly checked over her shoulder.

"It's OK," she smiled suggestively, then slowly pushed her lips against his, "I'll grab it for you, you're supposed to keep it with you all the time."

Still smiling, she left Leonard behind and headed out of Chamber 6.

"I'll check your bunk and come back," she said softly, starting to close the door, "Wait for me here."

Concealing the ID key she'd lifted from Leonard during the heights of his distraction, she calmly crossed the Drum.

"Just checking on Cathy," she called to Mike, who was monitoring Lana's progress at the auxiliary control console.

"OK," he called over his shoulder.

She closed the door behind her; if things were going to get a little rowdy, she thought, some privacy may be in order. From the sound of Mike's conversation, Lana was already approaching the CO_2 scrubber station; Eva realised she would have to move quickly.

She found Cathy at the far end of Chamber 4, just outside the airlock. Normally she would have engaged her in some meaningless chat, to give the semblance of a working relationship. Today she tried a different approach.

"Evening, Gant."

"Is it?" Cathy replied, and turned to face Eva, "I know we keep time with Houston-"

Eva interrupted her usual downbeat reply by punching her, hard, directly in the face. It surprised even Eva that Cathy had flown so far back; a result of the lower gravity, she supposed. But her fascination with the physics at play was short lived. Stepping across the airlock threshold Eva followed Cathy, who was only now hitting the floor.

Though Cathy and Eva had never really seen eye to eye, their tolerance of each other was reinforced by the cooperation required by the FLC's mission. They had exchanged heated words with each other over the years, but given the tight living conditions, it was inevitable. As an unwritten rule, and to a certain extent as a mark of respect, the crew had never exchanged blows; they all knew they were too valuable, as was the facility surrounding them.

In the heat of the moment, Eva thought the look on Cathy's face was priceless; the realisation that the unwritten rule had been so unceremoniously discarded. Eva's adrenalin unlocked years of frustration, and it now poured out of her. She grabbed Cathy round the throat and hauled her off the floor, the low gravity giving her a powerful assist.

"Get up!" she snarled, enjoying the power of the moment, slamming Cathy roughly against the airlock wall. With her other hand she took hold of the ID key chain hanging around Cathy's neck and pulled it so taut that she could see it dig into her skin.

It had taken her a few seconds to adjust, but now Cathy understood the new rules of engagement and adapted with equal satisfaction. She brought her knee swiftly up into Eva's stomach and pushed off the wall, sending the two of them off balance across the airlock. Eva lost her grip on Cathy's chain and she could finally speak.

"What the *fuck*, Eva?!" she managed to spit out, desperately trying to scramble to her knees, "We can't... do this!"

"No," spat Eva manoeuvring Cathy to get her arm around her neck, "*You* can't do this."

Cathy managed to thrust an elbow into her ribs, and Eva was winded for a moment.

"For… the good of…Mankind - " Cathy gasped, desperate for air, "one year left…"

With a stamp to the back of the knee, Cathy fell to the floor; Eva got behind her and looped her arm around her neck, putting her in a choke hold; but she was surprised to find that Cathy was, even now, putting up such a fight.

"You're just… Leonard's… common bitch!" came Cathy's constricted voice.

She tightened her hold around Cathy's neck, then ducked low so that she could speak into her ear.

"I am Eve!" Eva roared. "I will birth the new mankind. Born in the fires of the old, they will renew the Earth!"

She waited until Cathy became limp then snatched her ID key. She closed the airlock door behind her and entered the appropriate key combinations to set the airlock into a diagnostic mode. After confirming to the panel that there were no personnel inside the airlock she set the cycle running. She disabled the comm panel and strode away from the airlock, along the length of Chamber 4, heading back towards the Drum.

The excess of adrenalin had given her an authentic, flushed appearance with which to convince Mike of Cathy's rash actions. She had not accounted for the same adrenal excess in Cathy's veins though, which had already started to drag her back into consciousness.

As Eva was entering the Drum, she could hear that Mike was still in conversation with Lana out at the scrubber station.

"Don't be such a poor loser," he said, grinning over some private joke.

Eva deliberately took a few loud breaths and Mike turned suddenly, the smile draining quickly from his face.

"What is it?"

"It's Gant," said Eva breathlessly, "she's locked herself inside the external airlock, and she's disabled the comm panel!"

"OK," said Mike, "take the headset, Lana's at the scrubber, stay on comms with her. Get Leonard to meet me there?"

Eva nodded and sat down in front of the display, carefully positioning herself between Mike and the ID key he'd left inserted in the control panel. Mike gathered a few things together and exited the Drum, closing the internal airlock door behind him.

It was the work of a moment for Eva to lock him out.

DAY 187

17th August 2013

Inside the Mark 3 Field, Anna looked across the upper floor lab at the split-time clock. The first set of figures indicated the external date followed by the elapsed mission time, the second counted the days spent inside the Field:

17AUG2013+12.30 : DAY 187.5

Outside the Field was an identical clock on the hangar wall, it had been synchronised at the start of the journey but now it displayed:

17AUG2013+12.29 : DAY 187.5

"Douglas?" she called.

Douglas made his way up the flight of spiral stairs from the lower deck. Placing the Field's generator at the centre of the Field had always proved tricky when people needed to inhabit the space too, so as a matter of necessity the spiral steps had been constructed to sit around the enclosed tubular shaped generator. It was an approach duplicated in the architecture of the Node itself that was, even now, undergoing the final stages of its construction.

"Yeah?" he called ahead, before reaching the top.

"Take a look at this will you?" she pointed towards the internal clock and the one in the hangar.

He speeded up as he crossed the floor and actually grinned, "Yes!"

"What?" Anna laughed, "I don't get it. Aren't they supposed to be in sync?"

Douglas looked a little sheepish, "I tweaked the radius a bit."

"You did what?" she exclaimed, getting to her feet.

"I shrank the Field size by a quarter of an inch," he said, and spotting her eyes widen he hastily added, "just for a millisecond!"

"Douglas!"

"Everything's fine, Anna!"

He pulled forward a keyboard, intending to feed a message into the high-definition noticeboard that faced out towards the hangar. Previously, in the Mark 2 chamber, he had adopted the low-tech method of writing brief messages on a noticeboard and angling it to be visible through the observation port, and replies had come in the same way. Direct radio communication was still proving elusive, so they had resorted to a similar, albeit slightly upgraded, noticeboard.

"They'll notice the dip in the Field output any second now, so I just need to let them know that we're OK."

She laid a hand on his forearm and looked at him directly, "Next time, please tell me *before* you do it, Dougie."

Very few people called him that, and her message seemed to hit home more effectively. Generally, he thought, people tended to address him with a kind of ill-deserved reverence. To be addressed as an equal, and not an aloof genius was refreshing for him. He returned her smile and nodded.

She gently took the keyboard from him and began to type quickly, in preparation for the moment that the hangar personnel would react. She hit 'update' and sent the message to the noticeboard.

'Field anomaly within tolerance. Disregard. All vectors nominal. DW&AB.'

Outside in the hangar, the computer analysing the Field's condition would take perhaps a second to detect the Field variance and then alert those on duty. The personnel would no doubt find it odd to witness the arrival of a message from the Mark 3 in advance of the anomaly itself being discovered.

"Thank you," said Douglas, reading the message, "a little inaccurate, but…"

"…but shaped like an explanation," she smiled, "It would be easier if we could just use walkie-talkies."

"I think I've worked out why direct communication doesn't work."

"Explain it over dinner, I'm starving," she said. "I'll just go and slip into something baggy and shapeless."

Over the years he'd grown accustomed to her dry sense of humour, and he derived a certain comfort from their working relationship.

"I'll open ration pack 187C for the occasion," he quipped back.

During the meal, Douglas got back to the topic of direct communication using radio waves, or more specifically why it didn't work. An experiment with mice had once gone horribly wrong and had resulted in the generator being locked inside the Field for months until the power depleted. The Field's power supply had been remotely activated by a radio transmitter, but once the Field had been established, the radio signal could no longer penetrate it. Since then, the generator had always been put on a timer, or had a human operator, to deactivate the Field.

"I think it starts here," he said pointing to a line of equations on a second sheet of paper, "but it doesn't factor in Shapiro's predicted pinch points, which tipped us off about the -"

"Granularity and pocketing of the Field, yes - " Anna joined in, "We know the Biomag and isotope warps the Field - "

"Which is why we can move around in here without getting shredded," he picked up, "But what if you consider for a moment a hypothetical laser beam pointed from out there in the hangar, to in here?"

"OK," said Anna. She sketched a circle on the page then used a red pen to draw a thin line travelling through the circumference towards the centre of the circle, "So, our laser passes through the Field and presumably, with some sort of Doppler shift to the frequency, it continues on to our theoretical detector, just about here." She drew a box almost at the centre.

"Now," said Douglas, picking up a different pen. He started drawing dark patches inside the circle to represent the pockets where time had not been shifted at the same rate. In some places the patches intersected the red line. "Thanks to your isotope, you and I can walk through the Field and these pockets don't affect us; but for the laser beam, it passes right into them and gets scrambled as badly as anyone with no iso-protection. Radio waves get scrambled."

"You're forgetting about one very obvious fact though Doug."

Douglas seemed momentarily concerned, and began retracing his steps along his carefully constructed mental tree.

"What?"

"We can still see the light from the outside world," said Anna, and started adding in line after line of theoretical light beams entering the circle, "If the beams of light are getting scrambled, why can we see the outside world so clearly?"

Douglas was relieved, he knew this question would be raised.

"I'm glad you asked," he smiled, "Analogy blindness."

A frown had started to form on Anna's eyebrows, as though hearing a new concept for the first time.

"Our soap bubble analogy," he continued, "treats light as *entering* or *leaving* the spherical Field. What if it doesn't? I think we've become blind to our own analogy. Bear with me."

He pulled a small rectangular card from his pocket, and spotting Anna's slightly puzzled expression he explained why he had it with him.

"I like to keep this as a reminder of why we're doing all this," he said, handing her the card.

"You prepared for this didn't you?" asked Anna incredulously. Normally she would be the one to explain things to others using visual aids.

"My apologies," he smiled, "but I've learned from a good teacher."

She inspected the card. One side of it was matte black with small white text. The other side was a garish yellow-green hologram, depicting a round planet Earth. As she turned the card from left to right, she could see the planet from slightly different angles.

"Cute," she commented, returning it to him, "My cousin used to collect this sort of thing."

"You know the little planet isn't really on the other side of the card though?" Douglas pushed.

"Don't patronise me - "

"No, forgive me, it's all part of the, er -"

"Presentation. OK," she played along, "so yes, I know it isn't on the other side."

"But. What if, somehow, I'd arranged for a little planet model to be suspended behind a card *made of glass*. The effect would be the same and you wouldn't be able to tell the difference, would you?"

"Well no, that's the way holograms work -" she began.

But Douglas could see that the idea had taken hold, and that she had begun extrapolating in the same way that he had:

"Wait, wait, oh!" she said, her eyes beginning to widen.

"We can represent a three dimensional object" he said twisting the card, "on the two dimensional surface of the card -"

The grin on her face told him all he needed to know.

"So you're saying that everything outside the Field is only *represented* on the *surface* of the Field?" she smiled.

"Yes! We're not looking through a soap bubble wall, we're looking at a visual reconstruction of what is happening on the other side."

"But we can see them actually *moving* around out there."

"Two-D surface," he turned the holographic card from side to side, "showing Three-D object."

"Three-D Field surface," completed Anna, "showing Four-D space-time."

"And the same goes for their view out there. We are only *represented* at the surface of the sphere."

Anna took a gulp of water from her glass, then looked at Douglas through it.

"And with any representation, details get distorted," she said.

"If we knew *how* to look, then I think we'd notice a simplification in the information transmitted through the Field's surface. The radio waves can't be reconstructed once they've been simplified by the transition through the surface."

Anna beamed at him.

"OK, but does this help us with Field inversion?" she asked, starting to shuffle through the pages.

"I don't think so," he shrugged, "but my Dad told me once that there are no left over pieces, only things we didn't realise we might need later."

LIMA RELAY

25th December 2013

"Just tell me one thing," said Lana Yakovna, bringing the rover to a stop, "How did you know I had nothing?"

"What? And give away my only bargaining chip?" came Mike's voice from the FLC Drum, *"No way!"*

She could tell from his tone that he must be grinning from ear to ear.

"Don't be such a poor loser," came his mocking tone.

She would have to be careful in their next poker game.

There was something about the solar panel array in the west quadrant of the Coriolis crater that suddenly caught her eye. She half-recalled a conversation with Mike some years previously and experienced a sense of déjà vu. Several sections of the array were misaligned. Her sense of mild levity evaporated instantly.

"FLC, solar array look misalign. Run megawatt check."

She waited for Mike to bring up the relevant subroutines within Floyd's control program. She remembered that several years ago a few of the sun-tracking panels had suffered a delay, but what she was looking at now appeared to be entire banks of the array pointing in the wrong direction.

"Mike, what is take so long?" she stood still, "Mike? Over."

She checked her channel number before attempting again, "FLC this is Yakovna, at Lima-".

Her headset erupted with static. Almost instinctively she went to cover her ears but quickly corrected her reaction and reached instead for the control panel on her chest. She tried switching back to the FLC main comms loop, but found the same disruption. It did not take her long to realise that none of the conventional comms channels were operational.

Without a word, she remounted the rover and turned it around to go back.

Most of the FLC was, by design, buried under tonnes of regolith to shield against radiation, with only the airlocks protruding from the grey dust. As she got closer though, she could see activity at the airlock for Chamber 4. Someone was coming out, but at this distance she couldn't identify who. Hers was the only moonwalk scheduled for today, which made this an unauthorised exit from the FLC. Something which could be endangering the entire facility.

She anxiously pushed her right foot down, hard, on the floor of the rover, an old Earth habit which had no effect on her speed whatsoever; the vehicle was already travelling at its maximum speed. She was within a hundred yards of the FLC when she saw the lights suddenly turn off inside the airlock of Chamber 6.

TRIPS

11th March 2013

As Kate lay in the contained darkness, she decided she actually knew very little about the woman that she called Mum. It seemed that there were periods of their lives that were parallel and shared, but a larger, stranger part which bore little resemblance to the mother figure Kate had experienced.

Barely five minutes ago, in the space formerly occupied by the family dining table, a door had opened up in the kitchen floor, and her mother had escorted them down some steps that appeared to have been hewn from the chalk cliffs themselves. She had shown them to a plastic chute, drilled into the wall of the concealed room. She had then spoken about their destination, the need for a delivery container, and then wheeled over what looked like a metal casket, one for each of them and one for the man they were calling Benton.

"See you down there," came her mother's voice from the outside of the cramped capsule, followed by a double tap on the metal. Kate presumed that it was intended to reassure her but the sound was amplified inside the closed space and if anything it put her nerves even more on edge. She felt a tipping sensation but, being denied a window, couldn't tell for sure.

Then the bottom fell out of her world and she could feel herself plummeting.

The pathos of riding a fast moving, coffin-shaped box towards an underworld was not lost on her, and as the chute changed angle to allow faster travel she expressed these feelings by screaming for all she was worth. The vibration of the capsule was incredible - definitely not the smooth ride that Monica had hinted at during their swift briefing.

Then, after she felt that she must have been falling for a full minute, she was surprised again by the sudden arrival of her father's voice:

"Nearly there Katie!"

His recorded voice sounded from a speaker somewhere near her head. In the moment she felt a little comfort from knowing that long ago he had prepared this capsule specifically for the possibility that she would one day need to use it.

"Braking in three, two, one."

She felt a sudden deceleration as friction brakes outside activated, causing a screeching wail to transfer through the capsule. She could feel her head getting heavier and realised it was because the capsule had changed from a vertical to a horizontal position. And still the friction brakes wailed, though less intense now. Then the noise disappeared and she felt a slight bump down by her feet.

"Stay calm, you made it!" came her father's warm voice again, *"Sit tight and I'll open the door for you."*

There was a metallic unlocking noise from outside, and she had the sensation that the whole capsule had been lifted from whatever track had delivered her here. Then the capsule split along its length letting the comparatively bright light in, and silhouetting a figure reaching down to her. She half expected to see her father, but as her eyes adjusted to the light she could see that the silhouette belonged to Marcus.

"I hate your Mother," he greeted her.

Kate could see that he'd had a much rougher trip than her. Evidently he'd lost control of his stomach during the journey.

"Mr. Killer?" said Kate, sitting up and starting to swing her legs out.

Marcus jerked his head towards the other side of the small room, where another capsule lay, unopened.

A loud screech from behind them alerted them to the arrival of the final capsule.

It arrived at speed among a burst of sparks as it exited the chute and flew along a short section of track. A hook on the top of the capsule was caught by several stretched elastic bungee cords, and it slowed rapidly before bumping into a rubber piston at the end of the track.

Kate noticed for the first time that there were other people in the room, presumably those who had helped unload her capsule from the track, and they now sped over to attend to Monica.

"You know what?" Marcus said shaking his head, and watching them unload Monica's capsule from the track, "When this is over I'm gonna just sit in the sun and let the waves wash my feet."

"You might wanna wash your shirt first," smiled Kate.

Marcus smiled down at his vomit covered shirt, "Yep."

Kate watched as Monica was helped to her feet and briefed by one of the men who had helped with the capsules. As she watched, her mother's expression hardened, and she walked over to join Kate and Marcus.

"Chalk *Mole?*" asked Marcus, emphasising the latter syllable, and pointing at the chute.

"I thought it was apt," she shrugged, "The tour will have to wait. Apparently there'll be a televised announcement at eleven hundred hours."

"Is this it?"

"I hope not," said Monica, beckoning the man over, "If Archive do a global reveal it'll be chaos, and I don't need to remind you, we'll lose our insurance."

"Yes Ma'am?" said the young man arriving at her side.

"Dawson, we'll need to get answers quickly," she said, looking at Benton's capsule, "From the looks of things I think we'll need Arrivals Room Two, and get Woods up here on tech."

"Yes Ma'am," said Dawson and departed swiftly.

Monica could see the perplexed looks starting to creep across Marcus and Kate's faces again.

"We're a year away from Siva getting here. If we don't want Archive to dispose of us in the meantime, then we'll need more information to bargain with. We need to find out what's inside that man's head."

"Yeah I know all that," said Marcus, quietly grateful for things making sense for a change.

"Good. So what's up?"

"You told him to get some guy *up here*," said Marcus.

"And?" said Monica, impatiently checking her watch.

"If this is 'up'," said Kate, "then just how far down does this rabbit hole go, Mum?"

•

For the longest time, Miles Benton felt the sensation of falling and turbulence, a howling wind followed by a quiet he had never known. None of that seemed to matter now. He felt warm now. Secure. He could hear a voice calling to him, as though someone was trying to wake him, except he was already awake, or at least that's how it felt. He turned his head slightly and a bright square patch of light swam into view, then coalesced into a summer window, like the one in his room at the Pittman Academy. A picture of that nice lady appeared in his head, Mrs. Pittman, no she preferred to be called Aunty Dot. That made her happy. He liked to help people. It made him upset when he couldn't help people. That's why he had to take Aunty Dot's medicine, he could help lots of people if he took it. A face moved towards him covering the window, refocusing his mind he could see the figure becoming Aunty Dot.

"Aunty Dot?"

"That's right, but what do other people call me?" came the voice from Aunty Dot's face. It seemed slightly odd.

"*People call you Mrs. Pittman,*" thought Miles out loud, and then added helpfully, "*or Dorothy.*"

"*And what should I call you, Mr...Benton?*"

"*You can always call me Miles,*" he said and remembered something that made him laugh, "*I'm Miles, Ahead.*"

He couldn't understand why she didn't appear to be laughing, she seemed to have found it funny a moment ago, when she had given him the present for his fourth birthday.

"*I kept your present safe, Aunty Dot, and I never spent it, it's a special coin.*"

"*Do you mean this coin Miles?*" she said holding out a silver dollar that appeared to be sharper than anything else in the room. Sharper, even, than Aunty Dot herself. He could see the embossed picture of the bell and the moon with crystal clarity.

"*Yes,*" he found himself telling her whilst studying the coin, "*it means I am to help people keep their liberty, and protect our people on the moon.*"

"*And what do those words, E Pluribus Unum, mean to you, Miles?*"

"*It's Latin,*" he found himself proudly telling her, "*it means 'Out of many, one' because you said I'm special.*"

"*You are special Miles,*" said Aunty Dot's face. Now she presented him with a silver case, which looked as vivid as the coin. He flipped open the case and ran his finger along the groove in one half. It was hard and cold to the touch.

"*For the good of Mankind,*" he heard himself say.

"*Very good, Miles.*"

There was something unbalanced about the case, and he realised that all the vials were missing. For some reason he felt a rising sense of panic, but she must have seen his discomfort.

"It's OK, Miles, I have plenty more," she patted him on the hand.

"It helps me to help others," he heard his own voice say.

Aunty Dot smiled benignly and he felt the anxiety begin to drift away.

"I'll get you some more, but could you help me first, Miles?"

"Of course, I like it when I help you."

"Very good," she patted him on the hand again, "you are very special, and clever, and I know you can help me."

She was looking at a newspaper now.

"I'm trying to work out the answer to a crossword clue."

Miles liked puzzles. He enjoyed fitting things together, and seeing patterns.

"What's the clue, Aunty Dot?"

"Well I'm not sure. It has two words. Six letters in the first word, and four in the second," said Aunty Dot, studying the newspaper, "Oh excuse me Miles, the phone is ringing."

He hadn't heard any ringing but he watched as she raised what looked like a walkie talkie to her ear. It was slightly odd because it didn't appear to have an aerial. There was something very familiar about it though.

"Please," she was saying into the phone, "I said I didn't want to be disturbed, I'm with my good friend Miles. We're solving a puzzle together."

Miles felt a warm feeling flood over him, like happiness filling his very veins.

"Oh dear," she was saying into the cell phone. He didn't know how he knew the name of the walkie talkie phone but it seemed right. He could see the phone was making her unhappy.

"Is everything OK, Aunty Dot?"

"I'm speaking to the people on the moon, Miles, and they say the crossword answer is very important to them too. Can you help them solve it Miles? Six. Four."

If it would make her happy and help the people on the moon, then he would try his best. He looked at the phone and thought about an important message. The answer arranged itself obediently in his mind and he beamed from ear to ear. He liked to help others.

"Aunty Dot, is the answer Fallen Veil?"

"They heard you Miles, and they think you're right!"

Her smile gave him a warm glowing feeling all through his body.

"They ask, what does it mean on Earth?" she smiled down at him.

"It means we can tell everyone how we're going to help them," he said, proud that he could be so supportive, "We don't need to keep secrets anymore."

"Except The Node, of course," said Aunty Dot, "surely?"

Miles nodded his head enthusiastically. Aunty Dot was right, no one must know about the Node. He pictured a busy military base, hidden away at the top of the globe, and he started to feel chilly.

"Is it cold in Iceland, Aunty Dot?" he said.

"Whereabouts in Iceland?"

"Öskjuvatn Lake."

"Oh yes, it's very cold here, Miles," she smiled, "That's why we have to keep you all tucked up and cosy in your bed."

Miles looked out of the window, it wasn't summer any more, and it wasn't the window from the Pittman Academy.

"What can you see, here at The Node, Miles?" came her voice.

Miles strained to look out of the window, but all he could see was white.

"I… I can't see anything, Aunty Dot!" he began to panic, "It's all blank. White."

"Shh!" came her soothing voice, once more, "It's OK, Miles, the window shutters are closed."

That made him feel much better.

"Now," Aunty Dot squeezed his hand, "I'm going to let you rest, we've got a big day ahead of us Miles, and I'm just sure that I'll need your help again."

"I like to help, Aunty Dot," he smiled. He could already feel a warm sensation flooding all through him, telling him it was OK to sleep.

He could hear her voice continuing to talk, and he let the words into his mind without resistance.

DEEPER

11th March 2013

Very early on it was known that for the majority of the global population, the best hope of surviving the moments after a comet strike would be to hide deep underground. With this in mind, William Pittman's name had been placed at the top of an Archive list of wealthy individuals who already had potentially useful assets.

The Pittman family had large enough financial resources to help kick-start Archive itself, but if all else failed they also owned deep mining operation sites which could be used to temporarily shelter large numbers underground. Whether there would be a habitable surface to return to afterwards was, of course, another matter.

Discussions had inevitably turned to the idea of prolonging the period of subterranean survival, in effect creating generational bunkers; but with Archive resources stretched thin during the initiation of the Apollo program, it was agreed that ploughing resources into the development of tunnelling machinery would have to wait.

Having a flair for perceiving the chaotic patterns within nature, Monica Dean excelled in her field of geology. Archive put her to good use in advising the route, and then later project managing, the Eurotunnel; a rail network running under the English Channel between Dover and Calais in France. Archive learned a great many lessons from the project; in fact the resulting gargantuan tunnel-boring machines had also paved the way for the creation of other networks and subterranean caverns worldwide.

Another lesson learned was that, like water finding its way through tiny fissures in rock, Monica had a habit of finding ways into things that shouldn't concern her.

Monica had crossed paths with Douglas Walker at a fairly sombre party on New Year's Eve 1979. The event itself had been organised by Archive following an earlier briefing attended by those on a high priority evacuation order. In the event of an emergency before the completion of the underground survival villages, delegates were briefed on how to reach the closest nuclear bunker. The party had done little to raise spirits.

Monica and Douglas realised during their conversations that, although their approaches differed greatly, they saw solutions in very similar ways. What Douglas would visualise as a set of cumulative options, Monica would see as paths of least resistance. In an attempt to compartmentalise, Archive had tried to intervene in their fraternisation but were met with Monica's unobtrusive persistence. Four months later they were married.

After the completion of the Eurotunnel in 1993, Archive began work extending the tunnel on the UK side and excavating an artificial cavern, two hundred metres below Dover.

In preparation for her family's exit from Archive, Monica continued to direct, and where necessary misdirect, the project; adding extra tunnels and supports where she needed them to be. Nothing she did had compromised the integrity of the generational bunker, it had simply assisted in the creation of her own smaller, but parallel, ecosystem. In 2000, after a staged collapse of one of the side tunnels in the main bunker, Monica and Douglas began their negotiations to leave Archive, whilst continuing to make preparations for the time ahead.

Since leaving Archive, her preparations had continued apace, and the parallel underground facility she had helped to build was now nearing completion. While there was still free oxygen to breathe above ground, she had allowed the personnel to come and go, but in the next few minutes she would have to decide if she wanted to recall everyone. Her interrogation of Miles Benton a few moments ago seemed to confirm that Archive were indeed about to reveal everything to an unsuspecting world.

In a separate room, Marcus and Kate had watched through an observation window as Monica had spoken at length with Benton. The short conversation had taken well over an hour, with Monica seeming to deliberate over how to phrase the next question or statement, but when it was over she swiftly left the room, prompting Marcus to depart the observation room with almost equal speed.

"D'you mind explaining what the hell that was?" he called, catching up with Monica who was walking swiftly down the chalky, rough-hewn tunnel.

"Autosuggestive interrogation," said Monica, without breaking her stride, "with luma stimulation and a mild hallucinogen."

Kate had caught up with them both just in time to hear her reply.

"You're talking about hypnosis!" said Kate incredulously, her voice echoing down the hard walls.

"Certainly not!" said Monica ducking under a low hanging lighting cable, "Why would we want to put anything *into* his head? We want to read what's already there. No, we manipulate the environment, provide the right personal belongings, and he fills in the blanks."

Monica made a sudden turn left off the tunnel and they followed her into a small space, where a small, bearded man was reviewing the interrogation on a set of monitors.

"Well?" said Monica directly to him, as though continuing a conversation.

"I'd say there's no doubt," he replied, then glanced at Marcus and Kate with a quizzical expression.

"Yes, sorry," said Monica acknowledging the need for introductions, "This is Woods, he handles our, how should I put it? Arrivals and acclimatisation program."

Through a small flurry of handshakes in different combinations she added, "This is my daughter Kate, and her security advisor Marcus."

Marcus wasn't sure how he felt being called a security advisor, but it seemed an accurate, if somewhat emotionless, summation of his role so far.

"Anyway," continued Woods, "I'd say he's definitely an ego-morph, the vials tested positive for metathene; and then there's 'fallen veil', the very important message. I'd say Archive's about to shift into damage limitation."

"But at least now we know that Archive want to keep The Node secret, whatever it is," said Monica, "And that gives us our leverage back. We have confirmation of the Icelandic location, even if he's never been to The Node itself."

"Sorry?" asked Marcus, "How do we know he ain't been there?"

"Subjects tend to view the white square as a window, and that normally gives us a read on what they're experiencing," explained Woods, "he saw the back-lit white square in the Arrivals Room as plain white. There was no detail, it's not in his memory."

"Couldn't he be, y'know, faking it?" pursued Marcus.

"Through that much acid?" Woods snorted, "Not likely. The whole Aunty Dot fixation thing is odd though."

"Not really," countered Monica, "Dorothy Pittman ran the original Archive Academy. If he was deemed bright enough it's possible she selected him specifically for this role. In fact, given the importance he seemed to place on that coin,

I'm pretty sure she must have known the family very well. That gives us something to work with."

"Wait a minute," interrupted Marcus who had spotted a knowing look pass between Monica and Woods, "Ain't we got what we needed? Shouldn't it be, like, 'Thanks Mr. Killer, now kindly piss off'? What's all this about 'work with'?"

Monica made sure she had eye contact with Kate before replying to Marcus.

"I know that *Benton* has put you both through hell," she took care to emphasise his name, "but we - "

"But what, Mum? Marcus is right, he's dangerous, we should - "

"Hand him over to the *Authorities?*" Monica completed with a slight note of derision in her voice, then turned to Marcus, "Drop him off in the forest and hope he doesn't find his way back? I'm afraid we are *way* beyond that, we can't simply let him go."

Monica walked a step closer to the monitor showing Benton asleep in the other room.

"We have an *actual* ego-morph. In our possession. There *has* to be a way we can *use* him."

Woods started to catch on, and began tugging at the hair on his chin, "Hmm, it's possible that before all *this* he was just a really bright kid, but his psych-profile does seem rooted in a fundamental need to please. I suppose, if there was a way we could redirect that impulse, indoctrinate an alternative meaning for the imagery on his coin..."

"Can you even hear yourselves?" interrupted Kate, "Mum, tell me you're not actually talking about brainwashing?"

"Well, I wouldn't put it quite like - ".

"What if it went *wrong*?!" she shouted, her voice echoing off the rough walls.

Outside the room, fast-moving footsteps preceded the arrival of the young man they had met earlier.

"Yes Dawson, what is it?"

"It's the broadcast Ma'am," he threw a thumb over his shoulder, "It's starting."

"OK, everyone follow me," said Monica heading for the doorway, "Dawson, send the word out, get our people back here."

"Everyone?"

"Yes, everyone. And tell them to bring any supplies they can lay their hands on."

NIGHT SHIFT

25th December 2013

Leonard let out a long stream of loud, vicious words, screaming his anger into the confined space of the helmet around his head. Before Eva had cut him off, their dialogue over the comm panel had told him all he needed to know; he'd been manipulated.

He'd put on the spacesuit in case Eva's mental state persuaded her to vent the FLC chambers to the vacuum of space. When he'd attempted to contact Lana via the spacesuit's comms, all the channels had been filled with static. It seemed that Eva had also disrupted all the FLC's communications.

He felt utterly betrayed by both Eva and himself. Even at this great distance from Earth, primitive biological programming had asserted itself, overpowering his logic and convincing him that Eva actually had feelings for him.

Before him, Floyd's control console in Chamber 6 lay dormant. An accusing light flashed on and off to tell him repeatedly that the auxiliary console within the Drum had taken control. Leonard knew that transferring Floyd's access point required the consent of all the crew, or more specifically their ID keys. If Eva had all the keys then she also had complete access to the FLC's functions; a situation he was unwilling to accept.

Despite his best efforts to re-acquire Floyd's processing cores, so far he had only managed to access the lighting system. It might annoy Eva to strobe the lights throughout the FLC, he thought, but it was unlikely that she would open the Drum door to tell him to stop.

Without his ID key, he was powerless.

A thought suddenly struck him. It had the added benefit of definitely annoying Eva too.

•

Earlier that day, the traditional Christmas video call to the crew of the Floyd Lunar Complex had taken place. Alongside everyone else in the Houston Mission Control room, Lawrence Clark had watched the White House up-link that had commended the FLC crew. The President had delivered a heartfelt thanks for their continued guardianship of the most important task ever to be entrusted to the human race. Then everyone had simply resumed their mundane duties.

Lawrence scraped a few more unappetising morsels of over-microwaved turkey from the plastic tray, then added the last of his tiny roast potatoes to the mix.

"Merry Christmas, Larry," he grumbled to himself, shovelling the flimsy plastic spoon into his mouth. He looked around the Houston Mission Control Room and shook his head despondently. The state of disrepair, as with life in general, seemed to surround him. The glory days seemed hopelessly lost now, part of a more optimistic era.

He could see others who, despite being on duty for the 'Santa-shift', were already crawling under desks to their sleeping bags. The reality was that nobody checked, but he'd always had a strong work ethic, and prided himself on doing his best.

Before Archive had revealed its plan, he had been lecturing students in quantum mechanics at M.I.T.

Now he watched data.

In the cramped cubicles surrounding him, every one of his neighbours held at least one doctorate. He took some solace from the fact that his qualifications, though totally over-powered for the actual task, were at least providing him with food and shelter.

He returned his attention to the console in front of him. It was his lowly task to observe a continuous stream of data coming back from the FLC. Not the interesting data, he would be the first to admit, like voice comms or the Siva deflection system, but the more background grey-data of CO_2 levels, power consumption and sleep-cycles taken by the crew.

Not that he minded.

Since the great collapse, any work was better than none. Looking at this data all day long, all Christmas Day long, was better than the alternative. The fact of the matter was that people were cheap and plentiful, and therefore replaceable.

He had to keep telling himself that he was one of the lucky ones. All he had to do was watch over the data and he would be paid enough Habitation tokens to sustain him. If he worked hard, he may even earn enough Habs to enter the Lifeboat lottery.

If he stopped to think about it for too long he realised how unfair it all was. But in his experience, humans had always operated well on the basis of inequality of wealth. Whether he liked it or not, Archive had ensured that life had regained its purpose. Out of the depression that had followed the threat of global annihilation, once again people were fighting for their chance to survive; a Darwinian natural selection accelerated for a modern era.

On a display in front of him was a mostly horizontal line. He knew that in extreme close up, the line itself was not perfectly straight, it had a slight wave to it. This was normal, as it represented the internal power consumption of the FLC; as the crew slept or came on shift, the power would dip or rise accordingly. The display was set to cycle through a series of magnification levels, so that it could be easily seen if there was an over-voltage, or power outage.

Lawrence sat and stared at bluish glow of the display. There were worse jobs he supposed.

The horizontal line dipped to half its normal output, then returned to normal.

At first Lawrence thought it might have been a transmission glitch, where the signal from the FLC had been affected by some atmospheric anomaly. The display continued to cycle though its magnification levels, and at the scale he was now viewing, he could see no evidence of the drop.

"This has gotta be a...." he trailed off, switching the display to focus only on the zoomed-in level. There, clearly displayed, was the drop, followed by the continuous line again.

To his surprise, the horizontal line dipped again to half its normal output, remained at the lower level for a second, then returned to normal. Lawrence was now looking at two, separate, inverted spikes on the display. He watched for several minutes, and soon the original two spikes began to move off the left hand edge of the screen. Pretty soon he would almost be able to convince himself that he'd hallucinated the whole thing, which given the strength of the accumulated human body odour in the room, was an actual possibility.

Suddenly the spikes reappeared and more regularly now. As he studied the screen it began to dawn on him what it meant.

He glanced around the dimly lit room as casually as possible at the neighbouring cubicles to make sure that no one else had been watching. He could hear a few muffled coughs from the dark side of the room, but most had now adopted foetal positions under their desks or in corners, seeking the oblivion of sleep.

He turned again to look at the screen. This information had a material value for the person that discovered it, and he was determined that the person to report it would be him. He thought for a moment about how many Habs he could bargain for, without appearing to be a mercenary; maybe he could even get a private shower token. The spikes were persistent, he had something valuable.

He captured a screen-shot of the spikes, saved the image then turned off the display's power. As an added precaution he unplugged the power cable from the back, then quietly made his way out of the control room to the supervisor's office.

If anything, the corridors were slightly worse. Where fluorescent tubes had failed they had never been replaced, and others flickered on the brink of dying. The emergency lighting was always on now, giving the stale atmosphere a green-blue tint. His foot caught someone's sleeping bag, one of a series lining the left hand side of the corridor, but there was no reaction from its occupant - people were used to it now.

"Sorry," he whispered, more out of habit than anything else.

Three doors down was Todd Baker's office, he gave a polite knock and waited. After a few seconds there had been no response, so he knocked on the supervisor's door again.

The door suddenly opened a few inches and Todd's red face appeared, back-lit by a dim red light saturating the office beyond.

"What?" he panted, wiping white powder from under his nose.

Lately, Archive had turned a blind eye to matters of personal vice, as long as the task was accomplished they saw no reason to intervene; people were cheap to replace. In fact Lawrence had heard rumours that Archive themselves had controlling interests in all sorts of narcotics and mind-altering drugs. It made sense to him, with currencies being effectively rendered useless, the world had begun trading material assets again. Previously banned substances traded very well with a population wanting to mentally escape reality.

Lawrence hesitated too long.

"Speak, dipshit!" he sniffed.

"Sorry, Mr. Baker, Sir," apologised Lawrence, unnecessarily.

"Can't you see I'm right in the middle of someone?"

A girlish giggle came from somewhere behind the door, and Lawrence caught on. Todd had always made life difficult for everyone, using the position of supervisor to make them miserable. It was well known that he routinely docked Habs from everyone's pay, funnelling the excess into his own wallet. However, the chances that Baker's drug-addled brain would remember any of this conversation in the morning were slim, and Lawrence spotted an opportunity.

"Just wanted to wish you a *very* Merry Christmas, Sir," Lawrence smiled.

To a tirade of slurred expletives the door was slammed in his face.

Wasting no time, Lawrence sped down the corridor to find the Communications Director. His discovery was massive, and the more he thought about it, he was glad that

Todd had passed up the opportunity to listen. Hab tokens be damned, he thought, he'd have Baker's Lifeboat Pass for this.

•

Mike tried to quickly assess the useful contents of Chamber 4. Mostly, it contained the exercise equipment designed to protect the astronauts against both muscle atrophy and loss of bone-mass. There was also a modest sized area designed to hold the Z-bank, a genetic zygote super-sample of the biology of Earth. Under normal circumstances it drew its minimal power requirements from the chamber's electrical supply, but it also had a small internal power unit in case of external power failure. There were small evac-packs stuck to the wall in case of emergencies.

"What's your end game, Eva?" Mike said out loud for his own benefit.

If she had wanted to kill the crew, Mike knew there were easier ways. This meant her focus was the station itself. The purposeful locking out of the crew from the command centre seemed to support this. He automatically reached for his ID key, and realised with horror that he'd left it inserted in the Drum's auxiliary control panel when he'd left to deal with Cathy. Eva had planned this down to the last detail. Protocol dictated that all ID keys were kept within the FLC during moonwalks, so Lana would have left hers, which presumably meant that Eva now had it. He had definitely lost his key and perhaps, in the altercation with Eva, Cathy had lost hers. He couldn't tell where Leonard's allegiances lay, but it was now entirely feasible that Eva was in possession of *all* the ID keys. She could have full control of the station.

Abruptly the lights in the chamber went off and then, after a second, came on again.

"What are you doing?" he mumbled to himself. It appeared that she'd begun tampering with the lighting system.

In the brief darkness he'd noticed that the airlock panel had remained powered. The panel displayed a message:

'Diagnostic 1 of 1 - complete.'

He deduced that after locking Cathy in, Eva must have put the airlock into a diagnostic mode that ran through one complete cycle. The external door had opened, allowing Cathy to exit the FLC, then it had automatically closed again; after repressurising the airlock, the internal door had unlocked, completing the diagnostic.

After checking through the airlock's available options it seemed that Eva had remotely disabled the normal functions. But although he couldn't manually control the opening and closing of the airlock, he found that he could get the airlock to run a *series* of diagnostic cycles.

"The trouble is, Eva," he said, hurriedly keying in the new instructions, "you're arrogant enough to believe that no-one else can think like you."

He unhooked the long metal bar from the elastic resistance exercise bench, returned to the Drum door, and wedged it under the door handle. He unplugged the Z-bank, which instantly emitted a low-pitched, pathetic warning tone, and then he grabbed an evac-pack.

He took one last look around Chamber 4. The lights went out again, this time for slightly longer, before flickering back on.

"Always hated the Gym anyway."

He pushed the activation button on the panel and stepped swiftly inside the airlock with his luggage. The panel lit up with its new instructions.

'Diagnostic 1 of 999 - active'.

CELL

18th August 2013

Kate opened her eyes and saw that she was obviously in a holding cell, complete with bars and a food tray slot at the base of the door. The cell itself was barely big enough to hold the uncomfortable, hard, military-issue single bunk, and a single pace separated the bunk from the bars. The area beyond the bars was almost a mirror image of the cell she occupied, except that the blank grey walls were broken by a door that lead out of the holding room.

She heard footsteps approaching that door, and stood to face the bars. As the door opened inwards she could hear a brief exchange.

"But Mr. Benton, General Napier instructed me to wait outside the door."

"And did he also instruct you to hide that MP3 player in your top left pocket? Is that standard issue, or an unauthorised home comfort from your wife… no, not wife… girlfriend? Does your wife know?"

An embarrassed silence was followed by the sound of footsteps retreating as the sergeant marched to the other end of the corridor.

The familiar, calm figure closed the door purposefully behind him.

"I want to see my father!" she grasped the bars.

"That's good, Kate," he intoned, "They can see us, but they can't hear us."

She shook the bars again and turned her back on him.

"You're sure, Miles?" she said.

"Absolutely," said Miles, "I've checked the recording station next door already. Vision only."

"So, you think Napier bought my faint?"

Miles had triggered the exact timing of Kate's earlier feigned collapse from the chair by leaning and pointing at Napier. For someone as physically reserved as Miles, the action had signalled Kate to start the next stage of their plan; but to Napier it would have appeared as normal body language.

"Yes, and thanks to your superbly delivered outrage in his office, he leaked a fair bit of information."

"So do you know where my dad is?"

"And more. The camera's still recording, sit down or something."

Kate sat down on the edge of the bunk and faced Miles, then leaned forward to cradle her head in her hands, to conceal her face.

"When you stressed him about the Node," he continued, "his eyes flickered in a completely different direction to the one when you accused him of holding your father. I've had chance to absorb the layout of the base now, and from the shift patterns I think your dad is in a new-built hangar about a hundred yards from here."

Kate smiled into her cupped hands.

"There's something else though," Miles hesitated, "My observation may not be as sharp now, but - "

"But what, Miles?"

"It was just a flicker on Napier's face. It's possible that your dad thinks he's working *with* them, not *for* them."

"All the more reason to get him out," said Kate.

"Napier was lying about your dad being on an expedition - "

"Yeah, I think I worked that one out for myself Miles," she interrupted.

"But I think he was telling the truth about when he'd be back. I think your dad will emerge from that hangar before the day is out, and I'll arrange to intercept him."

"What about me?" she asked, getting up and prowling back and forth alongside the bars.

He placed the mug of tea he had been holding carefully on the ground and, using his foot, slid it through the food slot under the cell door.

"Seriously? You're giving me tea?"

"Just make sure you don't choke on the sergeant's key at the bottom of the mug," he smiled looking at the lock on her cell door, "When you've emptied the mug, hide the key and lie still on the bunk for a count of two hundred and twenty."

"Security camera loop?" she guessed, still pacing back and forth.

"I'm hoping it won't come to that, but yes, something like that," said Miles and left the room.

Kate dutifully drank her tea, manoeuvring the key with her tongue to put it between her teeth and cheek; both the tea and key tasted horribly metallic. She lay down on the bunk and started counting, when she hit two hundred and twenty, she continued to lie still. But shortly after she reached three hundred, she heard the sound of a distant siren.

DAY 689

18AUG2013+45.56 : DAY 689.0

Dim safety lighting within the Mark 3 allowed Anna to see well enough to walk from the top of the spiral stairs towards the observation window. She could see it was dark in the hangar beyond, the lighting system having dipped to black to simulate night.

Not wanting to wake Douglas downstairs, she carefully pulled out the chair from under the desk and lowered herself into it. She checked her watch and then turned on the console display in front of her. The iterative simulations were still running, slowly making their way towards deriving the equations necessary to calculate Field inversion. Once this was achieved, the Node could be made ready to make its leap over an entire epoch, within one generation.

The sheer number of permutations within the base field geometry equations were so high that all they could predict was a probable time to reach a solution. Both Anna and Douglas had agreed that a solution before ninety percent of the permutations were tried was unlikely; but they were honing in now, the number of evaluations currently stood at ninety-six percent. In theory the solution could happen any time from now until their power ran out in about forty days.

She heard a beep and immediately checked the screen again.

With a little disappointment, she realised that it wasn't the console that had emitted the tone, but the watch on her wrist. She tried to read it in the feeble glow of the safety lighting, but resorted to angling it towards the somewhat brighter console display.

She smiled at the date through watery eyes, "Lycklig femtionde, Anna," she said softly to herself.

When she had entered the Field with Douglas almost two years ago, she had allowed her digital watch to continue marking time in the normal fashion. Although the date outside in the hangar had progressed through almost two days, her watch read 7th July 2015. For Anna it was significant for two reasons. Should Archive's efforts fail, then Siva's predicted impact date of April 1st 2015 meant that she had already, and quite literally, lived beyond her years. The second and perhaps more poignant reason was that it was her fiftieth birthday.

Long before they had entered the Field, Douglas had once mentioned that marking an arbitrary number of solar orbits since first drawing independent breath should have no more significance than any other day. She found it hard to argue with his logic, and while inside the Field she hadn't marked her previous birthday in any obvious way. She knew that it would only be a distraction from their work and on a personal level it would also have made Douglas feel awkward.

Today, at this moment, in the extreme isolation of the Field she found it a comfort to indulge in a little sentimentality. She reflected on her past half-century, over half of which had been spent in the pursuit and research of this very Field. As far as she could see, Douglas had been mentally engaged with the Field all of his life; but she could still remember the day it had all changed for *her*. The day her parents had told her the truth about the approach of Siva and the need for her to contribute to Archive's solution.

Although life didn't necessarily get any harder after that, the knowledge seemed to alter her. It was as though an invisible burden had been placed on her ten-year-old shoulders, albeit a burden shared by many others. But like most of Archive's children, the burden of knowledge never unduly weighed her down; she was, after all, directly involved with the solution, and she found that the feeling of control was a positive force.

The Pittman Academy education she'd received in Sweden, along with the special supplements given to all pupils, had allowed her to focus and excel in all the academic subjects. She liked to think that even without the supplements she would still be just as bright, but it was a hypothesis she had no intention of testing now, particularly this close to the emergence of a Field solution. When she had asked Douglas why he never took supplements, he had said that he'd never needed to; and it certainly seemed to be true - he still appeared just as sharp as the day they had first met.

She straightened herself up and took a deep breath. The oxygen recycling worked well but it had a used smell to it, and she let it go with a sigh. The creaky ninth step she'd avoided on her way up the stairs sounded as Douglas reached the upper floor. She quickly ensured her eyes were dry and turned to study the Field calculations on the screen. Douglas ambled over and stood over her shoulder.

"I didn't mean to wake you," she apologised.

He patted her shoulder.

"Looklig Femtioarsday, Anna," he said, slightly hesitantly, "Did I pronounce that right?"

Her laugh caught in her throat, "Near enough! How did you… I mean… I didn't - "

"…celebrate it last year," Douglas completed, "You didn't say anything on the day, so I thought it best not to draw attention to it, in case it was, er, sensitive. But I couldn't let this one slide…"

He brought his other hand from around his back to present her with a gift.

"Variation on a theme," he said presenting the plate for her inspection, "Sorry I couldn't light them. But, you know, oxygen, fire hazard…"

Before her was a small ration of cake. In the top of the cake were three, small, wax birthday candles. Now that she looked more closely she could see they were the exact same candles she had used for *his* cake, over two years ago. Similarly, he had arranged them in a binary pattern of candles and holes to represent her age.

"You kept my candles?" she smiled through glassy eyes.

Douglas shrugged sheepishly, "Sorry you can't blow them out."

She puffed up her cheeks and blew across the black, brittle wicks of the candles.

"Don't forget to make a wish," said Douglas embellishing the charade.

She closed her eyes for several seconds, then opened them.

"Well?" he enquired, "Did it work?"

She turned to face the console.

"No," she smiled, tapping the screen, "Ninety-six *point two*. I guess we have to stay in here a little longer."

"Good," he said dryly, "I hear that the restaurant serves an excellent ration pack 689A."

"Really?" she joined in, "I've heard that the waiters are rude to anyone over fifty…"

Over an early breakfast the two of them discussed their ages, both in terms of the time that had passed for the rest of the world, and their own personal timeline. For Anna, she had entered the Field in her forties but would emerge from it in her fifties.

"It just makes me feel…"

"Old?" chipped in Douglas.

"I was going to say, what is the word in English? Obsolete."

"Hmm, I know what you mean," said Douglas though a mouthful of freeze-dried ice cream.

"Assuming we're successful in calculating the inversion," she explained, "when we get out of here, Archive will have a full set of Field Equations. Why would they need to keep us around once they have the information they need? I mean we're both pretty old, why save us a space aboard the Node?"

"I've been thinking about that," Douglas nodded and sat back.

"Any ideas?"

On more than one occasion Douglas and Monica had discussed the territory inside the triangle of Truth, Bluff and Insurance. Douglas had never been comfortable with the idea of deceit, but not in any moralistic sense. He just found it harder to factor the concept of false positives into his logical deduction.

"Yes, but I think I'll need your help."

COOPERATION

25th December 2013

Lana unclipped herself from the rover and made giant leaping strides over to the airlock of Chamber 4. Since last seeing the airlock on her return from the scrubber station, a second astronaut had joined the first outside the FLC. She couldn't tell who they were, because they were facing each other with their helmets pressed together. It took just a moment for Lana to recall some of her basic training.

With the FLC radio transmitting only static, and sound unable to travel in a vacuum, conventional communication was all but impossible. But by physically pressing together the hard glass surfaces of their face-plates the tiny contact area would allow the transmission of vibrations from one to the other. Provided they maintained contact, then by shouting they would be just about audible to each other.

Peripherally spotting her approach, the two turned to face her and she could see that it was Mike and Cathy. Cathy had a bleeding cut down her cheek, and both had deeply furrowed eyebrows. This changed matters considerably; with three of the crew now outside the FLC this constituted an emergency. She slowed her approach and beckoned them to huddle together, face-plates in three-way contact with each other.

"Situation report," she shouted.

"Eva's taken control," Mike called back, "We are locked out. FLC and Lima relay comms are down."

"Houston?"

"No. As far as we know, they have no idea."

"Cooper?"

"We don't know where Leonard - " started Mike.

"He's probably with that bitch!" interrupted Cathy, wincing at the pain in her cheek.

"Stop!" shouted Lana, "Assets?"

They were just piecing together their list of combined resources when they noticed the lights in the airlock behind them flicker off, and then back on again.

"I don't know what she's doing in there, but it cannot be good," said Lana.

"I told you," came Cathy's voice, "she was raving on about making a new Earth by burning the old one. I tell you, she's going to take out the FLC, so Siva can hit!"

The lights continued to turn on and off.

"Mike, what do you think?" Lana questioned, "Mike?"

Mike left the huddle and hastily grabbed the message board from his waistband, never once taking his eyes off the airlock window and the light inside it, and started to jot something down. The other two joined him to look at his notes. For every few bursts of light coming from the window he was writing down a new letter. Noticing them watching, he jotted a quick note across the top of the board:

'*Morse*' the scribbled message read, followed by the capital letters he had already decoded:

'*SOS FLC SOS*'.

After about twenty seconds the much longer complete message cycled. Mike realised it was Cooper's work and grinned as the lights continued to flick on and off. With all other forms of communication with Earth cut off, it was a long shot; but hopefully someone back on Earth was watching their power output.

EMERGENCE

18th August 2013

Steven Pike manned his station, keeping a close eye on the Mark 3's output levels. He'd lost track of the number of day-night cycles that the hangar had gone through, but currently it was daylight hours and would remain that way for another two minutes. Taking advantage of the light, Roy Carter tiptoed back over from the coffee stand.

"Hey," said Carter, handing him the plastic cup filled with lukewarm coffee, "that's the last of it."

"Good man," said Pike.

The two of them sat and watched quietly. From time to time a fast moving shadow would flicker past the window, or one of the lower level port-holes.

"How many you got so far?" said Carter, pointing at the observation window.

"Seventeen."

"What?"

"No, straight up," insisted Pike, "check my tally pad. I spotted the pair of them at the same window. Twice. "

"Bullshit, you did not!" said Carter, grabbing Pike's piece of paper to check.

"So that's fifteen, plus two triple scores," Pike totted up, "That puts me at twenty-one points. Read it and weep."

To relieve the monotony of their observation duty, they had started to count the number of times they saw either Douglas or Anna at one of the windows. The accelerated time frame within the Mark 3 made it quite a challenge and it wasn't long before they were competing with each other, and with the other shifts, to rack up the highest number of sightings.

"Shut up," said Carter, looking on at the window.

"No, I think that's a record -"

"Shut up! Why's the window grey?"

"Grey?" said Pike turning to face it, and saw the problem immediately, "Oh shit! Smoke!"

He slammed the 'Abort' button, immediately switching the hangar's lighting system into a fast strobe.

The purpose of the strobe was to alert those on the inside, but it also had the effect of triggering an alarm throughout the hangar and its neighbouring buildings. The siren split the air and within five seconds the hangar doors were being dragged open from the outside.

Carter dashed across the floor towards the Mark 3's airlock.

"Stop!" Pike shouted above the continual bark of the alarm, "The Field's still up!"

Carter skidded to a halt just outside a circle painted on the floor, then whipped around and dashed back to a nearby medical rack to grab a handheld oxygen cylinder. Colonel Beck arrived alongside him, dragging deep breaths, followed by the fire crew.

"Internal fire, Sir!" gasped Carter in brief explanation, then turned to shout, "Pike, how're we doing?"

"Not yet! Field's still up!"

"Charge the hoses!" Beck bellowed at the fire crew, "Damn it, they're going to burn before we can get 'em out!"

"Pike!" yelled Carter.

"No... wait... Field Collapse! Fifty percent! They've turned off the Field! They're alive!"

"Or they were, twenty minutes ago," muttered Beck, aware that for Douglas and Anna, time was moving faster.

"Hoses charged, Sir!" came a voice from within the fire crew.

The alarm and strobe lighting suddenly stopped, leaving the hangar in silence. The churning of smoke within the Mark 3 was now detectable rather than just a fast grey blur, but it was completely noiseless.

"Ten percent! They're slowing!" shouted Pike, "Fire crew, stand by!"

The pattern of smoke slowed again, and Pike could see flames now through the lower deck window. The Field, although weak, was still in place so there was still no sound accompanying the broiling inferno within.

"I see them!" yelled Carter, "They're in the airlock!"

"Hoses ready!" Beck directed the crew, "Airlock side, move it!"

"Five percent!" shouted Pike, "Four… Three… Two, oh damn! Get d-"

The Field collapsed, and the air from the hangar rushed in to feed the blaze, causing the Mark 3 windows to blow out and a ball of fire to erupt into the hangar. The heat, previously contained by the Field, rushed outwards along with the fire, rolled upwards into the roof space, and began to burn.

With his hearing replaced by a continuous whistle, Carter picked himself up from the floor. He had been standing in the shadow of the airlock during the decompression and had escaped the direct blast. Several of the fire crew had not been as fortunate, he could see Colonel Beck wrestling someone to the ground to smother out the flames on their clothing. Pike was waving wildly at him and pointing at the airlock.

Through the small porthole in the airlock door, Carter could see Anna frantically pulling at the internal door handle. He ran to it and pulled it hard. It started to move but a burning sensation in his hand forced him to let go; he should have realised that the metal was going to be hot. He gritted his teeth and, although he still couldn't hear his own voice, screamed loudly as he grabbed the handle again and pulled for all he was worth, the heat burning his hand the entire time. The airlock door suddenly gave way and he lost his grip; falling to the ground again he left a blackened layer of his own skin still attached to the handle.

Colonel Beck raced past him and caught Anna who was stumbling out of the airlock. Douglas tripped over the threshold after her and then helped Carter to his feet. Beck pushed all three of them in the direction of the open door, beyond which he could see General Napier briefing a small troop. To Napier's right was a man Beck hadn't seen before, wearing civilian clothing.

There was a flash of light from inside the Mark 3 accompanied by a low frequency shockwave in the ground, then the whole hangar shuddered and a burning panel fell from the ceiling, followed swiftly by two more. With large portions of the roof now missing, the convective effect of the heat escaping through the roof was causing more air to rush in through the open hangar doors, stoking the fire further.

The metalwork in the base of the Mark 3 started to sag under the thermal stress, and the tortured air began to carry a new high-pitched whine as the framework began to give way.

"Get out!" Beck yelled at Pike, who was crawling under the control desks to escape the falling debris.

The Mark 3 began to list and collapse to one side, then its momentum took over and started to roll the entire burning sphere slowly across the hangar floor. The hoses finally took a bite into the flames, but for the first few seconds the intensity of the heat simply converted the water directly to steam, reducing visibility in the hangar even further. Through the smoke and steam, Beck could just make out that the sphere had rocked itself to a halt lying on its side. He could also feel from the temperature that the vast quantities of water pumping into the hangar was having virtually no effect. Then a low persistent groan came from the roof.

"Fall back!" he yelled to the crew, and backed his way towards the exit.

The groan was suddenly replaced by sharp metallic snapping as the burning roof finally gave way. Half of it collapsed into the sphere below, and the remainder sliced through the control desks, crushing Pike in an instant.

Beck had seen death many times before, and no doubt would do so again, but the thing that haunted him most was the banality of it. The neutral expressions on faces that fully expected to live beyond that fatal moment.

Pike's face joined the others, and Beck turned to resume command.

DESCENT

4th July 2013

Monica's instinct to recall her personnel to the Dover facility had proved right. The broadcast announcing Siva's approach had triggered exactly the response that Archive had prepared for; as predicted it acted as the catalyst that allowed them to take control.

Three years previously, Alfred Barnes had headed a discussion group tasked with creating a mechanism to assume social control of a population. Manipulating the nuances, beliefs and ideologies of a population would require the simplest form of solution, so that each individual's self-preservation instincts would personally engage with it. The solution would also project the illusion of choice, and key into a primal fear, in order to motivate action.

The solution that Alfred Barnes devised was a simple one.

He suggested the creation of an Archive-funded terrorist organisation with ideologies that directly challenged Archive itself. Archive could be seen as a benefactor with a mandate to save humanity, whereas 'Exordi Nova' could be the menacing, unseen, foe.

The beauty, as Barnes had put it, was that with Archive controlling both sides of a war, Exordi Nova could be directed against any threat they wanted. As long as any attack could be interpreted as one against Archive's benevolence, they had another means to control people by force and fear.

Exordi Nova's first act was to publicly assassinate the British Prime Minister, shortly after his public address espousing Archive's Food and Shelter missions. World condemnation had been swift, as had Exordi's rise to prominence in the news. The exploding policeman's broken-circle tattoo began to appear all over Britain as large red graffiti; further spreading fear that Exordi Nova may be nearby. Neville Asquith went from harangued political leader to dignified martyr overnight. In terms of publicity, and an accelerated kick-start to Archive's usurping of power, they could not have hoped for better distributed propaganda. Through international news the symbol's effects quickly spread worldwide.

As the attacks continued to occur on seemingly random targets, news reports fanned the flames, pointing out that those carrying out the attacks were just normal people. The notion was sown that anybody could be Exordi Nova; your neighbour, your friends even your family.

Within one month of Fallen Veil, people's daily lives were dominated by multiple levels of fear. Most people experienced the fear of Archive failing to stop Siva, or the fear that Exordi Nova might strike at, or near you. But the greater fear was that of being labelled a 'Novaphile' by failing to report an Exordi Nova suspect.

It wasn't long before the need for vigilance twisted into the creation of vigilantes. Whilst governments encouraged and empowered people to report any suspected terrorist activity, they could no longer police the streets and were turning a blind eye to the execution of Novaphiles.

In addition to funding and recruiting for Exordi Nova, Archive recruited hundreds of thousands of people worldwide into jobs engaged in largely pointless activities. Though the size and scale varied, most of these enterprises revolved around people digging long, deep, tunnels in the dirt and then hand excavating rudimentary family shelters in the sides. Archive knew the facilities weren't deep enough or sturdy enough to escape a direct hit, but it supplied the shovels and electricity; it motivated people in their plight for self-preservation.

In Britain, alongside the wall-to-wall posters encouraging vigilance, others had popped up. Not seen since the end of the Second World War, the reappearance of posters proclaiming 'Dig for Victory' took on a new meaning. A few weeks ago, in an attempt to save power, street lighting had been turned off, further contributing to the war-time air of caution.

Marcus pulled the car in at the side of the road and turned off the headlights. The light rain drummed at the roof and ran down the windscreen, distorting the view. They were still a good hundred feet from the gate but he didn't want to attract attention.

"This is it," he said, somewhat redundantly.

"You sure?" said Kate, from the back seat, "Looks derelict."

"*Looks* derelict," said Miles, and got out of the car, dragging his rucksack with him.

The reprogramming of Miles Benton had taken over six weeks, and a further four to phase out the influence of the metathene he'd been indoctrinated to continually take. But even now, both Marcus and Kate were still not entirely convinced; he shot her a glance in the rear-view mirror after Miles had closed his door.

"I'm coming in with you."

"That's not the plan," she said, "Benton and -".

But he had already begun to exit the car.

"I hate it when he does that," she muttered, before getting out herself.

After a long and illustrious career, RAF Manston had closed in 1999. Its runway was the longest and widest in Southern England, but more importantly, being only twenty miles from Dover it was ideal as a departure point.

The thin sliver of moonlight allowed them to make out the entrance, where a dishevelled Spitfire aircraft now sat dormant and defaced; its RAF roundel graffitied with an additional dot in the outer circle. Kate and Marcus walked past it suppressing a sense of trepidation.

The gatehouse had been left to overgrow with weeds, and inside Kate could see that the road was peppered with potholes filled with rain.

"I hope the runway's in better shape," she said, pulling out her torch.

"I'm sure it will be," replied Miles, "Your mother is very thorough in such matters."

They walked the few hundred yards to the side of the runway and, as arranged, waited by a triangular orange flag staked into the ground. Marcus checked his watch and looked around nervously, the rain was continuing to drizzle making visibility poor. Quietly at first, then growing louder, a low engine noise came from the distance, and Marcus quickly turned to check the approach road.

"Torches off!" he hissed.

Kate complied quickly but, as far as Marcus could tell, Miles had switched his torch off before he'd even said anything. It was slightly unnerving to know that, even without his chemical assist, Miles seemed more focussed than Kate or himself.

The noise became louder, and Marcus realised that the sound was not coming from the road but from somewhere overhead. He turned his head in the general direction of the sound and saw a small pulse of dim, red light. Then, without warning, dozens of high-powered LED light clusters lit up along the edges of the runway. Spaced every fifty feet or so, they defined a long illuminated landing corridor in an otherwise pitch-black landscape. The engine noise from the approaching aircraft grew louder, but in the persistent rain they still couldn't see the plane itself; the blue-white LED light coming from the ground nearby had significantly reduced their night vision.

"It's the Cessna," said Miles.

"How can you even see..?" began Kate.

Miles just tapped his ear a few times.

Kate wasn't sure if it was the cold rain, or the slightly eerie up-lit effect on his face, but it caused her to shiver.

The pitch of the noise suddenly dropped and the single propeller Cessna 172 emerged through the rain and shot past them. A short squeal of rubber told them that the aircraft had made a swift touchdown.

"OK," said Marcus, turning Kate around to access her backpack, "Your mum said to give you this."

Kate felt him push something into one of the pockets.

"She said you'd understand when you open it," Marcus continued, turning her again to face him, "Don't ask me, I dunno. You take care of yourself, you get me?"

"I get you," she nodded, glancing over at Miles, who was busy watching the plane turning at the end of the runway.

"OK then," shrugged Marcus.

"Thank you, Marcus. I - ".

"Oh shut up," he exhaled, not knowing how to deal with the moment, "Just get back with your dad before the space rock does. Shouldn't be hard, you got, like, a year and a half."

The engine noise was returning now, so he turned to Miles.

"Benton?"

Miles turned to face him.

"You take care of her," he stared directly at him, "and just so's we're clear, I don't mean in the way that you would 'Take care of a problem', d'you know what I'm sayin'?"

"Marcus," Miles shook his head, "the man who pursued 'Blackbox' is gone. I remember him, and all of his... experiences... but he's not me."

The plane re-emerged from the rain; it rolled along the wet runway and stopped a few feet from them, the propeller idling at a low speed. Inside, they could see the pilot and one passenger.

"That'll be the new guest," said Marcus, straightening his jacket.

The man clambered awkwardly out of the small doorway holding a large, unwieldy suitcase, and walked towards them.

"Is that it?" asked Marcus, pointing at the suitcase.

The nervous looking man nodded, at this point he was obviously unsure who he should be talking to.

"Good. Wait over there," said Marcus, pointing back at the orange flag.

Without a backward glance, Miles swiftly manoeuvred himself and his rucksack aboard, leaving Kate and Marcus behind.

"Send word before you leave the Faroe Islands, yeah?"

"Will do," Kate replied, "Look after Mum?"

Abruptly the Pilot's window opened an inch.

"Any chance of us shiftin' a wee bit faster there?" came the thick, Scottish accent, shouting over the constant propeller noise, "We're lit up like a bloody Christmas tree out here!"

Less than a minute later, Marcus watched as the Cessna took off heading north. With the aircraft's transponder now out of range, the covert runway lighting deactivated again, leaving Marcus and his guest in the dark once more.

DRIVE

18th August 2013

Kate couldn't tell where the siren noise was coming from, but it was definitely outside.

"That's one hell of a signal, Miles," she muttered under her breath and tentatively stood up from the bunk, hoping that he had put the video security loop into place.

She pulled the foul-tasting key from inside her mouth and, threading her hands through the narrow bars, fitted it into the lock on the other side. The door unlocked easily and she stepped out of the holding cell. She walked as quietly as she could towards the door and slowly pulled it open. The siren became much louder now, and a quick check of the corridor confirmed that it was unguarded. Whatever it was that Miles had done to cause the distraction, she thought, appeared to have worked.

Ahead she could see a glass-panelled door with daylight visible beyond; a way out. She moved stealthily along the corridor, keeping to the side with the doors in it. She edged up to an open doorway and slowly tilted her head into the room.

The recording station was unoccupied, so she slid in.

She saw that the wall immediately behind the wastepaper bin was stained with coffee spatters. No doubt someone used the bin for target practice. Looking into the bin itself she saw that, in addition to coffee cups, it had several balled-up pieces of paper. That meant the room was usually manned.

"Not bad, Katie," she complimented herself on the deduction.

Her sense of triumph was short lived. With a creeping sense of dread she spotted the security monitor was displaying her *empty* holding cell with the door still left wide open. For some reason Miles hadn't looped the footage. Every aspect of her escape had been captured in detail.

The siren abruptly stopped.

"Think," she said out loud.

She could hear voices, some barking commands, and the sound of sprinting feet. Sprinting feet that were moving away. Good, she reasoned, they weren't for her then.

"They're gonna find you anyway," she whispered to herself.

Casting around for solutions she looked at the workstation. Next to the keyboard was an external hard drive, its tiny light blinking on and off in the surface of the black box.

Unbidden, the voice of Marcus Blake leapt into her head, *'Ditch the evidence.'*

On the other side of the desk she saw a stack of similar but disconnected drives. Either they had already been recorded on, or they were blank and ready to use. Steadying the stack, she pulled out the bottom one and swapped it with the one that was connected to the workstation. Immediately a message popped up on the screen:

'New media device detected, continue recording Y/N?'

She hit the 'Y' key, and then shuffled the original drive into position at the base of the stack.

She was suddenly distracted by the arrival of a new sound outside. A sound she couldn't readily identify, similar to thunder, but continuous, and much closer. She was just about to depart the room when she noticed the workstation screen:

'All media currently on the drive will be erased. Continue Y/N?'

"Yes! Just bloody *do* it will you?" she hissed, hitting the 'Y' key again.

In their haste to leave the room, whoever was on duty had left their coat behind. She grabbed it from the back of the chair and threw it on. Unsurprisingly it was several sizes too large, but it would have to do, she thought. It may still help her to blend in a little.

She left the room, walked swiftly along the corridor and cautiously pushed open the building door.

People were still running towards the commotion, and suddenly the smell hit her. Something was burning. The thunderous noise she had heard was the sound of a large-scale fire.

"Embrace the chaos, Katie," she said to herself, recalling something her mother used to say, then forced herself to go outside. She kept low to the ground and continually checked her surroundings. As she reached the end of the holding cell building, she saw it. A thick column of black and grey smoke rising into the sky, and beneath it was a large hangar, ablaze. The thought of her father somehow trapped inside the hangar, triggered her into a reaction; she knew she shouldn't do it, but couldn't help herself. The thought of losing her father, after all she had been through, was too much to bear, and she started running towards the burning hangar.

"Dad!" she shouted, carelessly, "Dad!"

It was only as she got closer that she became increasingly aware of a structure lying beyond the smoke. Her mind had identified and focussed her on the more primitive threat of the fire in front of her. Having no frame of reference to identify the vastly larger structure beyond the fire, she had filtered it from her perception.

Dwarfing the plume of smoke was the colossal and imposing dome of the Node, its sides curving impossibly away from her towards its apex. So large was the structure that the rounded top actually looked almost too far away; its details muted and less distinct than at its base.

As she continued to move forwards, people in front of her were staring at her, and some were even reaching for their side-arms. She was also becoming distracted by a voice coming from behind her - it was shouting instructions.

"Halt! I will fire. Halt!"

She had got no further than a few strides when she heard the gun go off.

GREY DATA

25th December 2013

Those who had been sleeping under desks received an abrupt awakening as the main lights of the Houston Mission Control room flickered to life again. Communications Director Ross Crandall strode purposefully to the centre of the room:

"Everybody up," he shouted.

People climbed hastily out of their sleeping bags and squeezed past each other to get back to their workstations. Above the low babble of the personnel who had obviously been caught off-guard, he turned to Lawrence.

"Why the hell are we only getting this now?" he shot.

"Sorry Sir," Lawrence spotted his perfect moment, "Mr. Baker said he didn't want to be disturbed."

"Didn't want to…" he fumed, "Sergeant. Get Todd Baker up here on the double."

The sergeant was about to leave the control room, and Lawrence decided to deliver his killer punch.

"It's OK, Sir! I've already decoded the message!"

The busy room fell quiet and even the sergeant froze in his steps.

"Say that again," said Ross, genuinely flustered. "I thought these were power fluctuations?"

"They are," said Lawrence, not missing a beat, "but they have a modulated pattern, that repeats. It's a Morse code string buried in the power output of the FLC. I think the comms system is down, Sir."

"Impossible," he blustered, and pointed at the communications personnel, "Relay station, confirm."

After a flurry of activity, they shook their heads.

"You," he said pointing at Lawrence.

"Larry Clark, Sir."

"Fine. Show me what you've got there."

It was now or never, Lawrence realised. He hesitated just the right amount of time before speaking.

"I'm sorry Sir, but shouldn't Mr. Baker brief you - "

"I'm not asking that powder-snorting sack of crap!" exploded Ross, clicking his fingers at the sergeant to resume his task, "He's finished! Now, Mr. Clark, what have we got?"

"Of course, Sir," he said obediently, but inside he was bursting with satisfaction.

He plugged his memory stick into a nearby console and found the screen capture he'd saved a few minutes ago. The image was projected onto one of main screens at the front of the room. A series of inverted white spikes of different widths, on a solid black background.

"Translate for us," said Ross.

Lawrence hesitantly sat in front of the console then typed the translated message under the image:

'SOS FLC SOS GO ANALOG SOS DRUM GRAY HOSTILE SOS MOON'.

"The message repeats, Sir," Lawrence announced quietly to the stunned room.

LOVE LETTER

20th November 2013

"How do I look?" asked Monica, adjusting her clothing. "Knackered," Marcus replied from behind the webcam.

"Thanks."

"You know what I mean," said Marcus adjusting the light from a desk lamp.

In the months following his almost surreal arrival at the underground Dover facility, Monica had increasingly sought his assistance. She had once explained that because he'd had no historical baggage, she could talk with him more easily than the others. His perspectives were not yet distorted by the constant need for deception, a rare trait. Having spent so long as an outsider, with few people he could rely on, Marcus benefitted from having a sense of community around him. And so the pair had settled into an easy symbiosis.

"OK, we're good," said Marcus getting out of shot, "if we don't get it right, we can always re-take."

"Ready when you are, Mr. DeMille," she quipped.

"What?"

"Never mind," she smiled, "Let's go."

Marcus clicked the record button on the laptop and Monica sat down at the desk in front of the webcam.

"My darling, Douglas," she began, "What can I say? It's been so long that I don't know where to start. I'm overjoyed that Kate found her way to you, and I hope they're treating you well. Things are pretty grim here I'm afraid, but Archive seem to be doing their best to feed us all.

"Talking with a few of the mobile volunteers, it turns out that they are using ex-Ordinance Survey map guys because they can find their way without GPS. I tell you, times change. I can still remember my dad telling us about the time he hired a beat up old Chevy Nova with Mum; the pair of them trekking across the States armed only with a paper map!"

She seemed lost in thought for a moment and smiled.

"They stopped at a diner with only sixty cents to their name. The owner felt so sorry for them that he gave them a full meal on the house. Ah, Douglas, those days are truly gone. When did I get so *old*? Memories eh?"

She continued in a slightly poetic tone.

"Memories, they 'entrance us with the glow of brighter days, but one still hopes in tactful ways'…"

Shaking her head, she sniffed.

"Sorry, my darling, there were days when I used to cry for the time we've lost. But you know me; most days I would just think to myself - 'Oh you nit-wit, Monica! No, get a grip!' - But now I can finally hope to see you again!

Her tone seemed to brighten again as she brought the one-sided conversation to a close.

"I'll keep sending these messages to you and our daughter. With any luck, you won't have long to wait until we're together again. It's over to you now, my darling, don't keep me waiting. I love you."

She placed her hand over her heart and, holding up her left hand, gave a small wave. Then she got up from the desk and walked out of the webcam's field of view.

Marcus hit the stop button.

"Well?" said Monica, suddenly businesslike, "Did I miss anything out?"

NOMADS

25th December 2013

The three of them put their heads together, literally, to discuss options.

"Maybe we can lure her out?" said Cathy.

"Kak?" replied Lana, before correcting herself, "How?"

"My airlock is still cycling, we can get inside if we need to."

"But Drum is still blok, yes?"

"I'd need Lenny's help," said Mike, thinking out loud, "but if we could rapidly depressurise all of Chamber 4, it might blow out the door to the Drum. The last time I saw him he was in Chamber 6."

"Let's go get him," Lana resolved.

The three of them took giant leaps around the mound of regolith until they reached the airlock at Chamber 6. They could see Leonard inside, at the far end of the chamber next to the Drum door. He had removed the comm panel, and appeared to be attempting to rewire it. Cathy picked up a chunk of moon rock and banged it against the metal of the airlock door. A rather startled Leonard looked round and then bounded over to the other side of the airlock. He slammed his message board against the small glass window:

'Eva Danger!'

When he took his board away again, he saw Mike's message board filling the other airlock window. The board was filled with Leonard's decoded Morse message. Leonard quickly wiped his own message, and wrote a new one:

'What now?'

Before any of the crew could respond, a static hiss came though on their headsets. For a moment they dreaded what Eva was going to say next. But the voice that followed the static burst was not hers.

"...do you read us? FLC crew this is Houston, broadcasting on emergency analogue channel one, do you read us?"

Lana switched channels.

"Houston, this is Lana Yakovna. We read you."

The message still took the same time to reach Earth as before, so Houston were still broadcasting their initial message when they received Lana's reply.

"We say again, FLC crew this... Lana?" came the voice, heavily distorted by interference, or possibly cheers from the Mission Control room, "We got your message, good thinking. Deliver situation report, over."

"Eva Gray has FLC Drum in lockdown. Leonard Cooper is internal Chamber 6 with no Floyd access. Mike Sanders,

Cathy Gant and myself are external, with the Z-bank and two evac-packs. Chamber 4 airlock unsecure with cyclical access available. Over."

After the customary round trip for the radio signals, Houston crackled through again.

"Understood. We read an unauthorised activation of the Siva deflection system, but have no telemetry can you confirm. Over."

Lana looked through the airlock window to Leonard who, along with the other crew, had been listening in.

"Houston this is Cooper. I confirm I am reading an activation of the Siva deflection system. I read a charge build-up in Larry, Curly and Mho. Current capacity of the fusion core is at forty-seven percent of maximum. Request immediate remote shut down. Over."

After an agonising wait, Houston replied.

"Roger. We've got the team running scenarios. What is the status of the protective cowl? Over."

Lana motioned Cathy to climb up the exterior regolith mound covering the FLC to check if the beam-combining prism was still covered by the protective cowling.

"Houston this is Yakovna. Gant is in ascent to the prism. Over."

"Roger."

Cathy's climb took less than a minute but, for everyone waiting, it seemed infinitely longer.

"Houston this is Gant at the prism. Cowling is still in place. Over."

A few crackles of static punctuated the silence. Even allowing for the radio round-trip the response was taking too long.

"Roger."

It was just one word, and one that they had heard a thousand times, but the crew could tell that Houston had no pre-calculated plan to counter this eventuality.

"FLC, be advised at this time we are unable to effect remote deactivation. We're still running numbers but order the immediate evacuation of the Z-bank and personnel to the RTO module. Over."

Lana and Mike just looked at each other in sheer dumbstruck silence, a mild static pop occasionally filling the void between the crew.

"Houston this is Cooper," Leonard broke the silence, "We read you. Be advised my airlock has negative function. I will remain at the FLC and do what I can to run interference. Over."

Almost too soon, Houston's reply arrived.

"Thank you Lenny, we'll keep this channel open for you."

ASYMMETRY

18th August 2013

Even at this distance from the hangar, the heat on their backs was still incredibly intense. Douglas knew they were lucky to be alive. Ahead he saw a troop disperse away from General Napier, leaving a figure standing at his side, quietly taking in the events with an air of calm.

Napier strode up to them, accompanied by the silent observer.

"Tell me you got out of there with *something?*" he demanded.

"Our lives, thanks for asking," Anna delivered with a cough, "Nice to see you too, General."

From Napier's perspective they had only been gone a day and a half, but for Anna and Douglas the claustrophobic trip had lasted almost two years. If he looked carefully, he could just about discern the additional grey hairs. Their faces looked more lined too, though this was probably more down to the smoke and ash than age.

"Sorry Dr. Bergstrom -" he began.

"It's OK," Douglas stepped in, "we only left you yesterday. We'll be fine."

Douglas fished a small memory stick out of his pocket.

"We did it," he said simply.

In the palm of his hand, Douglas held the Field inversion solution.

The ground under their feet shuddered.

A loud, metallic, shearing sound caused them to quickly face the hangar, and a moment later an angry ball of fire erupted through the roof. Activity around the entrance was now frenetic, with fire crews training hoses into the hangar, and still more troops were forming chains away from the building, passing supplies away from the blaze. Napier turned away from the chaos.

"This is it?" he pointed to the memory stick, looking also to Anna for confirmation.

She nodded, still distracted by the devastating scene, "Everything we need to invert the Field."

"Twelve hundred to one ratio," added Douglas.

Napier shook his head in disbelief and smiled, but looking at Douglas he could see there was something else.

"What?"

"There's an asymmetric issue we believe is intrinsic to the Field," said Douglas, closing his fingers around the memory stick.

The burning roof above the Mark 3 collapsed into the hangar, sending a new wave of heat in their direction, and a renewed sense of confusion into the air.

"As a consequence," explained Anna, "Douglas and I will need to oversee the activation of the Field."

The heat subsided slightly and, as the Icelandic chill started to reassert itself, Napier read between the lines.

"And, of course, you will need to be aboard the Node to do this," said Napier.

"Of course," said Anna, staring directly at him, "but where else would we be?"

"I think we understand each other," smiled Napier's mouth.

Against the background noise and commotion, Douglas became aware of a persistent voice calling from the distance. In the way that only a parent could know, he recognised the voice of his daughter as an isolated sound above the background chaos, and whipped around to find her.

She was running towards the burning hangar, unaware that she had an armed guard pursuing her. Suddenly the guard stopped.

"Halt! I will fire. Halt!" he shouted.

It was all happening too fast for Douglas to process. His long-dead daughter. Impossibly, right here. About to lose her life in front of him. All he could manage was a whispered, "No!"

The guard raised his assault rifle and aimed.

A single gunshot rang out.

But it came from behind them. As the round hit the guard's body armour, he twisted on the spot and then fell to the ground, cursing.

Miles, who had stood silently observing the situation, lowered the gun he'd just fired, and put the safety catch back on.

"My apologies, I didn't have time to ask your permission," said Miles, handing Napier's gun back to him, "He will be fine, and at least your asset is still alive."

Meanwhile, as more personnel converged on her, Kate had skidded to a halt and was raising her hands.

"Katie!" yelled Douglas and ran as fast as he could in her direction.

Kate heard his voice and turned immediately, but remained glued to the spot, hands and arms raised in fear. She saw him running towards her now and tried to call him again, but her throat had suddenly become tight and the words wouldn't come. He stopped a few feet from her, studying her intensely, desperately trying to make sense of the impossibility.

"Katie?" said Douglas, his voice breaking, "My little... is that really you?"

She became aware that five or six other soldiers had arrived, and had loosely surrounded the pair of them. Kate still couldn't speak, it was just too much.

She reached towards her trouser pocket, but spotting the reaction of those around her, temporarily stopped to raise her hands again to show submission. Then, slower than before, she pulled from her pocket a small, well creased, red envelope, and held it out to her father.

Hesitantly, and at arms length, he took it from her and read the writing on the front:

'External Variable'.

Monica's envelope was all the proof and explanation he needed. Douglas just nodded then closed the gap between them, throwing his wide arms around her and pulling her close. Despite the hostile situation, landscape and people, she felt shielded and protected by his arms. She felt about ten years old again; a life-time ago and a different world away.

General Napier swore under his breath as he watched both the hangar and his leverage go up in smoke. Many years ago, he had watched as Bradley Pittman had shown Douglas the faked photographic evidence of his family's death. Napier himself was complicit in the necessary cover-up that had inevitably followed. Douglas must, even now, realise his involvement.

"They told me you were dead," said Douglas, still squeezing her hard.

"Mum said the same about you," Kate managed, "she said it was to protect me - "

"Wait!" said Douglas suddenly and pulled away from her a fraction, "Monica's alive?!"

Kate nodded, and she saw that her father's eyes had started darting back and forth. During her childhood she'd seen this look a hundred times, usually when he was deep in thought or calculation or often both.

Suddenly he straightened, and his grip on her relaxed.

"Kate, come with me," he said with resolve, and turning on his heels marched towards Napier.

Napier saw him coming and straightened up too, drawing to his full height.

"Douglas - " he began, but was silenced by Douglas himself raising a single finger aimed at his face.

"Dylan," he countered, fixing him with a piercing stare, "Under Archive's Protected Lineage Directive in return for my Lifetime Services, I reassert my rights. My family is protected and included, either jointly or separately, in all Impact Event counter-enterprises."

Napier hoped that he could regain full control at some point in the year ahead, but for the time being, he realised that he must go along with it.

"Agreed, Dr. Walker."

Kate saw her father lower his finger and then step closer to the General. Against the background noise of the fire she couldn't tell what he was saying, but when he was done the General stepped to one side.

Without turning to either of them, Douglas said firmly, "Kate, Anna, with me."

Behind them, the remainder of the hangar slowly collapsed in on itself.

RTO

25th December 2013

In order to keep the one functioning emergency channel clear, only essential communication between the crew was permitted, so the quarter mile journey east to the RTO module had passed in silence. Lana and Cathy had taken the first of the two lunar rovers and Mike had followed in the second, accompanying the zygote bank. On some level they all realised that the decision to evacuate to the RTO module was not a temporary course of action, designed to give Houston thinking time, it was a final option.

The 'Return To Orbit' module presupposed the success of the mission and had been designed to lift the FLC crew from the Moon and return them to a stable orbit around Earth where they would await rescue. The actual technology was *old*, differing very little from the ascent propulsion system of Apollo 17 which had left the lunar surface some forty-one years ago. However, it had almost double the thrust capacity, in order to lift a theoretical six occupants. To Lana it seemed a cruel twist that, according to her revised calculations, the

1972 ascent system would have been perfectly capable of today's required 3-person lift.

They completed their final checks, having now compensated for the much lower mass aboard.

"Houston, RTO module. We are go for launch," reported Lana.

"RTO, Houston, we'll recalculate Trans Earth trajectory as soon as you're in Lunar orbit. Launch Commit."

The original flight plan had been created for a different date, over a year away, so it was going to require time and a fair bit of astromechanical dexterity to calculate a new Earth-orbit trajectory. Time they didn't have now.

"Roger," said Lana and without waiting pushed the countdown start, "Launch Commit."

Cathy opened her mouth to say something, anything, that would perhaps bring a sense of meaning to abandoning Leonard, but nothing came. The numb, cavernous void of the situation's cold logic had stolen the all the crew's words.

"two…one…" she heard Lana saying.

Then they all felt the hypergolic kick of the thrusters underneath the module.

Unlike on Earth, where perspectives changed relatively slowly on take off, the low gravity here and disproportionately high counter-thrust felt like the RTO module was nothing but an artillery shell. The course correction and manoeuvring phase would only arrive in about thirty seconds time.

Mike looked out of the starboard porthole, and caught his last view of the FLC. The mound of regolith they had called home was shrinking away incredibly fast as they continued their acceleration. From this altitude the tracks of the rovers had already disappeared; even the car-sized Regodozers, still blindly collecting precious Helium-3, looked like mere snails leaving thin tracks in an expanse of grey dust. A contrastingly colourful orange flash of light at the FLC suddenly redirected his attention. He saw a fireball erupt from the airlock end of Chamber 6, which was then immediately extinguished in the permanent vacuum. The regolith above it jolted and then collapsed into an alarmingly shallow trench.

Until this point he had been able to persuade himself that the situation was, at some small percentage of chance, retrievable. The finality of witnessing Leonard's fiery death brought home the harsh reality.

The FLC had failed.

The edge of Coriolis crater came into view and he realised that soon he would be required to step up and navigate the RTO module into lunar orbit. He forced himself to turn away from the porthole and face the controls.

Mankind's last hope was now no longer beneath them, it was strapped into Leonard's unclaimed seat, and still emitting its low-pitched, pathetic warning tone.

WALKERS

16th December 2013

Construction of the Node had continued patiently over the past four years; the various Field experiments continuing to develop in its ever-growing shadow. Each experimental Field had improved upon the last, with the eventual aim of providing the Node with a functional, full-sized and inverted Field.

Four months ago Field inversion had been achieved, bringing to an end the long line of Field experimentation. Although the Field inversion data had made it out of the Mark 3 intact, the hangar and the Mark 3 itself had burned to the ground.

Logistically the focus of construction had shifted solely to the Node, but with at least fourteen months to go before Siva's theoretical arrival, progress had suddenly slowed.

General Napier had discussed the matter with Alfred Barnes who had surmised that the personnel were still grieving for the loss of yet another life, whilst having no immediate focus for their efforts. Alfred had suggested a re-dedication service, where some form of physical monument could be placed on site. The monument would serve as a memorial stone to those who had lost their lives in the pursuit of saving humanity, and also inspire a proud continuation of what had gone before. According to Alfred, the emphasis had to be placed on '*continuation*' if the personnel were to maintain their belief in the long term goal.

In the cold morning sun of September the 18th, one month after the fire, all production work was halted and a base-wide service was held. During the one-minute silence, a dedication stone was unveiled next to the bridge in full view of the Node.

The words were chiselled deeply into the light grey granite:

'THE NODE, MARK IV'

In smaller text, above the names of all those who had died at Öskjuvatn Lake, ran the words:

'They gave their lives for the good of Mankind'.

It soon became customary among the personnel to touch the stone when entering or leaving the Node's small island.

Much to General Napier's relief, base operations began to return to normal.

Douglas had a much harder time adjusting to Bradley's malicious deception.

Try as he might, Douglas could not conceive of any probability tree that resulted in Archive being *unaware* that his family were still alive. He had known Bradley for decades and the sense of betrayal was immense. For days after Kate's arrival, he was mentally crippled; constantly reassessing his previous interactions with Bradley in an attempt to find some sense of meaning.

Kate's presence had helped him though.

Now effectively back under Archive protection, Kate had followed her father everywhere on the base. She would listen in a state of incredulity for hours as Douglas and Anna recounted the development of the Chronomagnetic Field; and although none of them had set foot inside the Node itself, Kate's talent for layering visual information had made light work of memorising the structure from the printed plans she had seen.

Douglas was convinced that Kate's continued presence at the base explained the rarity of General Napier's visits. On the few occasions that Napier had returned to check on progress he always gave them a wide berth. If they had to speak about any matters relating to the upgrading of the Node's Field generator, Napier always ensured that Colonel Beck was present too. Douglas thought that perhaps it was Napier's way of ensuring that the topic of 'faked family deaths' never arose in general conversation.

A week ago the final components of the Field generator had been put into place, and now the slow process of populating the Node had begun. In the unlikely event that the FLC failed in its mission to deflect Siva then there was still over a year to go before a launch of the Node would be deemed necessary. But Archive preferred to plan ahead. By assembling and training essential personnel now, ahead of the later Lifeboat Lottery winners, it would allow time for an orderly transfer of expertise and physical resources from around the world.

From the Node's island, Kate looked through the window of Hab 1 at the steady stream of people carrying, or wheeling, containers over the bridge from the remote shore.

Originally her plan had been to find her father and then somehow return to Dover. But when Kate thought back to her first supply run, up to the surface with Marcus, her enduring memory had been of a people now blinded by fear and hunger, burying themselves alive in dirt tunnels, and paranoia haunting the eyes of children. It seemed to her that the thin veneer of civilisation had all but disappeared; even if the FLC were successful, it may already be too late to restore the world to how it was before.

Here, at least, there was order.

Unlike the ravaged streets of Dover, here she had never seen a fight for drinking water.

"Do you think she'd come *here*?" she said over her shoulder, still looking out at the view.

Her father was experimenting with a wide pair of digital recording binoculars, and appeared lost in thought for a moment.

"What? Er…Oh, I see, your Mum? I don't think so," he shook his head, "But by New Year I should be done here, so we'll both go and work on wearing her down!"

Kate laughed, but in the short time she had spent beneath Dover she had seen, first hand, how stubborn her mother could be. The years without Douglas had undoubtedly hardened her, and went some way to explaining why Kate's own relationship with her mother had been so difficult. But this was a woman with a long-term plan; the scale of the facility under her mother's independent control was staggering.

There was a knock on the door and Miles entered swiftly.

"I don't have much time," he said in a low voice, "Napier's escorted Dr. Bergstrom off the base."

Douglas made to stand up, but Miles waved him to sit down, then swiftly continued:

"I've got ten minutes to get to the runway, I'm supposed to shadow Napier, but I'll make arrangements to ensure that I go where she goes."

Douglas suddenly remembered that immediately after the hangar fire, Anna had made a copy of the final Field equations.

"Miles, did she take her copy of the Field equations with her?" he said.

"It's unclear, but her quarters are empty."

"I thought Napier agreed you were both protected?" Kate jumped in, "Aren't you both supposed to oversee the Field's activation?"

They could hear footsteps approaching.

"Sorry, but I have to go," Miles cut in, "I'll find answers, and you know I'll do my best to help Dr. Bergstrom."

Miles quickly pulled a small thin memory card from his pocket.

"I was trying to find a less obvious time to get this to you. It's from Monica," he whispered. As the door behind him started to open, his posture changed to become more upright.

Without missing a beat, he continued with the tail end of a completely fabricated conversation, "Because, Miss Walker, my enquiries are authorised by Archive itself, and your continued favourable treatment here is contingent upon it."

Napier came to a halt next to Miles.

"What the hell are you doing, Benton?" he demanded.

As Miles calmly turned around to face him, he deposited the memory card on Kate's table. Among all the other pieces of equipment it didn't look out of place.

"General, I am continuing to monitor the Walkers, as per your instruction," he said smoothly, "and given the departure of *certain personnel*, I considered it prudent to make my enquiries now."

Kate could see that Napier wasn't entirely convinced.

"Benton!" she shouted, "I've got something for your enquiries."

As Miles turned around she spat at him.

He wiped the spittle off his face and walked from the room. With a blank expression, Napier followed.

Her demonstration had been effective, but it had left her with a hollow feeling at having treated him so badly. She was tired of the constant deception, and knew that her parents must have this feeling too, a hundred-fold.

They waited an hour before playing her mother's video file; the screen showed that the framing and decor had been arranged to exclude anything that would identify its location. Then Monica sat down into frame.

The first thing that Kate noticed was that she appeared much older than when she had left her barely four months ago; her hair was now cropped shorter and was grey in places, but her eyes still had a fire to them. Mostly the recording was for her father and he watched the message through tear filled eyes. Then, seemingly less than a minute later, it was over. She placed one hand over her heart and, with the other hand gave a little wave at the camera, before exiting the frame.

Kate knew that Douglas hadn't seen Monica since 2001, so it was at least a dozen years they'd been apart; but having since learned about the various experimental 'Fields' her father had been within, she couldn't begin to guess what that meant in terms of his own personal timeline. Kate looked over at her father, ready to comfort him.

"You OK, Dad?"

"Sorry Katie," he looked up at her, "I'll be fine. Would it be OK if I have a few minutes to myself? I'm so sorry."

"Sure," she replied, it had been a difficult morning, "I'll go and check Anna's room, she may have left something behind."

Douglas nodded and waited for her to leave the room. He waited until her footsteps had faded, then swiftly squared himself up to the screen.

"No ring, Monny?" he muttered, "What are you telling me?"

He scrolled back along the video to watch her wave, pausing it during her wave to the camera. On the ring-finger of her left hand was a band of skin that was much whiter than the skin surrounding it. As he scrolled backwards to the start, he noticed that throughout the video she had kept her hands placed on the desk in front of her.

He watched the video again, and saw that the same ring-finger twitched at random times throughout her message.

"Monny you're priceless!" he exclaimed suddenly. He stifled his own laugh and dashed around the other side of his desk to grab a pencil and a scrap of paper, "No redundant information!"

His initial thought was that it was some, slow, version of Morse code, but nothing seemed to fit. The duration of the finger twitches was the same each time. He needed to find the primer within the message. A coherent correlation. A self-contained truth. Then he saw it.

Her last three words were accompanied by three finger twitches, 'I. Love.You.'

She was highlighting syllables within her own message.

Hurriedly he restarted the video, pausing each time to write down the syllables she was indicating. Some of them were phonetic rather than written, and she had even indicated new sentences by raising both hands from the desk; something he hadn't even noticed the first few times. Within a few minutes the transcription lay before him among a mass of scribbled pencil lines:

'*Archive are Exordi Nova. House gone. Entrance one still intact. Cryo unit no hope. Keep our daughter with you until it's over. My darling I love you.*'

Five of the six sentences were essentially headlines, with ramifications he had yet to calculate. But the sixth one, even though she had said the same words in plain sight, she had chosen to encode again. It had been her way of placing equal importance on it.

"My darling," he sighed, "I love you, too."

EVE

25th December 2013

Eva felt the whole Drum shake violently as Chamber 6 explosively decompressed.

A few of the meagre Christmas decorations fell down in protest at the disturbance, but the integrity of the station held. The ID keys had allowed her to transfer Floyd's operation inside the Drum, so her plan was still intact.

"Goodbye Leonard," she said.

His departure seemed to tug at her, but not just because of their former intimacy, it was because out of all the crew at the FLC, she felt sure that Leonard had known nothing of the sabotage.

She had become aware of a problem back in 2010 after the first firing on Siva. An error had resulted in Floyd targeting the beam at the edge of Siva, rather than the centre. It had been a trivial matter for Eva to observe Leonard at work and then later recall his methodology in accessing Floyd's data logs. But when she had reviewed the logs herself, she'd found that as far as Floyd was concerned it had scored a direct and central hit on Siva, and not a side impact. From the time-stamps however, the logs appeared to have been altered *after* the event, to reflect the actual impact position.

Eva suspected that either the targeting system was wrong and the evidence had been suppressed, or that someone at the FLC had instructed Floyd to miss, by building in an offset to its aim. In either case she was no longer sure of who she could trust. After a while though, with no further anomalies, she had almost convinced herself that she had imagined it.

That was until the 2012 deflection, Leonard's so-called 'Mayan Calendar Reset'. The firing had been a complete success but the day after, a series of inexplicable minor faults began; malfunctioning lighting, CO_2 scrubber failures, and errant solar array tracking routines. In themselves they were insignificant and easily rectified by the crew, but for each of the events Eva could find no error logs. It was as though each of the systems were being tested. Her distrust of the crew became stronger.

One night she had woken while falling out of her bunk.

The fall had synchronised with her exit from a vividly disturbing dream; she had seen an unstoppable Siva ploughing through the Earth's atmosphere. She later reasoned that in all likelihood the image was drawn from her memory of Tenca's similar arrival.

It was not an uncommon crew nightmare but the cruel imagery, combined with her fall and the crew's traditional mocking, had been burned into her mind. In the moment itself, she had shrugged it off and even laughed along with them, but the experience had motivated her to increase her doses of metathene.

Before leaving Earth the low-level dose had been sufficient to balance her mental edge against her own humanity. But now she realised that she could not afford to have her analysis clouded by emotion. She'd reasoned that the metathene would allow her to perfectly simulate her own emotions to the rest of the crew. As far as they were concerned there would be no difference, but she would be able to assess them far more easily.

During one night shift, Eva had found another error. This one had been more significant; within Floyd's programming she could see that the beam deflection subroutines had been compromised. Eva saw that during the next scheduled deflection of Siva in 2014, 'Larry' and 'Curly' would be instructed to slowly widen their containment spirals. The end result would be that, although the FLC would register a full power transfer, the actual power reaching Siva's surface would slowly decrease to nothing.

Undeflected, Siva would hit Earth.

It also seemed that Floyd's programming had been altered at the root level; an action that should not have been possible without Houston's authorisation. Or perhaps, she thought, it had been *with* Houston's authorisation. Prior to both previous firings, Floyd's own diagnostic tools had returned no errors, and Houston themselves had confirmed the program was mission-stable. Eva found herself faced with the possibility that Houston could be compromised.

Over the following weeks, other minor errors continued to occur, but being unable to discuss it with anyone she began to dwell on a thought:

Who could possibly benefit from the failure of the FLC?

The further, logical extension was an even colder thought:

Who was trying to *ensure* that Siva struck Earth?

She knew that her ID key alone was insufficient to allow a root level alteration to Floyd's core programming.

To do this she knew that she would need all the crew's ID keys and, to avoid the possibility of Houston's intervention, she would have to disable communications to Earth.

The thought had terrified her, both in her waking hours with the crew and during her sleep.

The nightmares would always play out in a similar way, but with the same end result. She would see Siva's seemingly slow push through the atmosphere, triggering the feeble response of the Debris Cascade Protection network; hundreds of impotent explosions ranged against the unstoppable force. Then the inevitable impact, that forced her awake.

She had raised her dosage again.

She watched the crew and interacted with them, sometimes explicitly so, with a view to building a more thorough mental terrain. She calculated that if she could get the timing right, then acquiring the ID keys and excluding the crew from the Drum would be a trivial matter. Once she had full access to Floyd it should become apparent where the deception lay.

Then, one night, her recurring dream changed.

Despite the events still being catastrophic, the logical extrapolation of what she'd dreamt had given her a sense of resolution. It also became the basis for a personal mantra that she would mentally recite during stressful times. Within her new personal directive, she continued to watch the crew while preparing an alternative plan that she hoped she would never have to use.

With her metathene set to run out late on Christmas Eve, and being unable to trust even Houston, she'd decided to carry out her plan after the Christmas messages. She'd also reasoned that during the celebrations on Earth, the possibly less experienced staff may be slower to react to her actions.

So far she had been right.

An hour ago, after providing Floyd with the authorisation of all five ID keys, she had been granted permission to access Floyd's core program. She quickly discovered that the core program access record was either missing or had been deleted. During routine diagnostics this absence should have raised an alarm at the FLC and Houston, but it hadn't.

This made it impossible for her to determine who had accessed the beam deflection system, but she realised that it no longer mattered; her priority had to be the correction of Floyd's confinement beams.

Within a minute she had located the beam deflection subroutines and attempted to remove the errant lines of code. But as fast as she could delete the lines, the system would automatically reinstate them. Even with the combined authority of five ID keys, her direct instructions were still being overridden; something that should never have been possible.

After her fifth failed attempt to correct the programming she knew that the FLC had been hopelessly and irrevocably compromised.

With no one to trust and Siva still bound for Earth, it left her with one solution. The solution that had arrived in her metathene-fuelled dream.

Long ago she had made the promise that her actions would be 'For the good of Mankind', and that promise was still true now. Although she could not alter the confinement parameters of the beam, Floyd had no issues with her reprogramming the optics within the prism directly above her. With the permission of all five ID keys it also allowed her to begin the beam charging routine.

Then all she had to do was wait.

As she sat in the quiet of the Drum she ran through the calculations in her head again, but she found it difficult. She could tell that the final dose of metathene was starting to wear off; she could feel stray thoughts beginning to intrude within her ordered mind.

She reflected on the fact that no one would understand the motivation for her actions, yet.

All too soon, the moment arrived.

A tone sounded on Floyd's console indicating that charging was complete. She only had to press the button, and Floyd would carry out the remainder or her plan.

Her eyes began to fill up, and she realised that the cold guiding hand of her Christmas Eve dose must have already left her. In its place were only exposed, raw emotions.

She knew it was her decision, and hers alone. Her next action would mean the deaths of billions, but she knew it was the only way she could give the human race a fighting chance for survival, a chance to begin again.

She wept bitterly, knowing that she would be forever branded as a traitor to her own planet. A dim echo of her former ego reminded her that it was humanity's long biological chain trying to appeal to her vanity; desperate to force her into making a choice that might result in self-preservation.

As the tears began to blur her sight, she knew she would have to act quickly to override her own primitive instincts.

She slammed the button, and let herself fall to the floor.

"I am Eve," she wept, beginning to recite her private mantra aloud.

As she had planned, the beams fired and combined within the prism above the Drum.

"I will birth the new mankind," she sobbed, curling herself up into a ball.

As she had instructed, Floyd focussed the beams away from the black sky above, and downwards through the Drum itself. Immediately, the metal above her head began to vaporise.

"Born in the fires of the old," she whispered now, "they will renew the Earth."

The beam penetrated the Drum, and travelled towards her at the speed of light.

In the instant transition she felt no pain.

In a white hot flash of light, her atoms united with those of the beam as it burned downwards.

CHOICE

8th February 2010

"**S**o at some time on February 13th 2013, *before* the Tenca splinter collides with our atmosphere," Dr. Patil was saying to the group, "we're going to lose a percentage of satellites up there, but that's just collateral I'm afraid. The bigger problem is the amount of space-junk in orbit. I'm looking at you Bradley."

"Ah, bite me, Chandra," smiled Bradley Pittman raising his middle finger in salute, "What's it matter if our NASA junk gets junked?"

"Debris collisions," he replied, "A chain reaction cascading through orbit, annihilating everything up there."

"That would include the ISS, Dad," Sarah Pittman chipped in, "what have you got in mind Dr. Patil?"

"OK," he replied, "We don't have a precise plot yet, so we can't tell where Tenca will cut through, but we think it may be possible to put clusters of directed explosives in orbit - "

"Thought you said we couldn't blow it up?" cut in Bradley.

"It's a firebreak, Dad," Sarah translated, "We can't stop Tenca, but we can make sure that the damage doesn't spread. Is three years enough time?"

"Yes," shrugged Dr. Patil, "what other choice do we have?"

At that point, the door opened and General Napier followed Alfred Barnes into the room.

"Apologies, delays," Napier muttered taking his seat, "Dr. Barnes, you're up."

Alfred decided to recap a little, more for the benefit of his own, tired, brain than anyone else.

"We spoke about combating the panic that will follow the arrival of Tenca over Russia, and the need for Archive to impose a new, controllable, social order."

There were general mumbles of assent from around the table.

"We made an assumption that we shouldn't have."

Bradley opened his mouth, but then resisted the urge to be sarcastic.

"The most successful battles in history," Alfred continued, "were fought by a force that was united against a common foe, a foe that they feared."

Napier slowly folded his arms.

"After Tenca makes its demonstration in 2013, our enemy will become Siva. But even then it will be more than two years away from a *possible* impact. It's too distant, too intangible, to ignite action. We'll need to give the world something *real* to fear, something that will be happening *right now* for them, something to unite *against*.

"The anatomy of fear has its roots based in a breakdown of perceived order. We should not be seeking to create a system of social order," he summarised, "if we want true control, true fear, we should be imposing social *dis*-order, by creating our own foe. We need our own terrorist group."

It appeared that everyone in the room recoiled a few centimetres in their seats, drawing slightly deeper breaths than a moment ago.

"Out of the question," stated Napier, his arms forming a barrier over his chest, "What if we lost our control?"

"I'm sorry if that bruises your *Ego*," said Alfred tilting his head slightly, attempting to convey the intended meaning.

Napier's barrier lowered slightly, and Alfred knew his message had been successfully interpreted.

"Now hold your horses!" Bradley leaned forward, "Yesterday you yammered on about delusions of choice, all that monkey-brain motivation stuff."

"I mentioned the need to overcome the primitive instinct to hold onto the tree, rather than make a possible wrong choice in leaping to an uncertainty," Alfred re-paraphrased.

"So is all of that claptrap useless now?"

"All that 'claptrap', as you call it, is still true. All I'm suggesting is adding motivation by setting fire to the tree."

Recalling his sleep-deprived Greek Mythology dream from a few hours before, Alfred altered his approach for Bradley's benefit. He made sure that he used plenty of physical gestures to emphasise his points.

"When people are trapped in a maze of choices, where no single choice is any more valid than another, having more choices *impedes* escape. Options become *less* clear. So the more avenues we can give people to exert their 'free will' the better. For them, the focus of the primitive drive becomes about out-surviving an unseen foe inside the maze, rather escaping the maze itself. It will occupy their attention completely, while they labour for the benevolent Archive who are trying to save them."

Alfred went on to outline the requirements of creating what was essentially an Archive-funded terrorist group, including the importance of the right name and symbology. One that would be intentionally vague, but carry a meaning for those that cared to impose their own philosophy upon it. Eventually they settled on a circle, perhaps representing Earth's atmosphere, broken in one place by a smaller dot, which could be interpreted as Siva penetrating it.

Later, as the group left the room, Alfred signalled to Bradley.

"Have you got a moment?"

They waited until the room was clear, then Alfred cleared his throat and spoke in a low tone.

"Dr. Walker doesn't know his family's alive, does he?" he said, patting the Siva folder.

"No, and it stays that way," Bradley fixed him with a stare, "We need him focussed on the Node."

"Of course, of course," he nodded deferentially, "But Walker's parents, er…"

"Howard and Betty?"

"Yes, thank you. Were they ever part of the cortical enhancement program?"

"I… No," Bradley frowned.

"No. Of course not, sorry. It's just that I assumed that because Douglas himself is, well, er…"

"A genius?" laughed Bradley, "No that's all him, hundred percent genius. No artificial sweeteners!"

But as they both laughed, Bradley made a mental note to check his own, perhaps incorrect, assumptions later.

CORIOLIS EFFECT

25th December 2013

From Earth's northern hemisphere, the left side of the moon was in bright sunlight, whilst the right was in shadow. The RTO fled on, into the illuminated side, having completed its first half orbit.

"*RTO, Houston, over.*"

"Roger. Go ahead," said Lana.

"*Roger. Lana we're transmitting the new Trans-Earth injection plan, acknowledge? Over.*"

"Understood, stand by," said Lana turning to Mike.

Mike studied the console in front of him, and saw that the new orbital mechanics data was slowly streaming through. After a minute he gave Lana the thumbs up.

"Houston, RTO, we have received your course correction," she relayed, "Over."

Mike busied himself unpacking the data and updating the automated external thruster sequence.

Meanwhile, Houston still had not replied.

"Houston, do you read us," Lana checked, "Over?"

"RTO, Houston, we apologise for the delay. Be advised that we are currently mid-countdown on a second launch sequence. We're juggling here."

"This can't be right," Mike muttered, reloading the flight plan, "we're set to dock with the ISS, but it's not in the right place. Lana, can you confirm this?"

"Houston, RTO, please confirm Trans-Earth flight to conclude with orbital approach and dock with International Space Station. Over."

There was another long delay.

"What the hell are they launching out of Kennedy?" whispered Cathy, "I thought all the Shuttles were canned?"

"RTO, Houston," came the voice again, *"We confirm your rendezvous with the ISS. You guys may also have noticed the altitude difference of the ISS. Flight advises me that this will be consistent with your approach vector... I guess things have changed a little while you've been away."*

"Roger," said Lana, "Received and understood."

Mike was shaking his head.

"We might've been away for a while," he said in a low voice to the others, "But I'm guessing that physics still works the same way."

Before anyone could reply, Houston advised them again.

"We read one minute to LOS. Prepare for automated thruster burn sequence."

Mike loaded the data into active memory and flipped the toggle switch on the panel above his head from 'simulate' to 'live'.

"New flight plan accepted and locked," he reported.

"Houston, RTO, we are course locked," Lana relayed.

"Roger, Lana, we'll see you on the other side."

The loss of signal occurred on time, and miniature concussions accompanied the firing of the course-correcting thrusters. The second phase of the flight would take them directly over the FLC on their way around the moon, before a more continuous thruster burn would break them free of lunar orbit.

"This is it!" said Mike, who had been checking their position relative to the FLC.

At this altitude all that was distinctly visible was the solar array to the north. The mound of regolith covering the FLC did too good a job of camouflaging itself within the surrounding lunar landscape. At their relative speed, the visual inspection time had been ridiculously brief, but Mike was convinced the surface pattern within the local Coriolis crater had changed.

MOON

25th December 2013

Over the course of half a second, the sublimation beam continued to burn downwards through the floor of the FLC Drum. Designed to work in the vacuum of space, the inclusion of excessive oxygen in the vicinity of the beam had never been accounted for, and the air ignited.

In the next tenth of a second, the beam breached the Drum's air-tight containment and the combusting environment within it explosively decompressed, opening an instant, six-foot-wide, hole under the FLC. In reaction, the whole structure attempted to push away from the lunar surface below, but was held down by the weight of regolith piled above it.

The structural engineers who first put pen to paper would have been proud of the FLC's resilience; despite this central decompression, not a single internal airlock door was breached, allowing the fusion reactor to continue efficiently pumping energy to the beam.

The operation continued flawlessly with the beam persisting to burrow into the rocky surface. As was the original intention, a pocket began to form under the beam, allowing it to effortlessly convert the rock into a super-heated condensate.

As the beam ploughed on, the pocket of molten rock and gas continued to deepen. But after a few minutes a new balance point was reached, and the pocket's liquid mass prevented the beam from penetrating any further. Instead, the reaction entered a new phase of development; the relentless energy being poured into the process started to widen the pocket. Through conduction alone, the heat rose and began to melt the lunar surface directly under the FLC.

Under the weight of the regolith above, the FLC began to sink. From above, the entire liquefaction was concealed. The only clue that any reaction was underway was a change to the surface patterns of the Coriolis crater itself, as the underlying rock buckled and collapsed.

The seething hot soup now began absorbing the FLC structure itself. As the regolith above it was converted to liquid, it flowed in through the compromised areas first; the metal in Chambers 4 and 6 melting like candle wax. As the remainder of the FLC was dragged beneath the molten lunar lake, the heat build up within Chamber 1 proved too great and it exploded. The clockwise containment laser 'Curly' failed instantly, leaving its counterparts to take over.

Floyd, the Shen500 series computer, coped admirably; increasing the relative power flows to the remaining two beams. The additional boost of power to the central sublimator beam, 'Mho', allowed the pocket below to deepen again, and the FLC began to sink faster.

A few seconds later the structural integrity of the station as a whole failed and, with the directional prism now destroyed, 'Mho' cut straight through the chambers directly in front of it, neatly severing its own power supply. The laser's excavation stopped.

The fusion reactor however, separated from conventional matter by the electromagnetic field surrounding it, continued to operate, producing megawatts of clean energy from the Helium-3 pellets at its core.

As the engulfing, liquid heat searched for a way into the core, mankind's small, but beautifully formed artificial sun continued to sink towards the heart of the moon.

Then, through a slight imperfection in the magnetic field, a thin filament of super-heated matter pushed through to the reaction inside. It took only a millisecond for the reaction to breach and then overwhelm the containment. Armed with a much more efficient source of material, the fusion rate accelerated a thousand-fold, and the miniature sun detonated.

The surrounding rock could not escape at the same speed as the expansion, and the moon tore itself apart.

TRANSIT

27th December 2013

For a whole day after the detonation, the fractured moon dominated the night sky with a grotesquely beautiful celestial display; its brilliant, white internal starlight stabbing radially outwards through the random sized lunar segments, and casting impossibly long, dust filled, shadows.

Then the light had faded, as the fusion process used up the matter within its reach. With the dying of the light and the spreading out of the fragments, the shadows within began to move.

The fusion event had originated on the dark side of the moon, but the major fracture had travelled towards the Earth before the colossal pieces had started to separate. In addition to the usual surface detail, it was now possible to see the *interior* structure too; the very depth of the moon was easily visible with the naked eye. Rugged, Australia-sized chunks could be seen tumbling and impacting with smaller ones, in the expanding gap at the centre.

The GRACE mapping satellites confirmed that there *had* been a gravitational shockwave, but could not immediately confirm the likely consequences. The hypothesis at the time had been that, because the pieces of the moon were still in one place, the Earth would experience no large tidal consequences. However this did not stop the attempted mass migrations of millions of people deserting coastal regions, fleeing inland to escape theoretical tsunamis.

The truly imminent threat was the arrival of lunar debris, thrown in the direction of Earth, striking like meteorites. Although many of the smaller ones would burn up in the atmosphere, deep space radar had found a cluster of fragments that were large enough to cause widespread devastation.

The first would fall one day from now, with the others following a few hours later.

Arrivals at the Node went from once a week, to once an hour.

In the initial confusion, two approaching military supply aircraft were misidentified and shot down by the automated ground-to-air missile defence stations. To avoid any further unnecessary loss of personnel, the network had been deactivated. But the increase in air traffic brought with it different problems.

The sheer amount of military traffic converging on Vatnajökull glacier had attracted attention. Those fleeing the perceived threat of tidal waves headed inland, following the stream of helicopters, and trucks. The gun emplacements, set up to defend the ten-mile mark, had been quickly overwhelmed by the thousands of people converging on the base, desperate to escape, or find sanctuary.

The base's, now electrified, perimeter fence was still intact, and five of the six observation towers were still armed. The main purpose of the towers had been to protect the narrow access bridge that ran from the Node's island back to shore. But with a large population now breathing heavily through the surrounding fence, the tower marksmen had been given a wider remit. Earlier, they had been forced to open fire on a light-weight snowmobile. Somehow it had breached the fence that surrounded Öskjuvatn Lake and had made its way across the Node's frozen meltwater moat.

From his window, Douglas had watched as the vehicle had approached the island. He had heard a single gunshot and the snowmobile drifted to a stop near the island, a dead man at the helm. On some level Douglas was relieved that there were no children aboard, as he knew there would have been no exceptions.

Over the next hour he had waited anxiously by the same window, splitting his attention between his unconscious daughter, and the baying crowds being held back by the perimeter fence. As the situation developed he continued to assess options, examining different pathways through one of his mental decision trees.

He realised that he'd already cut away entire branches of potential futures.

He could feel this decision branch resolving right in front of him, and knew that he would soon reach the singularity; a single final decision.

He replayed Monica's coded message in his head. The message he'd never revealed to Kate. Most of the details he had now mentally filed away; they belonged to a future he could no longer access. The one message he focussed on now was *'Keep our daughter with you until it's over.'*

From the looks of things outside, it soon would be.

When news of the FLC's destruction had reached the Node, he had immediately acted to protect Kate.

For subjects to be successfully anchored within the Node's Chronomagnetic Field required two key components: A dose of Anna Bergstrom's isotope and a Biomag anchor tag. The Biomag could be simply worn around the neck, but the isotope had to be injected into the bloodstream to allow it to circulate throughout the entire body and become absorbed by the tissues. He had told her the isotope injection was merely a precaution against an unexpected early departure. What he had not told her was that the side effect of taking it was that, at least initially, the body attempted to reject it by running a high fever for around 24 hours.

Behind him, Kate stirred, and he turned from the window to be by her side.

"Dad?" she woke, groggily.

She tried to prop herself up on her elbows but found she ached too much.

"Ssh honey," he said, wiping her forehead again with a damp towel, "You've been fighting it for a while."

She groaned, pressing the palms of her hands into her eyes, "I have a headache like you wouldn't believe."

"No, I'd believe it," he comforted, "here, drink some water."

She drank the water gratefully and this time felt able to sit up. She studied the Biomag pendant round her neck. The device was about the size of a mobile phone, with a small, bluish crystal protruding from the surface. The digital panel beneath it displayed the number '1'. Recalling one of the Biomag briefings she had received here at the Node she knew this number was a ratio. At 1:1 they were in a *'temporally flat space-time'*.

"Hmm, I like it," she smiled, "But I'm not sure it goes with this outfit."

"Well at least your sense of humour hasn't got any worse," he smiled.

"OK, so what did I miss? Has the transport -", she faltered, spotting the daylight through the window.

"You've been out for about twenty hours," he said, anticipating her next question.

Kate swore and staggered over to the window. The scene before her now was much worse than before.

"When's the transport due?" she panicked, looking around for her things, "We've got to get to Mum!"

"Katie!" he raised his voice.

She stopped immediately.

"It's much worse than we thought," he said softly.

"But… Mum! We've got to go get her!"

He simply shook his head, and let out a long breath.

"What is it, Dad?"

"The fragments. They'll get here tomorrow."

Kate knew exactly what the words meant, but was incapable of responding.

"We'll need to leave," he said, "very soon."

"Great, let's leave! It may not be too late, Mum might…" she began again, but trailed off, seeing the tears building in her father's eyes.

"No, honey," he said as gently as he could, looking out towards the Node, "We need to… *leave*."

She could say nothing. She must always have known it would end. But unlike her father, she couldn't predict that it would end *exactly* like this. Soon they would step aboard and leave *everything* behind. Everything and everyone.

She turned to her father and saw that he was already wearing his Biomag.

The breath caught in her chest; she knew they were leaving right now.

Quietly he smiled and held out his hand. She took hold of it, and together they left Hab 1 for the last time.

90 MINUTES

28th December 2013

The RTO module had already completed three orbits of Earth, exchanging momentum to allow gravity to recapture it at the appropriate altitude. The process meant that during the final pre-docking orbit they would have to pass along the length of the International Space Station.

"Well that would account for the difference in altitude," said Mike, staring out of the starboard porthole, "the mass has changed. Just look at it."

"I am look at it," Lana shook her head, "but I am not believe it."

Even though the RTO module was travelling at a speed in excess of seventeen thousand miles per hour, its speed relative to the ISS was low, so the ex-FLC crew had the opportunity to take in the broad details as they sailed past.

"They never told us," said Cathy.

The main space station backbone looked similar to how they remembered it; a long central axis composed of smaller sub-modules, with a few spur-like chambers extending outwards at right-angles. But the new additions completely dwarfed the original construction.

Surrounding the original ISS was a triangular prism-like structure. Space Shuttle external tanks, identical to those used in the construction of the FLC chambers, ran along each long side, parallel to the central axis. The whole of this new structure was anchored to the original ISS by multiple support struts and access gantries.

At one end of the station, the tips of the three Shuttle tanks were linked to each other by a doughnut-like loop; the loop itself being anchored to the central axis by a long tube that spanned its diameter.

Then the whole structure swept out of view as they continued their final orbit.

"ISS, this is RTO, over," called Lana.

"Roger RTO, this is Commander Charles Lincoln, over."

For the crew it seemed odd to be interacting in real time, with no delay, over radio frequencies.

"Roger ISS, this is Commander Lana Yakovna," she replied.

"Yakovna, we're transmitting course trimming data, please acknowledge when you have received and activated the update. Over."

Mike saw that the update had happened almost instantly. He switched the sequence live, and gave Lana the thumbs up.

"We have received and updated our navigation. Over."

"Enjoy your round trip, we'll see you in ninety minutes for docking. Lincoln out."

The RTO sped on around the world.

The first lunar fragment was only five hours from Earth, but at their altitude the turmoil of the entire human race was invisible. The crew watched silently as the majestic and timeless landscapes swept beneath them.

Each of them knew it.

They were among the last to see the pristine, beautiful face of Earth.

Cathy placed her gloved fingers against the porthole glass.

"This is the closest we'll ever be to home," she whispered.

The others, lost in their own private thoughts and tears, didn't respond.

INTELLECTUAL PROPERTY

27th December 2013

As Douglas and Kate cleared the habitation building, they heard the sound of rotor blades approaching from the west. The helicopter slowed its descent and turned to land just inside the perimeter fence. The logo emblazoned on the side of the Bell 430 read *'Pittman Enterprises'*.

Still holding his daughter's hand, Douglas picked up the pace; but instead of walking towards the Node he pulled her in the direction of the bridge and the helicopter beyond. They hurried past the 'MARK IV' dedication stone without a second glance and quickly trekked onto the bridge. In places, because of the recent heavy traffic, some of the thick wooden planks were badly damaged or missing, and Kate could see the frozen melt-water in the chasm far below.

"Dad, what are -" she began, but he gave no attempt to reply.

They reached the other side of the bridge and set foot on solid ground. The helicopter's rotors were no longer powered but they were still spinning creating a strong downdraft. Most of the noise they could hear now was coming from the restless crowd beyond the fence a mere hundred feet away.

The side door of the helicopter slid open, revealing the plush interior, and several people inside. Two of the men, wearing long thick coats, jumped down and stood either side of the door, surveying the scene through slim skiing glasses. Then a small bespectacled man stepped down, dragging a large suitcase with him. Douglas recognised him immediately. He knew Dr. Alfred Barnes was involved within Archive across a range of projects, but having only met him a few times he didn't know too much more.

He walked towards Douglas wearing a weak smile and, he couldn't help notice, an active Biomag.

"Dr. Walker," he acknowledged, but then continued to walk past him towards the bridge.

Both Douglas and Kate turned to watch, as he made his way across the bridge towards the Node.

"Dougie!" came Bradley Pittman's voice.

Douglas whipped around to see him standing only a few feet away, flanked by the two long-coated men.

"How's that exhaustive inquiry going?" Douglas shot at him. He knew very well that it had been Bradley who had authorised the faking of his family's death. Whilst the logical side of him could see why, the other side wanted to make him pay.

"Why don't we go someplace warmer," said Bradley, still smiling.

"I hear the fires of Hell are quite warm," Douglas starred back.

Bradley's expression changed to match the cold landscape.

"You wanna talk *fires,* Dougie?" he stepped a little closer, "I know about the Mark 3. Your little barbeque? The one that conveniently burned all the evidence?"

Kate stepped a little closer too, unsure what was happening.

"Oh yeah, I know *all* about it. Anna 'n' me had a *real long* conversation about it."

"What's he talking about, Dad?"

"It doesn't matter," said Douglas, not taking his eyes off Bradley, "You've got Anna?"

"Sure I do!" he said definitively, then turned to Kate, "Did Daddy not tell you?"

"Kate, get going," said Douglas firmly, waving her in the direction of the bridge.

But Bradley continued to talk to her.

"They worked it all out when they was in the Mark 3! You don't need no specialist knowledge to *pilot* that thing. They just *said* that to protect their own asses! Thanks to Bergstrom and your daddy, it turns out that you can just push the 'go' button!"

Somehow, Douglas realised, they had coerced the truth from Anna. Their protection was gone.

"So, you're here to *push the button,* Bradley?" Douglas retorted, "Is that it?"

"Ain't you figured it out?!" he shouted, "Eggs in baskets! *This* ain't my basket."

Muted machine gun fire crackled deep within the crowd outside the fence. Screams echoed out, followed by a few retaliating single shots. The pitch of the crowd shifted and swelled in volume.

"Take a look 'round you Doug! Planet's *fucked!* The FLC's gone. If the moon don't kill us, Siva will! You wanna wait out ten thousand years inside your big bubble? Be my guest! Your prize'll be a big snowball in space! So, no, I'm not here to push the button."

"Then why the hell *are* you here?" he shouted.

"Well look who grew a pair!" Bradley snorted, "Look, I just want you to know this ain't personal."

"Personal?" Douglas shot back, "Your entire family owes mine! Without my father, no-one would have seen Siva coming!"

Bradley actually burst out laughing.

"Your father, the great Howard Walker?!" he continued mockingly, "Your dad was a regular rocket scientist, but it was *your mom* who was the star of the show!"

Douglas was lost for words.

"Sam Bishop *discovered* Siva!" Bradley spat out, "He threw your dad the *credit* for it, just to bring your mom and her *genius baby* into Archive! Or maybe I should say *back* into it!"

Douglas was truly adrift now, but Bradley followed up with a look of exhilaration.

"Ahh Dougie! It took me a fair bit of digging, but, well, digging is pretty much the family business. Turns out, your mom got given brain boosters before she popped you out. Did you never wonder why you was *so* smart? Why nobody could *think* like you?"

Douglas stood, debilitated in thought, trying to grasp at the shape of the information, but finding no grip. Kate took the step to his side and steadied him. The noise from the crowd grew louder as another single shot was fired, to be answered immediately by one from the observation tower.

Bradley started laughing, overjoyed to demonstrate his, for once, superior knowledge over Douglas.

"What? All this time you thought you were some kind o' miracle kid? Your mom spliced it into you, Dougie. It's a female thing," then he looked directly at Kate, "I'm here for her."

The two men either side of him moved forward a step, pulling back their long coats to reveal the concealed shotguns within.

"She's not going anywhere with you," said Douglas, pushing her behind him.

The voices within the crowd took on a more fevered tone and a wave rippled through it. The people closest to the fence were jostled forwards and a few fell onto it. Instantly, bolts of electricity arced through them, sending them into convulsing spasms, before collapsing dead.

Bradley's two men still had their shotguns grasped purposefully, but they were distracted by the crowd who were in a frenzy.

"You've just *told* me that you need me," said Kate, defiantly stepping out from behind her father, "You're not going to shoot, you need me."

"All I need is your genes, sweetheart," Bradley raised his voice over the commotion, "An' I can still get *them* while you're on life support."

He signalled the helicopter to start the rotors, and then turned back to Douglas.

"I wish it didn't have to be this way, Dougie. Truly, I wish it didn't," Bradley shook his head, "but one day, we'll need to rebuild the world and, like your mom, she's gonna be the star of the show."

WAITING ROOM

28th December 2013

All too soon, the time to bathe their eyes in the scenic orbit of the Earth was up.

They had approached the ISS superstructure along its central axis, trying to take in as much detail as possible from their new vantage point and greatly reduced velocity.

At this closest end, a circular framework linked the rounded ends of the three Shuttle tanks. It appeared to be the same size as the completed loop at the other end of the station, but was obviously incomplete. Within the circumferential structure, they could make out frameworks of doorways, access hatches and walkways.

There also appeared to be a much greater number of spur modules extending out from the central axis in all compass directions, filling the empty space framed by the triangular Shuttle tank supports.

One thing had not changed, the end module on the central axis was still equipped with a docking port and airlock, and the automated docking procedure had gone without incident.

Next, Lana, Mike and Cathy had waited.

And waited.

But had not been permitted to board the ISS.

The universal power couplings within the docking ring had provided them with power for the Z-bank, so at least the incessant whining tone had stopped. But there the comforts had ended.

"Sorry for the delay," Charles Lincoln's voice came through the open intercom, *"your arrival was earlier than expected. We need you to sit tight a little longer while we prepare to manoeuvre."*

"Let us in and we'll help you push!" quipped Mike.

"Ha ha, thanks but, no disrespect Mike, we won't have time to bring you all up to speed. We're just going to get her out of path of the fragments, and then you can come aboard. Both myself and Dr. Chen are very keen to meet you all."

"Looking forward to it, Commander Lincoln!" said Mike and clicked the intercom off, "I don't like it, Lana. The ISS is not equipped to make the orbit-breaking manoeuvre he's talking about."

"We're not dealing with the ISS that we knew, Mike," Cathy offered, "You saw the scale of upgrades. We don't know *what* we're dealing with now. But I can't see why they have a problem with letting us aboard, it looked like they have plenty of space."

"Lana, any thoughts?"

Lana was smiling, "You have missed his slipped tongue?"

The others looked blankly at her, hoping she would elaborate.

"He said that our arrival was *earlier than expected*."

"So?" said Cathy, "We got here a little early -"

"No, wait I see what you mean, Lana," said Mike, lowering his voice, "We've been on automated approach since leaving the FLC. They knew the timing, down to the exact *second* that we would dock."

"OK," said Cathy, "So maybe they weren't expecting us to be here before the FLC's final deflection?"

"So?" encouraged Lana.

"So they *were* expecting our arrival *after* Siva's deflection?" Mike said hesitantly.

"Well of course they were expecting us *afterwards!* This tin can was always going to rendezvous with the ISS. We're not physically equipped to go home," Cathy patted her own legs, "what are you getting at, Lana?"

Lana took a deep breath, and placed her fingers on her temples.

"OK, let us make theory?" she exhaled.

"OK," Cathy frowned.

"We imagine that the FLC worked. Then Siva is gone, and Earth is safe. Yes?"

"Yes," said Cathy, but then her frown disappeared, "Then why would the ISS need the *ability* to move out of orbit? In fact why would it need to be this *big* in the first place?"

"Da!" said Lana.

"So you mean, FLC failure or not," concluded Mike, "the ISS was being upgraded to go places."

Cathy was nodding, "Makes sense. It looks like they've been building out there for a while."

Their view of the ISS was restricted whilst attached to the end module docking port. But earlier they had all seen the extensive expansion that was still underway.

"Next question," said Lana, "Why are we so important?"

"We're not, we failed," shrugged Cathy.

"So why go to the effort of bringing us back from a doomed moon," said Mike, "to a planet that's just as doomed?"

"Because it's what we're *carrying* that's important," Cathy concluded, tapping the Z-bank.

"Da! So what do they *not* have?"

"They don't have our Z-bank," said Mike.

"No, I see what you're saying," said Cathy, "The ISS is big, they've been building for months, years, that means there should have been plenty of opportunities to ship up a similar Z-bank."

"Which means?"

"We have the Earth's *only* repository of biological life!" Cathy realised, "And they need it."

"Da!"

"I don't get it," said Mike, "The Z-bank made it into orbit just fine, and then they retro-dropped it to us at the FLC. Why send it all the way out to the moon, why not keep it here in orbit?"

"It actually *does* make sense to hold it as far from Earth as possible," Cathy shrugged.

"Agreed," Lana nodded, "But what does not make sense is *this*."

She lifted the weightless but bulky Z-bank and turned it to show them the power socket within its smooth surface. The power cable, now attached to the case, filled most of the wide socket, but left four exposed copper data terminals unconnected.

"At the FLC," Lana continued, "why would the Z-bank need a high speed data link with our Floyd computer?"

"It doesn't," said Mike, "Back at the FLC it just interfaces with a single -"

He stopped when he saw the additional socket terminals on the case, staring up at him. The Z-bank was a sealed unit and required only a power supply. There was no need for it to exchange data with anything before it was opened, at some future point, by the appropriate genetic engineers.

"But then it's been hooked up for months! It's been connected since they shipped up the -" Cathy froze, "it's been connected since we upgraded Floyd with the Shen 500 processors."

The three of them fell silent, trying to piece it all together.

"I am thinking," Lana spoke first, "that it is no coincidence Dr. Chen is here. Yes?"

"The name rings a bell, who is he?"

"Dr. Chen, is the genius behind the Shen series," said Cathy shaking her head, "Shit, Lana! You got all this from *'earlier than expected'* ?"

With a raised eyebrow, Lana replied, "I was not called the Ice Queen for nothing."

MINOTAUR

27th December 2013

He knew that the others must be here, he had arranged it himself.

'*We move separately, but as one,*' Maxwell's own voice reminded him.

He had travelled for many weeks, but he could feel the end of his journey was near.

He moved through the crowd, looking for the sign.

But the voice of doubt continued to nag at him telling him that he was in error.

On instinct, he reached inside his pocket, his fingers closing around the familiar shape.

He pulled the silver case out into the light and it pacified him.

He opened it, and ran his fingers along the groove in one half.

He knew there was something missing from the case.

But the nagging voice said that *he* was missing *something*.

He saw the sign within the crowd, and the doubt was quietened.

The tattoo on the man's hand; the symbolic broken circle, made whole by Siva.

The symbol provided mutual recognition, the man moved towards him.

'*Siva must complete its path*,' he heard himself say.

'*Our self sacrifice is just*,' he heard the man reply, taking out his gun.

He watched the man become absorbed by the crowd.

The persistent voice within broke through, shouting '*No! Protect Archive!*'

Unwelcome words from another life, he was not the same person now.

He heard the guns firing within the crowd.

He knew the others were here, making their sacrifice.

The screams of the crowd joined with those in his mind '*No! Error!*'

He heard the gun firing once more within the crowd.

He heard the loud reply from the tall tower.

'*There is no ego*,' he told the nagging voice.

But still it screamed inside his head '*Not your true mission!*'

He unzipped his vest, and began his walk.

He saw the crowd flee before him into the fence.

He saw chains of lightning erupt within the people.

The light welcomed him forward.

'*Siva must complete its path*,' he told the fevered voice within, '*my sacrifice is just*.'

'Your sacrifice is just wrong!' the voice shrieked beyond sound, *'It will mean The End!'*

'It will mean The New Beginning,' he told himself.

He felt his hand pull on the vest cord, and with his last breath roared:

"Exordi Nova!"

FLOW

27th December 2013

The horrific electrocution of several people and Bradley's complete lack of even a flicker of compassion, had fortified her resolve. Kate stepped out from behind her father.

"You're not going to shoot, you need me," she stared defiantly at Bradley Pittman.

The chaos within the crowd was amplifying. Kate noticed, as did the bodyguards, but Bradley seemed either unaware or unmoved by the unrest.

"All I need is your genes, sweetheart," he drawled, "An' I can still get them while you're on life support."

He turned to the helicopter and signalled the pilot to start the rotors.

Kate saw that a space had opened up within the panicked crowd and a man was walking slowly towards the fence. Kate pulled on her father's arm, and he looked at her. Using her eyes only, she looked purposefully towards the fence, and Douglas followed the direction of her stare.

"I wish it didn't have to be this way, Dougie. Truly, I wish it didn't," Bradley was saying.

As people continued to flee from him, the man stopped in front of the electric fence and reached for a cord on his vest.

Bradley, now apparently focussed on Douglas, continued unaware.

"But one day, we'll need to rebuild the world and, like your mom, she's gonna be the star of the show,"

A roar erupted from the man, and Bradley turned to face it.

With the bodyguards similarly distracted, Kate pulled her father in the direction of the Node.

As the words *'Exordi Nova'* punctured the already terrified air, the man's vest detonated.

Although excruciatingly loud, the explosion was insufficient to reach them and Bradley merely staggered.

"Son of a *Bitch!*" he yelled in shock.

The initial smoke started to clear, revealing the damage to the perimeter fence.

A small section of the fence, about three feet, wide was missing, surrounded by a mass of twisted metal.

"You'll have to do better than that!" laughed Bradley, and turned to the bodyguard nearest to him, "Shoot anyone dumb enough to try gettin' through."

He knew the perimeter towers would be honing their weapons on the breach, but he didn't want to take chances. He returned his attention to Kate but found she wasn't there. In the distance he saw that both Douglas and Kate had seized the opportunity to run, and were already half way over the bridge.

The helicopter rotors were now almost up to speed and the downdraft was considerable.

Behind him he heard the bodyguard's shotgun go off, and turned in time to see a woman collapse into the twisted metal within the fence's hole.

"Idiot," he shook his head.

A second person started climbing through the hole, his clothing snagging on the jagged fence. Others started to follow him through the gap, as they realised that the fence was no longer electrified. The bodyguard closest to the helicopter ran to get on board.

"Aw crap!" Bradley muttered and starting running the few feet back to the helicopter's open door.

The bodyguard nearest the fence managed to discharge his shotgun twice more before being engulfed by the flow of people.

"Get us out!" yelled Bradley as he dragged himself through the doorway.

The pilot complied and the rotor noise increased in pitch.

The crowd were no longer trying to use the gap in the fence. In the knowledge that the fence was no longer electrified they had taken to climbing it; first in the area above the gap, but very swiftly flowing outwards along the entire top of the fence.

The area closest to the gap collapsed under the immense strain, unleashing a tidal wave of people now clamouring to find any form of escape. The perimeter towers were now firing continuously into the crowd and the surrounding camp, but they were having little effect.

As the helicopter left the ground, the crowd flowed in underneath, desperate hands grasping at the hydraulic metalwork of the wheels. The rotor noise increased in pitch again as the pilot tried to compensate for the additional weight dragging at them.

Their ascent slowed as a chain of people continued to grow underneath them, anchoring them to the ground. The engine reached an upper pitch and their ascent stopped.

"There's too many!" yelled the pilot.

Bradley quickly sat down on the floor of the cabin and, looping his hand through the seatbelt of one of the leather seats, flung open the sliding door. Beneath him he could see a long human chain, stretching all the way to the primitive, howling sea of faces below.

On the flight here, not twenty minutes ago, he recalled Alfred Barnes had been yakking on about *being slaves to our evolutionary chains'*. He shook his head and, leaning a little further out, began kicking at the hands that were holding onto the landing gear, "I'm nobody's slave!"

He let loose his rage. Rage at all he had lost. Stamping his boot, over and over again, into the cloying, bloody, fingers until with a final snap, the man's wrist finally broke.

The chain fell away, collapsing into the seething mass below.

The helicopter instantly gained lift and began to rise.

Below him, Bradley could see the crowd pouring in through the overwhelmed perimeter, and flowing towards the bridge. He could see that Douglas and Kate had made it to the Node's main island, but the crowd would inevitably get there too.

SYNC

27th December 2013

Colonel Beck's attention was drawn to the arrival of a helicopter, hovering into position next to the perimeter fence. His tablet showed that the helicopter's transponder was Archive approved, but with the defence station identification system deactivated, they had no clear way of automatically correlating the personnel arriving at the Node.

"Can someone please explain who just parked their chopper in our front yard?" he shouted to the room.

With no-one able to answer his question, the bustle continued unabated.

Unsurprisingly, there had been no contingency plan to deal with the destruction of Earth's natural satellite; but with the basic functionality of the Node now complete, the schedule had been accelerated in an attempt to depart before the lunar fragments hit.

He became aware that a civilian was standing next to him and he turned to face her.

"General Napier's shipment has arrived, but the manifest doesn't show where to store it," she said.

Colonel Beck brought up the manifest on his tablet, but he couldn't find the details either. The sheer speed with which equipment was arriving at the Node meant nothing could be unpacked, it just had to be stowed. But stowed in a manner that would allow access to the most useful items first, once they were underway.

Napier himself was due to arrive in under two hours, with the penultimate set of delegates. He could ask him then for an appropriate stow point, but for now he just had to place it somewhere well out of the way.

"OK, put it in Sub-4 Alpha," Beck confirmed, "I'll handle the internal update."

"Thank you, er, Sir," she said, and departed at speed.

She was just some kid, he thought, no older than his daughter would have been; and she had been thrown into *this*.

"Sir," came the voice of Scott Dexter from the other side of the room, "Airlock 2, the one nearest that chopper, reports activation by a Dr. Alfred Barnes."

"Pre-registered Biomag?" confirmed Beck.

"Yes Sir," Dexter nodded, then returned to working at his console.

Pre-registered Biomag pendants had been assigned to many of the high-ranking Archive figures weeks ago when the Node's Field generator had been completed. Many had taken their isotope injection within an hour of the FLC's failure, in an attempt to be Field-ready before their arrival here. The

Node kept a stock of Bergstrom's isotope, but the reality was that anyone only taking it now would not have sufficient saturation to be anchored within the Field.

Beck waited for a few seconds for the personnel manifest to update with the new arrival, then brought up the profile on his tablet. It took him a few moments to recognize Dr. Barnes, who belonged to a different Archive project. He could only assume that for some reason he had been added to the Node at the last hour. Beck had a growing sense of unease, and over the years he'd learned to trust it.

"Carter?" he called out, "Have we had any communication from the General's Chinook?"

"No Sir," Carter replied, "Do you want me to try raising him on long range?"

"No, but let me know when the transponder is in range."

"Yes Sir."

"Webshot?"

It took Roy Carter a little longer to find the information this time, as it was a background computation process. "We're pulling down about a gigabit per second, Sir," he reported, "Our receiver station is fine, but the satellite link -"

"Breach!" shouted Dexter, silencing the chaotic room, "Perimeter Breach!"

Unrest outside the perimeter had been growing for hours, but this was even sooner than Beck had expected. He strode quickly over to the console.

"Where?"

Dexter redirected the CCTV feed from the closest tower, and zoomed in on the burning section of fence.

"Here!"

Smoke drifted across the camera's view and began to obscure the image.

The possibility that he'd dreaded since the FLC's failure was coming to pass. Beck knew it was all too soon, but there was no other choice. The Node was now under threat.

"Time to leave," he said quietly to himself.

"Say again, Sir?"

As the highest in the chain of command, he filled his lungs and lifted the Main Circuit public address handset.

"All stations. Departure conditions. This is not a drill. I repeat. All stations. Departure conditions."

The air became a frenzied blur of activity as personnel cleared from the room, whilst others arrived. He knew there would be casualties, but he had to hope that all would do their duty. As he must now.

As far as he knew, the single act of terrorism at the fence may only be the precursor to a more sustained and terminal attack on the Node. He crossed the floor to his own workstation and, after entering his authorisation code, re-armed the defence station identification system, along with the ground-to-air missile defences it controlled. If there was an attack from the air during their departure, there would be no time to react. Better to destroy the threat before they got any closer than the ten mile mark.

He returned to making his way down the mental list.

"Prime the core," he shouted, "Set departure status to commit."

"Core primed and charging!" answered a voice from somewhere within the noise.

"Commit!" came another.

"Sir!" came Carter's voice, "Dr. Walker is not aboard!"

Beck consulted his tablet, but found that the wireless link was down. The charging of the Chronomagnetic Field was creating too much disturbance.

"Did he enter the departure Field solution?" Beck discarded his tablet to a nearby desk and joined Carter.

"Checking," said Carter, "Yes. He filed it last night. We're good to go, Sir, but if we hit a problem…"

Beck let out a short, aggravated grunt, "Where is he? Can you locate his Biomag?"

"Checking," Carter lapsed into silence, then switched to a second monitor screen.

A slight tremor began to pass through the floor, and a shout came from behind Beck.

"Haken manifold horizon in progress!"

"Acknowledged!" Beck returned, "Activate primary stage containment."

"Activation confirmed! Field inversion event… contained!"

There were a few, short-lived, elated cries as the historic moment passed amid the general noise.

The tremor stopped to be replaced by the continuous hum of the core.

"I have him!" shouted Carter over the noise, "Dr. Walker's Biomag is just clearing the bridge, Sir!"

"What the hell's he doing out there?" Beck swung away and shouted across the room "Dexter, get me visual confirmation on that!"

"Already on it," reported Dexter, pointing to the far wall, "Main screen, Sir!"

Beck thought he saw Douglas just exiting the bottom right of the image, but couldn't be sure. From the angle of the CCTV view it looked like he was heading for the same airlock that Dr. Barnes had used a minute ago.

"Dexter! The moment he gets to Airlock 2 - "

"Yes Sir!" he shouted, but then his eyes widened as he saw what was happening on the main screen.

It was still showing the bridge that joined the shore to the Node's island, but now it also showed a crowd flooding through the collapsed perimeter and heading towards the bridge.

At that moment a repetitive tone pulsed from Beck's own workstation.

"What the hell?" he swiftly moved to check.

It was a perimeter warning from the ten mile mark.

The automated ground-to-air missile defences had fired on several aircraft as they had entered the airspace without the authorised transponder codes. As Beck watched the data, he saw that the stock of missiles was depleting rapidly. This could only indicate an organised and persistent incursion, rather than a stray aircraft testing their luck.

With the lunar fragments due to impact the Earth in a matter of hours, he thought, who could possibly benefit now from the destruction of the Node?

"Sir!"

The CCTV feed showed the crowds trying to squeeze through the narrow entrance onto the bridge. Beck could even see the characteristic muzzle flashes of machine gun fire erupting sporadically from within the massed crowd as the situation broke down into blind panic. The Node was under attack from at least two directions and Colonel Beck knew what must be done.

"Dexter. Close the bridge," instructed Beck, removing a key from around his neck.

"But Sir…!" said Dexter pointing at the screen.

The live feed showed that civilians had already started to cross the bridge towards the Node's main compound; men, women and children clambering over each other in a gunfire peppered desperate scramble. As the crowd's front line tripped and fell they were replaced by others trampling them underfoot.

"Close the damn bridge. Now!" shouted Beck striding over to Dexter's console and inserting the key.

"Sir, the people…" Dexter stammered, "We *have* capacity to -".

"When we depart, they'll all die!" Beck waved his own Biomag, "They're not tagged!"

On the bridge, the stream of human traffic had become too much and people were being forced off the sides.

The leading edge of the crowd passed the halfway point. He pushed Dexter aside.

"This facility. Must. Not. Fall!" he yelled, turning the key.

Anyone in the crowd, trying to force their way on, would have seen the central third of the bridge instantly disappear in a concussive explosion of livid red fire. The bridge, now a collection of splintered matchsticks and rivets, started to fall trailing thick acrid black smoke and burning corpses in its wake. Several people were alight and trying to flee, spreading fire back into the crowds. Yet more were trying to cling to the remains of the burning structure, but then flailing into the black smoke below.

The eerily silent CCTV feed dutifully relayed a grainy image of the unfolding horrific scene.

Dexter clapped his hands over his mouth, but couldn't prevent his stomach's convulsion; he bent double and vomited over the hard polished floor.

Against the background hum of the Node's core, a silence fell around the room.

Colonel Beck turned off the video feed and steeled himself to become what was demanded of him.

"We will have time to mourn. But unless we leave, now, the Human Race ends. Today."

The images they had seen would stay with them until their dying day, a continual reminder of their own survival. In a state of wide-eyed shock, people slowly began to move and breathe again, returning to their stations in sombre silence.

"Lieutenant Carter?" Beck said calmly.

"Yes Sir," said Carter, turning to face his console.

"Please sound the one minute external siren."

•

Although the detonation of the bridge had been a good hundred feet behind them, the force of the blast had knocked them off their feet. Kate had hit the ground hard, but found herself on her feet again and running towards the Node's airlock. She looked back and saw that her father hadn't got up. As the one minute siren sounded she sprinted back to help him. She was relieved to see that he was now staggering upright.

"I thought I'd lost you!" she panted, helping him stand again.

"Ha!" he coughed "Zero percent probability!"

"The siren…" she knew the Node was less than a minute away from departure.

"I know…," he glanced at her Biomag pendant hanging around her neck, and then flashed his best smile at her.

She returned his smile, but she knew that something wasn't quite right.

Her concentration was broken by a second explosion coming from the fiery remains of the bridge, evidently not all the explosives had blown at the same time. She could hear renewed screams now coming from below.

"We need to move. Now!" his serious expression was present again and he pushed her on.

She arrived at the airlock and threw her rucksack in.

He arrived a moment later and as she turned to face him she saw his pained expression. His eyes were darting from left to right and he was blinking erratically.

"What is it?"

He emerged from his thoughts and placed both his hands on her shoulders.

"My little Katie," he gazed at her face, as if wanting to burn every detail into his memory, "You have your mother's eyes, you know."

"Dad!" she interrupted, "We have to get in there - NOW!"

He shook his head gently.

"No," he said and brushed a stray hair out of her eyes. He pulled her close and hugged her.

This caught her completely off guard and she was unable to speak.

"Honey," he continued, squeezing her tightly, "I love you *so* much, I'm so proud of you..."

"Dad...I..." she felt him smooth down her hair and, comforted, she closed her eyes.

The thirty second siren sounded.

"Don't be angry with me," he said, releasing his hold.

Douglas realised that the singularity, that final decision he had feared for so long, had arrived.

"No more branches to my tree," he explained, "You fell over too hard and your crystal..."

"No more branches? What are you talking..." she pushed away from him.

In that moment she saw that her Biomag was smashed and lifeless; she had apparently landed on it heavily during the explosion. She then spotted that her father's Biomag was now hanging next to hers, fully intact.

It took her a second to process that, during his improvised hug, her father had looped it over her head.

That second was all he needed.

He grabbed both of her arms and, using his whole body weight, forcibly pushed her into the airlock; as she was still stumbling into the airlock's back wall, he hit the 'close' button and stepped outside as the door hissed shut.

She was on her feet again almost instantly and jabbing at the door control panel. She knew it was futile, the safety protocols wouldn't allow the door to re-open during the departure phase, but she screamed and pounded on the glass with balled fists anyway.

Outside Douglas could only see her terrified angry screams; the Node was far too well insulated for sound to escape. He couldn't bear the sight of her pain, and knew what he had to do next.

"Don't you turn away from me!" she yelled, her fists pounding at the glass. She watched him pull his rucksack on and clip the belt around his waist. He looked at his watch, then after a brief check of the sky he ran off in the direction of the main lab without a backward glance.

Knowing her father, he was attempting to get a replacement Biomag. She would now do her best to get the launch delayed by a few minutes. As the interior side of the airlock opened she turned on her heels and, recalling the layout, sprinted towards the control room.

•

The core's hum swelled louder and the whole control room shuddered suddenly.

Beck's tablet jittered to the edge of the desk and fell to the floor. He shot a glance at the core's lead engineer.

"Gyroscopic shearing! A few microgram-metres squared per second, tops!" he shouted, "We're still within tolerance. Good to go!"

"Core charge?" Beck resumed his departure checks.

"Complete!"

"Disengage geothermal exchanger,"

There was a slight additional vibration as the rods withdrew from the Icelandic landscape below.

"Disengaged. Power is internal, and holding."

"Sound the thirty second siren," said Beck.

The siren pulsed five times.

"Dexter, tell me you have some good news?"

He shook his head, "I'm sorry, Sir."

Beck picked up the public address handset, "All hands, prepare for immediate departure. Stand to!"

He hung up the handset, then turned to address the crew.

"Sir!" shouted Dexter, "I have Dr. Walker's Biomag signature confirmed in Airlock 2!"

"About time!" Beck let out a long breath of relief, "Thank you Mr. Dexter."

The core's hum changed pitch and then started to rise.

The vibration ceased momentarily, while motion phases within the core temporarily cancelled each other out, and then the vibration resumed, as the core started to enter a still higher range of pitch.

Over the noise Beck could just about discern a voice shouting.

"Field inversion synched! It's folding!"

•

By necessity the Node was laid out in a series of concentric segments, with the control room lying at the centre; so whilst the direct-line distance to the centre would never be more than fifty yards, in practice the curved corridors increased this distance.

It was this fact that confronted Kate now, she could never make it to the control room in time.

A little way ahead she spotted a communications panel and raced towards it.

She slammed the button marked 'Ops'.

"Abort the launch! Dr. Walker is NOT aboard! Abort! Repeat Abort!"

There was no reply, and as she began to push the button again she realised why.

This particular panel bore a yellow and black striped engineering tag with the label 'WorkOrder#3' clipped to it. In the rush to complete the Node, all non-essential works had been postponed until after the journey was underway.

The panel was still inactive.

The ever-present core hum changed pitch and continued to climb.

Suddenly she felt the hairs on her arm swing upright, and then a powerful and persistent tug began to pulse throughout her entire body.

'We must nearly be in sync!' she thought.

Remembering a slice of the briefings, she quickly stood bolt upright with her back and hands pressed against the wall. The theory was to orient the major organs to reduce the temporal shearing as the Chronomagnetic Field propagated outwards from the Node's hub.

The Biomag round her neck emitted a long, high-pitched tone, and she had the sensation that every one of her molecules had just aligned itself with the core, like iron filings in the presence of a magnet.

The core reached an almost ultrasonic pitch, followed by a deeply subsonic *whump* that she felt rather than heard.

'There it is...' she thought.

The core had fired.

The Chronomagnetic Field explosively radiated outwards from the core in an expanding sphere, enveloping the whole of the Node. The Field passed through Kate almost instantly, but the severe time deceleration had a disorienting effect.

Time smeared out in front of her.

'Like being a living watercolour' she thought.

She could see her own hands and arms outstretched and blurred in front of her as though she was studying them.

'This is wild...' she thought.

Abruptly the effect stopped.

She found herself, once more, standing bolt-upright in the corridor, with her back and hands against the wall.

On impulse she studied her hands to check that she was alright.

She experienced an overwhelming sense of déjà vu as her earlier perspective echoed itself.

"This is wild," she found herself repeating, before regaining her full senses.

The cacophony of the core was gone, replaced with a low-pitched hum.

There were no sirens.

There were no Biomag tones, it simply displayed the digits 1200.

The quickest route to the control room now was through the Observation Deck, in the next radial segment. She set off at a sprint, hoping that she could still halt the mission.

SURVEY

28th December 2013

Cathy remembered the earlier RTO conversation with Mike and Lana about the Z-bank. She also remembered the ISS manoeuvring thrusters firing, and the brief discussion about their disproportionate strength. Things became a little hazy after the airlock had finally been opened for them.

She knew there had been panic.

The image of Lana and Mike drifting in front of her, unconscious, swam back into memory.

The remainder of the memory poured in now; the sickly sweet smell filling the small airlock; her failed attempt to return to the RTO; then voices and hands tugging at her as she had lost consciousness.

She was awake now though; but on trying to raise herself up, she found she was completely immobilised.

She was obviously restrained, though she couldn't tell how, and her thoughts were slightly sluggish, which probably meant some form of drug.

"Ah, you're awake," came a voice from somewhere out of view.

Depending on her point of view, she determined that she was either lying in a narrow trench that ran the length of a cylindrical room, or standing in a recess within a cylindrical wall with a circular floor some way below her. The lack of gravity didn't help. Then again, she thought, the lack of gravity didn't matter; it meant that she was still aboard the ISS.

Now that her mind had adjusted to the new perspective she could recognize the familiar FLC-like curves. From the shape of the room she guessed that she must be inside one of the three Shuttle external tanks clustered around the original ISS.

"I am Dr. Chen. Despite appearances, I *truly* greet you as my honoured guest."

If this is what honoured feels like, she thought, he could keep it.

"Yeah about the honoured thing, I'd like to leave now. I brought some sentimental baggage aboard, could you fetch it for me?" Cathy found herself replying.

Dr. Chen closed his eyes, seemingly in sublime thought.

"The repository of *all human life* is more than mere sentimental baggage. It is the gift of a deity!"

"Wow," she sniggered, "you actually see the Z-bank as a gift from the gods? Ha! Cooper would have loved you!"

There was a brief look of mild confusion and then it vanished, "Ah Leonard Cooper, one of your former crew-mates.

He was quite the scholar, I was looking forward to talking with him. It is a great loss. I cannot bring myself to say the same for Eva Gray. Her actions have complicated matters."

"Complicated matters?" she stared at him with a look of sheer incredulity. He was referring to the Moon's destruction as a complication. The fact that it would bring about the premature annihilation of millions seemed a minor abstraction to him.

"Of course. But hopefully, in time, we can still wipe the slate clean."

"How forgiving of you," she said, being careful to let the sarcasm shine through.

His only reaction was another slight frown, as though she had misunderstood him.

"Ah, I see," he said as if making a mental note, "Now please try to answer my questions honestly, it will make your transition to life aboard much easier."

He pushed himself away from her and drifted up out of her limited view.

She could feel a momentary tingle in her scalp. Evidently he would be electronically measuring her response, she thought, perhaps some form of polygraph. She longed to reach up and pull off whatever wires were taped to her head, but the restraints were too perfect.

"You'll get my honesty pal," she shot at him, "don't you worry."

"Before we start, you should know that I am recording our conversation - "

"For training and monitoring purposes?" she almost laughed, it sounded too similar to the telephone helplines back on Earth.

"Exactly, very perceptive," he replied without a hint of irony. "Now, in your childhood did you ever dream of, one day, becoming an astronaut?"

She thought of her own induction into Archive. As a child, there was never really the opportunity to dream of becoming anything else. Her whole life had been dedicated to helping Archive achieve the goal.

"No," she said.

"Thank you," he replied from somewhere above her, "Now, tell me how does the destruction of the FLC make you feel?"

"Now let me think. Yeah I'd have to go with 'Quite Cross'," she over pronounced.

"Thank you," he replied, "Next, how -"

"What that's it?!" she interrupted.

"Yes," he replied calmly, "The difference between your stated response and your body's physical reaction to the stimulus has been accurately captured. Your honest response has been noted."

"And you don't think that your *mechanical marvel* could've mistaken my subtle and nuanced sarcasm?"

"My Shen Series do not make mistakes," he corrected her.

"It was a Shen500 that *caused* all this!"

"Continue," he said, drifting back down into view.

"If Floyd had hit Siva dead-centre, back in 2010, then there would have been no Tenca! No Tenca, there'd have been no Chelyabinsk impact. Everyone on Earth could have slept in blissful ignorance until we'd done our job! So don't try to tell me how *perfect* your silicon child is!"

He folded his arms patiently, while she continued to rage at him.

"Either your Shen500 made a *big* mistake, or it was instructed to miss."

Dr. Chen manoeuvred himself closer, then spoke slowly.

"My Shen500's do *not* make mistakes."

"Then -"

He seemed to study her as she grappled with the logical conclusion of his statement.

His intent had always been to subvert Siva's deflection.

Her strength left her.

"*Bastard*," she breathed, suddenly only able to whisper, "we could have saved the world."

"Saved?" he smiled benignly, "With a little patience I will inherit it."

He drifted out of her view, as she herself began to drift into dark sleep.

"Thank you, Cathy," he said, as the darkness took her, "we will talk again on our voyage."

RELATIVITY

27th December 2013

The design of the Node's Observation Deck was the crowning contribution of the science communities within Archive. It had been argued that, far from being a mere escape vessel, the Node represented an unprecedented opportunity to observe nothing less than the evolution of the planet.

As with all rooms within the Node, the Observation Deck was a radial segment.

However, unlike the other segments, it took up fully one quarter of the circumference of the Node and offered an uninterrupted vista of the outside world. The glazing stretched from side to side, and from floor to vaulted ceiling some fifteen storeys above, where the curvature also allowed a panoramic view of the sky. The large panels of glass that made up the glazing were directly bonded to each rather than a frame.

The overall impression was of being inside a soap bubble, overlaid with a spider-web thin lattice. Peppered with science stations, seats and soft mats it was a cathedral of science and quiet reflection looking out on all of creation.

Kate arrived at speed into this space, her sprint collapsing into a walk as she was overcome with the majesty of the sight that greeted her. Almost in a trance she crossed the Observation Deck floor to the window and placed her hands on the cold handrail, overwhelmed by the view.

Ablaze with a riot of colour, the Node's magnetic field had induced a vivid aurora in the night sky. The clouds appeared to coalesce and evaporate in a constant receding stream, like a time-lapsed movie. The stars were no longer pin pricks of light but tiny smooth crisp arcs lazily cart-wheeling around the North Star.

They had truly begun their journey towards futurity.

On any other night the sight would have been beautiful and serene, but she knew that devastation was already approaching over the horizon. The extreme shockwaves predicted to accompany each lunar impact would wreak havoc with Earth's ecosystem, and cause tectonic upheaval.

The lights on the observation towers surrounding the Node now seemed rock steady, whilst the environment pulsed and raced; it was an impossible sight. Her attention wandered to a bright source of light on the ground - it wasn't an artificial light but a large campfire that seemed to flicker in synch with the outside world. Beside it, standing almost motionless in defiance of time, was a lone figure.

Her father.

In here the decelerated time-frame meant that mere seconds had passed since he had pushed her into the airlock, but for every one of those seconds, twenty minutes had passed on the outside. Already he had been standing there for hours, and must surely have missed any opportunity to get to safety.

Why was he standing there just waiting for the end?

As if in answer to her own question, a memory of his patient voice echoed in her mind, *'There is no redundant information honey, just stuff we didn't realise we needed at the time'.*

He was standing in order to get her attention.

She dashed across ten feet of floor and grabbed some digital recording binoculars from the recharging bank of a nearby science station. She ran back to the handrail and hit the record button on the binoculars, before she'd even focussed them on him.

From his perspective, she realised, it must have taken just short of an hour to complete this simple task, and was kicking herself for not having reacted sooner. The binoculars auto-focussed on him and stabilised the image.

She was greeted with the sight of him holding a clipboard horizontally bearing a message in plain black marker pen.

'New Tree! Hit Record'.

She simultaneously laughed out loud and choked back the impulse to cry. Glancing up at his face she could see he had a standard pair of binoculars and was watching her. As she was already recording, she quickly flashed an 'OK' symbol with her thumb and forefinger. This brief action would take a good 10 minutes to play out for him. Not that he needed that long to prepare his next page.

'Hit Data-burst, and hold steady!'

She quickly dropped the binoculars, found the 'Data-burst' button, raised the equipment to her eyes again, and hit the button. The device started recording at a hundred times its normal speed.

She saw the briefest of pauses then the clip board text blurred and was replaced by a new message.

Before she could register what it was, it also blurred and was then replaced by another, and another.

And so it continued for about 5 seconds, a stream of hundreds of images, equations, graphs, no two alike, a bizarre animated flick book of information. Abruptly the clipboard disappeared from view, and she got the fleeting impression that he was checking behind himself.

He disappeared briefly and then reappeared with his rucksack.

Then just as suddenly he was holding the clipboard in place again.

The binoculars had gone, and he was just smiling:

'Gotta Go', another brief blur, *'I Love You Honey'.*

He continued to smile, occasionally he would flicker as he turned to check behind himself, or glance at his wristwatch. The faint glow of dawn was spreading into the sky erasing the night stars, and she realised that the first impact must already have occurred on the other side of the planet. The predicted earthquakes would hit Node Point just as dawn broke.

He continued his defiant stand, all the time smiling and holding his clipboard proudly.

She knew he would stand guardian over her to the very end if she continued to watch him.

She wanted desperately to write a message back, to tell him to find cover, to tell her father that she loved him too, but she knew he would never receive the message before dawn.

She suddenly realised the significance of the fact that he was no longer wearing his binoculars - he expected no reply.

If he was to stand any chance of reaching shelter, she would have to release him from his guardianship. She could hold back the tears no longer. She dropped the binoculars to her side, and with hot tears blinding her, she turned her back on her father.

Through closed eyes she sensed the whole Node tremor as the quake front impacted the site and inside she felt her heart rip.

FRAGMENTS

27th December 2013

Following the fusion-induced break up of the moon, a deep, ragged strip of the lunar surface, stretching from *Copernicus Crater* to the *Sea of Tranquillity*, had been ejected towards the Earth. Over the following days the former lunar surface broke into a long chain of fragments that had loosely followed the RTO module's trajectory.

Deep space radar imagery had confirmed that the fragments ranged in size from ones as small as bricks, to those at least five times the size of Tenca. Despite human civilisation on Earth drawing to a close, the larger of these super-fragments were documented and named according to their lunar origin; the hope being that one day the information would be rediscovered.

Copernicus and *Stadius* arrived first, ploughing through the cloud of satellites surrounding Earth. The Debris Cascade Protection system provided a pathetic firework display in orbit before expiring forever. Stadius fragmented into smaller pieces as it streaked through the atmosphere, but Copernicus was only stopped by the Pacific Ocean, initiating tidal waves, ninety feet in height, that travelled west towards Indonesia, and east towards Mexico.

Sinus arrived forty minutes later removing Malaysia and Singapore, and triggered tectonic shock-waves and earthquakes throughout the Indo-Australian and lower Eurasian plates. The resulting 120-foot-high tsunami ran north through the Bay of Bengal, reaching as far north as Nepal before the Himalayas absorbed the flow.

The tides caused by the earlier arrival of Copernicus fled north, washing over California, and ran inland towards Arizona. Meanwhile, the expanding cloud of debris in orbit continued to run unchecked, and satellite communications networks began to fail worldwide.

Palla, *Hyginus* and *Agrippa* arrived as a super-cluster, tearing through the atmosphere with ease and ripping a deep, new canyon through Africa, stretching from the Gulf of Aden to Nigeria. The tidal displacement created earlier by Sinus reached the east African shores then continued relentlessly into the newly created corridor of devastation.

Tranquillity, the largest and final super-fragment, struck Venezuela creating a temporary Gulf of Columbia. The resulting 180-foot-high tsunami radiated out through the Atlantic Ocean, towards the Norwegian and Mediterranean seas. A chain reaction of earthquakes began as the tectonic stresses equalised across four major tectonic plates.

North and South America parted company again as the Caribbean plate liquefied. The resulting shockwave travelled north along the Mid-Atlantic Ridge line towards Iceland and the Arctic Circle beyond, and west along the East Pacific Rise.

The uncharted minor fragments had continued to bombard the Earth throughout, ensuring there was a steady stream of terror for those attempting the futile exercise of escape. Aftershocks and tsunamis rippled around the world for days and triggered volcanic activity. Around the planet, hundreds of thick, churning, black ash columns rose; standing as burial markers for entire towns and cities swallowed by the pyroclastic flows. Then came the rains, carried far and wide by the new chaotic winds, their acid fell and burned.

And still, Siva advanced.

MINUTE ONE

Colonel Beck looked at the devastation outside the Node. In the moments after the lunar fragments had impacted the Earth, equatorial earthquakes had been predicted, followed by tidal waves that would lap around the world.

He could see that both had wrought their worst upon the landscape.

Öskjuvatn Lake, normally the home to relatively shallow melt-water, had been inundated by the combined swell of the Atlantic Ocean and Norwegian Sea pushing inland. The waters would recede in time, but already the landscape seemed part of a different epoch.

The Node's surrounding base and bridge were now mostly washed away, the only evidence of their former existence being the jagged tips of observation towers drowning in the time-smoothed, mirror-like water.

Beck pulled his eyes away from the sight.

There would be time for introspection later, time to determine the identity of those responsible for the attack on the Node. But now he must ensure their survival.

"All stations report in," he commanded, "Mission order,"

While each station reported in, he considered what lay ahead.

"Structural, intact!"

They would mourn the loss of a civilisation…

"Power, ninety-eight percent, holding!"

They would rebuild their lives and the world beyond…

"Field, twelve-hundred to one gradient, stable!"

Out of the fires of the old, they would begin again…

"Gravitational tether, fifty-nine milligals, steady."

On hearing the final station report, Beck lifted the main circuit handset.

"All hands, this is Colonel Beck. We are underway, report for roll call at duty stations."

He hung up the handset and returned to his own workstation.

The screen was blank.

The ten mile mark defence stations were no longer relaying any missile telemetry; radio frequencies had never worked through the Field.

He looked out at the Node-induced, purple-green aurora and the rising, but utterly destroyed, moon.

The fragments that were still in orbit had already begun to string out in a thin line. Before their departure he'd overheard that the lunar fragments may possibly fall into orbit around the planet, giving the Earth a Saturn-like system of rings. Now it seemed that this would become a certainty. He realised that the

Node's aggressor no longer mattered; whoever they were, they belonged to an already vanished world.

"Sir," came Carter's voice, "The Siva clock stands at four hundred and sixty days."

Beck realised that the countdown to Siva's arrival had already begun.

Over a year away, but now unstoppable, they must now prepare for the next onslaught.

"Internal Clock?"

Carter inhaled deeply before replying.

"In here, Sir, that's nine hours, twelve minutes."

A commotion broke out at the entrance of the control room as a young woman pushed her way in.

"General Napier, I need to speak with - " she gasped for breath.

"Wait! Let her through, it's Walker's daughter," said Beck, crossing the room to meet her, "Miss Walker? I'm afraid General Napier didn't... wait, where's your father?"

She just shook her head.

Beck shot an angry glance across the room at Dexter, who looked completely distraught.

"He's not coming," said Kate, still clasping her father's Biomag tightly.

The magnitude of the news was not lost on anyone in the control room.

Although each station knew their roles, no individual knew the Field equations like Douglas.

Beck was rubbing his head, in controlled panic, "This is *not* part of the plan."

"No, it's not," said Kate, now smiling in memory of her father, "but *this* is."

She held up the pair of digital recording binoculars.

"My Dad sent me a message."

ATKA

Atka turned away from the glare of the Orb to look at the scintillating rings that surrounded his world, and the stars beyond. Many had speculated that The Guardians came from those stars and may one day depart from here, taking their followers with them.

Hearing distant thunder, Atka turned away from the stars to focus on the present. Puzzled, he saw there were no storm clouds. A second growl of thunder split the air, and he realised that the sound was not coming from the sky but from the Orb. Without warning, the ground under his feet began to shake and he fell. The Orb's once steady light was now pulsating and the Sky-Spirits had almost vanished.

The whole Orb began to shudder and then slowly vibrate towards him, the forest floor crumpling and breaking up in its wake. It started to push against the first of the surrounding trees, vaporising each in a brilliant flash of violet light. Then, just as suddenly, silence returned to the clearing and everything was still once again; although Atka was not there to see it, he was already sprinting back to the village to alert the Elders.

However, he did not have far to run.

The Elders, presumably sensing the disturbance, had already begun their journey from the village and met him along the way. As Atka guided them back towards the Orb, they were joined by more of his people; eager to hear his tales of the Sky-Spirits' disappearance and of how the Orb had miraculously moved towards *him*.

When the crowd reached the bridge, they were instructed to kneel and bow in reverence to the Sky-Spirits who had now returned; once more the playful exchange of purple-green mists ebbed and flowed above the Orb itself.

Long ago the forefathers had repaired the bridge, allowing the Elders to reach the wooded island beyond. It was at the heart of this island that the Orb sat; but even from here its cold, ethereal dome was visible above the small trees.

The most senior Elder called forth Atka alone and together the pair began to walk across the long, wood and vine bridge. In the spaces between the wooden branches below his feet, he could see the chasm below and the still waters that ran deep and dark. He could see the strange jagged shapes, from a long-departed era, jutting out from the mirror-like surface.

Earlier, Atka had leaped from branch to branch in fear of the violent noise pursuing him. But now in the calm of his return journey to the Orb, he trod more carefully as the night's events began to take on more significance for him.

They reached the end of the bridge and stepped onto more solid ground. As was the custom, they touched the fractured, ancient carved stone that bore the inscription 'ARK IV'. Then they moved towards the Orb's light.

They knew not to tread too close to the impenetrable field surrounding The Guardians' domain, and stopped many footfalls short. But even at this distance Atka could feel its powerful force tugging at him. He was about to bow in reverence, but the senior Elder bade him stand.

Kneeling beside the cooling remains of Atka's campfire, the Elder scooped up a handful of the warm ash and then returned to Atka's side. Lifting his hand to his mouth he dropped a small amount of spittle into the ash and then invited Atka to do the same.

As the Elder mixed their spittle and ashes into a paste, Atka looked around at the perfect night; the bright stars and rings, the Orb and even the Sky-Spirits were here to witness his initiation. He became aware of his place within the long chain of his ancestors and their dedication to preserving this place.

Atka turned to face the Elder as he began the ritual.

Although the words themselves had lost their meaning to the depths of time, they knew the importance of saying them aloud.

"Arkiv," said the Elder raising the ashes.

"Exordi Nova," replied Atka, brushing the hair away from his forehead.

Dipping his thumb into the black paste, the Elder marked a circle on Atka's forehead then placed a wide dot to intersect the circumference.

The exact origin of the symbol was now long-forgotten knowledge, but Atka believed in what it represented now: The circle meaning the unbroken renewal of life and the dot depicting the Orb watching over each new beginning.

Atka felt the hairs on his arms stand upright, but it was not in reaction to the symbol being placed.

He turned towards the Orb and saw that within, a Guardian had appeared.

She was pointing at him...

Field Two

(Excerpt)

More details of the Field series are available at
www.futurewords.uk

*T*he feeling of falling was going away now. He felt warm and comfortable. He could hear a voice calling to him, as though someone was trying to wake him, except he was already awake, or at least that's how it felt.

"Hello Miles, we have spoken before, do you remember me?"

It was still dark and he couldn't tell where the voice was coming from but, when he thought hard enough, he was sure he recognised it.

"Is that you Aunty Dot?" he liked Aunty Dot and she liked him.

"Yes, Miles," said Aunty Dot's voice, "You're still very special to me, but do you remember why?"

"You gave me a special coin," he smiled proudly, thinking of the silver dollar she had given to him, "It said 'E Pluribus Unum' on it, which means - "

"Out of many, one," she completed, "That's right. Do you still remember when I gave it to you?"

Miles thought of his fourth birthday party, and Aunty Dot crouching at his side handing him a small, bright red parcel.

"It was at my fourth birthday party, Aunty Dot."

He could picture the scene clearly; the buzz of conversation in the air and people laughing. He also remembered a girl with a splinter in her finger, and the upsetting feeling it had given him when he knew that he couldn't help. For some reason he felt a rising sense of panic, but Aunty Dot must have seen his discomfort somehow.

"It's OK, Miles," her voice reassured him.

He remembered how, back then, Aunty Dot had put her arm around him to comfort him. He felt this same warmth again now as she continued to talk.

"Do you remember why I gave it to you?"

He remembered that she had not let go of the small red parcel until she had told him something. She had looked at him when she had said it, but he had to concentrate really hard to remember it. He pictured her saying the words.

"For helping others," he smiled, pleased that he had remembered what Aunty Dot needed to know. He liked it when he could help others.

"That's right, Miles. Will you help me, Miles?"

"Of course Aunty Dot," he beamed, "I like to help."

He remembered unwrapping her present and looking at the silver dollar. He remembered his fascination with the two dates, representing two hundred years of liberty. He pictured the coin in front of him now, and imagined running his fingers over the familiar embossed surface. He could see the Liberty Bell and the Latin inscription to its right. But above the inscription there was just empty space. Something was missing.

Or, he thought, he was missing something.

"Something's wrong," he heard himself say, and suddenly he felt cold.

"We'll speak again," came the voice from the darkness.

Then he was falling again.

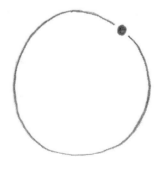

21396531R00298

Printed in Poland
by Amazon Fulfillment
Poland Sp. z o.o., Wrocław